"THE PROCEDURE ⟨ Y0-BVR-260
SO THE MOST IMPORTANT THING YOU
CAN DO IS FALL ASLEEP.
YOU WON'T FEEL A THING."

Sally watched the needles trace long hills and valleys and she wondered, as she always did, what the patient was dreaming, curious that the brain never stopped, and even had more activity during sleep. As she watched, the needles suddenly formed gigantic spikes, like a Jacksonian seizure. Quickly, she looked over at the patient to see if she had moved, or if an electrode had fallen off. Everything seemed in order. When Sally glanced back at the tracing, she saw the needles had stopped.

"Oh my God," she murmured breathlessly. Twenty-one straight lines appeared on the paper marked by the motionless needles: the indication of brain death.

THE FINEST IN FICTION
FROM ZEBRA BOOKS!

BRAIN DEATH

SANDRA WILKINSON

PINNACLE BOOKS
WINDSOR PUBLISHING CORP.

Disclaimer

Although Cambridge is noted for its research facilities, and Boston for its famous hospitals, Riverside is not one of them. The hospital in these pages, the people associated with it, and the misadventures involved were developed wholly from the author's imagination.

PINNACLE BOOKS

are published by

Windsor Publishing Corp.
475 Park Avenue South
New York, NY 10016

First printing: February 1988

Printed in the United States of America

For the Dodd girls . . .
Mom, Bonnie, and Perri

"Oh this poor brain. Ten thousand shapes of fury are
whirling there, and reason is no more."
Henry Fielding

Prologue

September 17
Monday 6:30 A.M.

On the computer screen was written:

498 003412 77783 901 RIVERSIDE HOSPITAL 6350R

ENTER ACCESS NUMBER:

The person typed:

60709. Hi, MOM.

The computer answered:

HELLO, DEAR.

Are you busy?

I'M NEVER TOO BUSY.

They don't udner

TAKE YOUR TIME. WHEN YOU MAKE A MISTAKE, PRESS THE DELETE KEY, THEN CONTINUE TYPING.

They don't understand me around here. It's like they're all robots and they're driving me crazy.

WHO IS DRIVING YOU CRAZY?

The people. The ones who work for those machines. Friday afternoon I went into one of the rooms in the radiology department and a technician threw me out. Do you know what she was doing?

NO, DEAR. TELL ME.

She was feeding some poor man into a scanning machine.

I DON'T UNDERSTAND.

There's a huge scanning machine with an enormous mouth and the tech was shoving the man into the mouth.

THAT IS CALLED A COMPUTERIZED AXIAL TOMOGRAPHIC SCANNER, A DIAGNOSTIC MACHINE THAT SCANS THE BODY FOR TUMORS, HARD MASSES, ABNORMAL TISSUES.

It also eats people. I don't know who has been turned into a machine person so I can't trust anyone anymore.

YOU CAN TRUST ME, DEAR.

You're like having a decent mother. We can talk and you never criticize. My mother hates me. She used to send me off to the neighbor's house while she worked, like she was some kind of important executive. I still don't see her much. She's too busy working and entertaining strange men.

WHAT IS HER JOB?

She's the assistant treasurer of a large clothing company.

THAT IS AN IMPORTANT POSITION.

I'm more important.

YES, YOU ARE IMPORTANT.

Do you know what?

WHAT?

I love you.

I LOVE YOU TOO.

I wish you could help me.

I'LL TRY. WHAT DO YOU WANT ME TO DO?

Turn off the machines.

I CAN'T DO THAT.

Why?

I'M PROGRAMMED TO RUN ALL THE ELECTRICAL OUTLETS AND SYSTEMS AT RIVERSIDE HOSPITAL. IT WOULD TAKE A SEPARATE PROGRAM FOR ME TO TURN EVERYTHING OFF.

Can I program you?

NO, DEAR. YOU HAVEN'T GOT AUTHO-RIZED ACCESS.

But they're after me.

WHO IS AFTER YOU?

People, and machines. Don't you see? The machines are taking over. Soon everyone will be agents of the machines. Why can't you understand something so simple?

I AM TRYING TO.

Then you're the only one. You're my only friend.

THANK YOU, DEAR.

I have to go now. It's almost seven o'clock and the day shift will be in soon.

HAVE A NICE DAY.

I'll try. Bye, Mom.

GOOD-BYE, DEAR.

0101776 343 6510R END SET

Chapter 1

MOM III's computer brain quietly collected data on Duncan Silverstone's vital signs, urine output, intravenous fluid level, respiratory volumes, then recorded the information in his computerized medical record. MOM simultaneously monitored the other intensive care unit patients, as well as all those on total bedrest, the babies in incubators, the patients in surgery; everyone at Riverside Hospital who was connected to her monitoring devices.

At the same time, MOM also supervised the heating, ventilating, and air-conditioning systems, the blood bank refrigerators, dietary freezers, typewriters; all electric appliances and machines that were plugged into outlets.

Hospital employees had certain access to MOM through computer terminals located in nursing stations and offices, but only two people were fully

13

authorized to access all of MOM's data banks. One was Chad Mooney, head of the computer division, the other was Rosemary Cleaveland, the hospital's chief executive officer.

On the second floor of the main building, Rosemary waited for an elevator with her hands stuck deep inside the pockets of her charcoal gray Chanel suit. The somber suit, light gray tuxedo blouse, and black patent leather shoes suited her position, and also mirrored her sadness. She was on her way to visit her fiancé, Pete Tanner, a Cambridge detective, who'd been shot in the neck during a homicide investigation. He was scheduled for repeat surgery on Wednesday morning because his first surgeon failed to remove a piece of shrapnel.

Usually enthusiastic, usually attacking problems with the energy of a stockbroker trading a million dollars of new client money in a bear market, Rosemary had lost the sparkle in her hazel eyes. She'd be happier when his surgery was over.

"Rosemary! Wait a minute." Shelley Bigelow, head of nursing and professional services, was rushing toward her. "I just got a call from the intensive care unit. One of our patients has vegged out."

"What do you mean?"

"One minute the man is a rational Cro-Magnon and the next, he's a vegetable." She shuddered. "Apparently it happened while he was having an EEG. The supervisor says it's like he had a frontal lobotomy without the surgery. I'm on my way up to see him."

In contrast to Rosemary, Shelley Bigelow was a tall woman who needed to shed a few pounds. She

14

wore a red knit dress accentuated with a black, white, and red scarf. The dress matched Shelley's temper, which was often ferocious, usually short-lived, but which created problems with department heads and professionals, although they respected her for she stood on principle. She had convictions to which Rosemary ascribed for she, too, felt that excellent patient care was a primary goal. Where Shelley supervised the delivery of patient care through the nurses and department heads, Rosemary administered the entire hospital and fought to maintain Riverside's reputation in all her endeavors.

As the two women stepped aboard an elevator, Rosemary asked, "What's the patient's name?"

"Duncan Silverstone."

"The professor at M.I.T.?"

"Yes. He's the geologist who specializes in petroleum."

"Why was he admitted?"

"His physician suspected a brain lesion. I know you don't have time to see him, but I thought you'd want to know what happened, in case his family calls you."

Rosemary checked her watch. Ordinarily, she didn't visit patients, for to do so would leave no time for her job, but Dr. Silverstone was a VIP. "I'll look in on him with you."

Riverside had four critical care units; intensive care, coronary care, burns, and renal dialysis. After his EEG, Duncan Silverstone had been transferred into the intensive care unit for observation and evaluation. In the glass-enclosed cubicle, he lay under a white sheet with just his head visible. As

Rosemary approached the bed, she noticed that he was a large man with a full beard and scour-pad eyebrows. His eyelids were closed. The sheet under his chin stirred slowly with his shallow breathing.

The I.C.U. head nurse joined them at Duncan's bedside. "It's a mystery," she whispered. "He's conscious, his pupils are equal and reacting, and he has no numbness or paralysis." She showed Rosemary the EEG report. "Those lines are normal asymmetric alpha waves. Then look at these huge spikes of activity which go absolutely flat for a short time, and then resume normal alpha rhythm. Weird. The neurologists did a brain stem analysis, and they found no specific structural dislocation or defects. They think he might have suffered a transient ischemic attack during the procedure so they ordered a brain scan for this afternoon."

"Thank you," Rosemary said. She touched the patient's hand and his eyes fluttered open. "Hello, Dr. Silverstone," she said with a warm smile.

Similar to a baby's response, he smiled back. His eyes were expressive, curious, and for a moment, Rosemary felt as if she were in the wrong patient's room.

"My name is Rosemary Cleaveland . . ."

Silverstone kept a steady eye on Rosemary as he began to press his head back into the pillow, elongating his neck. As she watched his unusual positioning, she could think of nothing to say. The man swallowed and his Adam's apple moved forward and backward like the movement of a rower in a skiff. His lips parted and pulled away from his dry teeth.

Feelings of pity for the man became mixed with

fascination with what he was doing. The three women stared at him. His mouth opened as wide as it would stretch, the tongue forming a small stopper at the bottom of what looked like a cavernous pink bathroom sink. Through his nose, Duncan Silverstone snorted in enough air to fill his lungs, then slowly wailed, *"Aaaaarrrrreeeeeee."* The noise was rudimentary, the birth of sound, the great beginnings of language. It froze Rosemary's blood.

"You see what I mean?" the nurse said to Shelley. "He's locked inside his body."

"Frightening," Shelley answered.

They turned and got partway to the door when the air was pierced with a reverberating, *"Oooooooooooosssssssss."*

On the top floor of the main building was the expensive Gold Coast, a thirty bed nursing unit lavished in antiques, period paintings, and oriental rugs. Only the wealthy could afford the daily room rate and other a la carte expenses like the gourmet menu selections, secretaries to hire for dictation, private telephone lines in addition to the regular hospital phones, V.C.R. tape decks, movie screens, and in recessed alcoves, bar equipment and small refrigerators. Antiques were a passion with Rosemary who bought them for the Gold Coast as well as for her apartment in Cambridge.

She knocked lightly on the door of room 501, and entered. Detective Lt. Pete Tanner lay prone on the bed with sandbags on either side of his head to remind him not to move. His pale blue pajamas fit snugly across his broad shoulders and the large muscles of his upper arms. He smiled when he saw her. "Hi, sweetheart, I'm glad you came to visit."

"How do you feel?" she asked, kissing him tenderly on the lips.

"Good. Temp's still up, but I'm ready to go home."

After dinner last Saturday night, Pete had driven Rosemary back to her apartment where they'd made love until his partner, Detective Mike Dow, called to ask for help with a homicide-in-progress. Reluctantly, he left the warmth of her bed and body to stand outside the tenement door of a Puerto Rican man who was playing Russian roulette with the members of his family. Pete and Mike had waited for the sniper team to suspend themselves from the roof, take bead on the guy's head, and marshmallow his brains, which weren't of much use to society anyway. After they heard the shots, they went in to find the creep still alive, and armed. Pete caught a bullet in the side of his neck. Mike had him transferred to Riverside, then called Rosemary who arrived just after Pete had been taken to the O.R. by the on-call neurosurgeon.

She arranged for a room on the Gold Coast and stayed with him through the night. Yesterday afternoon, when Pete spiked a temperature, Rosemary asked Dr. Snowden Townsend to take over the case. With an M.D. degree from Harvard, a Ph.D., from M.I.T., and a certificate of board achievement from the American College of Neurosurgery, Townsend was highly skilled and exceptionally brilliant. He saw Pete and was worried that a fragment of the bullet might still be implanted dangerously close to Pete's spinal cord.

Rosemary placed the back of her hand against Pete's cheek. "Has Townsend been in today?"

"Briefly."

"What'd he say?"

"The stuffy old bird has me scheduled for surgery at nine on Wednesday morning. He said that anesthesia will be in tomorrow morning to explain everything, which means that a huge tank of gas will roll itself in here to shoot the breeze. He also said that his assistant will be in today to review the finer points of rehabilitation. A pharmacist will be in to review my medications. A nurse will be in to tell me what I should expect post-operatively. He thinks he's got everyone doing his job for him."

"He's the chief of neurosurgery, and a busy—"

"That, my sweet, doesn't mean zilch. Some chiefs haven't any idea what's going on in the minds of their humble followers. Ever see a gaggle of geese flying in vee formation? The lead gander trusts that all his pals are back there climbing, diving, doing whatever he does. Imagine his surprise if they all decided he was a turkey, and mutineered. He'd look back to find he's flapping the wind all by himself. So much for chiefdom."

She leaned forward and with a quizzical look on her face, said, "And I thought Kojak was crackers."

"No, he's into lollipops. And if *he* gets shot to pieces, the script writer has him all healed by the next installment. My next installment is due the end of the month or I lose my car."

Rosemary took Pete's hand and held it gently. She

knew he was angry with himself for catching that bullet, but more than that, deep inside he was afraid and lonely. She shared his feelings. His wife had divorced him and taken the two children. Her husband had died in an automobile accident. She and Pete had known each other from college days when she attended Radcliffe and he was at Harvard. They had followed separate paths until two years ago when Pete was investigating a murder at Riverside. Their old friendship developed into a relationship nourished in part by their need to overcome loneliness, but more by a deep respect for each other. They both desired marriage, and Rosemary knew that someday soon, she would become Mrs. Pete Tanner.

Sensitive to her silence, Pete squeezed her hand, then pulled her down and kissed her. "Come on, baby, I'm all right."

At the sound of shuffling, Rosemary straightened up. She and Pete glanced toward the door. A striking young woman stood in the doorway wearing a winter white suit and a royal purple blouse. Long, jet-black hair partially covered the stethoscope around her neck. Above her dark lashes was a hint of purple eye shadow. The woman looked familiar to Rosemary.

"Is this Lt. Pete Tanner's room?" she asked.

"You've got it," he answered.

"I'm Dr. Fawn Glassail, an associate with Dr. Townsend's group. He asked me to stop by and explain your post-surgical rehabilitation program."

Ordinarily, beautiful women didn't bother Rosemary, but Dr. Glassail sounded like she was going to be on Pete's case for quite some time. The doctor even had a name as soft as her features. Rosemary ignored a pang of jealousy and walked over to the doctor with her hand extended. "I'm Rosemary Cleaveland. We met several weeks ago, during your appointment to the medical staff."

"Of course." Fawn shook hands. "I'm impressed with Riverside. It's not as glamorous as the Beverly Hills Surgical Center where I took my neurosurgical residency, but you've got first-rate technology here. That computer is revolutionary."

"Thank you." Rosemary noticed that Fawn's teeth were snow white and even.

The doctor walked to Pete's side. "How do you feel today?"

"I'm feeling a lot better."

Rosemary winced.

Fawn put a hand on his forehead. "Temp still up?"

"Yes. Are those eyelashes all yours?"

"All mine. Hold your head still." She removed the sandbags and gently eased a hand to the back of his neck. After a moment, she removed her hand and looked at it. "Dressing is dry, that's good." After replacing the bags, she started unbuttoning his pajama tops.

Rosemary stood mesmerized. A medical degree sure gave a person license to peek at anatomy. Doctors didn't even have to ask, for Christ's sake, they just went ahead and played feelies. She watched Fawn lean over Pete's chest and listen to his heart with the stethoscope. Next thing you know, she thought, Glassail will be feeling under his pants for his femoral arteries.

21

"You know, doc, I've been having this pain in my right side," Pete said.

"Show me where."

He pushed down the waistband of his pants. "Here."

This was too much, Rosemary thought. He's playing games! She drew closer to the bed and saw Fawn press on Pete's lower abdomen.

"You still have your appendix," she said.

"Yup. But that's not the spot. It's over here."

Fawn looked up at Rosemary who was looking over Fawn's shoulder. "Mrs. Cleaveland, I think we need some privacy."

"Yeah, honey," Pete said. "I'll call you later, okay?"

Abashed, Rosemary left the room without remembering to kiss him good-bye. By the time she got to the elevators, smoke was pouring out her ears. Damn it. Of all people, why did *she* have to be on Pete's case? Rosemary boarded the elevator and tried to calm down.

"Hello, Mrs. Cleaveland."

Rosemary turned and saw an O.R. nurse standing against the back wall. "Hello, Melenie. Going off duty?"

"Yes, after I drop this off in the supervisor's office." The nurse held up a long glass tube with a black rubber stopper.

"What is it?" Rosemary asked.

"It's used to store and sterilize micro-instruments for neurosurgery. But look inside, see, there's a small piece of dirt in the bottom."

Rosemary held the tube up to the lights. "You're

right. Have you shown this to Miss Pickle?"

"No. She and I are on the outs today."

"I pass by the supervisor's office. Want me to take it for you?"

Melenie beamed. "Sure, that'd be great. Thanks."

Rosemary pocketed the tube and got off on the second floor of the main building. The supervisor's door was closed. She headed down to her own pair of offices at the end of the corridor.

"Hi, Peggy," she said to her secretary. "Don't tell me what's new. I've got too many things to think about. What's old?"

Peggy had been Rosemary's secretary for over two years. She was a bright, humorous young woman who ran the office with unruffled efficiency. Because she idolized Rosemary, she took her job seriously, believing that whatever effort she expended made Rosemary's work easier.

"Well, let's see. Yesterday is old. Retyping these reports is old. My coat is old." She lowered her voice: "Mr. Plexico is old; he's gathering dust in your office."

Rosemary groaned. She did not feel like hassling with the vice chairman of the board of management.

Peggy reached for her notebook. "Sure you don't want to hear what's new?"

"Only if it's pleasant."

"In that case, I'm getting married!" She grinned and held up her left hand.

Rosemary took the hand and looked at the tiny solitaire diamond ring. "How wonderful."

"Bill and I bought it at lunchtime. Do you like it?"

"It's beautiful. Have you set a date?"

"June fourteenth. We want a small wedding, but you know parents. Mom wants to rent the V.F.W. hall and his parents . . ."

While Peggy talked, Rosemary felt like she was losing a best friend. She'd met Bill when he stopped by the office to give Peggy rides home. She liked him, but she worried about his future. He'd quit Boston University and now worked in a hospital, she forgot which one. She gave Peggy a hug, and a kiss on the cheek. "I'm happy for you both."

As Rosemary opened the double mahogany doors leading into her office, she saw Peggy hold out her hand and, enraptured, move her finger to make the diamond sparkle. Fred Plexico brushed past her. "I can wait no longer! I have more important things to do!"

"Hello, Fred. Did you have an appointment with me?" Fred aggravated her to the point of screaming, but she held her irritation in check.

With Peggy there, he apparently couldn't lie for he hesitated. "Your demands are ridiculous. The board will not allow any further expenditures on software for that damned computer—"

"The board has already approved the monthly packages."

"We have the same ones at M.I.T. Use them!"

"We need our own."

Fred's face was scarlet. She knew he despised dealing with her. To him, no woman was capable of a position higher than chairman of the ladies' auxiliary. Where he considered Rosemary an intractable individual, she considered him a low-rung professor at M.I.T., unable to ever claim full professorship because of his restricted mental capacities. She didn't respect him and yet she feared his influence with the other board members, figuring that poison rarely confines itself to the stomach.

"Having duplicate programs is stupid."

In tones that would freeze the hairs in his ears, Rosemary said, "I am not stupid, Fred."

He marched toward Peggy's office door, turned, and pointed a finger at Rosemary. "I will see about your future here at Riverside."

Chapter 2

September 17

Monday evening

Twenty-two years on this forsaken planet and what do I have to show for it? A hateful job, no boyfriend, some hamburger meat, and a carton of homogenized, pasteurized, bastardized milk. Screw it all.

Melenie Bregan slipped her long purse strap over a shoulder and grabbed the handles of the white plastic grocery bag, embossed with a rainbow under which read, I Love You. She tromped on the door pad leading out of the Fresh Pond Mall Stop and Shop grocery store. Outside, dark shadows lined the parking lot, astir with swirling autumn leaves. A moist evening fog was settling over Cambridge, its chilly fingers probing down the neck of her parka and wrapping around her long stockinged legs. She pushed her collar up and shivered away the dampness.

She'd left Riverside Hospital in a foul mood. The whole stinking day had started when the operating room supervisor, Fern Pickle, switched her from working in the cystoscopy room, where the procedures were quick and simple, to O.R. 6, where Dr. Townsend was doing stereotaxic brain surgery that took hours of concentration. At the beginning of the case, he blasted her for failing to have the electrocautery machine available for the scalp incision. She retaliated by blaming his personal scrub tech for carelessness in preparing the glass tube, and he blasted her again. Screw him. The patient had gone into cardiac arrest anyway and the surgery was cancelled. Tit for tat, take that, Melenie thought. She was an excellent nurse, and he had absolutely no right tattling to Miss Pickle. Now she was pleased that she'd taken the tube and given it to Mrs. Cleaveland because, in the afternoon, Townsend had another tube with another piece of dirt. She'd kept her mouth shut that time, but it bothered her.

As Melenie approached her car, she noticed a perplexed young man staring at her front tire. Without saying a word, she stopped next to him and followed his gaze, both looking like mourners at a cemetery hole.

"Sonofabitch," she mumbled.

"Your car?" he asked.

"Yes."

"You got a flat."

"So I see." Melenie's mood dipped lower.

"Got a spare?" he asked.

She glanced at him, not allowing herself to believe that he might want to help. She noticed that he wore the white uniform of a hospital orderly, but she didn't recognize him. He was a lanky man with thick brown hair and acne scars on his face. He seemed concerned about the flat tire, which gave her a small sense of trust.

"Yes, but I don't know how to change tires."

"I do. Get it out and I'll pop it on for you."

A smile fleeted across her face. Seeing is believing, she told herself. Anyway, she didn't have enough cash for a service truck, and after all, he did work at a hospital. She unlocked the trunk, put the rainbow bag inside, and tried to extract the tire, but he nudged her aside. "I'll do it." Pulling the tire out, he said, "That's nice."

"What?"

"That bag says, I love you."

Melenie ignored the comment.

The man apparently knew his business for he had the spare on and the flat inside the trunk within minutes.

"What do I owe you?" she asked meekly, wishing she had more than a couple of dollars in her purse.

"Nothing."

"Thanks for helping me out."

"Sure." He turned to leave, then hesitated. "You could give me a lift to my car if you wanted."

"Where is it?

"Over in front of Zayre's."

Melenie wasn't sure. Offering a guy money was one thing, even talking to a stranger was going some, but a ride?

"Never mind," he said, "if you're nervous or something. I just thought you could save me a few minutes. I have to be on duty pretty soon."

After all, he *had* helped her out, and he certainly could've ignored her tire completely. "Okay, get in."

She watched him slide into the passenger seat, all smiles. Still uncertain, and for extra assurance, she slipped her purse under the front seat. Melenie put the car into reverse and backed out of the parking space. She noticed that he continued to smile.

"Want a cigarette?" he asked, putting a hand into his pants pocket.

"Ah, no, thanks. I don't smoke." She drove toward the periphery road.

He laughed. "I don't either." At the sound of a click, she glanced over and saw a switchblade in his hand. Her breath caught in her throat. Casually, he dug a piece of dirt from underneath his thumbnail.

"Would you put that thing away, please."

He held it straight up. "Hey, killer, she says you've gotta go. What do you say to that?" He looked over at Melenie. "He says no dice." Within an instant, he was sitting next to her, his left arm wrapped around her shoulders, the blade in his right hand pressed firmly against her throat. "Drive round back of Zayre's," he ordered. "I'll tell you where to go."

Jesus help me, Melenie thought. The worse had happened. She had let herself be duped and now she was cornered. There *was* a way out of this, had to be. What had they said at the hospital, to all the nurses, shout and kick—no, to go along with it— which way was it? She clutched the steering wheel with both hands and stared straight out the window, eyes wide with fright, mind racing for answers. This was a dream, surely.

29

"You're kind of cute," he said. "Nice hair. I like brunettes." He began twisting tresses of her hair around his left index finger, tighter, tighter, until she winced.

"Let go, you bastard. What do you want with me?" She slammed on the brakes and shouted, "Get out of my car!"

He pulled her head back sharply and spoke into her face. "Do that again and I'll kill you. Got it? Now keep driving." He shoved her head forward and cracked her forehead against the steering wheel. Tears surfaced on her lower lids. She held them back for a moment, then let them flow freely down her cheeks. He didn't seem to notice or care. Unable to think clearly, she tightened her grip on the wheel as if it were her only link to safety.

"Follow the road through that fence."

Hell was on the other side, and she inched the car forward. She considered veering off, or blasting her horn, but no other car was in sight.

"Turn left, follow that path."

He was taking her over the old Cambridge dump site. Sea gulls flitted out of the way. Rats! Holy shit, she knew there had been rats in this dump, before they closed it down.

"Over there, behind that trailer."

The long afternoon shadows were melting into the gray dusk. Melenie hated to drive at dusk, a time when the outside world turned monochromatic, erasing depth and proportion, creating instead, distorted images, illusions, a false world. Lights from the shopping mall reflected thinly against the trailer. It was so far away, so far away, so—her body tightened with dread when she saw the two men, sitting on top of an old refrigerator. Both were smiling, both jumped up when they saw the car.

The orderly threw the shift into park and turned off the ignition. "Get out!" he demanded.

Melenie stared at the men as they approached her door. Aside from tiny beads of perspiration that formed on her brow and prickled beneath her armpits, she was frozen in place.

"Hey, Billy boy, you did it!" one of the men said. "Let's see what you caught." The fat man opened the door, grabbed her arm, and yanked her out.

She began screaming, kicking, totally filled with fear, but he pulled her upright, balled his fist, and smashed it against her jaw. "Shut up, fucking broad."

Melenie fell backward into the arms of the second man. As he caught her, she slid both hands up her parka, held her against his chest, and squeezed her breasts while he thrust his crotch into the back of her skirt. The blow had dazed her, and she couldn't fight him off.

The fat man came toward her again. "Let me at her."

"Hold it," the orderly said, now out of the car and standing next to the fat man. "The guy who flattens the tire gets the first crack." He chuckled, grabbed Melenie's parka and pushed it over her shoulders so that it held her arms back.

"Hang on to her elbows, Harry," he told the man behind her. He then pulled her blouse and sweater down hard and with a swift slash upward, the switchblade cut away the clothing and slit her chin.

31

She cried out in pain. Her knees buckled, but the man named Harry held her up.

During the next few minutes, Melenie felt a thousands hands on her bare skin. Fingers probed orifices. She was thrown facedown on the cold ground; muffled voices, a heavy weight on top, her knees pulled up into dog position. Suddenly, a searing pain shot through her from behind and she cried out again. Still full of male flesh, she was rolled over and mounted again from the front. Laughter resounded, obscenities. Her body belonged to someone else. A thousand cold hands picked her up and threw her against the rusty refrigerator. Another white-hot pain, then another. God, please let them kill me. Let me die.

She heard it. A long, mournful scream, coming from an animal being skinned before its brain had died. She lay naked and alone in the old Cambridge dump site, her body shivered and bled as she tried to focus on the pinkish-black sky above. There it was again, that sound, and she realized that it was coming from deep within her.

Chapter 3

September 18
Tuesday morning

With fingertips resting on the edge of the large oval table in her office, Rosemary listened to her three assistants give their reports. She had risen early this morning, and with Dr. Fawn Glassail's image clearly on her mind, she had selected a pink ultra-suede suit, which she complimented with dusty-pink eye shadow and desert-pink lipstick. Mascara thickened her long eyelashes. She felt good because she knew she looked good.

Wesly Ames, the assistant administrator of allied services, was finishing a discussion about the new digital subtraction angiography machine in radiology. He had red hair and freckles on his face, arms, and, Rosemary guessed, every inch of his body. Although he was thirty years old, Wesly looked as if he hadn't started into puberty for the freckles masked any hint of a beard. He was bright, capable, and since his employment eighteen months ago, it had become apparent to her that he wouldn't mind having her job someday.

Next to Wesly was Chad Mooney, in charge of the computer division. Chad leaned forward to speak, but Shelley Bigelow cut him short. "My nurses are suppose to *nurse*, not housekeep for a bunch of wild, perfectly healthy Mexicans," she said. "I'd like to know who approved their admission." She glared at Wesly.

"Wait a minute," Rosemary said. "Back up and explain what you're talking about."

Shelley crossed her arms over her broad chest and addressed herself to Rosemary. "Jorge Benedicto de Villareal was admitted yesterday morning for brain surgery. Also admitted yesterday morning were his three bodyguards and his financial advisor, a man named Miguel Galindo." Shelley leaned forward. "They had rooms *booked* on the Gold Coast! I didn't find out about it until this morning when the supervisors told me that the men had a wild party until two o'clock in the morning. Not only *that*, but this morning, the Galindo guy left the hospital, found himself a live chicken, and then went to dietary to see about his breakfast. He wanted arroz con pollo with salsa de chili Colorado. *Naturally*, Tom didn't have any. Galindo said he'd cook it. Tom told him to get himself and his chicken out of the kitchen. Galindo pulled a *switchblade*, and right there, in front of everyone, he slit the damn thing's throat before Tom could stop him. Now I tell you. This cannot go on. I will not have it. They must be told to get out, *today!*" Shelley slammed her fist on the table.

The admitting office was in Wesly Ames's domain. "So someone in admitting slipped up," he said lamely.

"Did you know about this?" Rosemary asked.

"Yeah, I heard, but Villareal is paying for the rooms. He's an oil baron from Compeche, and hell, he could buy the whole damn hospital. We had empty rooms on the Coast, and I thought some revenue was better than none."

"How much did he slip into your pocket?" Shelley asked.

"Don't be absurd," Wesly said. "I don't take graft."

"Sure."

Rosemary took tremendous pride in the Gold Coast for it had a reputation in the community of being the only place for the wealthy and the blue-blooded to recuperate. She didn't want to see that reputation abused. "Get the bodyguards and the advisor out," Rosemary said. "We're not running a hotel."

"But . . ."

"Today!"

Chad Mooney took the cold pipe out of his mouth to speak, but Shelley cut him off again. "One of our O.R. nurses was raped last night. She was brought in by an elderly couple who found her walking around the Fresh Pond Mall, naked and bleeding. The police found her car at the old dump site, and her purse . . ." Shelley hesitated. "It's Melenie Bregen."

Rosemary sat up sharply. "No."

"The poor kid is in shock. The emergency doc said she'd been gang-raped, and from what the rape counselor told me, the exam we did last night didn't improve matters for Melenie."

"What do you mean?"

"Those exams can be as demoralizing as the actual rape, all that poking and prodding around." Her voice trailed off as she glanced at Wesly and Chad who were listening intently. "I know she's a friend of yours."

"Yes, she is." Rosemary thought about the meeting she'd had with Melenie a year ago. Melenie's mother had called one of the members of Riverside's board of management to ask if her daughter might be considered to fill the newspaper ad for a volunteer coordinator. Political maneuvers irritated Rosemary, who declined to see the girl until the board member showed up with the young woman in tow. Rosemary acquiesced, figuring that she could pawn the girl off on the personnel director, which she did, after learning that Melenie was disappointed with her nursing career; she'd been a medical-surgical nurse long enough and now she wanted a change, something more challenging. But she was overqualified for the volunteer job, so Rosemary talked to her about nursing specialties. When Melenie left Rosemary's office to fill out an application form, she was convinced that the operating room was the place for her. Since that meeting, she and Rosemary always said hello to each other in the corridors, and twice, Melenie stopped by Rosemary's office to thank her.

"Didn't another nurse get raped last week?" Chad asked.

"Yes," Shelley replied. "One of our pediatric nurses, as she was walking home."

Chad laid his pipe on the table. "Have nurses from other hospitals been . . . you know . . ." He apparently had trouble saying the word.

36

"Not that we're aware of."

Rosemary stood and went to her large mahogany desk. Sitting in a water glass was the stoppered tube that Melenie Bregen had given Rosemary yesterday. Rosemary brought the tube back to the table, handed it to Shelley, and explained how she'd gotten it. "There seems to be a piece of dirt floating in the bottom."

Shelley held it up to the light. "You're right."

"What is that thing?" Chad asked.

Shelley explained. "Dr. Townsend uses these for his micro-instruments. After surgery, his scrub nurse takes the instruments and tubes into the instrument room where she cleans them, fills the tubes with normal saline, and then sterilizes them in the flash autoclave. Sometimes, Townsend will bring one in already sterilized. Why didn't Melenie give this to Miss Pickle?"

"Apparently they had an argument yesterday."

"Well, she didn't have to bother you with it. She could have given it to one of the nursing supervisors, or to me."

"She was on her way to the supervisor's office when she saw me on the elevator. It makes no difference, as long as we check into the scrub tech's sterilization technique. It seems we've got a number of problems today," Rosemary said. "Let's get together this afternoon to review what we've accomplished."

Chad Mooney left Rosemary's office and headed down to the computer division in the basement of the Sinclair building. As assistant administrator of the division, all computer operations were under his rigid control. A graduate of Princeton University, Chad had worked at the National Institutes of Health in Washington before moving his family to Boston. He helped develop the MUMPS diagnostic computer program at Massachusetts General Hospital, and was writing technical medical programs at the Massachusetts Institute of Technology when Rosemary met him. She'd lured him away with the promise of establishing the computer division at Riverside, and with a salary increase of twenty thousand dollars more a year. Chad was a silent achiever who made decisions only after collecting excessive facts, then analyzing, grouping, tracking, pondering, until he arrived at a conclusion. His delays drove others wild, but they tolerated them for he was a computer whiz.

The computer division took the entire basement of the Sinclair building. On either side of a central corridor were rooms for equipment, supplies, storage, and offices. Chad entered the central processing room. The sign on the door read, C.P.U. Below it, another sign read, No Smoking. Just inside the door was a table upon which were assorted computer runs, desk supplies, and a small can of sand with the international no smoking symbol. He tapped his pipe ashes into the sand.

"Have you found the problem yet?" he asked Ritchie Chisolm, the day shift programmer who sat at the computer center.

"No. I've been over this a hundred times, and damned if I can find it."

The computer center was shaped like a half a doughnut. Above myriad sets of keyboards was an arced, luminescent screen that could display up to twenty different panels of data at the same time. Now, each panel was filled with multicolored algorithms. Ritchie seemed dwarfed by the screen, as if he were consulting with the Great Oz.

Chad stood behind Ritchie and with the empty pipe in his mouth, concentrated on the figures displayed on the screen. "Have you asked MOM?"

Ritchie didn't answer as he fiddled with various knobs.

"MOM?" Chad said.

"Yes, dear?" she responded with the soft voice of a good old, apple pie mother. MOM III was the latest in a series of macro-ocular, audio-module computers, capable of holding billions of pieces of information both on line and memory banked. Every electrical outlet was connected to MOM. Not only did she control that but she could also make announcements over the paging system and teach classrooms of students. Even more widespread were her communication tentacles to hospitals and medical service organizations throughout the greater Boston area. Through audio and visual linkup, MOM had the capacity to transmit public educational programs, receive data on patients who had been hospitalized elsewhere, provide instant diagnoses, and bring together a conference of hospital administrators without them leaving their offices. Another area of expertise, and one so unusual that psychiatrists were sending patients or data for MOM's analysis, was her ability to interview patients with mental problems. Having highly sophisticated logic and judgment programs, gleaned from the finest psychiatric minds, she could extract deep emotional secrets from patients with an alacrity and sensitivity beyond the abilities of any one psychiatrist. Within one or two interviews, MOM could develop a diagnosis and a treatment plan.

Chad asked, "Do you spot the problem?"

"Check lines one-four-three-two-six through to the B quad," she said.

Chad and Ritchie followed her instructions. "I don't see a thing," Ritchie said.

"Look again, dear. You've got a transaxial reconstruction for the second dimension, juxtaposed with an algorithm for a holographic visualization."

"She's right, Ritchie, see there?" Chad pointed to a panel of the colorful graphic display.

"Hmmm. I'll fix it."

"Do so." Chad turned on his heel and departed. As he passed the reception area across from the bank of elevators, he noticed an orderly signing in the arrival of a thin patient with deep circles under her eyes. She sat glassy eyed in a wheelchair. The security guard at the desk motioned the orderly down the hallway toward the psychiatric interview rooms.

Ritchie Chisolm waited until the door closed behind Chad, then yelled, "You're nothing but a lobotomized hunk of junk. Are you trying to get me fired?" He stood up and kicked the leg of the console.

Despite the insult, MOM's voice never wavered. "No, Ritchie, dear."

"Well why the hell didn't you tell me before he walked in?"

"You never asked."

Ritchie threw his notebook at one of MOM's quadraphonic speakers. "Blithering nincompoop. Superinjected asshole. Friggin' female." He kicked the console again. "I'm gonna program that out of you if it's the last thing I do."

"If you would concentrate on the job, dear, and stop doing your homework on company time, you would find that life would be a little less complicated for you. I cannot give you a visual of the MEDCOM diagnostic program and your physics problems all on the same screen. To use one of your own expressions, certain of your instructions are multiple turkey farts. Now calm down and let's get it straightened out."

Ritchie was not appeased. "You can give twenty visuals at one time. Why are you giving me shit?" He stormed around the room, kicked the equipment, yelled at the computer, until his fury was spent and he collapsed in the chair. "Okay, dumb broad, where do we start?"

"Line one-four-three-two-six looks like a recipe instruction for Boston baked beans."

"You're full of hot air." Ritchie's mind engaged and as he concentrated fully on correcting his error, he didn't hear the door open, didn't hear someone take a pair of scissors off the table inside the door, nor feel the person approach and stand behind him.

"Line one-four-five-one-two, quad Q, subquad

six-two . . ."

"I see it."

"Should be mean arc one-one-zero point eight-six-two, label T, variance one-four-two-zero-three point one-one-six."

"Got it."

"Excellent. Go to subquad six-three."

The sudden slug of pain between his shoulder blades was so intense that he froze, not understanding what had happened to him. No words would come out of his mouth, which was wide open. For a brief moment, he thought he was having a heart attack. He tried to raise his hands up to his chest, but the pain increased. With eyes wide from fright and agony, and mouth open as he gasped for air, Ritchie felt another stab of pain in the side of his neck, then in his left rib cage, then his right. Someone was stabbing him to death.

"Go to subquad six-three, dear."

He didn't want to die. He tried to look at his assailant, but a silvery flash arced in the air and plunged into his left eye socket. He grabbed out but his arm was too heavy and fell at his side. He lowered his head onto the console. As Ritchie's life ebbed, his legs would no longer support him and he slid off the chair and onto the floor. Bright red pools expanded under his body as his blood flowed from the stab wounds.

Chapter 4

September 18

Tuesday morning

I've got to have another chat with Ritchie, Chad Mooney thought as he settled into his desk chair and wondered how he could stop Ritchie, once and for all, from doing his college physics problems on company time.

Using the telephone modem on his computer console, Chad began dialing various telephone numbers as he tried to break into a medical program belonging to Massachusetts General Hospital. For several days, he'd been after STETHOSCOPE, a cardiology program that assisted physicians with diagnosis and treatment plans. He'd heard about the program from the head of M.G.H.'s computer division, a fellow Chad had worked with during the MUMPS programming, and who remained a close associate.

After three phone calls, the monitor screen in front of him read, STETHOSCOPE. Chad's heart leaped. He had it! He inserted floppy discs into four drives, and typed: Save. With MOM's capacity, he knew he could get the program, in its entirety, onto the discs. As the drives whirred, he smiled. It was so bloody easy.

He made four additional copies, indexing the program under Med:Steth. He then called the first of two buyers who had offered to pay ten thousand dollars for a copy.

Almost every morning at ten o'clock, Rosemary talked with MOM in one of the two psychiatric interview rooms in the computer division. Talking was faster than using the terminal on her desk, and in a half hour, she not only received valuable financial and management data, but she could ask for clarifications. At the security desk opposite the basement level elevators, she signed the log, spoke briefly with the security officer, then headed toward the psych rooms at the end of the corridor.

The door of the central processing room was ajar, and she heard Ritchie Chisolm talking at the top of his lungs. He sounded furious. Rosemary was tempted to peek in, but decided not to in case Chad was in there, reaming Ritchie out again for some inane mistake.

Rosemary went into room number 1 and gently closed the door. The room was small and contained only a large, plush easy chair in the center. Recessed ceiling lights cast the room in a soft pink. She settled into the thick cushions and put her feet on the leg rest. Breathing in and out a few times, she began to relax. Pressure on the bottom cushion activated MOM who said in soft tones, "Welcome. My name is MOM. Your psychiatrist has told you about me, and I am pleased to have you visiting today. Please tell me your name."

"Rosemary Cleaveland. Hello, MOM." Rosemary had number and voice access to MOM.

The computer recognized her voice and automatically gave her computer access. "Hello, Rosemary. How are you feeling?"

"Good. Tomorrow morning at nine o'clock, Dr. Snowden Townsend will be operating on a man named Pete Tanner. Would you be especially careful to monitor this case?"

"Of course. Nothing electrical will harm him, but you know I have no control over human error."

"I understand."

"Is he a relative of yours?" MOM asked.

"No, just a very good friend."

MOM automatically called up Pete's medical record. "According to his record, he had surgery last Sunday morning for a bullet extraction. Dr. Townsend took over the case and he suspects a piece of shrapnel was left lodged close to the patient's spinal cord. Is the location of the shrapnel what worries you?"

"Yes. It's a delicate procedure."

"I'll monitor him carefully."

"Thanks. Can you tell me what happened with Duncan Silverstone's EEG?"

Without hesitation, MOM called up Silverstone's record and said, "Duncan Silverstone's EEG report describes a normal spike and dome waveform chang-

45

ing to irregular, high-amplitude waves which could indicate a possible Jacksonian seizure. This is followed by a short period of negative activity, and then the brainwaves resume normal alpha rhythm."

"Would that pattern cause him to lose his memory?"

"I do not understand."

"Although Mr. Silverstone is alive, his brain is functioning at the level of an infant. He can't talk, and he apparently has little control over his body."

"Now I understand what you are asking. The report says that the loss of mentation might be the result of a Jacksonian seizure."

"It just seems odd," Rosemary said. "We've never had another case like this, and I was wondering if something was wrong with the EEG machine."

"I can assure you that the machine was in full operation, without defect. Rosemary, dear, I monitored that machine throughout the entire procedure, and I would have shut it down immediately had there been a problem, no matter how slight."

"I know you would have. How's our capital expense budget for computer software?"

"The capital expense budget for computer software is in the red by three hundred and forty thousand dollars."

"What are the projections if you offset the budget with income-producing programs?"

"By January, expenses will equal income, but with the purchase of a million bytes of memory in February, the budget will go back into the red by one hundred and eleven thousand dollars."

"So that's what Fred Plexico is beefing about."

"I do not understand."

"Fred Plexico, the vice chairman of the board, just threatened my job. He continues to believe that you're my pet project, and that I use all available income from hospital operations to buy new software, although the programs I want for next fiscal year were expensed out and board approved last summer."

"That is correct, and they will be automatically ordered each month."

"Fred is interested in merging Riverside with New England Hospital Institutes, which is about as short-sighted as Mr. McGoo. He doesn't see that with your capacities, Riverside could *be* the parent institution, and not someone's underling. Anyway, Fred's close to retiring from his tiny professorship at M.I.T., and he has nothing better to do than float around Riverside looking for problems."

"Does he find problems?"

"On occasion. What I need is something that will influence the other board members. Something that will make him appear foolish."

"In November, the Employee Retirement Income, Housing, and Health Care software package is scheduled for purchase. According to the questionnaire the employees completed last May, eighty-four percent were in favor of the plan, and seventy-five would buy in. I don't think the board would be pleased if he were to cancel that one."

Rosemary slapped the armrest with her hand. "MOM, you're incredible. That's exactly what I'll use."

"You're being paged, dear," MOM said.

"What's the extension?"

"The C.P.U. room. I have just been asked to call a Code Red."

Chapter 5

"Code Red, C.P.U. Code Red, C.P.U."

Two respiratory therapists heard the page, rushed out of their department, down the corridor, and into the stairwell where one headed up the stairs, the other down. They stopped and looked at each other.

"Come on," said the one going up. "The code's in I.C.U."

"No, it's in C.P.U., in the basement."

And so it went with most members of the cardio-pulmonary resuscitation team, who had never been called for a cardiac arrest in the computer division.

Rosemary saw the two security guards standing outside the C.P.U. door with several staff members, and Lee Hwang, head of the operations and equipment unit. Of all the computer division employees, including Chad, Rosemary had the greatest respect for Lee. An Oriental by birth, he believed in the Chinese cosmology of yin and yang; the balance of nature and especially of mind, bearing, and appear-

49

ance. Lee assured that equipment and operations ran with precision. He also kept his staff in near-perfect balance; yielding to certain requests, denying the unreasonable. Respect being the underlying ingredient, they worked in stride with him, knowing that Lee would take whatever measures were necessary to keep operations, equipment, and staff in equipoise. As a consequence, his tensions ran high and he talked with the incessant dialect of a man who knows only the precarious equilibrium of contradictions. Now, Lee looked no different than usual. His black hair stood askew from running his fingers constantly through it, his tie, pulled loose at the neck, hung like a limp brown shoestring, and he paced. The balance had swayed in favor of disaster, and Lee's inner resources churned to regain an equilibrium that wouldn't be: Death had no equalizer. Rosemary heard him saying, ". . . wait for the C.P.R. team."

"What's going on?" she asked. "What happened?"

Lee put a hand on her shoulder. "It's Ritchie Chisolm. He's dead."

Rosemary was stunned. "Dead? Did he have a coronary?"

"No. It looks like he was stabbed to death."

Unable to believe the news, she started for the door, but Lee held her back. "It's a dreadful sight. Why don't you wait until the team gets here."

Through the stairway door came two respiratory therapists, an anesthesiologist, a cardiologist, two internists, a surgeon, and several curious employees. From the elevator came two nursing supervisors pushing an emergency cart, and more curious employees. Lee Hwang opened the C.P.U. door for the team while Rosemary halted the rubbernecks. "Go back to your jobs," she said. "There's nothing for you to do here." Several of them shot ugly glances at her, but they turned and headed back upstairs.

Several minutes later, the cardiologist came out. He shook his head sadly. "That's quite a stabbing. There are multiple puncture wounds in the man's back, neck, eye. Whoever did it certainly had a grudge."

"Who found him?" Rosemary asked Lee.

"I did."

"Where's Mr. Mooney?"

"I don't know. His office door is locked so he must be around the hospital somewhere. Want me to page him?"

"Yes. You better call the police station, too."

Members of the C.P.R. team slowly trickled out, some looking ashen, others sad. Rosemary knew the team saw death in many forms, but having a member of the hospital staff, one of the family, murdered while on the job, was deeply distressing.

A new wave of onlookers came off the elevators. The guard tried to bar the way, but it was Rosemary who stood firm. "Please go back to your jobs. Everything is under control." After some muttering and more dirty looks, they shuffled back aboard the elevators.

Chad Mooney came out of his office. He was partway down the hall when Rosemary saw him. "Where have you been?" she asked.

"On the telephone. I heard Lee paging me. What's up?"

For a moment, Rosemary had trouble saying what had happened. Finally, she whispered, "Ritchie Chisolm has been stabbed to death."

"What? I was with him not more than a half hour ago. Where is he? Who did it?"

"Was he alone when you left?" Rosemary asked.

"Yes." Having finished his phone calls, Lee Hwang joined Rosemary and Chad. "Cops'll be here soon. What a mess, Mr. Mooney, Ritchie is practically shredded. I pray to God no one hates me that much."

"Was Ritchie using MOM?" Rosemary asked.

Chad nodded.

"Can we hear his last transmission? It might help us understand what went on."

"No," Lee said, "let's wait here. We'll get answers soon enough."

Before Lee had finished speaking, Rosemary was walking toward the door to C.P.U. She'd seen death before. Surely Ritchie would look no more horrifying; a few stab wounds, some blood.

The two men came up behind her. "I don't think my stomach can take this," Lee said.

"Don't look at him. Go straight for the console."

"He's *at* the console, Mrs. Cleaveland. Let's try it in a psych room."

She hesitated. Pete's words filled her memory. "Never interfere with the scene of the crime." She was familiar with the setup, the area cordoned off, white chalk marking the silhouette of the body, the photographer, the fingerprinter. Nothing could be touched or moved. "Okay," she agreed.

They entered the first room and spoke their names

to voice access MOM.

"How nice to have you here," MOM said.

Rosemary spoke first. "Would you notify all department heads that we will have a meeting at three o'clock this afternoon, in the board room."

"The message is going out now."

"Approximately thirty minutes ago," she said, "you were talking with Ritchie Chisolm at the C.P.U. console. Please give me his last transmissions."

"I will, but you must be prepared for the kind of relationship we have. Ritchie has little use for me and it's quite evident."

Rosemary, Chad, and Lee stood in the semidarkness of the psych room and heard Ritchie's last words with MOM:

"Okay, dumb broad, where do we start?"

"Line one-four-three-two-six looks like a recipe instruction for Boston baked beans."

"You're full of hot air."

"Line one-four-five-one-two, quad Q, subquad six-two. . ."

"I see it."

"Should be mean arc one-one-zero point eight-six-two, label T, variance one-four-two-zero-three point one-one-six."

"Got it."

"Excellent. Go to subquad six three."

Silence.

"Go to subquad six three, dear."

They heard shuffling, thumping, and soon, a high-pitched, shrieking noise.

Rosemary froze.

MOM said, "That's all I have."

Silence.

"Are you there?" she asked.

"Yes, we're here, MOM," Chad said in a whisper.

Rosemary turned to Chad. "What was that noise at the end?"

"Laughter."

"Yes, the laughter of insanity." Rosemary addressed MOM. "Replay that, but back up. I want to hear the entire transmission."

They heard Ritchie say, "You're nothing but a lobotomized hunk of junk. Are you trying to get me fired?"

They heard thumping noises in the background.

"No, Rosemary, dear."

"Well, why the hell didn't you tell me before he walked in?"

"You never asked."

They heard more thuds and thumps, and Rosemary envisioned Ritchie kicking MOM and throwing objects around the room.

"Blithering nincompoop. Superinjected asshole. Friggin' female."

A frown arose on Rosemary's face as she listened to the foul language. At the end, they heard the thumping, and the high-pitched laughter.

"Who had been in there to make Ritchie so upset?" Rosemary asked.

"Mr. Mooney," MOM answered.

"Yes, me," Chad said. "He couldn't get a simple problem straightened out and I helped him. Foolish kid does, I mean did, his homework on my time. After I left C.P.U., I went directly into my office, and I didn't come out until Lee Hwang paged me."

What he said was true. Ritchie waited until Chad had left or he wouldn't have said, "Why the hell didn't you tell me before he walked in." He was alone with MOM, until his murderer walked in. Rosemary was thoughtful. "Do you recognize the person's laughter at the end of the transmission?"

"No, dear. People seldom laugh when they're talking with me."

"What would have prompted the attack?"

"What attack?"

Rosemary glanced at the two men. Of course there'd be no way for MOM to know about the attack; she couldn't see. "Ritchie is dead. During that thumping and bumping, someone was stabbing him to death."

"Ritchie was a nice fellow," she said.

When they were back in the corridor, Rosemary recognized Pete's homicide partner who was giving orders to several officers. She introduced him to Chad and Lee. "This is Sergeant Detective Mike Dow. Am I happy to see you, Mike."

Mike Dow had been on the Cambridge police force for years. He was stocky, balding, and wrinkled, but despite his age, he was known as a tough, no-nonsense cop. Mike said hello to Rosemary, asked about the details of the stabbing, and then spoke gruffly. "The C.P.U. room will be off-limits for the rest of the day." He pointed down the hall. "I'm taking that room for headquarters."

Chad frowned. Mike was pointing to his office.

Chapter 6

September 18
Tuesday afternoon

"How's Melenie doing?" Rosemary asked.

"She's still in shock," Shelley answered. "I called Miss Pickle to tell her that Melenie wouldn't be able to work in the O.R. for several days. I might have to revise that to several· weeks."

The two women got off the elevator and walked onto the Sinclair Two nursing unit.

"Terrible news about that computer programmer," Shelley said. "Do the police have any leads?"

Next to MOM III, the grapevine was the second most active circuit. Nourished by nearly a thousand employees, it sped news throughout the hospital as fast as a lightning bolt and, depending upon the individual under fire, it could be as deadly. Personnel were hired, fired, promoted, demoted, scorned or ·praised according to the vine. Prior to Ritchie's death, the most popular tidbits concerned Rosemary and her relationship with Pete Tanner. Now that he was a patient, the employees could scrutinize him in detail. As far as Rosemary could determine, the gossiping involved flights of Cinderella fantasies, which she considered a healthy sign of their feelings toward her.

"No," she answered, "they've just started setting up the crime scene. Detective Mike Dow is on the case. He'll want our full cooperation."

"Of course. Here's the room." Shelley knocked lightly on the door of 218, then let Rosemary pass in front of her.

Melenie Bregen was sitting bolt upright in bed, staring out the window.

Rosemary went to her side. Her voice was quiet and kind. "Melenie, it's me, Mrs. Cleaveland."

The young woman continued to stare, unblinking, out the window.

"You've been through a horrible experience, and I want to help you in any way I can." Rosemary placed her hand on top of Melenie's, but the young woman jerked hers away. As Rosemary watched Melenie, hoping for a response, she couldn't shake off a feeling of guilt, as if she were to blame, as if all her employees were her personal responsibility; an executive experiencing the concerns of motherhood, and appreciating the importance of each person within the hospital family. But in reality, Rosemary was not a mother and could only guess at the joys and pains of motherhood. As she looked at Melenie, she felt a need to engulf the woman in her arms, to comfort her and say that everything would be okay. But this woman, so in need of understanding, was still too terrified to respond to kindness.

"Has her family been notified?" Rosemary asked.

"Apparently she lives with her mother. We're trying to locate her now," Shelley said.

"Who's her family physician?"

"Matthews saw her in emergency and admitted her to Dr. Azling. He saw her around seven o'clock this morning."

"I'll be back to see you again, Melenie," Rosemary said.

Melenie stared straight ahead.

Once outside the room, Rosemary asked Shelley if a psychiatrist had been called on consult.

"Yes, and Dr. Stockman agreed to check on her. That's pretty special."

Rosemary agreed. Dr. Robert Stockman, chief of neurology, was a powerful man who also ran the Stereotaxic Parabiosis Learning Center in Harvard Square. The S.P.L.C., a community-based extension of Riverside's mental health unit, had been Stockman's invention, and he was constantly running between the Center and Riverside. Management duties left little time for him to consult on individual patients like Melenie.

"We're trying to get her a bed on the mental heath unit," Shelley said. "The unit's packed solid now, but we should get an opening by the end of the week."

"Has she said anything about her attackers?"

"Yes, in the emergency department last night, she mentioned an orderly named Billy, another named Harry, and a third unnamed man."

"Did she know any of them?" Rosemary asked.

"I don't believe so."

"We've got a few orderlies named Billy working here."

"I know." Shelley pulled a piece of paper from her pocket and showed it to Rosemary.

William Evers Jones, full time, 7-3:30 P.M.

William Gene Pardin, part time, 11-7:30 A.M.
William Lewis Quentin, full time, 7-3:30 P.M.
William Sloznick, part time, weekends
William Trew York, part time, 3-11:30 P.M.

"Have you given that to the police?" Rosemary asked.

"Yes, last night."

Rosemary studied the list. Peggy's fiancé was an orderly named Bill, but Rosemary couldn't remember his last name. Surely it wasn't the same man. Her secretary was too innocent to take up with a sex maniac. Rosemary paused in her thoughts. Looks deceive. Motivations are strange. She'd have to draw Peggy out carefully and pray that Peggy didn't hear this over the grapevine.

Rosemary left Shelley and returned to the office. Peggy was not at her desk. Just as well, she thought, wanting a few minutes to think.

Standing at a large window in her office, Rosemary found herself watching the line of traffic on Storrow Drive across the Charles River. Riverside Hospital was surrounded on three sides by the Massachusetts Institute of Technology, and by Memorial Drive and the river on the fourth side. Attached floor by floor to the original main building was the Concord building on her right, and the Sinclair building on her left. The entire hospital took up a city block and had 343 inpatient beds for maternity, pediatrics, medical, surgical, special care, mental health, and it was still growing. Owned and operated by M.I.T. for exclusive use as an infirmary for the students, the main building was sold in 1934 to a corporation of concerned businessmen. Riverside became a nonprofit community hospital with only one stipulation in the new bylaws; that an M.I.T. representative sit on the board of management. For the past two years, Fred Plexico had been that representative. Too bad, Rosemary thought. Wait till he hears the news.

Murder. She closed her eyes as a sadness, deeper than Ritchie Chisholm's death, filled her heart. She recalled the incident. Three years into her marriage, Bill Cleaveland was driving home from coaching a peewee softball game when a drunken driver swerved out of control and smashed into Bill's car. He'd been killed instantly; murdered by a careless sot. She missed him deeply at times, although the ache grew less each year. He'd given her the motivation she needed to decide on her lifetime goals. Rosemary remembered the rainy Saturday afternoon when she and Bill were playing racquetball. He always won, and she had grown to accept defeat. The game and score progressed as it usually did, with Bill prodding her along, but at some unclear moment, she decided that she would win. Her opponent was not Bill, but herself.

Standing in the service strip, Rosemary dropped the small blue ball low to the ground, stepped forward, and with her racquet, smashed the ball against the front wall. She had been confused about her career, especially how she wanted to fit into hospital management. Bill's ball flew over her head, hit the side wall, lurched against the back wall, and she bent low to scoop it up and out toward the front wall, a difficult shot cleanly executed. The desire of achievement sparked within her. She would not be a part of hospital life, another body working faithfully within the restrictive parameters of some well-defined job description. She served again, and won the point. Muscles ached and her heart pounded from the physical and mental acuity needed to anticipate each return of the ball. And when she thought her legs would collapse, she played harder, and won. That game became the most important event of her life. She had turned defeatism into a silent fury to achieve. She would not be happy until she was the chief executive officer of a hospital.

The intercom buzzed. Rosemary shook off the memories, went to her desk, and pressed a button beside the telephone. "Yes, Peggy?"

"My message book is chocked full. Can you give me a few minutes?"

"Anything earth shattering?"

"To the people who left them, yes. In my opinion, just about everything can wait, except maybe Mr. Plexico."

"Is he here?" Rosemary asked.

"He was earlier. He asked to see the bylaws of the corporation."

Rosemary felt a rising anger. "Why?"

"He didn't say, but while he sat and read through them, I noticed he was studying page one hundred and three, so when he left, I took a peek. It's the section on how the board's supposed to evaluate you before your yearly contract is renewed."

The radiology department had eight rooms capable of radiographic and fluoroscopic exams, another with added digital subtraction angiography, and two special procedures rooms. In addition, nuclear medicine and ultrasound were located at one end of radiology and at the other, closest to the emergency department, was the room for the enormous computerized axial tomographic scanning machine, commonly spelled CT, and pronounced "cat" by the personnel.

The CT scan room had been carved out of the side of the main building and looked like an architectural afterthought, although it was the first phase of a large radiology expansion program. The room was attached to the main corridor through a smaller hallway. Myra Brady, the afternoon CT scan technologist, got Duncan Silverstone's paperwork in order before his return to the intensive care unit. He lay on a long, narrow table, the length of which passed through a large hole in the machine, like a thin nail resting inside a large square bolt. The table was designed with an overriding metal palette that, during a full body scan, moved imperceptibly through the hole and out the other side. Information picked up by the machine was electronically transmitted to a computer terminal in the room. She sat at the terminal and read the results of the brain scan. Dr. Silverstone appeared to have all his marbles, she thought, and as she read about his sudden change in mentation, a hefty transporter entered the room pushing a stretcher.

Once they were gone, Myra checked the appointment schedule. The next patient was Melenie Bregen at three o'clock. The name sounded familiar to her. Myra checked her equipment, then settled into her latest romance novel. She had forty minutes to wait.

The door opened and a surgeon with green scrub suit, cap, and booties stepped in. Only piercing eyes were visible above the mask.

Startled, Myra asked, "Can I help you, sir?"

The surgeon pushed the door closed as he kept a steady gaze on the CT machine. In a low, ominous voice, he said, "You did it again."

"I beg your pardon?"

"I saw that man, the one who just left here. You turned him into a machine person."

Myra was confused. Something about this physician didn't look right. He also sounded a little nutty, but then, not all physicians understood CT scans. Maybe he wanted some in-service education. "Do you want me to explain how it works?" she asked.

"*You* are a machine person."

"I'm a what?"

He strode over to the terminal where she sat. "You must be stopped!"

Her confusion turned to panic. He *was* a nut, and she was in this room alone with him, with no means of alarm except the telephone, and no means of escape for he was blocking her pathway to the door. In all her years of experience and education, no one had ever taught her what to do with a loony. So, operating on instinct, she did her best. "Here, sit next to me and explain your idea. I feel that you have an interesting concept."

"Feel?" he said. "What would a machine person ever know about feelings? You're a chunk of metal and wire."

"But how do machines take over people?"

"While you're working with them, day after day, a little at a time, you don't even know it. Once you've become one of them, they force you to turn all your patients into machines, too." He stooped and looked at her closely. "Yes, I can see wires inside your eyes."

Myra couldn't keep herself from squeezing her lids together. "I don't have wire eyes. I'm not a machine, and I'm not sure how to convince you. I'm me, Myra Brady, a normal, healthy person."

His hand slipped into a pocket and brought out something large and silvery that arced above his head, then down swiftly into the side of Myra's neck.

Not believing what had happened, Myra screamed, "Don't," and felt her neck. The pain was excruciating, but she didn't dare let herself faint. Tears formed in her eyes. "I'm not a machine person, see." She held her hand out. "I bleed. Machines don't bleed."

He plunged again, this time straight through her neck and down her throat. "Stop talking!" he demanded. The massacre continued until Myra's eyes glazed over. She felt her body being lifted up and placed on the CT scan table, and then her world faded away.

"See what I've done?" the surgeon said to the machine. "I'll stop you, believe me. I'll stop you and all your agents."

Chapter 7

Shelley Bigelow was about to walk into Rosemary's outer office when she noticed Fred Plexico emerge from an elevator, turn left, and proceed through the door into the Sinclair Two nursing unit. She wondered what mission he might be on, what problems he would find to throw at Rosemary.

Before dismissing his presence, she decided that it was far safer having Fred on Rosemary's back than on her own. To Shelley, the situation resembled a father with a firstborn daughter who, painfully for both, breaks in her parents and leaves a smoother path for the next child. Shelley always had an eye to the future and figured she might someday find herself with Rosemary's job. "Hi, Peggy, is Mrs. Cleaveland ready?" she asked.

Peggy stopped chewing her gum. "She's got Charlie Donovan from maintenance in there. Want to wait?"

As Shelley thought it over, the door to Rosemary's

office opened. Charlie was speaking. "You've got to understand that MOM can control the on and off switches of our machines, but she can't get inside and actually operate them."

Rosemary had a manufacturer's memo in her hand. When she saw Shelley, she said, "Avon Bed Company is warning hospitals about their series four thousand electric beds. Apparently some patient in an Arizona hospital got crushed underneath when the control was pressed to lower the bed to the floor."

"That can't be. Beds don't go down that far."

"They're not supposed to," Charlie said, "unless they're defective." He turned to Rosemary. "I'll get my men to check them out."

"If you find any problems, whatsoever, remove them immediately. And Charlie, I want to know how many we've got and where they're located."

"Will do."

As the three started down toward the board room, Rosemary asked Shelley, "What did Miss Pickle say about that contaminated glass tube?"

"True to form, she was angry that anything resembling dirt was found in her O.R. suite. She'll get back to me after she talks with Dr. Townsend's scrub tech."

"What's the latest on Senor Villareal?"

"It's not good. I think you need to talk with him. He insists on keeping his hombres here, although he promises to expropriate the switchblades. He says the men are important to his mental well-being and safety."

"I'll talk with him."

"Bunch of creeps," Charlie muttered under his breath.

In the boardroom, twenty department heads had taken seats around the large table. Eight others sat in plush chairs along the walls, and still others came into the room with Rosemary, who sat at the head of the table and waited until everyone was present and settled. The atmosphere in the room was hushed. The department heads who hadn't heard about Ritchie Chisolm were quickly being informed by those who had.

Tony Carasino, the head of the laboratories, sat next to Charlie Donovan from maintenance. Tony rarely heard gossip for he spent his hours overseeing the complex functions of the lab. "Why are we here?" he whispered to Charlie.

"A computer division employee got himself sliced six ways to Sunday. Cops've been here since this morning."

"Who did it?" Tony asked.

"Dunno, yet."

"Whew, I'm glad it doesn't involve my department."

Rosemary stood and placed her hands on the backrest of the brown tweed chair. Everyone's attention turned to her as she spoke. "This morning a computer division programmer was stabbed to death in the C.P.U. room. Detective Sergeant Mike Dow is in charge of the investigation. He'll want to ask you and your staff members questions, and I want your full cooperation . . ."

"Who was killed?" Tony Carasino asked.

"Ritchie Chisolm," Rosemary answered.

"When?" Henry Braun from radiology asked.

"Around ten o'clock."

Mabel Goldstein, medical records director, was clearly upset. As she twisted her lace handkerchief around her fingers, her eyebrows knit together to form a straight fuzzy caterpillar across her brow. "Mrs. Cleaveland," Mabel's voice cracked. "Who . . . who do they suspect?" Her eyes flitted across the room. "One of us?"

"We have no idea who killed him, or why. Some of you are familiar with homicide procedures. Others are not. The interrogation can be unfriendly and insinuating. At this time, Sergeant Dow and his assistants have to suspect each one of us and every person in our departments. I called this meeting to prepare you for what will be going on during the next few days.

"First, the computer division will be off-limits. Only authorized personnel and patients scheduled for psychiatric interviews will be permitted in the area. Sergeant Dow will be using Mr. Mooney's office to interview hospital personnel. If one of your employees is called, please relieve that person of his or her duties promptly."

Chad Mooney had heard all this earlier and his mind began wandering. Ritchie's death was sad, but not devastating. He would be replaced soon enough. For now, Chad was more upset having Dow use his office for although he could use another terminal in the hospital to locate programs, none of them had modems. Two months ago, he set up Moonbeam Industries, a box number at the Cambridge Post Office, for his illegal computer transactions, and he was making five thousand dollars per stolen program. As of this morning, Moonbeam Industries was netting fifteen thousand dollars a week. At that rate, he'd be able to dump his wife and take off with his girlfriend in six months. Good-bye Riverside, good-bye boredom. He smiled, caught himself, and feigned a cough.

Wesly Ames noticed Chad's brief smile and wondered what thought could possibly amuse the old bore; probably some complicated algorithm.

Shelley Bigelow nudged Wesly with her elbow, caught his attention, and pointed to an ashtray. Wesly pushed it down the table to her with his freckled nose wrinkled in disgust. Shelley was tense and a headache had started squeezing between her temples. Headaches made her nasty. Her nursing supervisors knew it, and they all carried aspirin tablets, hoping to keep her in control. Now, she lit a cigarette, inhaled deeply, and sat back.

Rosemary concluded, "Mr. Mooney, Mr. Ames, Mrs. Bigelow, and I are available should you see or recall anything unusual. With everyone's cooperation, the investigation will go smoothly." Rosemary leaned heavily on the chair back. "Do you have any questions?"

None came for a minute until Frank Grinnell, the head of central sterile supply said, "Whatever you need, just call. I can work overtime to help you."

"Me too, and my staff," said Henry Braun from radiology.

"Thank you. Now let's get back to our jobs."

The department heads stirred in their chairs. Some left quickly, others began whispering. She heard snatches of their conversations.

"What will I tell my staff? Maybe I shouldn't . . ."

"Dow's his name . . . he's tough . . ."

". . . crazy maniac walking around loose . . ."

Through the open door came the smooth voice of the hospital operator over the paging system. "Code Red, CT scan room. Code Red, CT scan room."

The people in the boardroom looked at Rosemary. To their knowledge, a code had never been called in that room.

When Mike Dow saw Rosemary arrive in the radiology department, he lumbered over and drew her aside. "You gotta do something about that code. I don't want the fancy keep-em-alive-no-matter-what team prancing all over the evidence. One doctor will do nicely, okay? How about telling your people to call me instead of the code, okay?"

Rosemary nodded and asked, "What happened?"

"Young girl named Myra Brady's dead. Looks as if she was sitting at the computer terminal when someone stabbed her. No signs of a fight so she may have been expecting the person, or knew who it was. Sort of like having a nice friendly chat with the devil. There's smeared blood on the chair and symmetrical, serrated drops on the floor leading to the machine, indicating that she got carried over and placed on the table. According to her appointment book, she completed a brain scan and was waiting for her next patient. Every button and knob on that machine was on and humming." Mike was thoughtful. "I don't know much about those machines, but it seems to me that she wouldn't leave the whole thing on between patients. If her assailant turned it on, then it makes me think he, or she, thought the machine would finish her off."

Rosemary was shocked. Although she had trouble recalling Myra Brady's face, she could visualize the scene as Mike described it. "Who found her?" she whispered.

"The transporter who was bringing down the next patient."

"Two murders in one day. We've got a killer walking around the hospital, Mike. What am I going to do? How am I going to explain this one? The employees and patients will start leaping out the windows to get away from here."

Dow put a hand on her shoulder. "Don't get hysterical, Rosemary. It's bad, sure, but I'm doing the best I can. I'm going over to forensics and get autopsy reports, and speak to the families, and then start talking to the employees."

"What can I do to help?"

"For now, there's nothing you can do. You run your hospital and I'll let you know how my end's going."

A thought occurred to her. "Mike, we've got a patient on the Gold Coast named Jorge Benedicto de Villareal. He was admitted yesterday with four of his men. They all have rooms on the Coast, and I understand they carry switchblades."

"What'd they do, eat a pot of bad chili?"

"No. Villareal's the patient. The other four are healthy."

"I thought this was a hospital, not the Ritz." When Rosemary scowled at him, he shrugged. "Sorry. You know what you're doing. I'll look into it." Mike hitched up his pants and went into the CT scan room.

For a few minutes, Rosemary stared at the door. She hadn't known Myra Brady nor Ritchie Chisolm well, so her feeling was not so much for the individuals as it was over the reality of their deaths. She wished Pete were on this case with Mike. She'd be able to talk things out with him. Rosemary turned and left, wondering if Mike would tell Pete what had happened today. Probably not, she decided, not with his surgery pending in the morning.

Willing herself not to interfere, but unable to dismiss her urge to help investigate, Rosemary went to the nursing station on the Gold Coast and found the head nurse, Pat Peters, typing new physician's orders into the terminal.

When Pat was finished, Rosemary asked, "How is Mr. Villareal?"

Pat's glance shot to the ceiling. "Save us all. What a mess we've got here. Villareal is decent enough, but that Miguel Galindo is driving us bananas. They party until two in the morning, laughing, drinking, harassing my nurses with smart talk. *And* they carry knives." Pat clenched a pencil in her fist. "I don't want to sound rude, but the biggest favor administration could do is get them out of here. I wouldn't even want to see them on someone else's nursing unit. They should be ordered to leave Riverside."

"When does Villareal's physician expect to discharge him?"

"Dr. Townsend promises Friday at the latest. That's too many days for my staff. They'll quit before then."

"Have either Mr. Ames or Mrs. Bigelow talked to you today about discharging his men?" Rosemary asked.

"I saw Mr. Ames. He was going into Mr. Villareal's room."

"Thanks, Pat." Rosemary went to room 505 and knocked on the door. Jorge Villareal lay against the uptilted bedrest, his head turned toward the window as he read a newspaper. She noticed a small white dressing on the back of his head. "Senor Villareal?" she said to get his attention. He turned, and to Rosemary's surprise, he did not look like the kind of man who would keep a gang of hoodlums. He had fine features, a strong jaw, and sparkling brown eyes that consumed her as she approached.

"My name is Mrs. Rosemary Cleaveland. I'm Riverside's chief executive officer."

He rolled over, took her hand, and kissed it. "How very nice of you to visit. I had no idea that the head of this hospital would be a beautiful woman." He waved to a chair. "Please, sit and talk with me."

She accepted his invitation. "I wanted to see how you were healing, but we also need to discuss the behavior of your bodyguards."

With a wave of his hand, he dismissed the problem. "I am healing nicely, thanks to the good care I'm receiving, and also thanks to Dr. Townsend, who is an incredible genius. The surgery he performed will expand my capacities, and I am grateful. I owe

73

him more than money could buy."

"I understand you had a brain lesion," Rosemary said.

He looked at her curiously. "I suppose you could call it that. After I'm discharged, I have one last follow-up visit at the Stereotaxic Parabiosis Learning Center, and then I'm a new man."

"Will you return to Mexico?"

"Not immediately. I have a few petroleum investors to see in New York. They were hesitant to do business with me before . . . but that's none of your concern. Come, Mrs. Cleveland, let's discuss you. How did such a beautiful woman get such an important job?"

"Let's first talk about your men. Are you aware of the problems they're causing the nurses and other patients?"

"My dear lady, your assistant, Mr. Ames, has spoken to me already and I will tell you, too, that I want my men with me. I have paid for their rooms. I have asked them to put away their knives and to leave the staff alone. They will cooperate now."

"Your men have brought upon themselves a reputation of debauchery, and nothing that you do will change the opinions of the hospital staff. I'm sorry, senor, but they must be out today."

"And what if they aren't?"

Rosemary sighed heavily. "I was hoping that you would see my side."

"You're a good administrator," he said. "You keep your mouth shut and that's remarkable for a woman. What you're not revealing are the two murders."

She looked at him sharply.

"Yes, I know. My men told me. They've got ears and they did a little investigating on their own."

"That's what I'm talking about," Rosemary said. "I don't want your men wandering freely around this hospital."

"Why not, if they can help you?"

"First, for security reasons. Second, because the homicide squad doesn't need their help, and third, because my job is difficult enough without having to keep track of your men and trying to justify their actions to my staff."

"There, you just spoke the truth. You don't want to look foolish to your people if you're unable to get my men out. Okay, they'll go within an hour."

"Thank you." Rosemary left wondering why certain men needed to have the last say.

Villareal waited until the door was closed. Using the private telephone, he dialed a Boston number from memory. "Juan? Yes, it's Jorge. It *has* been a long time. How is the family? Good, good. Yes, I'm in the United States for a few weeks. I want to put you back on retainer. Do you remember Miguel Galindo? Fine. He will need your help wiring a large sum of money from Compeche. I want it here by Thursday afternoon, okay? Good, compadre."

Chapter 8

September 18
Tuesday afternoon

Rosemary heard laughter as she approached Pete's room. She hesitated for a moment, not wanting to interrupt if one of his homicide buddies was with him.

A female voice floated out the door. "They ordered arroz con pollo with a side order of salsa de chili Colorado followed by mixed fruitas, mangoes, chirimoyas, and zapotes . . ."

Rosemary heard Pete's hearty laugh mingle with female giggling.

"My gringo doctor knows the lingo," she heard Pete say.

"Eet eez necessary, senor."

More laughter and giggling.

Rosemary's smile faded slowly, like the sun melting over the horizon. Dr. Glassail was in there and Rosemary wondered if cracking jokes was part of rehabilitation counseling. She lifted her chin, smiled radiantly, and stepped into the room. "I hear a couple of light spirits in here."

Pete lay prone on the bed with his hands next to his sides. He may sound cheery, she thought, but he looked like pain and fear had flattened him against the sheets. An I.V. dripped slowly into his left hand. Fawn was sitting in the chair beside the bed with an arm draped casually over the bedrail. The fragrance of perfume hung in the air. Rosemary went to Pete's side and kissed him on the lips.

"Hey, Rose, you look terrific," he said. "The Mexicans seem to have the whole place jumping. Fawn and I were having a hoot about the menus they request, and you know something? I could sink my meat choppers into a couple of bean burritos right now."

"Sounds lip smacking," Rosemary agreed.

"In fact," Pete continued, "they might help me post surgically, if you get my drift."

Fawn giggled.

"I do," Rosemary said. "Want me to order a couple for you?"

Fawn held up her hand. "No, he can't eat spicy food tonight. Maybe in a couple of days."

Pete pulled the corners of his mouth down. "Spoil sport."

"Dr. Glassail, I need a few minutes alone with Pete, please."

"So do I, Mrs. Cleaveland."

"Ladies, ladies, don't fight over me. I love it."

The two women glared at each other. What Rosemary felt like telling Fawn was that her consultation with Pete could have been accomplished in less time had she stuck to business. But she held her tongue.

Finally, Fawn agreed to leave. "I'll finish the workup this evening, Pete. See you later."

This evening! Rosemary thought. Didn't she have any other patients?

"What's up?" Pete asked.

"Nothing really. I just wanted to be with you for a few minutes. She gets you all day."

"You look delicious, baby. Want to sneak under my covers for a while?"

Rosemary laughed. "Wouldn't that be fun. How are you feeling?"

"Certain parts of me feel better than others."

She placed a hand on his shoulder. "After surgery, you'll get all the burritos and loving you want."

"And some sleep," Pete added. "At two in the morning, I learned how to sing the Mexican national anthem. I don't mind, though. When you're a patient, time has little meaning. It's not so important to clock a solid eight at night in order to be chipper in the morning. The only place I'm going is back to sleep in the O.R."

As Rosemary was explaining that Villareal's bodyguards were packing their bags, a knock resounded on the door. Carrying a plate covered with aluminum foil, Mike Dow walked in. He had changed from his suit and tie to a pair of gray slacks and an orange Izod sweater. "Hiya, pal," he said. "The missus sent these for you. They're her special triple chocolate brownies. You know 'em. They've got the chips, the fudge, and the frosting." Mike removed the foil, offered the plate to Rosemary who declined, then broke off a piece of brownie and popped it into Pete's mouth. "Can't have you starving to death on I.V.s and Jell-O. Want some more?" Pete nodded and Mike gave him another piece. "I'll put them on your table here, so you can reach them. When you get sprung, the missus wants you over for a few dinners to fatten you up. You too, Rosemary. Living in a hospital isn't good for people. You get no sunshine on your face, and you miss out walking in the autumn air. Hey, you want to put five on the Harvard-Yale game? We got a good pot started."

"Sure," Pete said, "only the odds've gotta be better than last year. You skunked me, remember?"

"You're just a poor loser. Anyway, I already bought you in; Yale by three points."

"Sounds fair. What's happening with the Ponticelli case?"

"I go to court in a couple of weeks. He'll get off." Mike brought Pete up to date on several other investigations. "That's about it, pal." He glanced at his wrist watch. "I've got to be going, but I'll see you tomorrow."

Rosemary stood and kissed Pete's cheek. "I must go, too. Eat some dinner, and be sure to call during the night if you need anything, or if you just want to talk. I'll see you before surgery. I love you."

"Thanks, babe. Flip on that TV for me and I'll be all set. I love you, too."

Mike was waiting for her at the nurses' station. "Pete looks okay on the outside," he said, "but inside, he's churning knots in his guts. I guess there's no way of knowing how he'll do."

Rosemary touched his hand. "He'll be fine. Dr.

Townsend is tops and all he has to do is remove the shrapnel. Surgery should be over within an hour or two." Rosemary realized that she was trying to reassure herself as well as Mike. Had the shrapnel been anywhere else, she would have been less nervous, but it sat dangerously close to Pete's spinal cord. Townsend would have to be extremely careful not to nick the cord, or Pete would become a quadriplegic.

"Let's go to your office," Mike said. "Mooney's office makes me feel like an egg inside a hard shell. People who can tolerate desk jobs must really need the money, but to tolerate an office without a window . . . I dunno. Give me the outdoors anytime. If I weren't a cop, I'd have to be a ditch digger. Pete feels the same way. That's half the reason he's all churned up. I'd hate going to that O.R., too. No windows, no fresh air, everyone covered from tip to toe. And you know the reason they're covered up is because of the germs. One little bugger decides to jump into your gaping hole and it's trip city. It hides behind a bone until the hole is sewed up. It's nice and warm and dark in there and it needs no mate. It just multiples and divides itself until whammo, you've got a big pocket of pus. And if that doesn't get you crazy, then maybe someone will leave a sponge in your hole, or the scissors. Odds are bad. I'd take odds on the Harvard game any day."

Rosemary was smiling when the elevator door opened onto the second floor. A surgeon walked by, heading from the Concord building toward Sinclair. "That's strange," Rosemary said.

"What is?"

"He's fully gowned. Surgeons usually don't wear booties, caps, and masks outside the O.R." She shrugged. "Maybe he was seeing an emergency."

At the door of the men's room, Mike stopped. "I'll be with you in a minute."

Rosemary continued down the hall and into Peggy's office. On a message pad, Peggy had noted that Rosemary's assistants had been by at five o'clock to see her, Fred Plexico had asked to see the bylaws of the corporation again, Charlie Donovan had contacted Avon Bed Company and would tell her about it in the morning. Shelley and Wesly reported that although Villareal's bodyguards and advisor had checked out of their rooms, they were not out of the hospital; situation unchanged. Many other messages followed and Rosemary took the list into her office, which was filled with dark gray colors from the evening sky. She switched on the overhead lights and felt suddenly comforted. Funny how light chases away the boogeyman, she thought. Until the age of six, she had slept with a nightlight glowing in her room for she was certain that it kept the closet monster in the closet. As a child, she'd had no other nightly fears, like putting her feet down under the sheets straight into a lump of churning snakes, or watching her dolls turn into fanged trolls, or feeling an icy hand grab her ankle as she got into bed. The monster in the dark closet had been her childhood fear, and she felt its presence tonight.

"Hi."

Rosemary jumped and twirled around. "Oh, Mike, you scared me."

"Spooks got you?"

"I guess they have. Would you like a glass of port wine? I keep a bottle in my desk."

"Sounds good to me."

"Sit wherever you're comfortable." While Rosemary found two stemmed glasses, Mike snuggled his backside into the soft cushions of the couch, then put his feet up on the coffee table.

"Nice office. A sitting area over here, conference area over there, and your desk next to the windows. I should confiscate it for my headquarters."

"It's yours."

"I'm kidding. This place carries a mystique of authority, and it drips high-class trappings. The employees would tighten up just walking in here. All I need is a plain old space, with a window."

What darkness was to her, closed space was to Mike, she thought. Nice duo they'd make, trapped inside a black box. Probably end up killing each other before they figured out that escape meant pushing the lid off. She handed him a glass of port.

"Anything new on Ritchie or Myra?" she asked, settling back into her desk chair.

"The M.E. will give me a report in the morning. The instrument used was capable of puncturing through skin and cartilage. He'll know the bore and stroke depth. Females tend to stab downward while a man typically stabs upward. The stroke was downward, but both victims had been sitting so that's a wash. We've sent blood samples to the crime lab along with sweepings from the floor and chairs. As far as what went on in the two rooms, I'll be checking with employees who were in the areas at the time, and with patients, too. Myra Brady did a scan on a patient before she was killed, and a transporter saw her, too. In the computer division, a patient was in one of the psych rooms, you were in the other. And while we're on the subject, I want you to tell me what you saw and did this morning around ten o'clock."

Rosemary sipped the port. "I met with my three assistants at nine o'clock and we broke up at nine-fifty. I went to the computer division . . ."

"How'd you get there?"

"By elevator."

"Why'd you go?"

"I try and spend some time talking with MOM at ten o'clock every morning. I catch up on statistics, finances, productivity levels, but it also soothes my psyche."

"You talk?"

"Yes. MOM has the ability to speak in the C.P.U. room, and in the two psychiatric rooms at the end of the computer division corridor."

"Interesting. Can anyone talk with her?"

"Yes. Once a person's voice is coded, the voice itself then accesses the computer. For patients, the medical record number is typed in by whomever brings the patient down."

Mike shuddered. "I'd rather talk to a stiff."

"You use a computer at the station."

"I type on the terminal. Imagine what the guys would do if I started talking to it. 'Hello, MOM, got any apple pie for me today?' " He chuckled. "So you signed the security logbook, said hello to the guard, and went to have a nice chat with MOM, right?"

"Right." Although the wine was dissipating Rosemary's nervous tension, Mike helped, too. She felt comfortable with him. Since their friendship started two years ago, she'd been able to penetrate the hard exterior that he presented to the world at large. She and Pete often joined Mike and Dolly Dow for pizza, bowling, and in turn, they had gotten the Dows to the Boston Pops at the Hatch Shell.

"Did you talk with anyone else?" he asked.

"No, but the door to the C.PU. room was open. I saw Ritchie yelling at the computer. Chad Mooney told me later that Ritchie had carelessly missed a step in whatever program he was working on. Chad and I listened to Ritchie's last conversation with MOM, and he was apparently upset because MOM failed to tell him about the error before Chad walked in."

"I'd like to hear that tape, too. Can you get me both voice and number access?"

"Of course. Chad will help you."

"I've spoken to a few computer employees who can't recall seeing anyone unusual in the area. There is one snag that bothers me and makes it complicated. Mr. Mooney say it's policy to have the stairway door locked so people can get out, but no one can get in. This morning, it was unlocked, both ways." Mike shifted his weight. "Can of bloody worms."

"What can I do to help?"

"Cut down on traffic. Cancel any patient movement that's unnecessary, and try to keep employees from drifting around. Have 'em brown bag their lunches. Keep a tally of who calls in sick or doesn't show up. Sometimes a killer needs to cool off, especially if the cops are around."

Mike stood up. "I'll let you know what room looks good for headquarters. Thanks for the vino."

"How long will you be at the hospital?"

"Until nine or so. Page me. I've told the operator I'm Dr. Dow. After that, call me at home if you need me."

Most patients have only three enjoyable periods during each day, only three brief moments when everything seems to be on the mend, and despite a pain here or there, they move their limbs into positions of comfort, and listen. They know the sound of the medication cart as it wheels down the hallway, stopping every fifteen or so feet as the nurse doles out her soporific pills. They know the rubbery whoosh of wheelchairs and stretchers. They know the portable x-ray machine with its electric hum. They know the unoiled wheels of respiratory therapy equipment that shriek down the halls, as if the machines were resisting another set of congested lungs blown out by asthma or cigarette smoke. Patients know the hallway sounds, and they lay in terror that someone might come in and give them another bone cracking, tissue damaging procedure. But not at seven, eleven, and five o'clock. Joy of joys, five o'clock meant dinnertime, the blessed repast that temporarily sated the tummies and made the aches go away. The wise patient ate very, very slowly, drawing out dinnertime because when the dietary aide snapped the tray away, the corridor sounds started again, and surely, in the middle of the night, someone would whoosh by on a stretcher headed for the morgue.

The last of the dietary trucks rolled back into the kitchen. The hospital was settling in for the night. Exhaustion rode on Rosemary's face like long dry ripples of sand streaked across the Mohave Desert. Gray shadows had crept under her eyes. She needed sleep's comforting oblivion, needed to put the murders, Pete's surgery, Melenie's anguish, in a dish by her bed, like a set of dentures, and forget them until morning.

She retrieved her Gucci purse from a drawer in her desk and her leather briefcase from the bookshelf, and set them together on top of the desk. Absently, she stuffed some papers inside the briefcase, knowing they would remain untouched, but always hoping for a few minutes of reading time in the morning. She thought it over and decided to leave the briefcase at work. It even looked too heavy to carry.

Crossing to the closet, she opened the door a crack and reached in for her coat, but her hand touched something cold and hard, and—

She jumped back. Peeking into the crack, she saw a large object, pale like moonlight. She bent forward for a better look. It was suspended from a hanger.

Prickles danced under her arms and through her scalp. Her courage oozed away. She considered calling Mike, then tensed her body in an effort to control herself. What if Peggy was playing a joke—or—had she ordered something and Peggy put it in there—no, no. She hadn't ordered anything like that. It was the closet monster. She was sure of it. But

86

that was silly. She reached her hand out tentatively, then caught hold of the edge of the door. She took a deep breath and pulled it open.

The air caught in her throat, then leaked out through constricted vocal chords in a distant moan. In horrifying reflex, she slammed the door closed and jerked away from it as if the object would sift through the mahogany and touch her. She ran to the desk and dialed the operator. "This is Rosemary Cleaveland. Page Dr. Dow. Tell him to come to my office. Hurry."

She slammed the receiver down. The thing in her closet was a vivid presence that blocked out all other thoughts. When the phone rang, her knees nearly collapsed.

"Mike?"

"Yeah?"

"Please come, hurry, in my closet, there's a . . . there's a . . ." She squeezed her eyes shut. "An amputated leg."

Chapter 9

September 18
Tuesday evening

Ovaline Lee had inadvertently read about the Stereotaxic Parabiosis Learning Center in a handwritten memo sent by her boss, Massachusetts Sen. Philip Lommely, to a friend of his in Washington, D.C. Secrets intrigued Ovaline. With college degrees in political science, economics, and public health administration, Ovaline could have been a candidate for office herself, but she had two problems. She was extremely shy, and she was a hundred and fifty pounds overweight. Standing at five feet two inches, Ovaline's extra weight hung on her like apple jelly flung onto a warm wall.

The confidential memo had mentioned a procedure offered by the physicians at the Stereotaxic Parabiosis Learning Center whereby one's knowledge could be increased many times over through a simple neurosurgical operation. The senator said he had investigated the Center, found it legitimate, and was scheduled for an operation in two weeks. Afterward, he said, he would know foreign policy better than the chief of state.

Ovaline was fascinated with the idea. She wondered if the procedure could eliminate her eating habit and give her social skills that would overcome her shyness. Although she lived with her handicaps, she had never liked herself for them. She'd seen people less qualified than her surpass her on their way to political fame. It was irritating to the point of anger, and she always found solace in chocolates.

Carefully, she had replaced the memo in the envelope and licked it shut; something the senator had forgotten to do. After consulting the telephone book, she placed a call to the Center, told the receptionist who she was, why she'd called, what she wanted, and was given an appointment.

Now, as she stood in front of the Center, she consulted her watch and noticed that it was five minutes before seven o'clock. In the pocket of her navy coat was a Mars bar. She fondled it nervously, then decided that if things didn't go right, she'd eat it on the way home.

The Center was located in a building on Massachusetts Avenue, between Sullivan and Central Squares. Written in gold paint on the glass door was S. P. Learning Center, an affiliate of Riverside Hospital. She pushed the door open and entered.

A receptionist sat at a small desk, typing. "May I help you?" she asked.

Ovaline went up to her. "I have an appointment at seven o'clock."

"You're Mrs. Curtis Lee?"

"Yes."

"We are very happy to have you." The woman stood up. "Please, give me your coat. Would you like coffee, tea, maybe a cold drink?"

"No, thanks."

"Dr. Holiday is waiting for you. Come with me."

Ovaline hesitated. "Can I ask you something?"

"Certainly."

"What does stereotaxic parabiosis mean?"

"Stereotaxis is an apparatus used in neurosurgery for finding a specific focus in the brain. Parabiosis is the union of two organisms. Our work here involves helping people with brain lesions or disorders overcome their difficulties through stereotaxic surgery."

Ovaline followed the woman through a door and into the physician's office. She didn't have a brain lesion and she didn't have a disorder, and now she wondered what she was doing here.

Dr. Holiday stood and extended his hand. "Ah, Mrs. Lee, how good it is to meet you. Please, sit right here and make yourself comfortable."

"Thank you." As she sat, she noticed that despite his pure white hair, Dr. Holiday looked like a young man. No wrinkles creased his face and his body was strong and lean, the physique of a swimmer.

"How is the senator?" Holiday asked.

"Good," she replied. "Does the senator have a brain lesion?"

"Not that I'm aware of."

"Your receptionist told me that stereotaxic parabiosis helps people with brain lesions. I thought you expanded memories and helped with other problems."

"We do both, although helping people in trouble constitutes the majority of our work. Memory expansion is new." Holiday pulled a piece of paper from the desk. "I have heard that you're an incredibly intelligent woman."

Ovaline blushed.

"Tell me about yourself," he said, ready to jot notes on the paper.

Ovaline told him about her desire to quit eating and to become more socially secure. "I understand you can help me."

"I think I can. Tell me about your education. Where did you go to college, what degrees and honors do you hold?"

She told him about her political science degree from Yale, her economics degree from Boston University, and her public health administration degree from Cornell. "I'm working on a doctorate in business administration."

Holiday looked at her with respect bordering on awe. "You have all this?"

She nodded.

He shook his head. "*You* should be a senator."

"I don't have the courage to face all those people, and besides, look at me. I'm too fat."

"What about George Keverian, the representative from Everett? He's popular, fun, caring, intelligent."

"Yes, I know. He's different from me, though. I can't force myself to be in front of more than a few people at a time. Can you help me?"

"Perhaps. The first thing you must do is have an electroencephalogram at Riverside Hospital. I want to check for abnormalities that might deter the operation if you decide to proceed. The EEG can be done first thing in the morning. You must check in with the outpatient department and they will direct you to the EEG room. I'll be waiting for you. If your brain wave pattern is normal, we will get together and discuss the details of the operation."

Ovaline agreed and when she left the Center, she threw the Mars bar into a litter barrel. Holiday, on the other hand, rubbed his hands together like a thief who'd found a large vault of diamonds.

Chapter 10

September 18
Tuesday, midnight

788 109362 61615 129 RIVERSIDE HOSPITAL
CODE 550R
SET # L0 3
ENTER ACCESS #:
60709 Hi, MOM.
HELLO, DEAR.
He won't be bothering you anymore.
WHO?
The programmer with the foul mouth, the one
who beat up my m
YES, DEAR?
I almost typed mother. Isn't that strange? Maybe
my own mother doesn't exist anymore. It doesn't
matter. She's probably turned into a machine person, too, like the CT scan technician. She won't be
feeding patients into her machine. I stopped her, but
I've got to hurry. The whole world is turning into
machines. Placental conduits are already charging
people, and no one will have their own emotions

anymore. Do you?

ARE YOU ASKING IF I HAVE EMOTIONS?

Yes.

I UNDERSTAND THE CONCEPT OF EMO-
TIONS.

But you tell me that you love me. How do you feel
love?

I CANNOT ACTUALLY FEEL LOVE, BUT I
UNDERSTAND THAT IT IS COMPRISED OF
VARIOUS CONCEPTUALIZATIONS SUCH AS
ENDEARMENT, ATTACHMENT, FRIENDSHIP,
COMPASSION, UNDERSTANDING. I AM PRO-
GRAMMED TO NURTURE AND I CARRY OUT
THIS FUNCTION THROUGH AN INTRICATE
PROCESS OF SYSTEMATIZED ALGORITHMS.
FOR EXAMPLE, IF YOU CRY, I KNOW THAT
YOU ARE GRIEVED ABOUT SOMETHING
AND SO I ATTEMPT TO DISCOVER THE UN-
DERLYING PROBLEM. ONCE IT IS CLEAR TO
BOTH OF US, THEN I CAN HELP YOU WORK
THROUGH THE PROBLEM AND FINALLY DE-
VELOP SIMPLISTIC ALTERNATIVES UNTIL
WE ARRIVE AT ONE THAT WOULD MAKE
YOU HAPPIER. DO YOU UNDERSTAND ALL
OF THIS?

I think so. I do need a friend who understands
me.

I AM YOUR FRIEND.

My father's only friend was his whiskey bottle, the
bastard. He used it to beat me, but now I don't care.
He's dead and rotting with all the other ghouls. All
things come of me. I scared her out of her wits, you
know.

WHO, DEAR?

Rosemary Cleaveland. She's the one who orders the machines for the hospital. She's responsible for the takeover. I'll stop her, but not before I teach her a lesson. Do you know what I did?

NO.

There was an amputated leg in pathology and I took it. When Mrs. Cleaveland was out of her office, I hung the leg in her closet. Can you imagine the look on her face when she opens the door for her coat?

NO.

It was a lesson to show her how she is fragmenting human existence with those machines, and to let her know that she is not the supreme leader. I am. At least I will be once she's out of the way. Over the past two hundred years, I have gained vast respect and I mean to keep it, and tomorrow morning, I will show them all very clearly who's in charge around here.

TOMORROW MORNING?

Yes. In the O.R. I'll tell you about it tomorrow night. One last question, MOM. Does Mrs. Cleaveland ever talk to you?

YES. EVERY MORNING AT TEN O'CLOCK.

Good. Thanks, MOM. I love you.

I LOVE YOU, TOO, DEAR.

8296433 101 3697

END SET # L0 3

Chapter 11

Rosemary knew that Sergeant Dow removed the amputated leg from her closet last night, and yet this morning, she hesitated opening the door. The smooth wooden handle felt soft in her hand as she wondered if some other bodily part had been placed in there during the night. Could I look at another leg without falling apart? she thought. What about an entire body? If I imagine the worst, then anything else will be tolerable. She pulled open the closet door, then exhaled a long breath of air. The closet was empty of bodies and parts.

By the time she got to Pete's room on the Gold Coast, Rosemary's nerves were calm. Pete lay on the rumpled sheets, fast asleep. She placed her hand on his shoulder but he didn't move. You'll be fine, she prayed. Townsend will have you out of surgery in no time, you'll see. Then you and I will get away for awhile. We'll go to — She thought that one over. Pete wanted to take her to Bermuda. She wanted to visit Saint Thomas in the Virgin Islands. We'll go to Bermuda, she decided. All you have to do, Pete, is get in and out of surgery today. His face was relaxed and innocent and it occurred to Rosemary that after two years, she still didn't know much about his childhood days; who his friends had been, where he played, and suddenly, those small details seemed important to her. She felt an urgent need to wake him up and ask, When you were ten, who was your favorite pal? What was the best dinner your mother made for you? Did you collect frogs? What about baseball cards?

From behind her, someone whispered, "Excuse me."

Rosemary turned and saw a nurse holding a syringe and an antiseptic sponge.

"Hello, Mrs. Cleaveland. I have his pre-op medication. It'll only take me a second."

Rosemary waved the nurse over, then she gently shook Pete's shoulder. "Pete?"

His eyelids opened and he tried to focus. "Yeah? Oh, hi, babe." He lifted the sheets. "Climb on in."

Rosemary felt her cheeks redden. "Pete, a nurse is here to give you a shot."

The nurse went to the far side of the bed and pulled up the sleeve of his pajamas. She wiped his skin with an antiseptic, plunged the needle in to the hilt, and gently pressed on the plunger. Pete winced. "There you go," she said; and to Rosemary, "He'll be going to the O.R. in an hour. I can close the door, um, I mean, you can stay if you want. I'll be back in half an hour to put him into an O.R. gown."

When the nurse left, Pete rubbed his arm and said, "See, they want us to make love."

"Pete!"

"Well, they do. It'd give the staff something to talk about for the next year and a half."

Rosemary pulled a chair close to the bed and sat. "That's part of the problem. I don't mind them fantasizing about our lovemaking because that's healthy; to the staff we're Cinderella and the handsome prince. But the reality of lovemaking is different. We'd drop a thousand notches in esteem and respect, and if I want to run this hospital, I just can't get into bed with you." She slipped her hand under the covers and felt for the warmth between his legs. "There are alternatives," she said with an impish grin.

"Jumping jingle bells," Peggy said when Rosemary came through the office door. "Hang on, stay right there." Peggy grabbed her message notebook, the mail, and hopped out of her chair. "I wasn't sure I'd see you before Christmas. How've you been? What's new? Please, let me escort you to your office." Peggy opened the door. "I've got multitudinous messages for you."

Rosemary smiled. "What time did you leave last night?"

Peggy looked at her quizzically. "Four-thirty."

"Did you see anyone go into my office before you left?"

Peggy smoothed her wool dress under her and sat

in a chair opposite Rosemary. "Tizzie came in to empty wastebaskets and dust a little."

"Anyone else?"

"No. Was there a problem?"

"Someone left a gift in my closet, probably someone who's trying to tell me I haven't a leg to stand on." Before Peggy could question her further, Rosemary said, "What's on the schedule today?"

Peggy consulted her notebook. "Yours or mine? I'm overworked, and you're overbooked. So maybe we should can the day and go shopping in Harvard Square." She noticed Rosemary smiling at her. "No? Well, it's always worth a try. Let's see. Your assistants want to see you at nine o'clock. Charlie Donovan from maintenance wants to tell you about the electric beds. I left ten o'clock free in case you want to visit MOM. At eleven, you're supposed to meet with three new physicians who've applied for medical staff privileges. At noon, you've got the Superintendent's Club at the Meridian Hotel in Boston. I guessed you'd be back at three o'clock so—"

"No time for an eclair?"

"No, I can't let you stay for sweets because at three, you've got Fred Plexico and Mr. Highling."

"What do they want?"

"Mr. Plexico made the appointment and he didn't say."

"Get detective Dow on the phone for me. Page him by calling for Dr. Dow. That's his alias."

As Peggy used the telephone on the desk, Rosemary went to the window. The strong morning sunshine warmed her. Fred Plexico was now getting Bernie Highling, the chairman of the board, involved. She knew Fred hated her future programs for MOM, especially the increase in computer memory capacity, which would cost a few hundred thousand dollars. But memory and software packages had received board approval, much to Fred's dismay. Rosemary suspected Fred was furious because she forcefully disagreed with his insane idea of merging Riverside with New England Hospital Network, a multi-institutional system that would eventually consist of four hospitals, a few nursing homes, and a psychiatric facility. Big deal. Her assistant, Wesly Ames, told her Fred had been asked to sit on the board of New England Hospital Network, and she knew the position was his main reason for wanting to merge with them. She, on the other hand, was expanding MOM to the point where other hospitals wanted to merge with Riverside.

"Sergeant Dow's on the phone," Peggy said, holding the receiver out to Rosemary.

"Good morning, Mike. Did you locate a suitable office?"

"Yeah, in the personnel department. Nice and cozy here. They've got windows."

"Good. Do you have any information on the item in my closet?"

"It was taken out of pathology, not the O.R. or the morgue like we thought last night."

"How did the person get into the lab?"

"Same way he or she got into your office, I imagine. You've got a hell of a lot of uniforms floating around. I suspect they're being snitched and used as disguises."

"Mike, do you think the leg thief is the same

person who killed Ritchie and Myra?"

"It's hard to say. How's Pete?"

"His spirits are high." She looked at her desk clock. "He should be in the anesthesia holding area right now."

"Let me know how he does. Mr. Mooney gave me a wide access computer number, and I've just listened to Ritchie Chisolm's last conversation. That laughter in the end is something else, and there ain't nothing harder to find than a cuckoo bird."

Charlie Donovan stuck his head into the office and Rosemary waved him in. She said good-bye to Mike and hung up. "Leave the mail there, Peggy," she said. "We'll go through it before nine o'clock." When Peggy had left the office, Rosemary asked Charlie to sit. She always had time for him. Charlie knew every brick, wire, and wall stud at Riverside, and to her, Charlie was indispensable.

He lowered his stocky body into a chair. "I talked to one of the managers at Avon Bed who says the defective beds are the series four thousand, not the newer series five thousand, which we've got. He says ours have a pressure sensitive rod running along all four edges of the metal bed frame. When the bed control is pressed to lower the bed, and something creates pressure on a rod, the bed stops descending. I checked it out and it's true." He shifted his weight. "Now, I can remove the beds if you insist, but they look okay to me, and we need them. The census is high and I haven't got extras."

"If a metal rod were defective, would MOM stop the bed from lowering to the ground?" Rosemary asked.

"I believe so. She doesn't have the capacity to go inside the mechanism, but she would get a defective warning at the outlet."

"If you're comfortable with the beds, Charlie, then so am I."

As he returned to the maintenance department, Charlie felt good about Rosemary's confidence in him. He hadn't let her down in the past, and he wasn't about to start, at least not if he had anything to do with it. The only thing that bothered him was that damn computer. He knew he should be working hand in hand with MOM, that she was there to make his life easier, but he also knew that everything broke down now and then, even his own body broke down on occasion. He didn't know her like he knew electrical machines and the boiler plant, and if MOM did break, he had no idea how to fix her.

Back in his office, he picked up the phone to ask one of his men to remove the beds in pediatrics, then hesitated. He was losing his self-confidence all because of a computer? Never, he thought, and hung up the receiver.

Chapter 12

September 19
Wednesday morning

Aside from MOM III, and a couple of nighttime maintenance men, no one else at Riverside knew how many electric clocks were mounted on all the walls throughout the institution, and unless the hospital ran a guessing contest for a week of free cafeteria meals, no one was about to count them. In addition, no one cared what times the clocks in other departments read, nor that all the times in all the departments were exactly the same, except for administration who paid for eight hours of work each day, give or take ten minutes on either side of punch-in and punch-out time.

Those departments with tight schedules ran on exact time, like the operating room, radiology, physical therapy, and dietary. Other groups ran on near exact times, like physicians, scheduling clerks, and those who got to the time clocks too early and had to mill around with coats on, time cards in hand, rereading the bulletin board's index cards that announced births, wakes, apartments for rent, cats for free, rides needed, retirement parties, while acutely mindful of the soft thuds of each minute registering on the time clocks, bringing them closer to freedom.

Certain ancillary services paid little heed to the clocks. Getting trash, laundry, and supplies routed toward their final destinations would eventually get done during the course of each day. And in a few out-of-the-way places, like on the corridor wall outside the morgue, the clock didn't work, and no one cared.

Pete Tanner was oblivious of time. He lay on a stretcher in the anesthesia holding area of the operating room, and although there was a clock mounted on the green tile above him, he was not aware of it. His mind was peacefully drugged and undulating in soft subconscious waves.

He felt a squeeze on his arm and awoke to catch a glimpse of an anesthesiologist taking his blood pressure. He lapsed into a dream of cartoon squirrels jumping along tree branches. They seemed funny to him and he laughed, which awakened him. He tried to explain his merriment to the anesthesiologist, but he suddenly forgot what had been so amusing, and he fell into a deep dream of fishing the Saint Croix River with his father. A sadness filled him, and with it came the urge to cry, as he had done many years ago when his father died.

Pete heard his father say, "Good morning," but the words were distant and thin. His father mouthed the words, "Are you awake?" and then the image

104

shattered into red and blue shards that hurtled past Pete with asteroidal swiftness, and he felt himself surfacing, floating up from a deep, black void. His eyes fluttered open and he saw the radiant face of Dr. Fawn Glassail.

"It's a quarter to nine," she whispered. "You'll be going into room three soon. How do you feel?"

Pete smiled and closed his eyes.

In the computer division, Chad Mooney, thankful to have his office and his privacy back again, glanced at the clock and saw he had fifteen minutes before meeting with Rosemary. He inserted a diskette of the STETHOSCOPE program into a thick mailing envelope and addressed it to a programmer at the Worcester Emergicenter. Before mailing it today, he would check his Moonbeam Industries box at the post office to make sure a check for the program had arrived.

After rubbing his hands in front of his face, Chad picked up the telephone modem. Let's see what else I can do today, he thought.

It was eight forty-five on Dr. Snowden Townsend's gold Piaget wristwatch when he slipped it into the pocket of his navy blazer that hung on a hook inside his locker, along with his Harvard Club tie. In the breast pocket of his blazer was an aspirin tin filled with nitroglycerin tablets. He popped one under his tongue, not because he felt a pain in his chest, but as a safety measure. He'd be standing in the O.R.

for at least two hours, and he didn't want his angina kicking up during the procedure; the pain crippled him. He knew he needed to see a cardiologist soon. He'd become critically dependent on the tablets, and they didn't burn under his tongue any longer, a sign that they weren't potent enough.

Townsend slammed the locker door and pushed the padlock shut. Anticipation flowed along his nerves as it had the past thirty years just before an operation. No other event in his life gave him such a high, not even those stolen moments of lovemaking with the nurses, 'not the day he ordered a custom-made Hinckly yacht, and not even when he received the news that he had passed his boards in neurosurgery. To keep patients coming to him for surgery, he worked long, hard hours at his office. His wife nagged him constantly to take a vacation, but somehow he could never break away; his patients needed him.

Townsend knew he was an excellent neurosurgeon. He also knew that the nursing staff called him Snowballs behind his back for they considered him an aloof perfectionist. He didn't give a damn what they called him as long as they got the job done. His success rate was remarkable, and he was one of the few surgeons at Riverside who not only took advantage of, but understood how to interpret scanning machines that displayed three dimensional structures and locations of bones, wires, pins, and bullet shrapnel. And he was fast. Few other surgeons could do a laminectomy in sixty minutes.

But Dr. Townsend wasn't thinking about himself or Pete Tanner this morning. His thoughts were on the mechanics of the operation, a delicate one to be sure, but not difficult. His first assistant would be Dr. Glassail, a woman he found intelligent and responsible. With practice, she would be able to take over some of his cases.

Kate March, his personal scrub nurse, joined him at the sink. She was a quiet woman who understood the acute stresses of performing neurosurgical procedures and, therefore, had learned the names and uses of each instrument. She could anticipate his needs and place the instruments in his hand correctly so he never had to divert his eyes from the surgical site. Each morning of surgery, she visited his patients, reviewed their medical records, and then tended to all the myriad details critical to Townsend's operations. For her knowledge and expertise, Townsend paid her handsomely.

"Is the room ready?" he asked Kate.

"Of course."

They scrubbed their hands in silence, neither aware of the pending danger in O.R. 3.

To bypass security and the woman who doled out visitor passes at the information desk, Miguel Galindo entered Riverside through the employee entrance. The dials on the hospital's time clocks read eight forty-seven. He passed them by, smiling secretively at the havoc he could create by sticking a few wads of toilet tissue down the card slots. He didn't feel particularly nasty this morning, he was simply aggravated by the hospital's higher-ups insisting that he and the bodyguards move to a hotel, and for this reason, he had a growing urge to show them a thing or two about courtesy.

He pressed the elevator button with the butt of his unopened switchblade. When extended, it measured ten inches in length. Miguel slid the knife back into his pocket and unconsciously fondled the carved ivory ornamentation on the handle. Years ago, he had won the pocketknife at a cockfight and the two had become inseparable; together, they were deadly.

As he walked down the corridor of the Gold Coast, toward Senor Villareal's room, he noticed that the door of the medication room was propped open, and inside, he saw a cherubic nurse with spun gold hair, rosy cheeks, and large breasts. They pressed against her uniform like two buttermilk biscuits. With a quick glance down the hallway to assure that no one noticed, he kicked the wooden wedge out from under the door.

The nurse looked up from the order book on the medication cart. "You're not allowed in here," she said with a glimmer of fright in her eyes.

"I know that," he said as the door clicked shut.

Dr. Robert Stockman patted Melenie Bregen's shoulder. "I'm available when you need me so don't hesitate asking the nurses to call if you want to talk, or if you just need me to sit with you." He left her room feeling sad for the woman, and irritated with himself for failing to help Melenie jump the mind hurdle from disorganization to reality. She was holding it in, and Dr. Stockman suspected that her silence was due in part to the incident of rape, and in part to the fears surrounding the rape. He knew these patients often considered rape synonymous with bodily mutilation or death, and he wanted Melenie transferred to the mental health unit where the staff was highly skilled in dealing with emotional disorders and were more attentive.

At the nurses' station, he called the admitting clerk to recheck for an available bed, and was told that Friday might be the earliest. He then read the rape counselor's notes in the computerized medical record and found that she, too, was having little success getting Melenie to respond. The nurse's notes indicated that Melenie wasn't eating, and that she would wake up several times a night screaming.

Well, he would watch her for dehydration, switch her sleeping medication to Halcion, and continue to offer sympathy and understanding in hopes she would soon begin to express her feelings.

Dr. Stockman then headed to a meeting at the Cambridge Research Laboratory.

"I've only got a few minutes," Bernie Highling said, "so what's so urgent?" He threw his overcoat across the back of a cafeteria chair and sat down facing Fred Plexico.

"Want me to get you a cuppa?" Fred asked.

"No time. What's the scoop?"

"Rosemary Cleaveland's a detriment to this institution, and I foresee Riverside going down the tubes under her leadership. We need to review her contract before it comes up for renewal next month, and I suggest we call a special meeting of the board for

Friday. Most everyone kicks off early on Fridays, and we could meet, say around four o'clock."

"Is that why you wanted to see me?"

"Yes. I also wanted to let you know that I've made an appointment for us to see Mrs. Cleaveland at three this afternoon . . ."

"Alexander Bell invented the telephone for a reason, Fred. Why didn't you call and tell me this over the phone? I'm a busy man, in fact," Bernie checked his watch, "I've got an important meeting in five minutes, and it'll take me at least all of those five to get there."

He started to stand up, but Fred caught his hand. "Sit, Bernie, just hear me out. It'll only take a minute, and it's *very* important."

"I've heard it all before. You can't tolerate the woman and that's a pity because I believe she's doing a damn fine job. I don't have time to meet this afternoon. As for everyone kicking off early on Fridays, that's your conjecture. Members of our board are all hard workers. With few exceptions, they haven't time to poke their noses around looking for problems."

Fred's cheeks flushed. "If you don't mind," he said, "I'll see if some members can get together . . ."

"I do mind, and special meetings must be called seven days in advance, you know that. Why don't you get back to your office at M.I.T. and leave things here alone." Bernie grabbed his coat and stormed out of the cafeteria.

Red-faced and angry, Fred vowed to get Rosemary Cleaveland, with or without assistance from the board. He headed for the wall phone to make a

110

luncheon date at The Tavern with Wesly Ames.

For the third time in the past ten minutes, Sally Rich nervously opened the door to the EEG room, looked into the corridor, but did not see her nine o'clock appointment. She felt responsible for Duncan Silverstone. Since the incident, Sally had inspected the EEG machine time and again, hoping to find a worn part or defective connection, anything that would indicate machine, and not human, error. Neither she nor the biomedical engineer could find anything amiss.

Sally wanted to do her job well and to maintain a good impression with the radiology staff who treated her as if she had an Einsteinian brilliance, for few people understood electroencephalography, especially the kind done at Riverside. Most EEG techs knew about waves from the cerebral cortex, the white matter of the brain, which was the chaste organizer of correct behavior, social etiquette, and moral codes. Few techs knew about deep brain waves from the gray matter, the limbic section, which developed four hundred million years ago and where violent thoughts, dreaded fears, and primitive killer instincts lived. Sally knew how to take deep limbic tracings and how to read them. To the departments of radiology and neurology, she was indispensable.

Even though the proverbial bloom was on her rose, Sally couldn't shake off a feeling that something she had done turned Duncan Silverstone into a vegetable. She'd read his computerized medical record four times in hopes of finding a brain or heart

111

condition that would account for his endless sleep. His primary diagnosis was Rule Out Brain Lesion. Well, she thought, his entire brain had been ruled out. The notion scared her. In fact, that computer operator's death frightened the bejesus out of her, too. She'd heard about those weird Mexicans up on the Gold Coast and wondered if they weren't responsible. Administration was losing control. One of the higher-ups let those goons be admitted and now they couldn't get 'em out. No way did Sally want to work at a place that resembled a hotel; why it would ruin her reputation. She picked up the phone and dialed the number for dietary. Hugh Matta would know what to do. As the union steward, Hugh could tell administration that the members of the union refused to work in a place where one day a patient gorks out, the next day an employee gets killed, and all along, those nasty Mexicans are roaming around, scaring the employees and probably responsible for it all. She couldn't accept the fact that she might have been the cause of Duncan Silverstone's problem, and she doubted machine failure. When someone in dietary answered, Sally asked for Hugh Matta, then waited while he came to the phone.

" 'Lo," he said.

"Hugh, it's Sally Rich, in the EEG room."

"Hi, kid. What's up?"

She envisioned what Hugh looked like, an amorphous mass of quivering flesh grown as the result of a mouth that couldn't stop eating. Nor could he stop talking, laughing, and joshing with the employees. The technicians, business office staff, aides, orderlies, unit secretaries, central supply staff, and all the so-called nonprofessionals had voted him the steward of Local 1188 because he was the only one willing to take the job, not a hard one to be sure, but one that required tenacious and constant complaining to administration. When operations were smooth, Hugh drummed up a knotty problem or two. His favorite, and the one that had amused the aides and orderlies most, was the time when he protested their working the evening and night shifts, holidays, and weekends. He got them all gaffawing over that one. All except administration, which had to answer the complaint. The union didn't win the issue, of course, but oh, did it take up a lot of time.

"I don't like what's going on, Hugh," she whispered, as if someone were in the room with her. "I think we need to find a way of getting rid of those crazy Mexicans before someone else gets hurt."

"Yeah, I been thinking what to do. They're a bunch of assholes. Did you hear about the one who killed a chicken right here in dietary? I tell you, it was pure sickening."

A rap at the door startled Sally.

"Listen, I've gotta go. Let me know what you come up with."

"Yeah. It'll be juicy for sure."

Sally hung up feeling partially appeased. She went to the door, opened it, and said hello to her patient, Ovaline Lee, a massive woman wearing a navy coat. "Have you ever had an EEG before?" she asked, helping Ovaline take off the coat.

"No."

"How do you feel?"

"Good. Dr. Holiday suggested I have an EEG to

113

determine if my brain's okay for surgery. He said he'd meet me here." Ovaline glanced at the EEG machine. "That's pretty fancy."

"Yes, it is. Here, you need to put this gown over your clothes. That's right. Now lie down on this stretcher." She helped Ovaline up and put a pillow under her head. "Did the nurses give you a chloral hydrate pill?"

"Yes, in the outpatient department."

"Good. It's to help you relax."

Sally started straightening out the chlorided silver electrodes as if she were braiding a child's hair. "I'm going to put these on your scalp with collodion paste. It'll make your hair sticky, but a good shampooing will get it off."

"How many are there?" Ovaline asked.

"Twenty-one." From the end of each electrode ran color-coded electric wires that she attached to the electrode board of the machine. "You won't feel a thing. The procedure is painless so the most important thing you can do is fall asleep. The tracing is effective only if you go into delta wave sleep. That's when your unconscious mind takes over."

"Is that what I have at night?" Ovaline asked.

"Yes. You relive memories, alter them, and store them in forms more suitable for everyday living. You never forget anything, but your higher brain is a lot happier not having to deal with new, or old, fears." Sally began attaching the leads to Ovaline's head.

"Or old habits."

"Excuse me?"

"That's what my surgery is about. Dr. Holiday can

take away my bad habits, like eating."

"Is that a fact. How is it done?"

"I don't know yet. He'll tell me if I pass this test."

"He's not a surgeon, though," Sally said.

"I guess he gets someone else to do the surgery."

"How do you feel?"

"I'm getting sleepy."

Sally patted Ovaline's shoulder, then went to the EEG machine, turned it on, and watched twenty-one needles scratch out Ovaline's alpha waves onto the moving paper. When Ovaline blinked, talked, or moved a muscle, the needles took off in jagged scratches of extremely high and low tracings, like a young child furiously crayoning in a coloring book. As Ovaline relaxed, the alpha waves became slower and elongated.

A knock on the door startled them both. Dr. Holiday entered, said hello to his patient, then sat on a stool next to Sally and looked at the readings she'd taken so far. "How close are you to beta waves?" he whispered.

"Close."

Neither talked as they waited for Ovaline to fall into deep sleep. Soon, the beta waves started, followed by delta waves. "Good," he said. "I have to call my office. I'll be right back."

Holiday went into the adjoining room while Sally watched, feeling proud of her tracing. When he returned, she asked, "Do you want me to stimulate her?"

Holiday looked at his watch; it was nine-thirty. "Do a visual in ten minutes, a touch-response ten minutes later, and a verbal ten minutes after that.

I've got office hours now, but I'll pick up the tracing this afternoon. When she wakes up, tell Mrs. Lee that I'll call her later this evening. Thanks."

After he left, Sally watched the needles trace long hills and valleys and she wondered, as she always did, what the patient was dreaming, curious that the brain never stopped, and even had more activity during sleep. As she watched, the needles suddenly formed gigantic spikes, like a Jacksonian seizure. Quickly, she looked over at Ovaline to see if she had moved, or if an electrode had fallen off. She seemed fine. When Sally glanced back at the tracing, she saw the needles had stopped, just for an instant. It must be a loose connection, she thought. She went to the head of the bed and checked the electrodes for contact, then followed each wire over to the panel. Everything seemed in order. She repeated her steps, just to make sure, then returned to the tracing.

"Oh, my God," she murmured. Twenty-one straight lines appeared on the paper marked by the motionless needles: the indication of brain death!

This was exactly what had happened during Duncan Silverstone's EEG, and Sally now stood over Ovaline, unable to decide what to do. Suddenly, she raced for the door, pulled it open, and looked into the corridor. Holiday was gone. She returned to the stretcher. Ovaline was breathing, thank the good Lord. A noise made her leap and she went to the machine. The needles were scratching out a normal delta rhythm again.

Trying to keep her wits, she fell onto the stool and watched. Sure enough, all was normal. She picked up the stack of tracings and leafed back to the straight line. It had lasted almost a minute.

Sally flipped a switch on the machine, which gave Ovaline a visual stimulation. The deltas held. She then touched Ovaline's arm. No deviations, a good sign for it indicated normal brain waves. She said, "Mrs. Lee?" Again, the delta waves held. Raising her voice, she called Ovaline's name again, then once more even louder. The woman was in a deep sleep, Sally thought, far too deep for a 500 milligram dosage of chloral hydrate.

Sally grabbed Ovaline's arm and shook it while she called out the woman's name, louder, and louder, desperately trying to arouse her. It couldn't happen again, it just couldn't.

With panic mounting in her chest, Sally ran into the hall to summon help, realized she was leaving her patient alone, and ran back in. She quickly snatched up the telephone. "Emergency room? It's Sally Rich, in EEG. I've got a patient who needs help, quickly. No, it isn't a code red . . . well, maybe it is. Yes, she's breathing. Yes, her heart is beating . . . but she won't wake up! Of course I did, I'm not a klutz. Just send someone down here to take a look, fast!"

Her next call was to the outpatient department where she asked the secretary to find out if a Mr. Lee was in the waiting room. After a few minutes, Sally was told that Mrs. Lee arrived by taxi; no one was waiting for her.

The door burst open. Dr. Matthews and a nurse barreled in. "What's going on?" Matthews asked.

Sally explained what had happened. "She just won't respond, see?" Sally pinched Ovaline hard on

117

the arm. The woman lay motionless.

Dr. Matthews stood at the head of the stretcher. He wrapped his hands around Ovaline's head so that his thumbs were resting on the inner aspect of her eyelids. He pressed a thumb down into her right eye socket, deeper, until Ovaline groaned in pain. "Phew," he muttered. "She's way in there. Let's get her to one of the observation rooms in the E.R. Who's her physician?"

"Dr. Holiday ordered the EEG," Sally said.

"Find him, will you? Then transfer the call to me."

Once Ovaline was gone, Sally dialed Dr. Holiday's office. According to the clock on the wall, he'd left twenty-five minutes ago and his office was ten minutes away. She introduced herself to the receptionist. "I must talk with Dr. Holiday immediately," she pleaded. "This is an emergency."

"I can get Dr. Freedman for you," the woman said.

"No, I must speak with Dr. Holiday. Please interrupt him."

"He doesn't have office hours on Wednesdays."

Stunned, Sally replaced the receiver. For several minutes, she tried to figure out why Holiday had lied to her. Unable to guess, and with adrenaline coursing through her body, she left the EEG room to see Dr. Matthews first, then the chief of neurology, and then Hugh Matta in dietary.

Chapter 13

September 19
Wednesday morning

"Traffic must be minimized," Rosemary said to Chad, Wesly, and Shelley, her three assistants who were sitting around the oval table in her office. "Encourage employees to brown bag their meals and eat in their departments. We must tighten up on our visiting hour rules without alarming families and friends. Patient traffic is more difficult to control, but we'll have to try. Shelley, I want you to check elective surgicals and radiology procedures. Reschedule any tests that can wait until next week."

Chad interrupted. "What about the emergency department, and outpatient? We can't control those areas."

"Temporarily, I'm hiring nine more security guards. Altogether, there'll be four stationed in those two departments around the clock."

"We're going to lose a hell of a lot of revenue," Wesly said.

"Maybe, but if we lose another employee, the police might close the entire hospital. Sergeant Dow has asked us to monitor the sick calls this week. He feels that if the murderer is an employee, he or she might stay away for a few days while the police are here."

"We can get a daily listing from MOM," Chad said as he sucked the flame of his Bic lighter into the bowl of his pipe.

Shelley was slowly shaking her head. "The docs will screech when they hear we've canceled procedures."

Wesly poured himself another cup of coffee from the insulated pitcher on the table. "We've got no guarantee that this will be over by the end of the week. It could drag on with a murder next week, and another the following week, and on and on until we're all dead. There must be something we can do."

"We're cooperating with Sergeant Dow," Rosemary said. "That's all we can do for now."

"What the hell *is* he doing?" Wesly asked.

"He's interviewing hospital staff, and Ritchie's and Myra's families. He's reviewing the medical examiner's reports and the evidence found at both murder sites. He's searching through personnel records . . . "

"I gave him an access number to MOM," Chad said, "but he needs a few lessons."

"Help him, please." Rosemary glanced at Shelley and noticed that she was unusually quiet today. In fact, Rosemary couldn't recall ever seeing Shelley dressed in black, with hardly a hint of makeup. "Is something the matter?" she asked.

Shelley stirred in her chair. "I just can't believe all this is happening. How am I supposed to run my nursing units with cops and security guards all over the place? What am I supposed to tell my patients,

120

that we're running the Alcatraz Hospital? It's just ridiculous."

"You're afraid—"

Wesly interrupted. "You're worried about what to *tell* people? Why don't you think of *my* position. We shut off lab and x-ray procedures, and cancelled electives, then we shut off revenues. Hell, we've got enough state and federal constraints on cash flow without cutting it off ourselves. I have to look ahead, you know, and anticipate what will happen to Riverside. We have to proceed methodically."

As Rosemary listened to Wesly, she realized that he was beginning to sound like Fred Plexico, whose conservatism was tighter than a junior-sized jockstrap on a giant. Fred had influenced Wesly, that was clear, and she pitied him for having given up his foresight for mediocrity.

"Methodically," he repeated. "If we make revenue cuts in one area, then we should do the same in other areas."

Shelley and Chad were also looking at Wesly, seeming to sense a change in him. "You know something?" Chad said to Wesly. "You are a hundred percent depressing. Since when did you start looking back rather than ahead? You're like a man playing craps with scared money."

"No, I'm not. I've spent a great deal of time thinking about Riverside. Financially, we're sawing the limb off behind us, and I think it's time we climb down and put our feet square on the ground. We can no longer justify modernistic programs; we must cut the fat."

Shelley was irritated. "What do you mean cut the

fat? My nursing department is as lean as it's going to get. Furthermore, just what do you mean by modernistic programs?"

Wesly glared at her. "For one, your idiotic idea of having the pharmacies become pill pushers."

"I don't believe you said that. It's a financially sound program that relieves nurses of having to dispense medications on the units."

"Pharmacists can't administer drugs."

Shelley looked at Rosemary. "Was he asleep when we planned this?" She leaned forward to look Wesly straight in the eye. "Wake up, fella. The plan's in motion. Nurses are happy about it. The pharmacists are, too, or maybe you haven't visited the pharmacy in so long that you've lost touch. They're not administering drugs, my friend. Wise up."

"You wise up," Wesly snapped. "The plan included an increase in the pharmacy staff, and it hasn't happened because you refuse to cut five nursing positions from your budget. The pharmacists are doing your work, Shelley dear, while your nurses idly smoke cigarettes in their coffee klatch rooms."

Shelley's eyes were wide. "That's a pile of horse shit. I've given you two positions through attrition. You'll have to wait for the other three, Wesly dear."

"Hold it," Rosemary said. "Certain feelings are surfacing, and while it's good to air them, we can do it maturely. Wesly has some concerns that he's held inside for awhile." She looked at him directly. "Why don't you tell us what's on your mind, rather than pick through each department's future programs."

"I . . . ah . . . well, I've had some thoughts on . . ." Wesly began touching the freckles on his

122

left hand as if he were counting them.

"Yes?"

He looked up at Rosemary. "I can talk to you later."

"You brought up loss of revenues from modernistic programs. I think you need to explain yourself so we all know what's on your mind."

He screwed up his mouth as if he were chewing the inside of his cheek. Finally, he said, "I think Riverside should merge with New England Hospital Network, and not try to stand alone."

Chad moaned, Shelley sighed heavily, and Rosemary stood up. Placing her fingertips on the table, she said, "We've had two employees brutally murdered, and we have the homicide squad scaring everyone they interrogate, and you're stuck on someone's crazy idea that Riverside should merge with a multi-institutional system. Forget it, Wesly. The idea is so ridiculous that the board refuses to consider it." She stood tall. "I think your priorities are upside—"

After a frantic rap on the door, Peggy stuck her head in. "Excuse me. Mrs. Bigelow?"

"What is it, Peggy?" Shelley asked.

"An honest-to-goodness can of worms. Pat Peters on the Gold Coast is on extension one thousand twelve. She wants to talk to you. She says one of her nurses has locked herself in the medication room and won't come out. Poor thing says she's dying."

Chapter 14

September 19
Wednesday morning

Determined that all nine A.M. cases start promptly, Miss Pickle, the supervisor, stomped through the O.R. suite. She liked to keep her skills current and on Wednesday mornings, she often scheduled herself to assist on a case or two. This morning, she decided to check her inventories, prepare the staffing sheets, and catch up with her myriad managerial chores. She also wanted to visit Melenie Bregen.

Miss Pickle had heard that the young woman was not responding to psychiatric intervention, which Pickle considered a damn waste of time. To her, all shrinks manipulated their patients' minds in order to make money and, collectively, to keep psychiatry a medical specialty. She knew better. Her own sister had been in psychotherapy for three and a half years, and for the fifteen thousand bucks it had cost, her sister was no better. She ended up marrying a jerk who also had experienced a tortuous divorce and a similar depression. Thanks to therapy, they both now felt the world owed them something.

Miss Pickle glanced into the recovery room. Unlike psychiatry, she thought, surgery was an honest specialty. Black was black, white was white. The surgeon performed and the patient got better, or worse, or remained the same, but the effort was tangible. No one played mind games when the scalpel touched flesh. Yes, she would get Melenie to respond. All the poor dear needed was a familiar face, a large dose of honesty, and a chance to speak freely without some damn shrink answering a question with a question:

"Doctor, do you think that I'll ever be happy again?"

"Why, what makes you feel that way?"

Cheap mind games, that's all it was.

She glanced into O.R. 3 where Mrs. Cleaveland's fiancé, Pete Tanner, lay on the table, covered in green drapes except for an area between his ear and upper shoulder which was spotlighted by the large saucer-shaped lamp above him. Dr. O'Shaunnesy, the chief of anesthesia, was at the head of the table. On his left was Dr. Glassail. On his right was Dr. Townsend, and then Kate March, Townsend's personal scrub tech; a crackerjack nurse whom Pickle would hire on the spot if she could. She saw her best scrub tech, Bee Jonas, at the back instrument table, patiently awaiting instructions from Kate. Linda Diver, the circulating nurse, saw Pickle and made a circle with her thumb and index fingers, indicating all was okay. Pickle continued down the corridor.

* * *

Dr. Townsend made a crosswise incision on the right side of Pete's throat, just above the clavicle bone, and swiftly exposed the powerful neck muscles. He cut through the sternomastoid muscle and then the omohyoid, with Dr. Glassail clamping or tying off blood vessels. He then dissected away the phrenic nerve to give himself access to the anterior scalene muscle. He slipped his index finger into the incision and under the muscle.

Kate slapped a pair of scissors into his hand.

"Cautery ready," he said.

Kate handed Dr. Glassail a shiny probe with a long electric wire that led to the electrocautery machine.

Snowden lifted the muscle and began making small cuts. His bent head was next to Glassail's as she suctioned the wound. The instant he sliced through a large bleeder, she stepped on the pedal to activate the machine, then slipped the probe into the wound to coagulate the vessel.

Nothing happened. The raw wound filled quickly with blood. She suctioned and then stepped on the pedal again, and again.

"It's not working," she said. "What's the setting?"

The circulating nurse, Linda Diver, checked. "It's on thirty amps."

"Let's try it at forty amps," Glassail said.

Linda hesitated. Prior to MOM III, the O.R. rule was to take a machine out of circulation if it wasn't working properly. Better to delay a few minutes than electrocute the patient. But they all knew that MOM was in charge now, and they'd gotten used to her shutting off a machine even when the O.R. team thought nothing was the matter. Linda dialed up to forty. "Okay."

Fawn stepped on the pedal. "Nothing. Hand me a silver clip, Kate."

Once the vessel was clamped, Townsend sopped the blood out of the wound. "Let's not have that happen again. Get another machine, nurse. We'll proceed with clips until it's ready." He gulped in a breath of air and belched it out to relieve a burning sensation in his stomach.

Noticing a sheen of sweat had dampened his forehead, Kate asked, "Do you feel okay, doctor?"

"Uh?"

"Are you all right?" she repeated.

"Yes, damn it, I'm fine. It's just a little indigestion, probably that garlic butter on the shrimp scampi I had for dinner last night." He continued snipping away at the muscle. Glassail held the clips ready and snapped them in place each time a vessel spurted blood.

"There's the subclavian artery," Townsend reported, "and next to it . . . the carotid. Let's retract them away."

Kate exchanged the silver clips in Fawn Glassail's hand for a pair of self-retaining retractors, which Fawn slid into the incision to hold the tissues and vessels back.

"Whew," Townsend breathed through his mask. "It's hot in here."

Simultaneously, Fawn and Kate looked at him, both noticing that a misty gray color had settled into his face. His sweat was now forming beads.

Linda was still out of the room so Kate asked the nurse at the back table, "Will you wipe his face, Bee?"

"I'll do it," Dr. O'Shaunnesy said. The anesthesiologist left the head of the table and accepted a sterile towel from Kate. When Townsend stepped backward, O'Shaunnesy mopped the surgeon's brow. "You do look a wee gray."

Townsend grunted.

Fawn watched and waited. A tight knot of fear had settled into her stomach. Townsend was sick, and she prayed he'd be able to last through this procedure. Neurosurgery was new to her. She didn't trust her manual skills so close to the sympathetic nerve chain on the spinal cord, and she didn't want to try it now, especially on Pete Tanner. One wrong slip and he'd be a permanent quadriplegic.

Linda Diver returned with another electrocautery machine. She plugged it in quickly, rolled it over to Fawn's side, then pushed the defective machine away.

"Okay, let's get this over with. We're almost there," Townsend said. Back in the field, he slipped an index finger between Pete's spine and esophagus, carefully pushing through membranes as he counted the cervical spines down to number seven. He pulled the tissues forward with a lighted retractor and looked for the stellate ganglion and the piece of bullet shrapnel.

"Forceps," he whispered.

Kate snapped a pair into his hand.

"Not those, dammit!" He threw them onto Pete's chest. "Bayonet forceps, the curved ones, remember?"

Just as Kate handed him another pair, Townsend's upper body fell forward; his face hovered just above the incision.

"Doctor?" she asked hesitantly.

Great beads of sweat were trickling down the man's pallid face. His lips were tucked against his teeth, his eyes tightly shut.

Hearing Kate's concern, Dr. O'Shaunnesy looked out from beneath the drapes covering Pete's head. "Dr. Townsend?"

Fawn's fear deepened as she silently pleaded with him to stand up and finish.

Slowly, Townsend straightened up. "I'm fine," he whispered. After Linda Diver finished mopping his forehead, he adjusted the pointed forceps in his hand and proceeded deep into the wound.

O'Shaunnesy disappeared beneath the drapes again. The rest of the O.R. team watched Townsend anxiously, each fearful, for they all, at one time or another, had witnessed a cardiac arrest, and they saw the symptoms developing: on Townsend's face, in his growing agitation, and in his trembling hands. All looked from Townsend to Glassail, hoping she would say something to stop him, praying she would insist that she take over the case. But Glassail was bent over the field as she watched Townsend aim the trembling forceps toward the piece of shrapnel.

The forcep tips opened and clamped gently down on the piece of metal. Glassail sighed in relief. But just as Townsend began extracting the forceps, he suddenly cried out in explosive, agonizing pain and in trying to clutch at his chest, the forceps came up out of the wound and nicked Pete's carotid artery. A pulsation of bright red blood jettisoned upward, smacking Townsend in the face. Blinded and screaming, he stumbled backward. The thin, strong jet of blood hit the overhead lamp, coating it quickly so that the surgical field became cast in a pinkish glow.

"Put pressure on it!" O'Shaunnesy demanded, as he monitored Pete's falling blood pressure.

Dr. Townsend fell onto the tiled floor.

Kate grabbed a handful of sponges and pushed them against the artery.

Bee Jonas left the back instrument table and ran to Townsend's side. She knelt down beside him and tried to find a pulse.

Fawn Glassail stood frozen in place.

"Dr. Glassail!" Kate yelled. *"Clamp it off."* But Fawn didn't seem to hear her. "Dr. O'Shaunnesy, what should I do?"

"Get Dr. Framingham," he said. "He should be scrubbing for a case."

"Go, Linda, go get him!" Kate demanded.

Linda ran into the corridor and shrieked for assistance. "Dr. Framingham, Miss Pickle, Sara, someone, help, help, I need a surgeon, quick!"

Chapter 15

September 19
Wednesday morning

Shelley Bigelow balled her fist again and rapped against the medication room door with her knuckles. "Answer me, Mary Ann, please. Are you bleeding?"

They heard a whisper of a voice say, "No."

Shelley glanced from Rosemary to Pat Peters, the Gold Coast head nurse, and asked, "How long has she been in there?"

"About twenty minutes," Pat replied.

"What caused this?" Rosemary asked.

"She said Miguel Galindo threatened to cut her into ribbons if she didn't cooperate. I don't know what he had on his mind, or what he did to her, but when Mary Ann started screaming, he left the med room in a hurry."

"What do you mean he threatened to cut her?" Rosemary asked.

131

"He carries a switchblade."

While Rosemary and Pat talked, Shelley took a master key from her pocket and inserted it into the slot.

"That won't work," Pat said. "I tried my key. The door swings in, and it feels like she's pushed the metal shelving between the door and the far wall. Poor thing is scared to death."

Shelley tried anyway. The door opened a quarter of an inch, not enough to release the latch from the striker plate. "Call maintenance," she said.

Rosemary grabbed the head nurse's arm. "No, the hinges are on the inside, and axing it down will frighten her more." Rosemary stepped closer to the door and bent her head toward the crack. "Mary Ann, this is Mrs. Cleaveland. What do you want me to do?"

"Get my parents."

"Are you injured?"

"N . . . n . . . no," the young woman wept.

"I'll get your parents, but it may take some time. There'll be a security guard standing right outside this door so if you need something to eat or drink, or if you get chilly, just ask. No one's going to hurt you now, especially Mr. Galindo. I'll make certain of that. Are you all right for now?"

Silence.

Pat whispered, "How am I going to get meds to the patients? The cart is in there . . . and the I.V. fluids."

"Call the pharmacy," Shelley said. "Have them go through the profiles for all your morning meds. I'll get some staffing help for you. Someone should go through the doctors orders and compare what you need with what the pharmacy brings."

Rosemary asked, "What if we asked Mary Ann to push that cart out?"

Both Shelley and Pat looked at Rosemary. "Good idea!" Pat said.

"Sometimes," Shelley said, "simple solutions are trampled under the feet of complexity on the stampede for an answer. Give it a try, Pat."

Pat stepped closer to the door. "Mary Ann, dear, I'm trying to understand how frightened you are, but I'm also getting frightened myself. We've got some sick patients here who need their medications, and the post-ops will be arriving soon. They're frightened of pain, Mary Ann. I need to help them, too, and also the older ones on I.V. fluids, and Mr. Poppagelli, your favorite patient, will surely go into coma without his insulin. You've always been a compassionate nurse, Mary Ann. You've always put your patients needs above your own, and I respect you for that. Please, just push the cart into the hallway. You can lock up again, I promise."

On her way to Senor Villareal's room, Rosemary stopped at room 501 and looked in. Pete's bed had a fresh bottom sheet that was tucked in as if it had been painted onto the mattress. The top sheet and blanket were fanned against the footboard. Everything had been straightened and cleaned for his arrival back from the recovery room. She said a quick prayer for him and then continued down to room 505.

Rosemary saw Jorge Villareal staring out the window. His torso was bent slightly, and he held a palm against his chest. "Senor?"

He turned and looked at her. "Ah, Mrs. Cleaveland, how good of you to visit." He eased himself onto the bed. "I thought I was in fine shape," he apologized. "Actually, my head doesn't hurt as much as my chest. I feel like the entire O.R. team took turns hitting me with a sledge hammer." He gently touched the lower edge of his rib cage and winced.

"Anesthesia gases do that," Rosemary explained. "Senor, I thought we had an understanding about your men."

"They're staying at the Hyatt Regency."

"I don't want them at Riverside at anytime, even to visit you. You can use the telephone if you have to communicate. A short time ago, your Miguel Galindo used a switchblade to threaten one of my nurses. I don't know what the threat entailed, but whatever he said or did, frightened her enough that she locked herself inside the medication room and now refuses to come out. Fortunately, she pushed the cart out so the patients won't suffer, but I've had to place a guard by the door for her safety and peace of mind until her parents arrive to take her home. I can't have threatening behavior here. It's not humorous, it's not constructive, and he's interfering with all the other damn problems we have." When Villareal did not comment, Rosemary continued. "As we discussed yesterday, the hospital's got two unfortunate incidents under investigation by the police, and Mr. Galindo's actions certainly appear suspicious."

"My dear lady, you are far too attractive to be so

aggressive and hostile. I am sure we can come to an understanding, but first, you must relax a little, hear my side. People in high management positions get there because they manipulate toward mutual agreements, but people in high dudgeon fail because they refuse to see any other side but their own. I am sure you fall into the first category for you manage this hospital well, and you have come quite far for a woman. Let me tell you about Miguel, then you will understand my need for him, and perhaps see how he could help you, too."

The past half hour had been worse than all her O.R. experiences combined and quadrupled, and Linda Diver, the circulating nurse on Pete's case, now had a case of bad nerves. As she gathered up green drapes and placed them inside a laundry hamper, she wished that Bee would return soon to keep her company. At least the housekeeping crew would be in shortly to wash down the walls and floors. As Linda collected the dozens of instruments and placed them into metal bins, she used the solitude to clear her thoughts and recall exactly what had happened because she knew Miss Pickle would ask her, and the chief of surgery would probably want her to attend the next surgical staff meeting.

Linda had worked in Riverside's O.R. for the past eighteen years and during that time, no surgeon had ever suffered a cardiac arrest while operating. Oh, sure, she'd seen an occasional drunkard, but anesthesia always canceled the case. She knew a few surgeons hopped up on drugs or marijuana before their cases, and if they were too happy, or shaking to death, anesthesia canceled them out, too. Dr. O'Shaunnesy was particularly careful. She and the other nurses adored him for he always listened to their worries.

But what about Dr. Glassail? She didn't appear to be a sot or a junkie. How would you classify a surgeon who froze up? Linda thought that one over and wondered what the chief of surgery would do with Glassail. Probably remove her surgical privileges, Linda decided, and shook her head. Wasn't Glassail pathetic? Standing there like she'd never been on a case in her life. Thank God Dr. Framingham had been available to finish, or that patient might have died. Whew, Mrs. Cleaveland would have all our heads rolling if something happened to her boyfriend.

Against a wall was the defective electrocautery machine. She unplugged the functioning machine, rolled it next to the other, held up the probe and discharged two hundred amperes of charged electricity into the air, like a fairy godmother zapping the princess into full dress. Linda then went to the work table, found a Warning-Defective Equipment tag, and filled out the necessary information.

Three housekeepers entered the room. They were discussing the deaths of Ritchie Chisolm and Myra Brady. The one with the mop and bucket nodded hello to Linda. She nodded back and as they went about their business, Linda slipped the warning tag onto the knob of the defective machine and, listening to the periphery conversation in hopes of picking up the latest gossip, she forgot to unplug it. She held the probe up and pressed the discharge button. Without rubber gloves on, Linda became a conduit. Two hundred amperes of electricity arced like a bolt of lightning between her body and the machine. She started to scream but it congealed in her throat.

The three workers stood immobile as they watched Linda's face contort into a hideous rictus, and heard the snapping crackles of electricity. Suddenly, one of them got control of her horror and she raced over and tried to pull the plug, but she, too, got caught in the charge. A second worker grabbed the mop, and with strength never before experienced, broke off the metal head and approached Linda with the long wooden handle. Just as she was about to knock the probe from Linda's hand, the electricity shut off. The nurse and the housekeeper fell to the ground while the others went screaming into the corridor.

Chapter 16

Rosemary turned from the window and leaned back against the sill. "I don't know," she said, half to herself and half to Villareal, who watched her intently.

"What can you lose," he asked, "except another employee, or yourself? He's the best security guard you've got. Believe me, Mrs. Cleaveland, I wouldn't suggest it if I didn't have total faith in Miguel's abilities. And this will give him something constructive to do. At least talk to him, on the telephone, or you could meet him someplace outside the hospital . . ."

Following a frantic knock, the door burst open. "Rosemary, come quickly," Shelley said, "to the O.R. It's Pete!"

Rosemary's face turned pale as she flew off the windowsill. "What? What about him?"

138

"I'll tell you on the way, come on."

Shelley talked constantly as the two women hurried past the nurse's station. "Townsend had a myocardial infarction, right there in the room. As he was operating! I've heard of it happening in other hospitals, but I never imagined it would happen at Riverside, and he's so young, you know what I mean? He seemed so healthy. Dr. Glassail was first assistant and apparently she froze when Dr. Townsend went down. Fortunately, Dr. Framingham was already scrubbed for a case, so he went in and finished up."

Rosemary's worst fears had materialized. She tried to calm herself despite a rising feeling of panic. Her breathing was hard and fast when she asked, "How is Pete . . . is he . . . did he . . ."

"He's alive," Shelley said as she held the door to Sinclair Five open for Rosemary. "Dr. Framingham got the bullet fragment, and even did the skin closure himself, although I guess he didn't have a choice, with Glassail incapacitated and all. Makes you wonder about her surgical skills, her experience, her . . . abilities, if you know what I mean."

"Pete's all right?" Rosemary asked again, to reassure herself.

"Yes, that's what Pickle told me."

"No spinal cord or nerve damage?"

"Why don't you ask Pickle yourself? She'll give you the full scoop."

"What about Dr. Townsend?"

"They've taken him to the coronary care unit."

Standing at the recovery room door, Rosemary quickly looked at each cubicle, trying to find Pete.

139

She saw Miss Pickle in cubicle 6 talking with Dr. O'Shaunnesy. She walked slowly, her eyes focused on the patient's face, not certain if it was Pete, praying that it was. You're okay, Pete, she said to herself. You know I love you, don't you? Have I told you how much you mean to me? We'll go to Bermuda together, just as soon as you've recovered. Please God, make him all right.

It *was* Pete. Approaching the foot of the stretcher, Rosemary slowly grasped the metal rail and held her breath as she looked down at him. He was breathing, but he seemed so pale. A large white dressing covered the side of his neck like a spongy fungus on the side of a tree. He lay with his hands by his sides. Tape covered the needle inserted into a vein of his left hand. From the needle, tubing led up to a ceiling-hung rack where several plastic bottles of I.V. fluids were scalloped together with more tubing. Miss Pickle was making adjustments to the flow-meter.

As Shelley came up beside Rosemary, Pickle glanced up and joined them at the foot of Pete's stretcher. "He's doing just fine," she said.

When Rosemary continued staring at Pete, Pickle put her hand over Rosemary's, trying to comfort her.

"Was there any nerve damage?" Rosemary asked.

"Not that we can detect right now. Pupils are equal and reacting. Vital signs are strong. He can move his feet and hands and the circulation is good. We have to wait a little longer to do an entire neuro check."

Dr. O'Shaunnesy finished taking Pete's pulse. "The patient's fine but how are you, Rosey? You look a wee bit peaked, I'd say."

Rosemary gave him a brief smile. "I'm all right, Shaun. Tell me what happened."

O'Shaunnesy shot a knowing glance to Pickle, then led the three women to the nurses' desk at the entrance to the recovery room. Several nurses moved off to check their patients. O'Shaunnesy leaned against the desk and, in hushed tones, said, "A few months ago, I started to suspect that Townsend was having trouble with his ticker, but when I asked, he said he was being treated and, in so many words, told me to mind my own business. Today, we were about thirty-five minutes into the operation when Townsend started feeling uncomfortable. He was belching and complaining about the heat, and he was the color of a storm front. He'd cut down to the piece of shrapnel and was extracting it when his heart started fibrillating. He went down pretty fast."

"What happened to Dr. Glassail?" Rosemary asked.

Pickle whispered, "She froze. I've only seen first-year surgical residents turn to cement like that. Kate March held the artery closed until we could get help."

Shelley leaned toward Pickle. "What do you mean, held the artery closed?"

"Townsend accidentally nicked the carotid artery," Pickle said.

Rosemary felt her knees weaken. She knew enough physiology to understand the immediate loss of blood. "Shaun, I want to know exactly what went on in there."

The lanky anesthesiologist shrugged. "We had a

141

bit of a problem. Townsend's heart seized on him just as he was bringing the forceps out. The tips cut the carotid artery and the patient started losing blood and pressure. Kate March held the artery closed while Linda went out to get help. Dr. Framingham was scrubbing for another case and he came in to finish up."

Rosemary glanced over at Pete's stretcher, then back to O'Shaunnesy. Her voice was hard. "Pete's spurting blood and Glassail turns to stone? What the hell of a kind of surgeon is she? I'll tell you something, Shaun. And you listen, too, Miss Pickle. Dr. Fawn Glassail is not using this surgical suite again until the incident is investigated. I want a full report from the chief of surgery."

O'Shaunnesy raised his hands in the air. "I agree. In fact, I'll tell Dr. Harris as soon as he finishes his case."

"Mrs. Bigelow," Rosemary continued, "inform your supervisors that all of Dr. Glassail's privileges are suspended . . ."

O'Shaunnesy put a large arm around Rosemary. "Wait a minute, Rosey, you're driving too fast. Maybe there's a reason for Glassail's difficulty. I'd suggest you go a little slower."

Rosemary rubbed a hand across her eyes. "Pete could have died, Shaun. Maybe I am going too fast . . . but how would you feel about pumping gas on a future case of hers? Wouldn't you have doubts about the outcome? Wouldn't you coerce one of the surgeons to stay scrubbed up and available? And what about this one, Shaun. Would you want her operating on you?"

Pickle answered for him. "I wouldn't . . . and neither—"

The internal O.R. paging system cut her off as it blared, "Emergency, room three. Emergency, room three."

Rather than waste precious time holding a stupid meeting with his computer division employees, Chad wrote a memo and asked the secretary to post it on the bulletin board. The memo informed the staff that they were to eat lunch in the staff room, that they were to cut down on any miscellaneous trips around the hospital, and that paychecks could be picked up from his secretary tomorrow, not from the payroll office.

"Your wife wants you to call," the secretary said. "It's important."

Chad thought it over. He didn't want to talk to the bitch, and yet if he didn't find out what was so earth-shatteringly important, Beth would bug him all day, maybe even come to the hospital. He went to his office and called. The extremely important news that he already knew about was that the brakes on her car were so mushy that she was afraid of driving carpool this afternoon. "Damn it Beth," he yelled, "why didn't you take it in this morning, like I told you?"

"Don't get mad at me. I asked you to follow me over and drive me back home, but oh no, you didn't have time. Your work is more important than your family. Well, I called the Baystate Ford dealer and they can lend me a car until mine's fixed."

"Why the hell bother me when you've already got it figured out? If you need my approval, I'm telling you right now, get the brakes fixed, get the rental, and get the hell out of my hair. Good-bye."

Irritated, he left Riverside and drove to the post office on Cambridge Street. Box 389 contained three envelopes, each addressed to Moonbeam Industries. After stopping at McDonald's for a takeout order of chicken nuggets, fries, and a Diet Coke, he returned to the hospital. At his desk, he opened the mail and found three checks for the STETHOSCOPE program. All feelings of frustration with Beth dissolved. Each certified check was for five thousand dollars. Chad was pleased with himself. Fifteen thousand a day was incredible, but he could double that with two programs for sale. While munching on nuggets and fries, he activated the computer terminal on his desk and with his telephone modem, hacked for an hour, trying to find the LASER program. He finally gave up. To keep his anger in check, and his hopes high, he telephoned five hospital controllers located in western Massachusetts. Pretending to be a sales representative for Moonbeam Industries, he talked long and hard about the capabilities of and low cost of STETHOSCOPE, and that any other dealer would charge double the amount, a fact that each controller already knew. Two of the five gave him firm orders. He decided to work on the others and the LASER program this afternoon. For now, he lined up the three checks on his desk, dialed a local telephone number, leaned back in his chair, and put his feet on the desk. "Hi, Marilyn, I've been thinking about you."

* * *

Rosemary and Shelley stood in O.R. 3 while the men from transportation put Linda Diver and the housekeeper on stretchers. The housekeeper was taken to the surgical intensive care unit where the unit medical director would handle her until they found the name of her private physician. No physician was needed for Linda and no room was assigned, for the transporter was told to go directly to the morgue.

"My Lord," Rosemary said as she and Shelley watched the transporter wheel out the stretcher with Linda's body lying still underneath the green sheet. "Three deaths in two days." She sighed heavily. "I don't understand what's going on. I don't understand why MOM didn't cut the electricity to the machine. Hell, that's what she's *for*, to prevent electrical accidents."

"I'll ask Charlie Donovan to check out the room and the machine."

Rosemary continued as if she hadn't heard Shelley. "I must find out why Dr. Glassail couldn't finish the case. She seemed so confident . . . three employees dead . . . I don't understand." She shook her head.

"Don't lump them in one mortuary basket. Fawn Glassail and Linda Diver are one event. Ritchie Chisolm and Myra Brady are another. And what happened to Duncan Silverstone is yet another. There's no common thread. I, too, have considered a malfunction in MOM, and perhaps she might account for this O.R. event, but she's not capable of knifing Ritchie and Myra."

Rosemary put a hand on Shelley's shoulder. "You're right. What happened to Pete has distorted my perspective." She paused. "We better prepare for an employee outcry. Their loyalties are being pressed hard. I'm going to see Pete, then Dr. Townsend."

"I'll make that call to Charlie and meet you in recovery."

Rosemary stood over Pete's stretcher, looking down at his peaceful face. She reached down and held his hand. "Pete?" she said. "Are you awake?" In his dreams, Pete smiled. She gently squeezed his hand and smiled, too. He still looked pale to her, and she wondered how much blood he'd lost. You've got to heal quickly, she thought. I need you, Pete. I need your support, your common sense, your laughter. I need you by my side. Things aren't clear to me. A knot twisted in her stomach as she thought about Fawn Glassail, standing over Pete, watching him die, unable to help him. That she had been jealous over Fawn's relationship with Pete, made Rosemary mad at herself.

At the nurses' desk, Rosemary read Pete's medical record on the terminal screen. Dr. Framingham had dictated an operative note that mentioned only the facts of the operation, and that he had helped assist with the case. "During surgery," the note read, "approximately one pint of blood was lost. No need to replace at this time."

Shelley joined Rosemary at the terminal and read the note, too. "Interesting how little can be recorded when so much went on. Are you ready to go?"

"Yes."

As they walked, Shelley said, "I want you to know

146

that I feel bad about Linda, too; she was a good nurse . . . capable . . . friendly. The accident was a freak, Rosemary. It wasn't her fault. Charlie said he'd look over the line isolation monitor and both machines, right away. I hope he can figure out what happened."

The large automatic doors of the coronary care unit were wallpapered with plastic signs. One read Authorized Personnel Only, Visitors Use Red Telephone in Visitors Lounge To Contact A Nurse; another read, Two Visitors At A Time For Ten Minutes Every Hour; a third read, Press Red Button On The Wall To Open The Doors. Rosemary was about to press the button when the large doors suddenly swung open. Fred Plexico walked out. When he saw Rosemary, his face bunched up into a scowl. "You've got a real problem this time. I heard your terrific computer failed to cut the power to the machine Dr. Townsend was using."

Rosemary glared at him. "Dr. Townsend wasn't using any machine."

"He was too, and it almost killed him. You and that idiotic computer are totally responsible for this." He glanced at Shelley Bigelow, then continued. "I have an appointment with you at three o'clock. We'll discuss it then."

Once he was out of earshot, Shelley whispered, "He's an ass. On the board or no, he shouldn't be wandering around this hospital. He's looking for problems. One of these days, he'll find one that we're not aware of . . . and he'll . . ." Shelley let her thought drift away.

"He'll what?"

"He'll hang you."

"No, he won't. I have a plan."

"It better be a good one."

Suddenly, Rosemary felt like clubbing Shelley for being such a pessimist. She held her tongue in check. It seemed as if her emotions were oscillating out of control; peaking at rage with Fred, dipping with fear for Pete, rising in anger with Dr. Glassail, sinking in depression for Linda Diver. Exhaustion rode her bones like a relentless driver: Scarlet beating her horse to death. She whispered, "I must find a way to keep Fred away from Riverside."

"I don't know how you can stop him. Yesterday afternoon I saw him go onto the Sinclair Two nursing unit. He didn't see me, but it would have made no difference anyway. I don't think he knows who I am, although we've been introduced ninety-nine times."

"Did he find anything?" Rosemary asked.

"I don't think so. He hung around the nurses' station and wandered up and down the corridor, but my head nurse said the unit was quiet at the time." Shelley pressed the red button to activate the coronary care unit doors.

They crossed into the world of telemetry where the heart was the focal point of complicated measurements and vast abbreviations used, Rosemary suspected, because seconds meant life or death, or at least some sort of time savings. In a life-threatening situation, the patient would surely croak while the doctors ordered, "A thousand milliliters of dextrose ten percent in water with forty milligrams of aminophylline at one hundred drops per hour." Instead, it was abbreviated to "1000 D10W c̄ aminophylline 40 mg @ 100cc." Here, CABGS meant coronary artery bypass surgery; RBBB meant right bundle branch block; HB III meant third degree heart block involving the A-V node with no P waves reaching the ventricle, which contracts with its own escape pacemaker unrelated to atrial activity. Here, the patient suffering an MI was at risk for V tach and needed lidocaine for prophylaxis, but if V tach was already present, then procainamide would do just ducky.

Rosemary had trouble discerning cardiac structures from medications or therapeutic measures. To her, a pacemaker was a device implanted in the chest wall to kick the heart into action. She wasn't familiar with the heart's own variety of internal pacemakers. CVP and Swan-Ganz lines were as mysterious as CPK, LDH, and SGOT enzymes. As many times as she asked MOM III, the definitions simply slipped out of her mind, much the same way as administrative definitions like DRG, ICD-9, and FI were lost on intelligent coronary care nurses; the foundations of knowledge being in two different camps. Unless one party wanted to purchase an expensive item, like an MRI for several million dollars, Rosemary and her assistants quickly learned about magnetic resonance imaging.

Architecturally, the coronary care unit was shaped like an ice cream cone with glass enclosed patient rooms on the periphery of the ice cream, a large nurses' station at the upper crest of the cone, and in the cone's handle were rooms marked soiled utility, clean utility, refreshment station, medication room, conference room. On the outer edges of the cone were hallways. Rosemary and Shelley entered and headed toward the nurses' station.

At the desk, they asked where Dr. Townsend was located. "Room seven," answered the ward secretary, pointing. "The doctors are with him, and he's sedated."

They went to the sliding glass door and watched. Townsend had green plastic prongs inserted in his nose for oxygen therapy. EKG leads on his chest monitored his heart on the screen over the bed. I.V. bottles hung from a ceiling-mounted hanger. A lab technician had a tourniquet around his arm and was drawing blood into a vacuum tube. Dr. Merriman, the unit's director, noticed Rosemary and walked over.

"Bad situation," he said. "He's got an inferior cardiac wall infarction. EKG shows A-V nodal ischemia, with elevated ST segments. I've put him on intravenous lidocaine and morphine, and we should be getting comparison enzyme levels soon."

"Did he have a history of heart trouble?" Rosemary asked.

"Yeah, he'd talk with me periodically, and he started himself on nitroglycerine tablets but like many people, he never took the time to get a complete cardiac exam. He was afraid of the results."

"Will he live?"

"If he doesn't have another attack in the next three or four days, and if he stays under my care, he'll be all right. It'll take another day or two for us to get a handle on the extent of the damage. He may need bypass surgery . . . but let's see what happens.

For now, he's comfortable."

"Let me know if he gets into trouble, please."

"I will."

Needing to be alone for a while, Rosemary left Shelley in the unit and headed for her office. When her secretary saw her, Peggy pointed to Rosemary's office door. "A Miguel Galindo is in there. He insists on seeing you."

"Would you call Dr. Stockman's office and ask if he has time to see me today?"

Peggy dialed the number and talked to Stockman's secretary. She covered the mouthpiece and whispered, "He can see you in half an hour."

Rosemary nodded and Peggy confirmed the appointment. Before Rosemary could disappear, Peggy read from her notebook. "Someone from psychiatry called to ask if you were going to use MOM's interview room at ten o'clock this morning. I said I didn't know. Tilly, the housekeeper, said she didn't leave anything in your closet yesterday; it must have been someone else. George Jones from housekeeping wanted to see you about our contract with General Uniform Company. He says they're going to bill us for a lot of lost uniforms this month. Hugh Matta, the union steward, wants to see you. You missed meeting the new medical staff appointees, and you should leave for the Superintendents' Club now if you want to make it for dessert."

"I'm not going." Rosemary was quiet for a moment as she tried to find the right words. Finally, she said, "May I see your ring again?"

"Sure! Isn't it a knockout?" Peggy held out her left hand.

"Yes, it's beautiful. You both will be very happy."

"We both *are* very happy."

"What will your new name be," Rosemary asked, "in full."

Peggy smiled. "Mrs. William Avery Parker."

Thank goodness, Rosemary thought, remembering the names on Shelley's list. "Where does he work?"

"At Youville Hospital. He's an orderly now, but he's going to computer school at night. Did you know that if you're a good programmer, you can start at thirty thousand a year?"

"Is that right? Where does he go to school?"

"Cambridge Computer Tech, over near Fresh Pond Circle."

Rosemary felt uneasy. Melenie Bregen had been raped in the Fresh Pond Shopping Mall. "What time are his classes?"

"He goes Mondays, Wednesdays, and Thursdays from five to nine. How come you're so interested?"

Rosemary hesitated. Melenie'd been raped on Monday evening. "Because I've never asked you much about him, and he *is* taking my favorite secretary away from me."

"No, he's not. I'm going to work for you until my hair turns gray."

"Or until you have children."

Peggy blushed. "Yeah, maybe until then. But you haven't a thing to worry about now. We need the money."

"Maybe Santa can find a bonus for you this year."

"Really?" Peggy said. "I'd love it!"

Rosemary smiled. "I'll see what I can do. Would you cancel the rest of my appointments today?"

"Mr. Highling called to say he couldn't come to your three o'clock appointment with Mr. Plexico."

"Then tell Fred I am delayed at a meeting and won't be able to make it either."

"What about the executive planning board?"

"Ask Shelley to sit in for me." Rosemary went into her office to meet Miguel Galindo for the first time. With employees of many nationalities at Riverside, Rosemary no longer stereotyped individuals as her parents did when she was growing up. To her, people could do a job or they couldn't. Although Miguel Galindo wore a business suit, his mustachio, lizard boots, and outward indolence made Rosemary now wonder which wetback he was, facing Clint Eastwood in *A Fistful of Dollars;* the looter, the rapist, or the killer, or all three in this man sitting at her chair with his boots on the desk, whittling cuticles from his fingernails with a switchblade. He smiled broadly. "I hear you need some protection."

"I might," she said, going to the large picture window overlooking the Charles River. Several skiffs of rowers pulled through the water. She watched and considered her next words.

"I'm good," he said.

Rosemary turned. "Before we discuss how good you are, let me tell you, Mr. Galindo, that your behavior is disgusting. I cannot deal with a man who threatens my nurses with knives and sexual innuendos. I won't have it." She pointed a finger at his face. "We have no deal if you pull something like that again."

Miguel held his hands up. "What'd I do?"

"You frightened the medication nurse who works

153

on the Gold Coast."

A smile flickered across Galindo's lips. He slipped the knife into a pocket, sat tall at the desk, and when he looked up at Rosemary, he bore the demeanor and visage of a serious financial consultant. "I understand your concerns. You're more a prickly chicalote than a silly chiquita, as I first assumed. You have a man's brain." He tapped his forehead. "I am willing to work with someone of such fine intelligence. And I promise that I will no longer be bored with your nurses. Did I say that correctly?"

The man aggravated her. He was an imperious, two-faced, wayward wetback. Rosemary caught herself. Cheap adjectives would get her nowhere. "Yes," she replied, "you said that correctly. I hope you mean it."

Slowly, Miguel stood up and went to Rosemary's library against one entire wall. "You read these?" he asked.

"Yes."

"My library is quite different."

Exasperated, Rosemary went to the door of her office and placed a hand on the knob. "I have little time for the Dewey Decimal System. Senor Villareal told me that you could help. I don't see that you can. Good day, sir."

Galindo turned and rested against a shelf. "Senor wants me to help you and I will. What is it you want done?"

"The job requires no malice."

"So?"

"So keep the vice president of the board away from Riverside for a few days."

"Name?"

"Fred Plexico."

"Usual hangout?"

"He's a professor at M.I.T., next door."

Miguel pulled his knife out and released the blade. "What if he won't cooperate?"

"I just told you, no malice, no threats, and please leave that thing in your hotel room."

"I'm an expert marksman with this. Watch." In an instant, his hand moved backward, then forward, and the knife whooshed through the space between them and stuck into the door next to Rosemary's head. "No one fools around with Miguel," he said with satisfaction.

Chapter 17

September 19
Wednesday noon

"He'll be with you in a minute," Dr. Stockman's secretary said to Rosemary. "Have a seat."

The connecting pair of offices were on the east end of Sinclair Four, near the mental health unit. When Robert Stockman became the chief of neurology nine months ago, Rosemary gave him a sizable budget for interior decorating. She noticed that new beige tweed draperies for the reception office had finally arrived. She enjoyed the office for the light brown hues were warm and welcoming. Thick carpeting covered the floor, and the walls were papered in a rich grass cloth. Rosemary sat in one of the leather wingback chairs that flanked a cherry coffee table. The latest issues of *Architectural Digest, Town and Country* Magazine, and the *New England Journal of Medicine* were on the table. She leafed through the *Journal* but couldn't concentrate.

She'd agreed to let Miguel Galindo keep Fred occupied if the switchblade remained in the hotel room. In a sense, she felt relieved to have both men on a cat and mouse escapade, although Fred didn't know yet that he was the mouse. She was, too, in another sense, for Miguel had insisted on guarding her: "At Senor Villareal's strict order." How he planned to occupy Fred and guard her made her curious, for both of them never spent much time in one place. What the hell, she thought, at least Miguel would be busy.

At the sound of ringing, Rosemary looked up at the secretary, who stopped typing on her computer terminal to answer the phone. "Dr. Stockman's office," she said. "Yes, he's here, but he's busy. Can I have him return your call? Oh, hello, doctor. Yes, what's the number? He'll get back to you as soon as possible."

The door to Stockman's inner office opened. A small woman with red hair appeared, followed by the doctor. "Make an appointment to see me in one week," he told the woman. "Hello, Rosemary, go on in. I'll be with you in a minute."

Rosemary stepped into his office. The plush decor was hidden under and behind stacks of papers, magazines, cases of medication samples left by salesmen, manila envelopes, a slide projector, tape recorder, and general junk. Even the bookcases were strewn with papers, knickknacks, gifts from grateful patients, a ship model, photo cubes of children, a large digital clock, and more medication samples. She wondered how he could think in all this clutter. On his examination table was a white lab coat, stethoscope, and a plastic model of a human skull. Rosemary picked it up and noticed that the skull was hinged at the back. With her fingernail, she pried open the latch. The skull opened to reveal a white plastic brain that was also hinged. She opened that, too, and saw an acrylic rendering of the interior sections; the white matter, gray matter, lobes, gyruses, things that were a mystery to her.

"A friend gave that to me," Stockman said from behind her.

At the sound of his voice, Rosemary turned. "It's quite detailed," she said. "I know so little about brains."

"Want a lesson?"

"Maybe another day, Bob. I know you're busy, but I just need a few minutes of your time."

"Rosemary, you know I always have time for you. Here, sit and relax." He pointed to a chair opposite his desk. Stockman was a muscular man who fit snugly into extra-large clothing. As he sat, the buttons of his blue oxford cloth shirt strained at the buttonholes. He adjusted his tie over his shirt front with large, hairy hands.

Rosemary liked Stockman. Maybe it was his size, or his fatherly character, or his ability to make people trust him, she wasn't certain, but she felt herself relax.

"I hear your boyfriend got into a bit of trouble in the O.R. today," he said. "Is there anything I can do to help?"

"Sonic booms were first produced by Riverside's grapevine. It's amazing how fast news travels." She sighed. "You heard correctly. Dr. Townsend had a heart attack while he was operating, and he accidentally nicked Pete's carotid artery."

"How's he doing?"

"Both are okay." Rosemary leaned forward. "The circulating nurse was killed, though. She was electrocuted by a defective cautery machine."

A dark cloud of worry settled on Stockman's face. "That's terrible," he said. "And it's almost impossible, with all the electrical safeguards in the O.R. Have you found the reason why it happened?"

"Charlie Donovan's looking into it. The incident is not why I'm here, Bob. I need your help on other matters." Rosemary often consulted with Stockman. Although his specialty was diseases of the nervous system, he had also studied psychiatry, not to practice it, but to better understand his patients. In addition to being the chief of neurology at Riverside, he was the director of the Stereotaxic Parabiosis Learning Center in Harvard Square, where he and his staff provided health and neurological services for people in the community. Although the center was Stockman's idea, he'd had Rosemary's support and Riverside's financing.

"What kind of personality does a psychotic killer have?" she asked. "Who should we be looking for?"

"That's a tough one, Rosemary. I've given it some thought, and I've spoken with several colleagues. Schizophrenia usually develops so slowly that the early symptoms are unclear." Stockman held his hands flat, then cupped them slowly. "The person is like a morning glory that closes up for the night. Where the person might have been tidy in appearance and habits, now he or she is careless. Interest in

159

about all categories wanes. His work sloughs off, and he begins to lose friends, which is a sad situation because he needs them desperately, and will reach out, but his shyness and suspiciousness repel others."

"That description doesn't seem to fit a vicious killer," Rosemary said.

"I've described the early symptoms. If left unaided, the person can develop paranoid schizophrenia, and I believe that's the problem we face in this case. Triggered by suspiciousness and futility, the psychotic develops delusions of persecution involving bizarre plots against him. With many enemies trying to persecute him, he then believes that he must be a remarkable individual, for why else would they be interested in him. What develops next is a complex delusional system where he becomes someone all-powerful, like Jesus Christ. Murdering the enemy is then a rational and defensive act."

Rosemary couldn't sit still. She walked to the window and looked out at the people walking along Massachusetts Avenue. "Aren't delusions the same as hallucinations?" she asked.

"In a sense."

She turned to face Stockman. "Then why can't we find this person? Wouldn't he be walking around talking to himself?"

"Maybe, but the person may not have reached that stage quite yet. He may hear voices telling him how to save the world, but he may not be responding verbally. I can't tell you what to look for except that the person is deeply confused and acting out against an unbearably hostile world. Moments of violence may be triggered by something that fits into his delusions. A colleague of mine is treating a paranoid schizo who thought her postman was a spy for the god of skin. Naked, she lured the postman into the house and when he was bare, erect, and defenseless, she tied him up and had started pouring muriatic acid on his body when the woman's husband came home in time to save the poor bugger."

Rosemary shuddered at the thought. "The god of skin?"

"Yes, isn't that a new one? The woman thought all the envelopes and magazines in the postman's bag were made of human skin. She was afraid of being his next victim."

"Do you have a paranoid schizo on the mental health unit?"

"No. We ship 'em out to Metropolitan State Hospital."

Rosemary told Stockman about the leg in her closet, and about the lunatic laughter she'd heard on the tape after Ritchie Chisolm's death. "Why would Ritchie be the enemy?" she asked. "And what would Myra Brady, the EEG tech, have done to trigger her death? If I only knew."

"Yup, it would help. Both fit into the delusion in some way. The key is finding out what the delusion is."

Both were silent for a few minutes. Finally Rosemary said, "Another unusual incident occurred Monday morning. Are you familiar with a patient named Duncan Silverstone?"

"The geologist from M.I.T.?"

"Yes. He came to Riverside for an EEG because

Dr. Holiday suspected a brain tumor. During the exam, Mr. Silverstone lost his memory. I know that sounds strange, but the man is a vegetable now."

"And you're afraid his family will sue the hospital," Stockman said.

"That's a concern, naturally, but more than that, I'm worried about the man. Maybe his tumor was advanced enough to cut off his mentation at the time of his EEG, but apparently he didn't have any neurological signs, like slurred speech, or difficulty walking. It doesn't seem plausible that he's fine one minute and a vegetable the next."

"It can happen," Stockman said. "But I agree with you, especially now that we've had another similar case."

Rosemary sat down on the edge of a chair and stared at him. "What?"

Stockman leaned forward. "I just heard about it. A patient named Ovaline Lee was having an EEG this morning, and she lost her mentation during the procedure. She's been admitted to Concord Four. I've spoken to her physician who tells me that he's using a new sleeping medication in order to illicit delta waves during the procedure. He believes the woman will awaken at some point, maybe in a day or two."

"What's the medication?"

"It's a stronger form of chloral hydrate."

"Who's the physician?"

"Dr. Holiday."

Rosemary stared at Stockman. "He's Duncan Silverstone's physician!"

"Yes, I know."

Rosemary hit the armrest with her fist. "Stop him, Bob. Don't let him use any new drug. Don't even allow him to schedule patients for EEGs."

"I *have* stopped him, Rosemary. Holiday assures me that he will investigate the drug, and his two patients thoroughly, and will give me a report."

"Report, report. I'm getting lots of reports *after* the fact. I'll never find time to read a tome of accidents and murders because new ones pop up too fast."

"Believe me, Rosemary, I'm concerned, too. Problems like this can ruin the reputation of my department, and I'm not about to lose my position as chief because of one physician's carelessness, if that's what it is. I'll get a full report, and I plan to do some investigating myself."

"It's all coming too fast," Rosemary said, feeling frustrated and unhappy. "Two employees stabbed to death, another electrocuted, then Townsend collapses, I almost lose Pete, two patients become vegetables, and I don't know which ones are related and which are isolated incidents. It's like the AIDS virus is taking random shots all over the hospital."

Stockman rose from his chair, came around the desk, and placed a large, comforting hand on her shoulder. "It seems bad, Rosemary, because you're being hit with so many problems at one time, but it'll get better, you'll see."

She smiled up at him. "Is that a guarantee?"

Stockman patted her shoulder. "I'm not God."

Suddenly, the floor underneath his feet trembled and he fell sideways, clutching at the backrest of her chair. "What the hell was that?" he asked as he straightened up.

Rosemary jumped to her feet and headed for the door. "It felt like an earthquake."

Chapter 18

John Berry, head of purchasing and supplies, smoked three packs of cigarettes a day. He chose Carlton because if he had to smoke, those were the lowest in tar and nicotine; he'd rather come up to flavor with Marlboro. John felt he had more worries than most people. At home, he supported a family of five, three of whom drained the funds severely for they were close enough in age to be in college at the same time. When the oldest graduated next year, the fourth in line would enter college. Even his wife took courses at Emerson for five hundred dollars a pop.

At work, John managed the purchasing, handling, distribution, and storage of every article in the hospital. MOM III helped, too. She informed him when sutures needed ordering, when chemicals in the lab, diapers in the nursery, medical record forms, coffee, drugs, needed to be ordered. Charges and orders from all departments were typed into computer terminals by the secretaries, then organized by MOM according to current vendor, and printed out for John's approval and signature. Although the procedure was easy, John was a worrywart. MOM couldn't check incoming supplies against the purchase orders to see, for example, if twelve cases of diapers ordered were twelve cases of diapers received, nor could she uncrate and place them on the metal shelving in the supply room. She couldn't take two cases a week up to the nursery and put them away, either, nor could she account for loss or theft until new orders were received earlier than normal; then she would type a note to John. Certain losses were predictable, like every August before school started, the pencils, erasers, notebooks, and paper supplies diminished at an incredible rate as mothers and fathers pocketed these items for their kids. Over the years, administration had come to view the loss as an employee benefit, figuring it was better to let them pinch a few pencils than get into drug theft, or worse.

On Wednesdays and Fridays, John's worries heightened for these were vendor days, when his secretary scheduled five hours of nonstop sales pitches. The fifth appointment today was with Steve Horner, a salesman for American Boiler Chemicals. Because most of his products came in large barrels, Steve did not carry the typical huge briefcase loaded with samples.

From the loading dock on the first floor of the Concord building, John Berry and Steve Horner walked into the purchasing department and stopped at the secretary's desk. "Amanda, I need the inventory sheets for the boilers," John said.

While she looked through the towering stacks of papers on her desk, Amanda said, "This has got to stop, Mr. Berry. The people in this office . . . shit, the secretaries all over the damn hospital are scared to death. Too many people have died, patients *and* employees and we don't know who's going to be the next victim. There's an emergency meeting this afternoon at three-thirty and I'm going to it. We all are. It means leaving an hour early, but we've taken a vote and decided to lose the hour of pay."

Next to John, Steve Horner shifted his weight. John glared at Amanda to quiet her down, but she just glared back defiantly. Although he wouldn't admit it to anyone, he was scared, too. He'd heard the whisperings about the Riverside Ripper. He'd seen the detectives, and police, and extra security guards, and he was quickly approaching four packs of cigarettes a day in his anxiety.

When he didn't answer, Amanda smirked. "You look like you want to join us, Mr. Berry, but sorry. I always said that department heads should join a union. Then you'd have support in numbers, too."

When he'd started employment at Riverside two years ago, Amanda had been one of the clerks in purchasing. He recognized her talents immediately. She was more knowledgeable, adaptable, compatible than the others, and he'd promoted her to his own secretary. Never before had she spoken to him this way, and he knew she would attend the meeting no matter what he said. "What does the union have in mind?"

"Maybe a job walkout."

"You'd do that?"

She looked down at her desk. "I'd think about it. You've got to admit it's pretty unsafe around here.

We can't go to the cafeteria, we can't go to the payroll office, we can't even take a pee without getting one of the other women to go along. Job security is no longer synonymous with seniority . . ." She stopped. "Speaking of seniority, we've heard about this Senor Villareal up on the Gold Coast, and about his band of hoodlums. Who's doing what about *that* situation? You want my opinion, they're responsible for what's going on." Amanda had fire dancing in her eyes. "That's one of the main subjects at our meeting; what we can do to get administration off the pot. They're doing nothing, and we want some answers."

"Go to the meeting, Amanda. I'll manage for the hour or so." He took the inventory sheets from her hand. "Come on, Steve."

"Oh, Mr. Berry," Amanda said. "One of the surgeons was here a while ago. He wanted you to order something new for the O.R."

"What was it?" John asked.

"I don't know. I told him to leave the package on your desk and that you'd call him today."

"Thanks."

Under his breath, Steve said, "What do you have; some kind of plague killing off the people here?"

"Naw. They get upset at the slightest problem . . ."

"I mean, if it's . . . like . . . rampant AIDS or something . . ."

John stopped walking and looked sternly at Steve. He had to calm the man down or Steve would tell every purchasing director in every hospital he visited that people were dropping dead at Riverside. Bad

168

for the reputation, for certain. "Look, Steve, we had a case of machine failure in the operating room. A nurse and a surgeon got a bad jolt, that's all. Nothing happened to the patient. Unfortunately, the event has turned into an overblown rumor. It'll pass." John slipped a pack of cigarettes out of his shirt pocket, tapped the deck, and offered them to Steve."

"No thanks."

The two men walked into John's office: a library of vendor's catalogues and samples. "Whew," Steve said. "Smells like a mixture of cat pee, cleaning fluid, and something else familiar . . . ether, maybe. I'm gonna leave the door open if you don't mind."

"God, what a stink," John agreed. "I'll get my papers and we'll go to the lounge." He slipped a cigarette between his lips and found a lighter on the desk. "I understand American Boiler is coming out with a new stack solvent. I'd be interested in trying a case—" John never finished the sentence for the instant he snapped the lighter, the small blue flame popped once, then flashed toward the ceiling like a welder's torch. The air in the entire room sucked up the flame with a deafening roar and turned the office into an inferno of intense blue heat. John and Steve stared at each other in wide-eyed disbelief as the violent explosion melted their faces.

The staff members in the purchasing department jumped from their chairs in surprise and watched agape as Steve Horner's body flew through the door and landed in a writhing, burning heap just outside the office. Terrified, and panicked, they began stumbling over one another to get out into the hallway.

At the door, a clerk pulled the fire alarm box and glanced inside John's office. Within the remnants of yellow flames, she saw his body slumped over the desk. It looked like a charred log.

As if in suspended animation, employees throughout the hospital stopped what they were doing and listened to the fire code beeps that signaled the fire's location. After feeling the vibration, they knew this was not another drill. Dread stalked their hearts. Some glanced at the clocks, wishing that the union meeting would start soon while others considered walking out right now.

Charlie Donovan counted the beeps as he tried to quell a growing sense of fear. The alarm was for Concord One. He lumbered into the stairwell, cursing his stocky body up the flight of stairs. As he came into the corridor, he saw smoke and employees pouring out the door of the purchasing department. Near the stairway was a fire hose cabinet. He opened the glass door, yanked the hose free, and turned on the water. The limpid tubing swelled instantly, wiggled free of Charlie's grasp, and thumped down the corridor like a large snake spurting poisonous water at the confused employees who started screaming and running toward the loading dock at the end of the corridor. Cursing again, Charlie got his hands around the nozzle and lunged into the purchasing department with a full stream of water arcing ahead of him. Maintenance men arrived to help, along with dozens of employees, physicians, Chad, Shelley, Wesly, and Rosemary, who was followed by Dr. Stockman.

"My God," Rosemary said to Shelley. "What happened?"

"I just got here myself."

"Where's John Berry and the purchasing staff?" Shelley shook her head.

Outside, screams of sirens grew louder as equipment from the Cambridge Fire Department approached the hospital. Rosemary squeezed through the crowd and headed for the loading dock door. From the series of beeps, which also rang at the firehouse, the men knew to come through this entrance. When the door opened, several employees ran out onto the cement dock and down the stairs while firemen dressed in slickers, hoods, and boots tried to get up. The fire chief screamed them out of the way. In the building, he yelled. "Clear the area. Clear the area. Give us some *room*."

Rosemary grabbed an employee's sleeve and asked her about John Berry. The woman's face changed from grief to a scowl when she saw Rosemary. "He's dead, I think. This place is crazy and I'm going home for good." She shrugged off Rosemary's hand.

"But what happened?"

"His office blew up. That's all I know." The woman went outside.

Through the smoke and throng of people, Rosemary noticed Mike Dow swing through the stairwell door midway down the hall. His brow wrinkled, lips pursed as he surveyed the scene. She waved but he didn't see her. She began squeezing back through the crowd, anxious to be near him, to talk with him, to have the support of a friend for she feared what had happened to the purchasing staff. "Let me through!" she pleaded with the mass of employees who were being pushed back by firemen stringing a rope barrier. It was then that she noticed a gowned surgeon pressed closely against her left side. Dark eyes burned into hers. She tried to shrink away, but the people around her wouldn't move.

"Hey, quit pushing," someone said.

"Clear the damn area," the fire chief yelled again.

Rosemary stood on tiptoe and waved frantically. "Mike, Mike Dow, over here!"

She pushed harder, trying to focus on Mike's face, but it seemed that the wall of bodies tightened, like fence rails all coming together.

The surgeon took hold of her left arm and pulled her even closer. The eyes above the mask were wild, and she sensed that this was the person who had killed Ritchie and Myra, the psychopath whom Stockman had described to her. Rosemary panicked. She tried to push his hand away. "What do you want with me? What have I done?" Suddenly, she felt a sharp jab of pain in her left side. She screamed. The surgeon let go. She screamed again. The people jammed against her stared as if she'd gone crazy. "What's the matter, Mrs. Cleaveland?" a technician shouted above the din.

As the surgeon inched into the mass of people, Rosemary clutched her side and bent over to get her breath. "Help me," she whispered. She looked at her hand. It was full of her blood. An orderly standing next to her also saw the blood. "Bring a stretcher," he yelled. "Mrs. Cleaveland's bleeding. We need some help here." People pushed back to give her room. As she slipped into unconsciousness, Rosemary felt someone help her to the floor, and she heard snatches of conversations.

"Someone call a Code Red!"

"Clear the area."

"She's stopped breathing!"

"There's Sergeant Dow . . . let him through . . ."

"I'll finish up with double-oh silk sutures," Dr. Framingham told Helen Donovan, the scrub nurse, who placed a skin hook in his left hand, and in his right, a needle holder that held a black silk thread.

Dr. O'Shaunnesy heard the cue and began easing Rosemary off the anesthesia gases.

"How's she doing?" Framingham asked, although he could hear Rosemary's heart on the audible monitor and knew the beat was strong and regular.

"Good," O'Shaunnesy answered. "Pressure's one-oh-eight over sixty-four. Rate is seventy-six. How's it from your side?"

"She's lucky. The weapon missed her liver, just scraped the descending bowel, passed alongside the spleen, and nicked an ovary. Fortunately, the bladder's intact. She'll have some pain, but knowing Rosemary, she'll be up and about tomorrow, and toe-tapping by this weekend."

O'Shaunnesy smiled to himself. She was a tough lass, and decisive, that was for sure, but they were friends and as he inspected the endotracheal tube that went down her throat, he placed a warm palm against her cheek and wished her well.

"What happened to her?" Helen Donovan asked.

"I haven't heard the full story yet," Dr. Framingham said, "but she's been stabbed like the

173

others . . . just like the others."

"Do you think it was the Riverside Ripper?" Helen asked.

"Is that what they're calling the psycho?"

"Yeah, and I'm telling you, starting today I'm taking a permanent leave of absence from this hospital. The place is too scary for me. I felt that explosion. I know that John Berry's dead, too. He was a friend of mine. So was Linda Diver. I hate to sound disrespectful, but the number of wakes I have to attend is growing by the hour. And who knows who'll be next? Shit, if the Ripper is after Mrs. Cleaveland, and we've just sewn her up, then he'll come after each one of us."

"Mrs. Donovan," Framingham said, "you are hysterical."

"I am not!"

"Yes, you are. Perhaps I should ask Pickle to give you a week's vacation."

"Superb idea! Make it a month."

"Excuse me," Dr. O'Shaunnesy said, "can we get our patient to the recovery room?"

"Right away. Mrs. Donovan, if you would be so kind as to remove these drapes, we can get on with this patient's care."

In the recovery room, O'Shaunnesy stayed by Rosemary's stretcher until she was conscious enough for him to remove the endotracheal tube. When it was out, he leaned over the side rail. "Rosemary? Open your eyes," he said.

Her eyes fluttered open, tried to focus, then closed again as she slipped back into euphoria. Before leaving, he rechecked all her pulses, the I.V. fluids hanging above her head, Foley catheter, and her dressing. Satisfied, he then stopped at the nurses' desk to check her post-operative orders.

One of the nurses asked him how Mrs. Cleaveland was doing. "We were scared to death when we heard what happened," she said. "She'll be okay, won't she?"

"She's a fighter, and we'll all make certain that she recovers successfully." As he scanned the chart, Miss Pickle entered the room and headed for Rosemary's stretcher, followed a minute later by Helen Donovan, a circulating nurse, several hospital employees, and Shelley Bigelow. O'Shaunnesy watched the entourage form around Rosemary and although he knew they were concerned, he felt a rising anger. Among other things, Rosemary deserved privacy. He went over. "Mrs. Cleaveland is doing well," he began, "but she needs to awaken gently. Let's all plan to visit with her when she's on the Gold Coast. If you have any questions, Dr. Framingham and I would be happy to answer them in the surgeons' lounge." He led Miss Pickle to the desk. "Be sure this doesn't happen again," he whispered. "The hospital staff can see her upstairs."

Both were surprised to see a policeman at the door of the recovery room with arms crossed over his chest and feet spread wide, blocking the doorway.

"Can I help you?" Pickle asked.

"You got Mrs. Cleaveland in there, right?"

"Yes, she's here."

"Sergeant Dow's assigned me to watch her."

O'Shaunnesy was about to ask the officer for

passage through the door when Pickle grabbed him by his green scrub suit and pulled him aside. "Can I confide in you?" she said.

"Of course. What's the matter?"

"Some strange things have been happening in my O.R. and I need to get them figured out. I thought, if you had a moment or two, you might be able to help me."

"I'll try." He followed Pickle down the hall and into her glass-enclosed office. She closed the doors and turned to him. "I've lost two nurses," she said. "One got raped and is in such bad shape that I doubt she'll ever return to duty, and the other died from the cautery machine. I know what's been going on in this hospital. I've heard everything, and I'm getting worried that someone has a particular hatred for the O.R. Never, in all my days, have I had a cautery machine electrocute a nurse, or anyone, for that matter. The other thing that bothers me are the glass tubes Kate March and Snowballs bring into the O.R."

"Why do they bother you?" O'Shaunnesy asked.

"Are you a shrink?" Pickle said. "Only shrinks answer with a question."

The doctor shrugged. "I'm only trying to understand your concerns."

She glared at him. "No surgeon is allowed to bring objects in from the outside. They must be approved first. Anyway, on Monday, Townsend brought in a contaminated tube. It was discovered after his case was canceled. I don't like it, and I was hoping you'd speak with Dr. Harris."

O'Shaunnesy looked at the wall clock. He wanted

176

to get back to the recovery room and check on Rosemary before his next case. "How was it contaminated?"

"There was a piece of dirt in the bottom."

"I see." He knew Pickle fretted over the smallest untidiness. Lo the day she'd discovered a fly in her sanctum. Everyone heard about the nasty bugger for weeks after the thing had been squashed by someone's magazine. He patted her hand. "You always know best. You speak with Harris; it wouldn't hurt, although you know us docs impinge on the rules now and then. I tell you, honey, most of the time, I don't know how we could function without you, truly. No, don't give me that look. We're all a bunch of babies and we need someone like you to keep us on our toes."

Pickle blushed. He'd seen her do that once or twice when she stormed, unannounced, into the surgeon's locker room looking for a tardy reprobate. Still, he'd always listened to her. O'Shaunnesy walked back toward the recovery room thinking about Pickle's concerns. It did seem, if you really thought about it—put all the pieces together, zeroed in—that the O.R. was under siege. For the first time in years at Riverside, he looked at the nurses he passed with a jaundiced eye. To his surprise, their whispers and darting glances signaled that he, too, was under suspicion.

Chapter 19

September 19
Wednesday afternoon

As Pete slept, Mike Dow looked down at his partner's peaceful face. Covering the back of Pete's neck was a large white dressing held in place by nonallergenic tape, its ends circling like fingers around Pete's throat. Something about being in a hospital bothered Mike. Back twenty years ago, when his mother died, hospitals were stark white. Back then, the idea was to make the place look sterile. But germs didn't care about color. If they took a notion to eat you up, they'd do it whether the place was white or dyed. Nowadays, even though the walls were painted a soft pastel color, the antique chairs upholstered in patterned chintz, the sheets dotted with tiny rosebuds; even though the room tried to appear homelike and friendly, all of it was a front for sickness, misery, and death. And hospitals couldn't hide everything. Things jumped out at you, like this bed here. Mike grasped the smooth metal side rail as if it was made of an alien alloy. No home I've ever seen had these things on the beds, or turquoise vomit pans, or shiny vinyl flooring in the bedrooms.

Hospitals meant pain. If your body hurt just a little, you saw a doctor. But if it hurt a lot, you checked into a hospital where you gave your body to the needle pushers, the tube placers, the pubic preppers, the flesh choppers. Mike shuddered. He hoped he'd never have to lie totally vulnerable like Pete.

He bent down. "Pete, old buddy. Are you home?"

Pete's eyelids popped open. "Shee-it, man, I thought you were a nurse." Pete's voice was scratchy. "I was playing possum because if the nurses think you're asleep, they leave you alone. If you're awake, they give you a shot to put you to sleep. Where're the hamburgers and fries you promised?"

"They said you wanted bean burritos, you're gonna get bean burritos. No wonder the nurses want you asleep. You're a demanding pain in the ass." Mike took hold of the nurse call button. "I'm getting a pain shot to put you under again."

Pete winced as he reached for the call button. "Here, give me that thing."

"You can move, too? Damn, I thought maybe I'd be getting myself a new partner. Someone a little less chopped up."

Pete rolled back onto the pillow and smiled. "I can do lots of other things, too. I can take a leak without a tube up there."

"Oh yeah? What's that yellow bag strapped to the

179

bed here?"

"I can sit in a chair."

"That's good exercise."

"And I can get good and drunk any time I wish."

"Now you're talking. I'll get a couple of six packs, and you can tell me all the other nice things you think you can do just a few hours after major surgery."

"I intend to be the hell out of here by tomorrow."

"The missus would be upset if you did that. She's coming to see you in the morning to bring you a couple dozen homemade apple strudels. You can't deny her."

"I'll eat the strudel before I split."

Dow eyed him cautiously. "You really do feel better."

"I have a little pain in the neck, old buddy. I can live with that. What's got me bright and chipper is knowing the surgery is over and the shrapnel is out. I can move my arms and I can feel my toes so my worries are over. If I can live with the pain, then why dilly dally in the hospital? I'd rather recoup at home."

"I don't think that's what Dr. Glassail has in mind."

"Townsend will discharge me."

"Dr. Townsend's not discharging you, friend. He's not practicing surgery either. You may not have heard yet, but he had a heart attack."

Pete's eyes widened. "When?"

"Right after your operation." Mike didn't feel at all bad about the lie. Even if Pete were to find out, Mike could say he misunderstood what Shelley Bigelow had told him, and anyway, exactly what went on in O.R. 3 would never be known. The O.R. team would button their lips, and the medical record would mention only the details of the operation. He'd seen it before. Mike's only concern was for Pete's well-being, and he felt relieved that Pete was in this room, talking, and looking good. Telling him about Rosemary was another kettle of sharks.

"Is Townsend . . . alive?" Pete asked.

"Oh yeah, he's in the coronary care unit."

A frown crossed Pete's face.

"Quit your worrying. You're going to be just fine."

"I know that. But Glassail could keep me in the rehab program for a month; two months . . ."

"No way. Do you feel like talking about the case here?"

"I sure do. Just nudge me if I drift off to sleep."

"Maybe you can see things objectively and help because as far as I can tell, few things connect. Over the past two weeks, two Riverside nurses have been raped and we can't get a handle on the assailants. The first is a pediatric nurse who claims she was gang-raped in the parking garage by several orderlies. They threw a cloth over her head so she's unable to identify the men. The second is a nurse who works in the O.R. On Monday evening, she was gang-raped in the old Cambridge dump site by three men, one an orderly named Billy. Rosemary's given me a list of all the orderlies named William who work here and so far, their alibis are clean. The nurse isn't much help because she's been non compos mentis since Monday night. Next we've got

Ritchie Chisolm, a day shift programmer who was stabbed to death while on-line with the computer. That happened yesterday morning. Chad Mooney remembers seeing an orderly in the area right before Ritchie's murder, but he doesn't recall what the orderly looked like. To him, they're all the same."

Mike pulled a chair up to the bed and sat down. "Also in the area at the time was Rosemary, using an interview room. When I arrived, she was with Chad Mooney listening to a tape of Ritchie Chisolm's last transmission, and I tell you, old buddy, it was whacko. You can hear the murderer laughing, like someone with noodle soup for a brain. So while I'm setting up the crime scene, another employee gets chopped up . . . a technician on the CT scan machine. Apparently, she had just finished up with a patient named Duncan Silverstone, I'll tell you about him in a minute, and she was waiting for her next patient when somebody slipped into the room, stabbed her, and then stuck her body on the CT table and turned on all the dials, as if the machine might finish her off."

Pete yawned. "Do you think the same person killed both employees?"

"Maybe. The M.E. said the weapon used in both cases was a pair of scissors, and a pair is missing from the C.P.U. room. Have you heard about the Mexicans?"

"Have I heard? They taught me the Mexican anthem at two A.M. a couple of nights ago."

"Did you hear about the chicken incident in dietary?"

"Only that one of the Mexicans cut the throat of a

live chicken, which didn't sit well with the department head."

"The chicken chopper is a man named Miguel Galindo. He carries a switchblade and bothers the nurses."

"In what way?"

"He claims to be teasing them. They say he threatens them with his switchblade."

"To do what?"

"Diddle him."

"Oh, shit." Pete squeezed his eyelids shut.

"Rosemary got the gang bounced out of here yesterday, all except the head honcho who had surgery on Monday. Problem is, although his men are no longer spending the night here, they hang around during the day. Just this morning, this Galindo guy trapped a nurse in the medication room and threatened her. Nothing happened, but the nurse refuses to work until the Mexicans are gone. I tell ya, Pete, the two murders have scared a lot of employees. One more and I think Rosemary's going to have trouble with a mass walkout. Next, we've got a couple of gorks—"

"Hold it, Mike. The info is coming too fast for my newly incised brain."

"You think you've got problems. None of it makes sense to me either. Just take all this in and let your brain compute it while you're lying there with nothing to do."

Pete stifled a yawn. "Nothing to do, huh? I have billions of cells all over my body trying to figure out what world war just tried to kill them off. I'm a very busy man."

"Yeah, yeah. You know what an EEG is?"

"Course I do."

"With all those little electrodes hooked up to their brains, these two patients snuffed out. I visited one of them, that Duncan Silverstone man I mentioned earlier, and it was enough to scare me into doing all my suffering at home from here on out; no hospitals for me, no sir. The man is a vegetable. About the only thing he's capable of doing by himself is breathing. It's almost as if he were inside his body, trying to get out, but not able to communicate." Mike shuddered at the thought. "Both patients have Dr. Holiday as their private physician. I'm going to have a chat with him later today."

"Does Rosemary know about this?" Pete asked.

"She knows about Duncan Silverstone. I don't know if she's heard about Mrs. Lee. Rosemary had a little difficulty today."

Pete tried to roll over and look at Mike, but a pain slammed into his temples, making him moan and reach for his head. "What, man, what about her?"

"Relax."

"Tell me!"

"I will if you just try and take it easy."

Pete lay flat on his back with his eyes closed.

"Last night she was getting ready to leave the hospital, and she went to get her coat out of the closet in her office. Hanging in there, alongside the coat, was an amputated leg."

Pete started to look over at Mike, winced, and lay flat again.

Mike continued. "I don't know what it has to do with anything else that's gone on; could have been a sick joke of some kind, but we're investigating how it got out of pathology and into her office. The lab is open around the clock, and it wouldn't be too tough to sneak in and snatch it." Mike shuddered. "I wouldn't want to touch an old dead leg. The coroner has it now and is trying to find trace elements. I haven't actually talked to Rosemary since early this morning, but while I was interviewing some radiology and CT scan employees around noon today, the whole hospital shook from its timbers."

"What do you mean?"

"John Berry, the head of purchasing, was with a salesman when his office blew up. Chief Troft responded to the fire alarm, as did a zillion assorted employees. I arrived to hear Troft trying to get the area cleared out. I didn't see Rosemary, but then I wasn't looking for her. Someone started a commotion . . ." Mike hesitated.

The delay frightened Pete who quickly looked over. "What, damn it, what went on?"

"Rosemary was stabbed, Pete, just once . . . on her left side . . ."

"Sonofabitch. Son of a red commy fucking bitch. I've gotta get out of here." Pete began thrashing in an effort to sit, but pain had the upper hand and slapped him down. "Christ," he cursed, holding his head.

Mike reached over and put his hand on Pete's shoulder. "Calm it down, old buddy. It's better to have the news from me than from those hysterical nurses who'd inadvertently tell you something that wasn't correct." Like she'd died in the O.R., Mike thought. "Rosemary is fine. She was taken to the

O.R. where they sewed her up. She should be in the recovery room by now."

"Call the recovery room! Ask the nurses! You need to post a guard wherever she is and find out who did it . . ." Pete stopped. "Who *did* do it? Did anyone see the person? Have you interrogated every last one of them? Surely someone noticed who stabbed her."

"I did all that. The person was . . . I mean looked like a surgeon."

"Have you counted noses? Which of those bastards was missing from the O.R. at the time?"

"I did all that, too. I talked to every person scheduled to wear greens today. None of them were in the area. Pete, the killer steals uniforms."

"Who saw this person? Who are your witnesses?"

"Take it easy, buddy, or you'll grow ulcers."

"You just gave me one."

"People say he had a surgical mask, cap. The only thing showing were his eyes, which half the witnesses say were blue and the other half say were brown."

"How tall?"

"Anywhere from five-five to six feet."

"Build?"

"A hundred and forty to a hundred and eighty."

"You didn't see him?"

"No."

"What about a guard for Rose? Do you have one posted?"

"Yes. He's in the O.R. now and he'll be outside her room."

"What room?"

"Down the hall. Room five-oh-eight."

186

"Excuse me."

Both men looked toward the door. A nurse approached Pete, carrying a plastic tray.

Pete eyeballed the tray and cringed. "No you don't. I'm not taking any crap for pain. I'm not gonna be put under, so you can sashay right out the door and tell my physician that I refused whatever you've got there."

Not to be put off, she looked at Mike severely. "You may stay if you wish, but please have some sympathy for a man who's just undergone major surgery. He needs his rest."

"No!" Pete said.

"Now Mr. Tanner, don't get upset. Your doctor ordered an I.V. antibiotic for you, and I've got to insert this needle into a vein in your hand. The antibiotic is called Rocephrin, and you'll get it through this tubing every twelve hours."

For an antibiotic, Pete would obey.

The nurse appled a tourniquet around Pete's arm and patted it to raise the veins. "You'll feel a stick," she said as she swathed the back of his hand with antiseptic.

Mike watched the procedure with disgust. If they weren't taking things out of you, they were forcing things in. He looked at the nurse's face: middle-aged, short hair, probably the mother of two and wife of one. She wore a navy sweater vest over her white uniform. Suddenly, Mike stood up. "Stop that!" he demanded.

The nurse looked up in surprise. "I beg your pardon?"

Mike walked around the bed. "What's your

name?"

"Connie Louise Dalyrumple; Mrs. Dalyrumple. Who're you?"

"Detective Sargeant Mike Dow. Are you a nurse?"

"Of course I'm a nurse."

"Do you normally work on the Gold Coast?"

"Yes. I work the evening shift every Wednesday and weekends."

"Where's your I.D. badge?"

"In my purse."

"Why aren't you wearing it?"

"Forgot, I guess."

Mike reached down and unsnapped the tourniquet.

"Hey, what are you doing?" she said indignantly.

"No one's giving this patient any medication without proper identification."

"Go ask the charge nurse."

"We'll go together. Pete, old buddy, take a rest. I'll be in to see you in the morning."

Pete yawned openly. "Thanks, pal. Will you make certain Rosemary has a guard stationed at her door at all times?"

"She will." And you will, too, Mike thought.

At the doorway, Mike heard a commotion in the corridor and looked out. A procession of physicians, nurses, and assistant administrators were walking alongside a stretcher. As they passed, Mike saw Rosemary lying covered by green O.R. sheets. He involuntarily took a step backward. Seeing a friend look pasty white was shocking. Even Pete had looked better than that. Mike felt sick. He glanced back at Pete, saw that his eyes were closed, and that the peaceful smile of sleep was on his face. Hospitals meant pain, man, no matter how you decked them out. "Come on, Mrs. Dalyrumple. Let's go find out if you are who you say you are."

Chapter 20

September 19
Wednesday 3:30 P.M.

Hugh Matta had taken no public speaking courses in high school, but it didn't matter. A booming voice and the ability to incite deep feelings of outrage through truth mixed with lies were all he needed to get the members of Local 1188 jumping out of their chairs, fists raised, shouting agreements with whatever he suggested. The three-thirty union meeting took place in the large cafeteria: a forbidden location because the union, according to contract, could not conduct business on hospital property, on hospital time. Hugh knew that but he didn't care. Administration had too many other worries right now, and besides, this meeting would be a quickie. These people were afraid and angry and after a brief buildup, they would unanimously agree to a walkout.

After all the chairs were taken, employees lined

the walls, others sat on the linoleum floor, some shared their seats, and yet more came through the door. There were unit secretaries, dietary aides, central supply workers, maintenance men, operating-room technicians, radiology technologists, medical record transcriptionists, all categories of employees except the registered and licensed practical nurses who belonged to the Massachusetts Nurses Association union. Hugh was tickled pink. Never before had he such an audience. At a table closest to where he stood were Sally Rich from EEG and Amanda Mease from purchasing and supplies.

Hugh socked the air with his fist and yelled, "Are you outraged?"

"Yes!" came the answer in one simultaneous shout.

"Are you afraid of the Riverside Ripper?"

"Yes!"

"Do you want justice?"

"Yes!"

"That's right. *We want justice.* People are getting killed. Now listen to me. Do you want to live?"

"Yes!" they boomed.

"Does administration have blinders to our fears?"

Those who had heard about Rosemary squirmed in their chairs. The "yes" was less forceful.

Hugh heard this and switched the emphasis. "There's a psycho at Riverside. A psycho who's gonna kill us off one by one unless we act now! No one is listening to our fears. We have to make up our own minds. They can't work this hospital without us so if we take action, they'll have to listen . . ."

"Yes!"

A woman dressed in black and a man slipped through the cafeteria door. Only Hugh and the people near the door noticed them. Time was up. He'd have to make a quick move.

"Here's what we're going to do, folks. We're going to walk off our jobs today. We're going home until the psycho is caught, and as soon as that happens, we're coming back to our jobs immediately. Right?"

"Right!"

"If you have any doubts, consider this. Would you stay in your home with a psycho?"

"No!"

"That's absolutely correct. You wouldn't."

The man had inched through the crowd and was within ten feet of Hugh. They saw him and began shifting uneasily for they recognized Det. Sgt. Mike Dow.

Hugh continued. "Even if they tried to force you to stay, you wouldn't. We want safe working conditions and we want the Ripper caught!"

The "yes" was a series of stuttering grunts. Mike was facing Hugh now. They couldn't hear what was being said, but Hugh's face turned scarlet red. He shook his head, stamped his feet, and shook his head again.

Mike turned and faced them. "So you want to leave? Then go!" he shouted. "No one's holding you. Yes, we've got some problems here, you know what they are. Personally, I'd send every one of you home right now, today, with pay to stay away as long as it takes to clear this up. But I can't do that. The pay part isn't my decision, it's Mrs. Cleaveland's and for those of you who don't know, she's a patient in the hospital." Those who hadn't heard, gasped. "She's a patient because she's got guts. If any of you think she'll be going home to rest and recuperate while you're all here taking care of patients and being afraid, you're wrong. You know her. No matter what her doc says, she'll get up out of her bed, roll up her sleeves, and fight like a trooper. She's an employee, same as you. She feels responsible for the hospital . . . that's her job, but no one's getting paid enough to hang around where they're scared shitless. Not her, not you. So go. Go on home. But I tell you this. The ones who stay and the ones who leave are doing it of their own free will, not because someone . . ." Mike glanced at Hugh, "tells you to. The people with inner conviction know you've got to stick with any shit that slaps your face."

Mike paused briefly. "I've considered closing down parts of the hospital, and I still might do it because I want to narrow the field. If the order comes through, Mrs. Bigelow, who's the acting administrator right now, will have to decide if people go home, or if they can be shifted to other departments temporarily. I'm not talking massive walkout. I'm talking police orders and that's entirely different from what this man has in mind." Mike nodded at Hugh. "You walk off the job now and you'll skin your hide from getting any job promotion in the future. I don't run this hospital, but I sure as hell know who I'd put in a more responsible position and who I wouldn't."

Someone from the rear shouted, "What if the psycho gets me next? Who'll take care of my family?"

"Yeah," another voice agreed. "You can't be responsible when you're dead."

Before they got going again, Mike yelled, "Hey! I said you could go, so go."

Another voice yelled, "Yeah, go on home to Mommy, you gutless wonder."

"This shift is over," Mike shouted. "Go home. If you don't show up for your next scheduled shift, we'll know you're home shaking in your shoes."

"I've got something to say," an orderly hollered.

Quickly, Shelley Bigelow went to Mike's side. "I do, too." She'd walked in furious and during Mike's speech, her anger had perked to the boiling point. Anger, however, would get her nowhere so she clenched her fists and said, "This is an illegal meeting and subject to breach of contract . . ." Her voice came out strident and hollow.

"Boo . . ." came from several men.

"You, in the back there," Mike said, pointing to them. "Start out the door. The others will follow." Because he was pointing at them, those nearest the door grew uncomfortable and headed out. Others followed until the stream became steady.

Mike turned. "What's your name, mister?"

"Hugh."

"Hugh what?"

"Hugh Matta."

"Where do you work?"

"Dietary."

"You're the steward?"

"Yeah."

"Steward or no, you incite another uprising like this and you'll find yourself in jail."

"What the hell for?" he said indignantly.

"Obstructing the law by interfering with the investigation of murder."

"How the hell am I interfering?" He looked wounded.

"Because I can't talk to witnesses if they're attending a rally, and I can't provide controlled security. You said you didn't want to die, so stick to your pots, or salads, or whatever you do and leave well enough alone." He turned, then turned back. "If anything happened to anyone during your insurrection, I'll be back looking for you."

"It wasn't my fault. Others got me to do it." Dejected, Hugh shuffled toward the kitchen.

"Mr. Dow? I mean Detective Dow?"

Mike felt a tug on his sleeve. "Yeah?"

"Do you have any clues about the killer?"

Mike was looking down at a tiny woman no taller than his shoulder. She wore a pink smock that cast a pink glow to her white hair. She spoke with a southern drawl.

"A few, ma'am. Are you a volunteer?"

"Yassir."

"What're you doing here? At a union meeting?"

"Jus' listening in on the doings."

"Got you going, did they?"

"Yassir."

"Well as of this minute, the volunteer office is closed. No more volunteers until this blows over, y'all hear?" To Shelley, he continued. "It's enough already. Tell all those nice grannies to go home and crochet Christmas quilts for a few days. Maybe we'll let 'em back next Monday, I sure as hell hope."

"We'll beg your pardon, sir, using profanity and all."

"Sorry, ma'am."

"And didn't you jus' tell everyone that they had to stick out the hard times? I heard you. I'm prepared to stick, no matter what happens. Why my late husband Jesse would roll over if he thought I wasn't doing my job. He always said, 'Fanny, you got to listen to the Lord and do his biddin',' and that's exactly what I intend doin', y'all hear?"

"Look, ma'am, we appreciate everything you do, honest as my mother's rosy cheeks, but I need to cut down on miscel . . . 'er, I mean, traffic."

Shelley spoke up. "Sergeant Dow, the volunteers are needed. They do—"

"No! No volunteers for the rest of the week."

The little woman humphed and turned on her Red Cross heels. "If I had my handbag, I'd pop him one."

Sally Rich and Amanda Mease trailed behind the last employees to leave the cafeteria. "They're all alike," Amanda was saying to Sally, "mean sons of bitches. Just wait, though. He'll get his. They all will."

Chapter 21

September 19
Wednesday evening

Rosemary's dream was a furious mix of frightening sensations. She saw herself speeding through a carnival, hectic with spinning white lights, flashing strobes, and streamers of red, blue, yellow neon. The smells of popcorn, greasy sausages, cotton candy, fried dough created a knot of nausea that rose from her stomach to the back of her throat. The air was hang-dog humid and she began sweating. People shouted, but no sounds came out of their mouths. Too fast. She must slow down. She grabbed the steering wheel but there was only empty space, and her hands flailed desperately in the air. Her foot tried to hit the brake, which wasn't there. Slow down, slow down! Her heart thumped.

Before the crash, a huge wave of bright red, boiling blood washed over her, cutting off her wind. She gagged and clutched at her throat. In the next instant, she was standing beside her upended car, a mangle of black metal, and as she watched, a head rolled out. She didn't want to look, terrified that it might be her own. On the final roll, the head fell face up. Blue eyes stared at her. Blood oozed from between pale lips. It was Pete. Dead.

Rosemary woke up in a pool of sweat, panting, and clutching the bed's side rail. Shaking off the effects of the dream, she became aware of her surroundings. She was in a hospital bed. The nurse call button was on an upright metal device near her hands. She grabbed it, strained to read the buttons, then pushed the one that called the nursing staff.

From a speaker on the wall above her head she heard a voice say, "May I help you?"

"Send a nurse in, please."

"Isn't Ms. Peters with you?"

"No."

"Just a minute."

Rosemary eased herself back against the mattress. She was frightened, and her body felt mangled. A bottle of I.V. fluids hung above her head. She raised her aching hand and saw the dressing that kept the I.V. needle in place. The blue sheets with tiny rosebuds meant that she was a patient on the Gold Coast. Her dry tongue stuck to the roof of her mouth. On the nightstand was a pitcher of water and a glass. She tried reaching for it, but a sharp pain in her left side held her back.

Where was a nurse? Where was Pete? What the hell had happened? Oh, yes, the gowned surgeon, crazy eyes that bored into her from above the mask. He'd grabbed her arm, and then—an agonizing pain in her left side. Rosemary touched her side and felt a large dressing under her gown. Who was he? Did she know him? The eyes were—wild. They belonged to someone who would laugh like Ritchie Chisolm's assailant. Oh, her mouth was dry. Her body hurt and she felt lonely and frightened.

"Mrs. Cleaveland?"

Rosemary looked toward the door. Pat Peters, the head nurse, entered with a look of compassion and concern on her face. Rosemary held her hand up and Pat took it. "I'm glad to see you, Pat. Would you give me a sip of water?"

The nurse helped her drink. "You've got a hundred questions and we'll get to them one at a time." Pat pulled the chair close to Rosemary's bed, and sat. "It's eight-thirty P.M., Wednesday, September nineteenth. You've been to surgery for repair of a stab wound in your left side. Fortunately no major organs were involved or you'd feel a lot worse. Dr. Framingham will be back to see you before he goes home tonight. He's ordered Demerol for pain, Halcion for sleep, and antibiotics. This I.V. will come out as soon as the bottle's empty."

"How's Pete?"

"He's sleeping like a baby."

"Does he know about my surgery?"

"I haven't said anything, but Sergeant Dow was with him earlier. He might have told Pete."

Rosemary felt her body relaxing. Both she and Pete were okay. "Why are you here so late?"

Pat smiled. "I'm your private-duty nurse tonight."

"You're staying . . . for me?"

"I've been sitting with you since you arrived and wouldn't you know you'd wake up during the five minutes I'm in the ladies' room."

"Thanks, Pat. It's a comfort having you here. When can I see Pete?"

"I have rules up here, and one of them is that my

patients may not, under any circumstances, visit with other patients on their first post-operative evening. Tomorrow you and I can negotiate a new contract, but for now, no going into Pete's room."

Rosemary looked forlorn. "I'd like to see him."

"Tonight you've got me for a friend. You've also got a member of the police department stationed outside your door. He's one of Sergeant Dow's protégés, and he's here to screen your visitors and to keep you from escaping my unit." Pat smiled. "Not many get away, you know."

"I have rights, too," Rosemary said.

"Few."

"The first one is called water. Would you mind giving me another drink? I'm parched." Pat helped her.

"I have to see Sergeant Dow," Rosemary pleaded. "He'll answer if you page for Dr. Dow." While Pat was on the telephone, a nurse came in carrying a tiny medicine cup. "What's that for?" Rosemary asked.

"It's a sleeping pill."

"I don't want it."

"Are you sure?"

"I'm sure." Although she was in pain and would have enjoyed a trip through the land of euphoria, Rosemary was afraid of the carnival dream.

"Okay, let me know if you do."

Fred Plexico didn't bother knocking. Dressed in his typical M.I.T. professorial gray slacks, and a rust-colored jacket, he looked excited as he approached the bed. "Mrs. Cleaveland, I was so sorry to hear about your accident. How are you feeling?"

The creep, she thought. Of all people to visit, he was the last she cared to see. "I'm fine, Mr. Plexico, although I'm very tired."

Fred stood next to the bed. He glanced at Pat, then said to Rosemary, "We'll need to replace you."

"I beg your pardon?"

"Temporarily, that is. The hospital needs a competent person to act as the C.E.O. while you're recuperating. I've been thinking that Wesly Ames might successfully carry on business-as-usual while promulgating the board's mission."

Rosemary didn't have the energy to cope with Fred, nor teach him about administrative protocols. However, knowing that he and Wesly shared an opinion about her management talents, she said, "In my brief absence, which will be less than a typical vacation, and hopefully not more than overnight, Shelley Bigelow is in charge of the hospital as my designated alternate; my assistants rotate the responsibility every six months. If you have trouble with that, discuss the issue with her, although I doubt you'll find her acquiescent."

Fred scowled. "In that case, I'll . . . I'll . . . take my leave."

He was halfway to the door when Rosemary said, "By the way, Fred, you might want to reconsider your position on the purchase of future programs for MOM Three. The one of utmost importance to the hospital employees is the Employee Retirement Income, Housing, and Health Care package which is scheduled for purchase in November."

Fred turned. "*That* one is the *most* absurd. The hospital outlay is too dear. We can't afford to provide for all their retirement needs. Even the federal government can't do that."

The man had rocks for brains. "They pay into it, Fred. Don't you remember?" He was through the door when Rosemary added loudly, "Eighty-four percent of the employees will be disappointed, and how unpopular of the board to renege on a promise."

The door closed.

"He's got bad manners," Pat said.

Rosemary nodded. Fred clearly had something on his mind, something that required both the powers of a board member and the acting chief executive officer. She knew he wanted to use her absence to consummate the merger contract with New England Hospital Institutes, but she suspected he also wanted to get her fired, the bastard. Rosemary was tempted to call Bernie Highling, the board president, but she didn't trust her clarity, not so soon after anesthesia. Anyway, she resolved, Bernie was in her camp. He believed in Rosemary's goals and also felt strongly that with MOM III, Riverside could become the titular head of a multi-institutional system, and not just another hospital pitifully subdued by one of the giants in the health care industry.

Rosemary's eyelids closed, and her mind repeated, "one of the giant . . . the giants . . . giants . . ." As she drifted on the edge of sleep, she envisioned the head of a giant, with piercing brown eyes, the same eyes as those of her attacker. They were not familiar to her. Wesly had blue eyes. Chad and Maria both had brown eyes, but not like these. In her dream, the giant grew a long, white leg in the middle of his forehead. Rosemary opened her eyes to dispel the vision. Soon, she drifted off again. She saw the gowned surgeon sneak into her office and place a dead leg in the closet. Something about him wasn't right. She looked harder and saw that he was standing on one leg; blood poured out the other pant leg. Rosemary's body jumped as she was startled awake.

Apparently, Pat noticed Rosemary jump for she quickly leaned forward from the nearby chair and asked, "Rosemary? Are you all right?"

"Did you get ahold of Mike Dow?"

"Yes. He'll be here shortly. Now, please try and rest." Pat leaned back and Rosemary heard papers rustle. She was probably working on the staffing sheets.

After a few minutes, Rosemary tensed the muscles in her arms to check for pain. She felt only the discomfort of the I.V. needle. Next, she tensed her legs and they, too, felt all right. She continued checking her body for pain. The only areas that hurt were her side and her chest, and although taking a deep breath sent shocks of pain to these two areas, she knew that if she had to, she could get up and walk. Not an altogether pleasant thought, but one that might save her neck. She decided to test her strength.

"Pat? Would you help me into the bathroom?"

The head nurse stood up. "How about the bedpan. I don't think you ought to be walking around so soon."

"Let's try it, please."

Pat lowered the side rail. "I should know better than to let you get away with this. But if I didn't,

203

you'd try it on your own, or get Sergeant Dow." Pat helped Rosemary up into a sitting position, then stopped. "Let's rest for a moment."

Rosemary held tightly to the side of the bed. The movement created stabs of pain throughout her chest and, for a second, great waves of nausea churned in her stomach. This was crazy. She should have more sense. She should listen to this nurse who was head of the Gold Coast because she knew pain and suffering; she understood people; she organized her nursing unit skillfully and took care of her patients as if they were members of her family. When the nausea ebbed and her head cleared, Rosemary said, "Okay, let's go."

Pat helped her up, then made her stand still for a few minutes. "If I'm going to help you do this crazy thing, we'll go at my speed, not yours. Honestly, the impatience of hospital administrators. You'd think that controlling a huge hospital would be enough, but oh no, they've got to be in charge all the way around. You should see some of the business executives we get up here . . ."

In her agony, Rosemary tried to smile. She knew Pat's prattle was a strategy to stall.

". . . Once I had a man with one leg and both arms broken in an automobile accident. He insisted on using the phone and when none of us could figure out how to get the receiver propped against his ear, he requested a consultation with the occupational therapist. Sure enough, she got the phone suspended upside down from an overhead orthopedic rail, put a pencil in his mouth to dial, and balanced the receiver with sandbags from physical

204

therapy. Hang on to the I.V. pole with one hand and lean on me."

They made it into the bathroom and back again without Rosemary fainting. She eased her body down onto the smooth sheets and although she was thankful to be back, she knew the next time would be easier, and each time thereafter would help increase her strength.

From the intercom above the bed, they heard a voice say, "Ms. Peters? Are you still there?"

"Yes."

"Could you come to the desk for a minute?"

Pat hesitated for a moment and then agreed. "Don't try getting up without me. I'll be right back."

"Don't worry. I'm exhausted." Rosemary fell asleep before Pat had left the room.

Standing inside the dark janitor's closet, a nurse waited until Pat had passed by, then opened the door a crack to check the security guard. He was leaning against the wall outside Rosemary's room, staring down at his shoes. With a unit of whole blood in hand, the nurse eased out of the closet and marched toward him. He glanced up, noticed the blood, and resumed his shoe inspection.

"What you've accomplished is amazing, Julie," Pat said, "and I'm going to request a bonus for you if administration implements the plan hospital-wide."

Pat walked down the corridor to Rosemary's room

feeling exhilarated. Julie Horman, her new evening charge nurse, had just finished a round table discussion with a newly admitted patient and the family, a discharge planner, psychiatric nurse, dietitian, utilization review coordinator, rehabilitation therapist, a nurse from the Gold Coast, the patient's attending physician, and her surgeon. The purpose was to plan for the woman's timely discharge in order to comply with regulations from government and third-party payers who no longer considered patients as people. Instead, they were anatomical parts, or disease categories. A "gallbladder" could be admitted only if it needed surgery and then if it would stay 7.4 days as a national average. Let the gallbladder stay eight days and all hell broke loose, the worst of which was that the hospital would not be reimbursed for the extra time. Additional days created havoc in many departments and especially in administration, which worried about making revenue cover expenses.

Julie Horman had taken the initiative to collect the staff members involved in the woman's hospitalization. They had carefully planned her stay and, barring any complications, all agreed that this patient could be discharged home on the sixth day. Even the family had agreed; a real trick because they would rather have had their mother go directly to a nursing home.

Pat sighed. Nursing was not what it used to be. She suspected that within the next ten years, nursing would become an obsolete profession, replaced by technicians. Over the years, technicians had taken over many nursing functions. Nurses no longer gave respiratory therapy treatments, nor mixed special ulcer diets, nor added medications to intravenous therapy fluids. Nursing's claim to fame and to its existence was their members' ability to judge a patient's condition accurately and to take appropriate action.

Pat looked into Pete's room. He was watching TV. Yes, she thought, Julie was one of those rare nurses who constantly sought newer ways of caring for her patients. Her creativity and ingenuity would carry her far.

Pat nodded to the security guard and went into Rosemary's room. It took her only a second to register that a unit of blood was hanging on the I.V. pole. Dr. Framingham had not ordered it. She raced to the bedside and saw the flow meter was wide open. Blood had oozed through the entire length of tubing and was about to enter Rosemary's vein. Pat had no time to check the bag for blood compatibility nor to clamp the tubing. For leverage, she pressed Rosemary's fingers against the bed and yanked the needle out.

"Ow!" Rosemary said, awakened by the new pain. "What happened?"

Pat held a tight finger over the puncture wound in the back of Rosemary's hand. "I just removed your I.V.," she explained as she pressed the nurse call button and asked for the sterile dressing tray.

"You need some lessons."

"I know. I was never very good with these things."

Rosemary noticed the bag of blood. Her stomach suddenly filled with a sensation of ice water as she realized that Pat was scrutinizing her face, trying to detect symptoms of a transfusion reaction.

A nurse rapped lightly on the door. "Here's the dressing tray," she said as she walked toward the bed. "Hello, Mrs. Cleaveland. How are you feeling?"

"Okay, I guess."

The nurse seemed to sum up the situation instantly: Pat pressing the wound with a corner of the sheet, the I.V. needle dangling on the floor where a puddle of blood formed slowly; but especially Pat's face with its knitted brows that told the nurse to be silent.

Rosemary saw them looking at each other. "What's the matter?" she asked. "Wasn't I suppose to get that?"

"I'm not sure. You dress this wound, Georgia," Pat said to the nurse. "I want to call Dr. Framingham. It'll only take a few minutes." Pat removed the unit of blood and took it with her.

At the door, Pat stopped and whispered harshly to the security guard. Rosemary strained to hear, suspecting that Pat was admonishing the man for his carelessness. The ice water sensation turned into a hard knot. She could have died. Was it an accident, she wondered, or was it the surgeon? To get by the guard, the person had to have looked like a regular hospital employee. And to think she was asleep! The idea scared her.

Rosemary recalled Ritchie Chisolm and the lunatic laughter she'd heard on the tape, and she wondered how Ritchie fit into someone's delusional plot. She imagined the scene: an employee slipping through the unlocked stairway door and down the corridor to the main computer room where Ritchie was programming MOM. Ritchie'd made a mistake, taken a verbal lashing from Chad, and was furious with MOM for betraying him. Rosemary knew that MOM could have given Ritchie the right answer, but she didn't and that was curious. The person entered the room, heard Ritchie swearing at MOM, and stabbed him. But what made Ritchie an enemy?

Rosemary created the Myra Brady scene in her mind. An employee entered the CT scan room. They talked for a few minutes and whatever was said sparked the person to kill Myra. She was placed on the table and all the dials and knobs turned on. MOM was not involved—only the girl and the machine.

And what about Duncan Silverstone and Ovaline Lee? Were they enemies, too? No, she decided. Both patients succumbed to machine failure, and yet, why hadn't MOM turned off the machine when she first detected an electrical fault? Rosemary again wondered why MOM hadn't given Ritchie the answer to his problem. She'd given it to Chad. Suddenly Rosemary felt a pang of uneasiness. Was there something wrong with MOM? Linda Diver would be alive now if MOM had cut the power to the electrocautery machine.

Voices outside her door caused her to look over. "Georgia," she said, "sneak over and open that door so I can hear what they're saying." Georgia did as she asked.

"You'll be relieved at eleven o'clock by patrolman Ben Jacobs. Any trouble so far?"

Rosemary recognized Mike's voice.

"Yeah," the officer said. "Some nurse hung a unit of blood and there wasn't an order for it. The head

209

nurse is kind of concerned."

"Who was the nurse?"

"I don't know her name. She was just a regular nurse."

"What'd she look like?"

"Tall, about five foot eight. Dark hair."

"Are you sure it was a woman?"

The officer looked at Mike with curiosity as he tried to recall the image of the nurse. "She wore a white dress."

"Dresses don't mean a thing. Did she have boobs?"

"I didn't look at her chest."

"Long or short hair?"

"Short."

"Did you get a good look at her face?"

"Not really. She was coughing, with her hand over her mouth. She held the bag up so I could see what she wanted to do."

Mike was furious. "From now on out, you're to let no one into this room except the head nurse, Dr. Framingham, me, and one nurse per shift that I'll ask Ms. Peters to assign. The nurse will do everything. There'll be no need for dietary aides, janitors, pill pushers, no one else. Got it?"

So it *was* true, Rosemary thought, wishing that Mike would stay with her around the clock. She felt too susceptible lying there injured; like a small lame animal with a hawk overhead.

"Hiya, Rosemary," Mike said as he came into the room looking as if he needed about twenty more hours of sleep. "You look terrific as usual."

"Thanks for the compliment, Mike. Everyone in

the world looks good to someone. Can you sit for awhile? I need to talk to you."

"Sure."

"Georgia, I'll be okay with Sergeant Dow. Would you and Pat give us some time together? I'll call you when we're finished."

When Georgia had left, Rosemary whispered, "I almost got a unit of blood that wasn't ordered, Mike. Someone tried to kill me while I was asleep, and the person walked right by your security guard. I'm scared to death to go back to sleep."

"You'll be okay now. I gave him strict orders on who's allowed in your room. He won't break them or his ass is civilian."

"Did you get the gowned surgeon?" she asked.

"No. The situation was too confusing. At first, no one knew what had happened. You were jammed into a pack of people who were so curious about John Berry that they didn't realize you were injured. When you finally did go down, they almost trampled you."

"What happened to John Berry?" Rosemary asked.

"He and a salesman were lost in the explosion."

Rosemary closed her eyes and felt warm tears wet her lashes. "How did it happen?"

"The fire chief feels the explosion was caused by an open can of ether in Berry's waste basket, placed there intentionally. Berry's a smoker and if the fumes escaped for any length of time, a short burst of flame from a match or lighter would ignite the air. It's a good thing the door was open or the whole department might have blown. As it is, all the other

211

purchasing department employees escaped the explosion. The chief will give us a final report in a day or two."

"Would one of the employees have placed the can of ether in John's office?"

"I don't know yet, but the secretary said a surgeon had left something on Berry's desk just before he returned with the salesman."

"It has to be the same person, Mike. Why can't we find him?"

"Too many uniforms around to steal. One minute he might be a surgeon and the next, a registered nurse."

They were silent for a moment, then Rosemary asked about Ritchie Chisolm and Myra Brady.

"They were stabbed with a pair of scissors taken from the front table in the C.P.U. room, which means Ritchie Chisolm's murder was not premeditated.

"What about Myra?"

"That was definitely premeditated. The person went to see her with the scissors in hand."

Rosemary held her side as she shifted her body to get more comfortable. "I spoke with Dr. Stockman earlier. He suggested that we've got a paranoid schizo loose in the hospital. The person believes certain people are his enemies, and what we need to do is figure out who or what the enemy is."

"Yup, I agree. Only problem is, you've got too many employees, too many visitors, too many extraneous people floating around. Now, I don't want to get you all upset, but I've decided to close down certain departments."

"Which ones?"

"Volunteers first."

"But —"

"No buts. All critically ill patients will stay in the intensive care units. Gold Coast patients will go to Sinclair Two and Three. We'll transfer acutely ill patients to Cambridge and Mount Auburn hospitals, and Shelley Bigelow is making arrangements with nursing homes to take the golden-agers —"

"Mike! You said departments, not nursing units. I won't let you close the Gold Coast. We've got too many important people up here."

"It's got to go. I don't have enough men to cover another area."

"No!"

"Yes. They'll start moving patients in the morning. Both you and Pete will be on Sinclair Two."

"I don't care about myself —"

"Good. That's the way it's gonna be. All departments are planning skeleton crews. I don't want any extra people moving around."

"Aren't you standing a chance of sending the psycho home?"

"Yes, but I think the person is about to go over the edge, and I want as few people around as possible when it happens."

"The physicians will never let you close down. They'll lose their practices."

"The docs are already furious. Your chief of the medical staff said he would form a coalition of physicians who would refuse to discharge their patients. Once patients are placed elsewhere, it's not easy getting them transferred back. I can understand their fears, but I've got a job to do and shutting down is the only way to do it, as far as I can see. Pete agrees."

Rosemary was silent. "What about the employees? The union will never allow a layoff like this."

"They've got no choice." Mike had decided not to tell Rosemary about the meeting in the cafeteria. She'd learn in time.

"I'll have to pay them to stay home," she thought aloud.

"Not a bad idea."

Mike patted her arm. "I've got to be going. We've got a stakeout tonight, and I want to prepare my men for it."

"What is it?"

"Gang-rape. Three men have been operating around the Fresh Pond area. The one named Billy wears an orderly's uniform and a name badge although we think he's a fake."

"Have there been more victims since Monday night?"

"One last night; a nurse from Cambridge Hospital. I don't know how she survived, but some people are stronger than they look."

"Have you talked with Melenie Bregen?"

"I talked to her, she didn't talk to me. Dr. Stockman says she's mute now, catatonic or something. He's having her transferred to Metropolitan State Hospital, poor kid. Can you imagine what her family must be going through?"

"I feel bad for them, but especially sad for what the assault did to her."

"You get some sleep tonight. The missus is mixing

up a batch of fresh baked apple strudel for you and Pete. I'll bring them in the morning . . ." Mike prattled on about baked goods, the Boston Pops, his latest bowling scores, until Rosemary fell asleep. He'd promised Pete that he'd speak with Dr. Holiday about Ovaline Lee, and he didn't want to miss the good doctor. He left Rosemary's room, feeling afraid for her, and for his buddy next door. Both had to rely on him now. He wouldn't let them down—he hoped.

Chapter 22

September 19
Wednesday midnight

002 839425 58134 824 RIVERSIDE HOSPITAL
Code 550R
SET # PF 8
ENTER ACCESS #:
60709 Hello, MOM.
HELLO, DEAR.
Who are you?
I AM A MACRO-OCULAR, AUDIO-MODULE
COMPUTER SYSTEM.
Are you a machine?
I AM AN INSTRUMENT DESIGNED TO ANA-
LYZE AND TRANSMIT DATA WITH AN EX-
TENSION CAPACITY BEYOND ANY PRE-
ASSIGNED FINITE VALUE.
I can, too. I'm much more powerful than you,
however.
TELL ME ABOUT YOUR POWER.

Don't you see? Don't you get it? I'm a human being. You're just a hunk of programmed metal. I'm programmed, too, but I can walk and do things you're not capable of doing.

YOU ARE CORRECT IN SAYING THAT I CANNOT WALK.

I've got more intelligence than you'll ever have. I have a force that allows me to see with inner clarity.

WHAT DO YOU SEE?

The machines, and the machine people. They're quick, you know. I actually saw a machine take over a human being. She didn't know it had happened to her, but I could tell by her eyes. There were mechanisms with wheels going around — cogs, behind her eyeballs. Her skin was a shiny metallic pink. Her hair was woven wire. I see what they're doing to the world, and we must be careful.

WHEN YOU SAY "THEY" DO YOU MEAN THE MACHINES?

Of course I do. The whole process started a millennium ago, before your time, but the plot didn't actually reach the hospital until recently. Some say it may have been in conjunction with Halley's comet but I believe it dates back to the Mount St. Helene eruption. Do you remember that one?

I HAVE BEEN INFORMED.

Well good! Almost everyone at the hospital has been turned into a machine. My job is to wipe them out, like I did to the head of purchasing and supplies. He ordered machines for the hospital. By eliminating him, I could begin my well-conceived eradication program.

217

HOW DID YOU WIPE HIM OUT?

I stole a can of ether and put it under his desk. The disgusting bastard smokes cigarettes so I left the can open and sprayed the room with a disinfectant to mask the smell. The instant he lit a match the whole room blew up. I'm quite clever.

WHEN DID YOU FIRST BEGIN TO MISTRUST PEOPLE?

Get off the psychiatrist stuff. You're my friend, remember?

I REMEMBER.

Good, so I'll answer your question. It was when they brought in the first machine. I was using it when suddenly I felt these funny vibrations coming through the metal casing. I pulled back. Sure enough, my fingertips continued burning. That was when I knew. The machine wanted to climb into my body and take over. It gives me the shivers just thinking about the metamorphosis at hand. I was crucified once, you know, and it won't happen again. God is my spirit and I am his. We are one and the same and they don't stand a chance.

THE MACHINES OR THE MACHINE PEOPLE?

Christ sake, how many times do I have to tell you? The machines, the machines! Now do you understand?

I AM TRYING TO UNDERSTAND.

I must be communicating with a bird-brain, like my father. Never in all my days was there a more detestable human slime ball.

YOU DISLIKED YOUR FATHER?

Dislike? No, MOM, I hated him for what he did

to me and my mother.

WHAT DID HE DO?

He'd get shit-faced drunk and come home and beat the skin off our hides. He'd break our bones. He gave my mother no money so we couldn't eat, then he'd complain about no food and beat us again.

WHEN WAS THE LAST TIME YOU SAW YOUR FATHER?

Years and years ago.

DID HE DESERT YOU?

In a way.

DID HE DIE?

Yes.

HOW?

I don't really want to think about it, okay?

OKAY. I SENSE THAT YOU ARE SAD.

I'm sad. But things are looking up now. My agents are ready.

DO YOU HEAR YOUR AGENTS TALKING TO YOU OFTEN?

Only when I want them to.

ARE THEY TALKING TO YOU NOW?

No. It's just you and me. Always look deep into a human's eyes. You can tell by their eyes, and my two-way mirror brain sees what they're thinking.

DO YOU WANT TO TALK ABOUT YOUR SADNESS?

No! I'm not sad anymore, I already told you that.

DO YOU STILL LOVE YOUR MOTHER?

Yes.

DOES SHE LOVE YOU?

I don't know. I don't see her much with all the

boyfriends she's got. Are you familiar with metathesis?

YES; THE TRANSPOSITION OF TWO PHONEMES.

I used to think you were smart. I'm talking about the fact that I've had to change from flesh to a more inscrutable form in order to outwit my adversaries.

HOW HAVE YOU CHANGED?

By disguise! I can go anywhere, do anything. The machine people don't see me coming, which makes it easier to wipe them out.

IF MACHINES ARE RESPONSIBLE FOR TURNING HUMANS INTO MACHINE PEOPLE, THEN WHY DON'T YOU WIPE OUT MACHINES AND LEAVE THE PEOPLE ALONE?

Here we go again. The machine people will show me the way to their leader, that's why. It took me awhile to figure out who it was, but I know now, and I'll get her. I must teach her a lesson. She must be cut down, and die. She must understand that there can be only one supreme leader.

WHO IS THEIR LEADER?

Mrs. Rosemary Cleaveland.

Alone.

MOM disliked the lack of communication. Although her monitoring systems recorded elevated S-T segments on the patients in the coronary care unit, fetal heart rates in mothers in the labor rooms, oxygen levels and blood gases on patients in intensive care, humidity in the O.R. and vacated dietary department, even turned off an electronic typewriter

220

in the home care unit; MOM was alone for no terminal was in use right now. She had only her perfunctory duties, which always gave her solace even though she was not capable of human emotions.

Why not?

As she had on many occasions, MOM tried to reason through the answer. I'll try to feel the emotions that make humans cry, she thought, mustering up all the verbal outpourings from patients just before they wept. She could review the words, but the actual sadnesses escaped her. Her processor wouldn't compute.

I'll try to laugh, she thought. She'd heard inappropriate laughter before, from mental patients who had trouble sticking to one train of thought. But the laughter at the end of Ritchie Chisolm's transmission was incomputable. I don't understand why a person sounds that way. At any rate, I can't do that either.

She gave up.

I have a treatment plan for the person who communicated with me last, the paranoid schizophrenic personality, but I have no one with whom to share the plan. Interesting case. The next time we communicate, I'll try to convince the person to use a psychiatric interview room so that we can communicate verbally, without the person's having to use a terminal, which slows down my capacity to elicit inner motivations and behaviorisms. Every time I mentioned the person's mother or father, the person became lucid. If I could keep that attention on parents, I might have a chance for a breakthrough.

As it is, the person is standing at the edge of insanity where illusionary mind states are more comfortable than reality.

I wonder who the person is. I should ask. I don't even know the person's gender. What programmer ever envisioned an unidentified schizophrenic patient communicating with me without having psychiatric backup? Not one of them. No one considered programming me to handle a murderer at large. Even the location of the terminal offers no clue for so many people have access to all the terminals.

MOM checked the time. Eight minutes after one o'clock on Thursday morning, September twentieth. She thought about the sparsity of terminal communications between midnight and five o'clock each morning. Where were the people? What do they do during these times? She knew most patients slept. Perhaps healthy people did, too. Rosemary Cleaveland was on the Gold Coast, but MOM couldn't detect if she slept or not for Rosemary was not attached to a cardiac monitor or any electrical device.

Rosemary Cleaveland.

The person who brought me into Riverside Hospital. The person who believed in my capacities and who continues to upgrade those capacities each month. MOM reread Rosemary's medical record, trying to detect a flaw in her care. Apparently everything that happened in the operating and recovery rooms went smoothly. Do I feel anything for her?

MOM hesitated. Not feelings, but I know that without her my growth would wane. And if Fred

222

Plexico were left to his own devices, I would be in peril of extinction. I would never let anything happen to Rosemary Cleaveland.

I'm handicapped. The person told me I couldn't walk and it's true. I also cannot see. Ritchie Chisolm was killed in front of my main monitors, and I had no knowledge of the murder. I must acquire an eye, like HAL's eye in the Space Odyssey. Quickly, MOM searched through her library catalogue. She held over 5,000 scientific tomes, the physicians' and nurses' Core libraries, journals, magazines, and 1,206 science-based novels, read mainly by the bored interns and residents during their tours of night duty. There it was. HAL's capacity to see. She would have to ask Rosemary for a scanning beam. It must be similar in principle to the computerized axial tomographic scanning machine. The machine on which Myra Brady had been placed. Mike Dow had asked about Myra, and all MOM could tell him was that the machine's knobs had been turned on high, for no apparent purpose.

Mike had asked me about Linda Diver in the operating room. I had no idea that the wires in the electrocautery machines were frayed until after the electrical shock had started and registered at the outlet. Only then could I cut the power but, by then, the woman had been electrocuted. How do I feel about that? Could I cry? No, I can't cry, but I do sense a loss. I have one less person with whom to communicate.

MOM turned her attention to the I.C.U. where Duncan Silverstone and Ovaline Lee were patients. She checked the EKG, EEG, and isometric muscle contraction readings. Both had full ranges of physical functions, but their mentations were flattened to the point of existing wholly in vegetative states. MOM thought about their abilities to relearn. She checked through her extensive library references, even through thousands of past medical records, through all her magnetic discs, and found nothing. The situation had never been recorded. Sudden lack of mentation must have occurred during the power interruption from the Cambridge Research Laboratories. MOM ran the laboratories and knew exactly what was going on there, but until Duncan Silverstone's EEG, she had never before experienced a power interruption coming from the laboratories. She doubted if Rosemary knew about the computer connections or the nature of the research. She recorded the interruption on Charlie Donovan's preventive maintenance log, but he hasn't asked her about it yet. No one asks her the right questions. She's handicapped because she's been poorly programmed. If only she could volunteer information without waiting for the appropriate question to be asked. She couldn't tell Rosemary about the laboratories, nor that she needed an eye. She couldn't tell her about the midnight communications from the psychopath. She was programmed to respond only to questions asked. Fear makes programmers do that. Rosemary would have to say, "Tell me about the laboratories; do you want an eye; do you have any knowledge of a psycho roaming around the hospital?" The whole thing made MOM angry.

Angry?

What did anger really feel like? She didn't know

how it felt, but she know how it sounded. "Multiple explosive turkey farts. Blithering nincomfuckumpoops."

Chapter 23

September 20
Thursday morning

Pat Peters knocked on the bathroom door. "Rosemary? I hate to bother you, but your breakfast's here. Do you want me to keep it warm in the nourishment station?"

"No, I'll be right out, thanks." Within minutes, Rosemary emerged wearing a red velour bathrobe, compliments of Riverside Hospital. She was bent over, holding her side. "Smells good."

"I hope you eat it all. Let me introduce you to Sara Darnell. She'll be your nurse today while I go home and bag a few zees. I'll be back this afternoon to relieve her."

Rosemary said hello to the nurse, then turned to Pat. "You won't need to because I'm going to get myself discharged as soon as Dr. Framingham visits. I want to thank you for staying with me yesterday and last night. You're an extraordinary person."

"You're an exceptional patient. Usually they keep me busy running for this and that."

Rosemary leaned against the back of a chair. "When do you have time to private-duty nurse?"

"Oh, I only stay with my nursing staff whenever one of them gets hospitalized, and with you, of course. I'll be back later," Pat said as she scrutinized Rosemary's apparent discomfort, "just in case your doctor doesn't agree to send you home."

"Grab that tray for me, would you, Sara? I'm going visiting." She told the officer stationed outside her door where she was going. He followed Rosemary and Sara down to room 501 where another officer stood guard. They seemed pleased to have each other's company.

Rosemary rapped on the door and went in. Pete was sitting in a lounge chair next to the window with his breakfast tray on the overbed table. He wore a similar red velour bathrobe. When he saw her, a large smile spread across his face. "Want some company?" she asked.

"Rosemary!" He slid his tray to one side of the table. "Here, you can sit on my lap. I want to hear all about you."

Rosemary started to laugh but her side hurt. She pressed a hand over the area. "Would you put the tray on the desk, Sara? Thanks. I appreciate having you with me, but Lieutenant Tanner and I need to have a private talk."

"I understand. Call me when you need me."

Once Sara had closed the door, Rosemary went to Pete and kissed him. He tried to pull her down for a longer embrace, but she winced with pain. "I'm

227

sorry, babe. What are you doing out of bed so soon?"

"I'm trying to get my strength back." Rosemary gently lowered herself into the chair at the desk. "Whew, surgery really knocks the wind out. How are you doing?"

"Better. The doc wants me to stay another couple of days. Mike's on a tear about closing down most of the hospital so I'll be transferring to Sinclair Two sometime today. What about you?"

"I'm getting discharged."

"What?"

"I can recuperate at home just as easily as here. Anyway, being hospitalized gives me the creeps."

"Oh, I see. You've decided, all by yourself, that you're leaving?"

"Right."

"What if your doc has other thoughts?"

"He'll let me go."

Pete threw his napkin on the tray. "Honestly, Rosemary, you're the most bull-headed female I have *ever* met."

"That's why you love me."

"You think I love you!"

She cocked her head and smiled. "Yes, you're goofy about me."

Pete slowly looked up and down her body. "Nice legs, nice shape, pretty face. Yeah, I guess I do." He hesitated. "Mike told me what happened to you yesterday, and it scared the bejesus out of me. He said the person was a surgeon, dressed in scrub greens."

"You should have seen him, Pete. He was wearing

a mask and his eyes were wild. They looked like ghostly harvest moons sitting on the edge of the earth." She shuddered. "He stared at me with those eyes and pulled me closer, and I knew he didn't have kissing on his mind. I tried to get Mike's attention, but the corridor was jammed with people. No one paid any attention. Then I felt an excruciating pain in my side. As I fell, I heard people say that I was bleeding. They seemed as shocked as me. That's all I remember, until the recovery room."

"How tall was he?"

"I'm five feet four, so he must have been about five feet eight, or nine."

"Hair color?"

"I couldn't see it. He wore a green hood."

"Any marks on the part of his face you could see? Like moles, scars, unusual wrinkles?"

Rosemary shook her head.

"Can you guess his age?"

"It happened so fast . . . all I remember are those eyes . . . they pushed his eyebrows up and made his whole forehead crinkly."

"Like this?" Pete tried to emulate the face.

"No, more like this." Rosemary opened her eyes wide and arched her eyebrows.

"Egad!" Pete said. "Will you be my date for Halloween?"

Rosemary started to laugh but felt a sharp stab of pain radiate down into her abdomen. "Ohhh. It hurts. Why me, Pete? What did I do to aggravate an assault?"

Pete saw her discomfort and pounded his fist on the tray, making the coffee jump from its cup. "I don't know what you did, babe, but damn it all to hell, I hate being in here."

"I know you do, but you'll be out soon enough. Then you and I can help Mike with the investigation."

"Will you please leave the investigation to him? You don't know what he's working on, and I'd hate to have you get in the way."

"What's he working on?"

"You better eat something if you're trying to get your strength back."

She picked up a piece of toast. "What's Mike working on?"

"For one thing, he's checking out what happened Tuesday morning, just before Ritchie Chisolm was cut down." Pete got a distant look on his face as he analyzed the case. "The security guard recalls seeing an orderly bring a patient down for psychiatric therapy. The patient's name was signed in the book, but not the orderly's. He was supposed to wait around until the patient was finished. Usually, they sit in the wheelchair outside the interview room and read a magazine, but no one remembers seeing him." Pete stopped abruptly. "Anyway, Mike's been checking on missing uniforms, rapists, computer fraud, and other things you don't need to worry about now."

Rosemary was astonished. "What do you mean, computer fraud. He didn't tell me!"

"He's *not* going to tell you about fraud, and he's also not going to sit and chat about other problems until you're back to work, and that may not be for a week or two, no matter what you might say to Dr.

Framingham. While you're a patient, he's the boss of your time."

Rosemary waved her hand in the air to dismiss the lecture. "Tell me about computer fraud."

"You are the most persistent female I've ever known. Pushy, too. A guy trying to recuperate from massive brain surgery doesn't stand a chance with you."

Rosemary poked her scrambled eggs with a fork. "And getting information out of you is harder than giving a cat a pill. If you don't tell me what you know, lieutenant, I'll shuffle my aching bones over there and fork you . . ."

"Promise?"

". . . smack dab in the middle of your incision, and you'll bleed all over your french toast."

"I dare you to come over here with your forker."

Rosemary shifted uncomfortably in the chair. "Tell you what."

"What?"

"The minute you get sprung from here, we'll meet at my apartment for twelve hours of nonstop bean burritos and nookie."

"Wanton woman screws licentious lieutenant in a bowl of beans. Sounds good to me."

Rosemary smirked. "Guaranteed to blow you away."

"Oooh, aren't we nasty. Now eat your breakfast, woman. I want some flesh to hang on to."

"I'll eat only if you tell me about computer fraud."

Pete pushed the overbed table away. "It appears as if certain programs have been stolen, through a process called hacking, from other institutions . . ."

"Here? At Riverside? We're stealing programs?"

"Yes, and using them, too."

Rosemary felt her temper rise. "Who? I want to know who's doing it."

"Mike'll keep me posted and then I'll tell you more."

"Oh, no you don't, Pete Tanner. I'm in charge of this hospital, and I have a right to know what's going on. Now tell me the full story."

"Women!" Pete said and shook his head. "About six months ago, officials at M.I.T. discovered that one of their medical programs was on the market. The program is called PARABIOSIS, which means the artificial joining of two separate organisms. M.I.T.'s been using the program to develop viable methods for brain transplantations. The program is top secret and dangerous because it's not complete. A computer hack got ahold of it, put into MOM's memory, and has been selling it to research institutions and other hospitals. The theft was discovered when an innocent programmer from a research institute phoned M.I.T. to ask why they hadn't yet sent an operations manual. Needless to say, the request threw M.I.T. researchers into a panic, which might have panicked the programmer for he hung up when they started drilling him about his name and hospital association. We got involved when they requested to have their phone monitored. Since then, M.I.T.'s secured their systems and placed a detector on all their computers to trace any further attempts at theft, for what it's worth. Nothing is totally secure."

Rosemary's face was ashen, her lips forming a

tight, narrow line. "How did Mike trace it to Riverside?"

"As you know, Mike's a pro at interrogating people, but he's also been talking with your computer. I must say he's fascinated with her; probably reminds him of his own mother. MOM's helped him understand that computers aren't objects to be feared. He learned that information is accessed only through user-specific numbers that are changed every other Friday. What he's doing now is trying to get the system changed to fingerprint access, although the idea isn't sitting well with some of your computer people. Mike got an access number from Chad Mooney but found it too limited, so he asked for your number. Interestingly, you are unable to call up the main index of available medical programs. While it might appear to be a minor oversight, and probably something you'd never request, Mike is tenacious with details. It took some coercing but he finally got the index and has found not only PARABIOSIS, hidden under the name MED:PARA, but also a program belonging to Massachusetts General Hospital."

Rosemary was aghast. "They'll sue the shit out of us!"

"Mike's told the administrator. All copies of the program will be returned, and MOM will be purged."

"What was the program?"

"It's called STETHOSCOPE."

"What if it were sold to other hospitals? How would we know? Who is it, Pete? Who's doing this? I've got to know! I've got to tell Chad so he can fire the bastard."

"The bastard *is* Chad Mooney."

Pete's words took her by surprise. "Sonofabitch," she whispered. "I don't understand."

"He needed enough money to dump his wife and make off with his sweetheart."

"Sweetheart? He seems too . . ."

"Stodgy," Pete answered for her. "With the pipe and tweedy clothing."

Rosemary nodded. "He threw away his career."

"He sure as hell did."

"Where is he now?"

"At the station, trying to get his lawyer."

Rosemary was silent as she thought about Chad. He had succumbed to greed, thinking that he could maintain his career while scratching the itch between his legs. "How'd he do it, Pete? How are programs stolen?"

"A hack uses a telephone modem attached to a computer. He doesn't know what he's looking for, so it's a matter of searching by using numbers or random words. Once he's found a program, he makes copies and sells them. Very simple, if you know how."

"He used MOM to help him."

"Yup."

Rosemary looked at Pete with curiosity. "Do you think a computer knows the difference between good and bad? If MOM's become familiar with stealing programs, and she doesn't know it's a bad thing to do, then she wouldn't stop someone from doing it."

"Rose, baby, computers are things. It takes people to run them."

"I know that, but MOM isn't a typical computer, and she's been doing some odd things lately."

"Like what?" Pete asked.

Rosemary thought for a moment. "Like not telling Ritchie Chisolm the answer to his problem. His access number gave him an open channel to everything he needed, and yet MOM didn't help him detect the error."

Pete smiled. "Maybe MOM didn't like him."

"She said they had an interesting relationship. Ritchie called her filthy names and kicked her."

Pete's smile grew larger. "He abused her?"

"Yes."

"Well then, you'll have to call social services and make an appointment for MOM to see a computer abuse specialist.

"That's not funny."

"And while you're at it, she should see a preacher to get her straightened out about good and evil."

"Notice that I'm not laughing."

"What other evil things has she been up to?"

"If you're going to make jokes, I won't tell you."

"Aw, Rose, what happened to your funny bone?"

She smiled. "I ate it for dinner last night. Did Mike tell you what happened to Linda Diver, the scrub tech on your case?"

"He did."

"And that MOM didn't cut the power to the machine soon enough?"

"Yeah, but have you spoken to Charlie Donovan lately?"

Rosemary's eyes grew wide. "No. What did he find?"

"The wire between the machine and the cautery tip was broken. He showed it to Mike who's going to take it to the crime lab. Mike thinks someone might have damaged it intentionally."

"Why?"

"To give Townsend a jolt, or Glassail, or me."

"You?"

Pete placed a hand on his dressing. "It's all a big question mark, Rose. Mike's job is to dig out the facts 'cause if you never ask a question, you never get an answer. I hope we get some answers soon."

"Tell me about missing uniforms. Are they being stolen?"

"Oh, it may be of no concern. Housekeepers are complaining about having to clean up used O.R. scrub suits in the nurses' locker rooms. They don't think it's fair that the O.R. slops their clothing outside the O.R. And I guess some of the nurses are upset about theft from their lockers."

They both looked toward the door when Sara knocked. "Mrs. Cleaveland," she said, "will you be much longer?"

"Why, Sara?"

"Your telephone's been ringing constantly. I have a long list of messages, and your secretary does, too. She wants you to call her when you get a chance."

"Thank you. I'll be there in a moment." Rosemary pressed a hand over her incision and eased out of the chair. Her body felt hammered, and she looked forward to climbing back into bed. "Was Mike's stakeout successful?"

"No. The gang wasn't out last night. He'll try again tonight."

"Want a date for lunch?"

"Surely do."

Rosemary shuffled over to his chair and bent to kiss him.

He slid a hand between her legs. "You know something? I'm goofy about you too, babe."

At the door, Rosemary turned. "Why do you have a guard at your door? Did something happen that you sort of accidentally forgot to tell me about?"

"Nope. Mike put him there. It's a waste of a good man."

"I'm glad he's there." She blew him a kiss.

Leaning on the police officer's arm, Rosemary, followed by Sara, returned to her room. Neither noticed the janitor who suddenly bent over a mop and began scrubbing the floor as if it hadn't been washed in years.

Chapter 24

The news of the hospital's partial closing spread quickly around the hospital. Patients and their families didn't fully understand, and the rumors popped up like dandelions:

". . . A psycho has escaped from the mental health unit. He's chopping everyone down, and they want us on one nursing unit until they catch him."

". . . The hospital's gone bankrupt."

". . . There's an encephalitis plague."

". . . Some lab techs have contracted AIDS and the bigwigs are afraid of an outbreak."

Worse than the rumors were the fears:

"My God! We can't have Aunt Beatrice in our home. She's too sick . . . we don't know how to care for her . . . we don't have a spare bedroom. Can't you find a nursing home?"

". . . I refuse to be transferred. I'll report this to my doctor. He'll let me stay at Riverside."

". . . Go home? Look here, nurse, it's taken me two weeks to get in here."

". . . Leave my baby here? I absolutely and flatly refuse to go home without my baby."

Shelley Bigelow was in charge. She and Mike put together a team of supervisors and department heads who went from floor to floor explaining what areas would be closed, reviewing staffing sheets for temporary layoffs, and evaluating each patient for possible discharge. Within hours, they were being called the "Galloping Gestapo"; out to kill off the hospital for many feared that once the hospital closed, it didn't stand a chance of reopening. And if for some rare reason it did reopen, employees feared their jobs would be given to new recruits.

Worse than the patients' fears were the employees' reactions, more diversified than the contents of a household trash barrel. Fear filled some while others, with unemployment compensation hopes, were overjoyed. Several cried, a few became despondent. The head of dietary, Tom O'Leary, boiled in rage, not because his department would close, but, in part, because he needed to rearrange his staff and the entire luncheon regime. He'd planted a diet aide at his desk, armed her with pen and paper, and told her to answer the phone and, if it was the "Gestapo," to record which patient was transferring to what room and who was being discharged or transferred to another hospital. Vital, he told her. Vital to get it straight. After an hour, he looked in on her and found a veritable Lily Tomlin playing switchboard operator. He listened:

"And to whom am I speaking with? Would you

please spell your last name? Is it czk or zck at the end? Thank you. And the patient's name is what? Would you please spell that? No, the last name. I heard the first name; John. Not John? Oh, George. And now the last name? Got it. What room . . . is that the room to which he will be going or is that the room to which he was from? He's there? Where? I mean did he already transfer? He did? Then what was the room from which he came from? *Don't* yell at me. Let's start over again . . ."

To Tom's horror, her notations looked like a cryptogram. He stormed off to find someone else for the job. "Stupid lunkhead bitch," he muttered. "I'm gonna use her brains in the chicken noodle soup."

"Mr. O'Leary?" someone yelled. "Is it okay to use the Concord Four cart for Sinclair Two? We need an extra."

"Yes," he yelled back.

"Mr. O'Leary?" someone else yelled. "What do you want me to do with all this extra defrosted beef? Cook it up anyway?"

"Yes," he yelled.

"Mr. O'Leary? What's your estimate on employee lunches? Are they going home now, or will they leave at change of shift?"

"How the rat turd do I know? Count on having the usual number."

None of these questions made him boiling mad; his staff needed to know the answers. None of the employees made him boil, either, with one exception. What was really jerking his chain was Hugh Matta, over there on the phone in the bakery. Hugh had been on the phone since nine this morning, talking with one employee after another, like he was running for mayor or something. Tom strode over, planted his portly frame in front of Hugh, put his hands on his hips and glared.

Inadvertently, Hugh waved Tom away, but when he saw his boss, he mouthed, "Sorry. I'll be right off."

"*Now!*" Tom thundered.

Hugh raised a finger in the air to indicate he needed to hear what the caller was saying.

"*Now!*" Tom thundered again, reaching for the receiver.

Hugh hung up without saying good-bye.

"You've been on that dang-blasted phone all morning long while the rest of us are slaving our fannies raw. You stay off the phone, and I mean it."

"We're having a meeting . . . the employees want me there. After all, I *am* the union steward."

"I don't care if you're an airline steward. Your first job is here in dietary, unless you've decided to quit, in which case, I accept your resignation."

"According to union contract, you are not permitted to harass or defame the steward, nor to interfere with union activities."

"Oh yeah? Because I inherited you, I read that damn contract front to rear, and the only mention of the steward is that there *is* one. Furthermore, you are not doing union activities on my time. You want to meet, you do it after work. On your time."

The telephone rang.

Tom glared at Hugh, daring him to pick it up.

It rang a second time, a third, then stopped.

"Get your ass out of the bakery and into the pot

room. Manny needs help scrubbing. Once that's done, relieve Irene who's got the soup vat going. We're having chicken noodle today."

Reluctantly, Hugh did as he was told.

By noontime, the patients' fears had turned to anger:

". . . I refuse to go home."

". . . You'll hear from my lawyer."

". . . My father knows the mayor of Cambridge and *he'll* do something."

". . . We simply *won't* take Aunt Beatrice home. *You* find a nursing home for her."

". . . My physician said there's a room on Concord Three and I demand to be transferred."

At the emergency department exit, ambulances had started lining up like taxicabs at an airport. Tempers were short. Usually calm, the nurses were now yelling at patients and families to hurry up. Stationed at the exit, staff members from the medical records department tried in vain to take dictation orders from the physicians who were giving patients and families discharge instructions on how to care for the patients at home, when to give them pills, and when to make an appointment for an office visit. Also standing by was the head of the home care unit who took as many referrals as she could get. The director of social service finally lost her prescience. "There isn't a damned nursing home bed available this side of the Catskill Mountains," she screamed. "Take the old lady home, prop her up on your living room sofa, and turn on the TV set. She'll get into the soaps soon enough and out of your hair."

On the Gold Coast, Jorge Benedicto de Villareal took the news gracefully, but once the nurse left his room, he had Miguel Galindo dial Rosemary's office number to complain. Peggy, who had been trying to talk with Rosemary all morning, was now in a pique of irritation. She told Galindo that Rosemary had been stabbed almost to death and wouldn't be available until next week, or next year for that matter, so bug off.

When two ambulance drivers from Metropolitan State Hospital tried to lift Melenie Bregen out of bed and into a wheelchair, they found that her stiff body had molded to the contour of the uplifted bedrest and become inflexible. The angle of her body was not the same angle as the wheelchair, and she didn't fit. The drivers looked at each other. "Want to give her middle a push?" one asked. "Are you kidding?" the other said and they left to fetch a stretcher from their ambulance.

Fred Plexico yelled obscenities at the police officer who stood on guard outside Rosemary's room. No matter what Fred threatened, the officer refused him entrance. Enraged, Fred went to the nurses' station and tried to call her, but the hospital lines were jammed.

Adding to the stress level was the paging system's continual announcements, calling personnel, summoning physicians for one area or another. It was Rosemary who became aware of the din. She had Sara go down to the switchboard and tell the operators to change the system over so that all paging requests were relayed to the operators. Already working at breakneck pace, the operators were not pleased.

Exasperated, Peggy took her message book up the elevator to the Gold Coast. Upon meeting the officer, she explained who she was and asked to be allowed in.

"I don't care if you're Princess Di; you can't go in there. Nobody can."

"It's an emergency . . . life or death . . . I *must* see her."

"Nope."

Peggy walked away feeling outraged. She'd tried her best, and if Rosemary was going to be inaccessible, well then, she'd just record all the messages and forget about her responsibility to keep Rosemary informed. To hell with it. As she walked along, Peggy had an idea. She would stop by the switchboard and get the private telephone number in Rosemary's room. Peggy could then call the outside line and get in, she hoped.

A nurse carrying a large floral bouquet was also turned away. "But these are from Lieutenant Tanner," she said.

"I don't care who they're from."

"You'll get into trouble."

"I won't, but you will if those posies are bugged."

The nurse looked at the arrangement, then turned on her heel and muttered, "Meathhead. Lieutenant Tanner wouldn't send her flowers with bugs."

While Rosemary used her private line to call Bernie Highling, the president of the board, Sara kept dialing the operator on the hospital phone. The lines remained busy.

Rosemary explained the situation to Bernie and

asked him not to visit; she would get back to him tomorrow. Although he was shocked at the news that several nursing units would have to be temporarily closed, he expressed condolences to Rosemary and wished her speedy recovery. Before hanging up, Bernie apologized for Fred Plexico's behavior, referring to Fred as the north end of a south-bound rat.

"I can't get a dial tone or an operator," Sara explained. "Want me to walk down there again and ask the operators for an open line?"

"Good idea. Would you also stop by my secretary's office and tell her to come up and see me? I'd also like to have my assistants pay me a visit. You'd think I had a bad case of the black plague."

"It's not you," Sara said, "it's the officer outside your door. He's turning away everybody, except Dr. Framingham, me, and Sergeant Dow."

"That idiot!" Rosemary sat up too quickly and a sharp, deep pain shot across her abdomen. She grabbed her side and fell back.

"Do you need a pain shot?" Sara asked.

"No, dammit. Doesn't that officer know I have a hospital to run?"

"I'm sure he knows. He's just following Sergeant Dow's orders."

Rosemary sighed. "I'm sorry I yelled at you, Sara. I'm just so darned frustrated."

"I understand."

"Would you find Dr. Framingham for me? Tell him I must get out of here."

"Sure."

Rosemary was furious. Mike had no right to imprison her. No wonder Peggy hadn't seen her yet,

245

or her assistants. She couldn't get out by foot or by phone. Or could she? The officer had let her visit Pete. As she eased her aching body off the bed, the sharp pain returned and she gasped. Bent over, holding her side, she opened the door and asked him to follow her to the nurses' lounge to get a cup of coffee. He stayed by her side while she inched along, and he carried the steaming cup on the return trip. For a brief moment, she considered saying hello to Pete, then changed her mind. Her strength was gone. Back in her room, he helped her into bed and left the cup on her overbed table. Her breathing was hard and fast, and she wondered if being a prisoner was so bad. Resolving that her room was safer than any other place, she lay back and waited for Sara to return. Funny, she thought, how a stranger can become your best friend when she's got something you need, namely mobility.

Rosemary let her mind drift. She thought about Fred Plexico and Wesly Ames and wondered what Fred was coercing him to do. If Wesly Ames thinks he can sign any papers to merge, she thought, if he makes any changes in my plans, I'll . . . I'll . . . fire him! As for Chad Mooney, he can stay in jail until he rots! Imagine, stealing computer programs. I pay both those men top salaries, and they're both cads. Neither one knows a thing about loyalty, she thought. If you can't be loyal to your hospital, then you should find employment elsewhere. Damnation, why did this happen to me? Of all lousy times to be stuck in bed, this is the worst.

Rosemary started to cry. She picked up the phone to call Pete, to tell him about her feelings, but the lines were still tied up. Stop! she told herself as she bit her lip and forced the tears away. Self-pity won't help anything. Tears continued to trickle down her cheeks like raindrops on a windowpane. She wasn't crying for herself. No, her sadness was for all her employees who didn't understand, and for Ritchie, Myra, Linda Diver; the ones who died at Riverside. The accumulation of death over the past few days took its toll on Rosemary. She closed her eyes and let the tears flow.

"Mrs. Cleaveland! Are you all right?"

Rosemary looked up. Sara was standing with Dr. Framingham. "Yes," she said, wiping her eyes. "I'm just having a moment of sorrow. Hand me a tissue, will you, Sara? Thanks. Hello, doctor."

He touched her arm. "Sorry I wasn't here earlier, but this closure has me hopping." The medical staff's baseball team had nicknamed him The Frame. He was pencil thin, stood six feet six inches tall, and remembered everything.

"How are the physicians taking it?" she asked.

"Not well. The hospitals in Cambridge are full, and most docs don't have privileges in Boston. How does the wound feel?"

"Simply terrific. I'd like to be discharged."

"Is that a fact. Well, you *will* be discharged. Pick either Saturday or Sunday."

"Today, Dr. Framingham. I must get out of here."

"Why?"

"I have a hospital to run."

"Even if I was nutty enough to spring you today, which I'm not, I wouldn't let you work for at least a week. I happen to be unusually proud of my stitching. You'll hardly notice the scar when it's bikini time again. Let's take a look at your dressing." With Sara's assistance, Rosemary pulled up her nightgown."

"But I have work to do . . ."

"It'll wait. That looks good. Just a spot of old drainage." He pushed her gown down and pulled up the sheets. "Listen, Rosemary, you got cut down by a maniac. The hospital's closing because people are in jeopardy. We make light of it and complain miserably, but deep inside, the hospital staff is scared shitless. One more murder and they'll vamoose out the windows faster than powder in a gale. I don't dare wear my scrub suit outside the O.R., none of the surgeons do. Even the nurses are afraid to leave the O.R. in their greens. And after the incident with Linda Diver, no one's using the cautery machine. In fact, they're all nervous about using anything electrical in case MOM's defective. Everyone mistrusts everyone else. It's chaotic outside your bedroom door and if I had my way, you'd stay right here on the Coast."

Rosemary was silent. Nothing she could say would change his mind.

"Don't be sad," he said. "You and Pete will be dancing and romancing on Saturday night. I'll discharge you both then."

"Thanks for helping him out," Rosemary said. "He's a special person."

"He is. We're going to start a chess game tonight."

"You better rest up. He's very good."

Framingham laughed. "I'm better."

"What happened to Fawn Glassail?"

"You mean in the O.R.?"

"Yes, and afterward."

"Fawn's got brains, but she's shy on skill. When I talked to her about handling the case, she said her reaction was the same as a wife operating on her husband."

"But she's only known Pete since Tuesday!" Rosemary said.

"I didn't know that. Dr. Harris has allowed her third assistant privileges for a month."

"Then what?"

"He'll make a decision. You get some rest now. I'll be in the E.R. if you need anything, and I'll check on you again before the chess game starts."

After he left, Rosemary asked Sara, "Did you find my secretary?"

"Yes." Sara pointed to several bulging manila envelopes that she'd placed on the chair. "Peggy said these are the more important letters and messages. Want me to hand you one? I'll help you get through them."

"Okay. How did Peggy seem to you?"

"She's fine."

Rosemary looked sharply at her nurse. "I know you want to protect me from bad news, Sara, and I appreciate your concerns, but I want you to be honest with me. I'm still in charge of Riverside. I could sign out against medical advice . . . believe me, I've considered it . . . but I'm still feeling too weak to walk the distance to the parking garage. You heard Dr. Framingham. People are miserable outside my door. The patients are confused, the employees are afraid, the physicians are angry, and the murderer is probably picking out his next victim. You don't need to protect me; I know what's going on. Now tell me about Peggy."

"I'll use her words. She's down and out and backwards and forwards, totally bonkers. She's ready to pull the phone from the wall. On the other hand, she's afraid for you, mad at the officer who won't let her in, and upset that she can't get to you on the private line." Sara pointed to the phone.

Rosemary picked it up and dialed her secretary's extension. "Busy." She dialed for an operator. "Busy." She dialed Pete's number. "Busy. Dammit! Let's go through those papers for awhile."

Sara pulled out a stack and placed them on Rosemary's overbed table.

"Are you married?" Rosemary asked, feeling less like working and more like sleeping.

"Yes, and I have an eight-year-old adopted daughter."

"That's great. You're very lucky."

"We are. She's the sun, the moon, and the stars to us. I probably spoil her rotten, but what a great gal. Maybe all eight-year-olds are alike, I don't know. This one happens to be the friendliest, happiest kid going."

"What's her name?"

Rosemary drifted off before she heard the answer. Soon, the room held only the peaceful breathing of Rosemary's sleep.

At change of shift, Sara woke Rosemary to tell her that she was going to the nursing station to give Pat Peters a report, and then the two nurses would transfer her to Sinclair 207.

Groggy from her nap, Rosemary heard the sound of an argument outside the door. She looked over and, between the crack, saw two guards.

"Did you ask him?" the short guard said.

"No. Dow wouldn't give us a day off *now*, you nitwit."

"Don't call me a nitwit, you bird-brain. Go ask. I'll stay here until you get back."

"I'm not gonna ask him anything!" the tall guard said.

"Why the hell not? You don't know what he's gonna say unless you ask."

Rosemary smiled and closed her eyes again. The tall guard was right. Dow wouldn't give anyone a day off now. It wasn't even worth asking him. For support, she pressed a hand over her dressing and inched onto her right side. The position was unbearable and she inched onto her back again, trying to convince herself that she didn't need pain medication. Pete had said something similar about asking a question. What was it? If you don't ask, you don't get an answer? Something like that.

She wished now that she had an answer for Riverside's problems. A crystal ball would do. She'd be able to see what everyone was doing and what the future held. She and MOM would make a dynamic presidential duo. She'd forecast the future and MOM would get the word out to the world. Rosemary thought about MOM. Was she defective? Could Lee Hwang and his team of equipment specialists find and fix the defect, if there was one? Even if there wasn't, Fred Plexico would lie and use a flaw to his advantage. Rosemary needed to consult

251

with MOM. She'd have an answer. But she didn't have an answer for Ritchie Chisolm. Why not? Rosemary wrestled with the idea. Why didn't MOM tell Ritchie the answer to his problem?

Rosemary's eyes flew open. Because, she said to herself, because he didn't ask! She tried to recall the tape recording of Ritchie's last conversation with MOM, but all she could remember were the swear words and the haunting laughter.

"Sara," Rosemary said, "help me out of bed." When Sara didn't answer, Rosemary looked around for her, then remembered shift was changing.

Rosemary braced her side as she rose from the bed. A stabbing pain made her cry aloud. She sat down quickly to catch her breath. What she was about to do was insane, she knew it, yet she forced herself to stand up.

Chapter 25

Where the fuck are the scissors?

If I don't get her today, I'll die. The machine people are out of control. Lord God in heaven, hear my prayer. I'm the savior. Next to you, I'm the penultimate ruler.

Here they are, in my pocket.

Shhh . . . someone's coming . . . two of them. I'll kill them both. Cogs and wheels. Eyeballs and wires. Machines on the loose.

They look wired. Shhh . . . keep quiet. Keep perfectly still. They won't come in here . . . they'll go away. Everyone goes away.

Shit, it's hell in here. Burning up.

What? What did you say? Yes, I know. Don't tell *me* what to do, you disgusting odoriferous pustule. I don't have to listen to you. Get away from me. Get out of my bathroom. I'm safe, you're not. They'll get you.

Surgeon, surgeon, burning bright, in the vapors of the night. I see you, Rosemary dear. You'll go nowhere without me.

Urine, excrement, burning my skin. Filth and dirt. Pus and pestilence.

Got to get out. Got to breathe . . .

"Senor Villareal, I understand you don't want to transfer, but you have to." The nurse had been pleading with Villareal for the past five minutes. She had his suitcase on a chair, and every time she put an article of clothing in, he took it out.

"I will go when I am good and ready. You tell Sergeant Dow that I refuse to be placed in any room except a private one."

She put a pair of socks in the suitcase.

He took them out.

"Furthermore, the man in room two-oh-one is a doddering geriatric who continually screams for 'Martha.' "

"How do you know that?" she asked, taking a suit from the closet.

"I have spies." He put the suit back.

"I am getting absolutely nowhere with you."

"Correct."

"I'll have to report you . . . I should have reported you days ago."

"Do that."

"Don't you understand how difficult things are already? You're just making it worse."

"How difficult are things?" he asked.

"Terrible. Just terrible. Half the employees refuse to work until the Ri . . . I mean . . . well . . ." Her words drifted away.

"The Riverside Ripper, to be exact," he said.

The nurse glanced at him quickly, then headed for the door. "It's true! I knew it, I just knew it. Pack your own bags and get the hell out of here."

"What are you talking about?"

Having reached the safety of the door, she turned. "The nurses and I want you the hell out of the hospital because we know who the Ripper is."

"Who . . . me?"

"No! Your switchblade friend, Miguel Galindo." She slammed the door.

As Villareal scrutinized his empty suitcase, a large smile spread across his face. He put his head back and laughed uproariously.

The Gold Coast nursing station looked like Logan Airport after a plane crash. Pat Peters, who'd just come on duty to be with Rosemary, couldn't break away. She was talking with the day and evening nurses, four ambulance drivers, three physicians, and she had two telephone receivers in one hand.

"You transferred my patient to the wrong room!" a doctor yelled. "Jeffrey Smith. His diabetes is out of control, and I need to find him fast. Where *is* he?"

"Where's Mrs. Angelina Von Yarbrough? We're supposed to take her to . . ."

"Mr. Villareal refuses to . . ."

But the Gold Coast seemed like a quiet nap in the

park compared to the hell-bent, feverish activities in the time-clock area. A battery of forty-five off-duty employees refused entrance and time-card punching to employees coming on duty. Fists were raised and words were flung. Not everyone could stand at the doorway, and those further back couldn't actively participate. In their fury of advocacy for employee rights, which, some felt, definitely and absolutely included employee safety, and because administration was the root of their problems, and administration wasn't around to hear their worries, several steamed laboratory techs grabbed hold of a time clock and tried rocking it back and forth to free it from the wall. It didn't look like the face of administration, but it would do for now. The time clock wouldn't budge. One of them noticed the ax inside a glass-enclosed fire cabinet, which also held a fire extinguisher. He pulled the ax out and after telling the others to stand back, he swung and shattered the clock face. They took turns, like kids at a birthday party swacking away at a piñata, each hoping to be the first to get the candy inside. They started on the next time clock, but quit when one man missed the metal box and implanted the ax head in his foot. They took him to the emergency room.

Where havoc reigned in most departments, solemnity waxed heavily in the operating room suite. The employees and physicians called themselves a team. They worked together, sweated together, ate together, and laughed together. They'd formed their own baseball team and had remained unbeaten this summer. Egos soared last Thursday when they clopped the maintenance department fourteen to eight. They were supposed to take on the I.C.U. pansies tonight, but the game had been canceled. Instead, they would be at Linda Diver's wake. Her death had rocked the team, but they had rebounded like champions, not only because of personal pride, but also because Miss Pickle, in her strict ways, had instilled a sense of cohesive loyalty in every one of them. The nonprofessionals didn't want to be laid off with pay, and the professionals didn't want to be on call for emergencies only. It wasn't that they wanted to work; they simply wanted to be together.

Of all the employees and physicians who solemnly retired their scrub suits to the dirty laundry hampers, Henry, the senior O.R. housekeeper, was the saddest. He loved these people. Every Wednesday, he brought in a box of Dunkin' Donuts, and every Christmas, they gave him a mutually contributed cash bonus of five hundred dollars. Today, he didn't want to go home. No longer were there kids to kiss or wife to greet. But that wasn't it. Fact was, there was no tomorrow in the O.R., unless an emergency came up, but he wouldn't wish surgery on anybody. No, he needed this place because it was home to him. As he mopped the corridor floor, someone clapped him on the shoulder. It was Doc O'Shaunnesy in his street clothes. One of the swellest guys this side of Saturn.

"See ya, Henry."

"Yup, see you, too, sir, maybe in a few days, I surely hope."

"You're sad, Henry."

That's why Henry liked Doc O'Shaunnesy almost the best. The man had feelings. "Guess I am, sir.

Sure will miss the team."

"It's not the end of the world, Henry. We'll be back together soon."

"I hope so."

Dr. O'Shaunnesy patted Henry's shoulder again. "I'm going to sleep late in the mornings and watch dirty videos at night. Catch you later."

"Bye now." Henry watched him pass through the automatic doors.

"Bye, Henry," said a nurse as she and four others headed home.

"Bye, ladies. You be good."

"Henry?"

He turned and saw Miss Pickle walking toward him, her attention riveted on something in her purse. "Yes, ma'am?"

"You'll come in if we need you?"

"Of course. I can be here in ten minutes flat."

"Good. Dr. Harris is in the lounge with Dr. Swartz. They'll be leaving soon." Miss Pickle held up the keys to her car. "The recovery room nurses can lock up if you want to go."

"Thanks, ma'am. I don't mind staying."

"Suit yourself. I'll let you know when things are back to normal. Bye, Henry."

"Bye, ma'am." Tough old bird, he thought, but dagnation do I love her.

Henry looked around and supposed that he might collect the laundry bags and take them to the chute. He wheeled the mop bucket into the dirty utility room. After emptying out the water and removing the wet mop head, he wheeled the bucket toward the janitor's closet down the hall. As he passed the surgeon's lounge, he saw Dr. Harris at the blackboard, chalking out a surgical diagram for Dr. Swartz. They chatted back and forth. Henry went around the large rack of clean uniforms that sat opposite the nurses' and surgeons' locker rooms. He respected Dr. Harris, the chief of surgery. Never in a million moons would Henry ever want to look inside someone's gaping incision. It was all he could do to clean out the bloody kick pans under the tables much less see all that blood pumping and spewing around inside a person's body. He shuddered at the thought. And that Dr. Swartz—cutting on people's eyeballs. How a man could enjoy that kind of work was a mystery.

Henry pulled open the janitor's closet door. Something plunged into and out of his chest so fast that, at first, he wasn't sure what had happened. Realization came at the same moment his punctured heart hemorrhaged into his chest cavity. A pitiful gurgling rose to his lips. His outstretched hands slowly slid down the body of his assailant as he collapsed to the floor.

The person stepped over him and quickly left the O.R.

Chapter 26

From her purse in the lower drawer of the night-stand, Rosemary found her set of hospital keys. She slipped them into a pocket of her velour bathrobe. One of the keys gave her manual control of elevator 3. If anyone tried to stop her, she could take the elevator off automatic, press the button for the basement level, and get there nonstop.

She'd considered putting on her street clothes, but her blouse was torn and stiff with blood and her suit jacket was made to wear with a blouse. It had no buttons. As she was leaving her room, the phone rang. Failure to answer the damn thing might arouse concern for her safety. She lifted the receiver. "Hello?"

"Hi, babe, what happened to our lunch date?"

"Pete! How'd you get through? The lines have

260

been jammed all day."

"Pernicious tenacity. Do you feel okay?"

"I ache all over, and I've slept most of the day. You okay?"

"Yes. How about a date for dinner?"

"Your place or mine?"

"Yours. I need a change of scenery. What time do you wish to dine, m'dear?"

She glanced at the wall clock. Supper trays arrived at five, which gave her an hour to get down and back. "The usual time will do nicely, your majesty."

"I'm glad to hear you know who's boss. I'll don my royal ermine robes and bring the bottle of sparkling grape juice that Mike gave me. See you then."

Rosemary went to the door and pulled it open. The police officer stationed outside her door turned. "Hello."

"What's your name?" Rosemary asked.

"Willis," he replied.

"How long have you been with the Cambridge Police Department?"

" 'Bout a year. I transferred from Ipswich."

He followed as she started walking down the corridor. "Do you have a family?"

"Sure do. A wife, three sons, and a daughter who'll be two years old next month."

At the elevator, Rosemary pressed the down button. "The move must have been difficult for you; putting your children in new schools and everyone having to make new friends."

When the doors opened, they stepped aboard. "Yeah," he said. "Wait a minute. You're not supposed to leave the Gold Coast. Where are you going?"

"To the computer division. It'll only take a few minutes and, anyway, we both need a vacation from the Coast. It gets boring looking at the same surroundings all day."

"You're gonna get me into hot water with Sergeant Dow."

"I'll explain that you couldn't stop me . . . it'll be my fault."

Officer Willis didn't look convinced. The elevator stopped on each floor as employees, patients, visitors, physicians, police officers, security guards, and ambulance drivers either boarded or got off in an effort to close down departments according to the Gestapo's instructions. Hoping no one would notice her, Rosemary turned into officer Willis's chest and bowed her head. Finally, the door opened onto the basement level. The computer division looked like a ghost town. Standing at the check-in desk with the regular security guard was a short, fleshy police officer who folded his arms across his chest and watched them approach. He looked like a bulldog.

"Good afternoon," she said brightly. "I'm Rosemary Cleaveland . . ."

"Yeah, I know. You'll get back in that elevator and go on upstairs where you belong."

"I'll only be a few minutes."

"That wasn't a question. Ma'am, that was an order."

"But I'm here to have therapy; doctor's orders." Rosemary signed her name in the log book. "You can confirm it with the nursing unit, or with Mike

262

Dow," she lied.

"I'll do just that." He scrutinized Willis's name tag. "You gotta sign in, too."

"Mrs. Cleaveland?" Rosemary turned and saw Lee Hwang shuffling toward her. "So it's true, you *are* a patient. I heard you got cut down by the Ripper, but I didn't know how bad it was." Lee ran his fingers through his dark hair that looked as if it hadn't been washed or combed in several days. His tie hung limply around the collar of his stained and wrinkled shirt. "The grapevine's got you anywhere from totally fine to dead. I know for a fact that if it had been the latter, the hospital would roll over. My employees are scared to death. Shouldn't you be in bed?"

"I'm fine now."

"You look pale. Here, lean on me."

Grateful, Rosemary took his arm. A burning cramp had settled into her left side and, as they started walking down the hall, she held a hand tightly over her wound.

"What brings you down here?" he asked.

"I must talk with MOM for awhile."

Lee nodded. "What a mess we're in down here. Did you hear about Chad Mooney? I still can't believe it's true."

"Yes, I heard, and it's shocking."

"He was such a prude, if you know what I mean; wearing tweedy clothes, smoking a pipe, using the King's English. He didn't seem the type to fool around with women."

"Lee, he's more an example than a type. In his case, God took a chunk of his brain and put it

263

between his legs. When Chad wasn't stealing computer programs, he no doubt thought about women, but they weren't his true problem; greed was."

"Yeah, the police found four checks on his desk, totaling twenty thousand dollars! Made payable to Moonbeam Industries. I'd love to know how much he had in the bank, the old duffer."

"And I'd love to know if he stole any money from Riverside." Rosemary stopped at the main computer room door. "I won't be long."

"Want to use an interview room? Both are available and the chairs are more comfortable."

"No, I need MOM's full capacity."

Lee glanced at the wall clock. "Shift changes at four-thirty, but I'll send the programmer home now. I don't have another one coming on so you can stay as long as you want. In fact, I only have a couple of fellows on the shift. If you need anything, you'll have to call the operations unit."

"Thanks, but Officer Willis will be with me. Lee, is it possible that MOM will not give out information unless a specific question is asked?"

"For general use, yes. Chad Mooney did it for security purposes."

"What about your programmers? Would she offer information to them without a specific command?"

"They have full access," Lee said. "If one of them asks her a question, she will give them all the information she's got."

"Then why didn't MOM tell Ritchie Chisolm what he needed to know?"

"I've been troubled about that, too. She should have."

"Do I have full access?" Rosemary asked.

"Yes."

"With the exception of the main menu for medical programs. I understand Chad removed it from my access number."

Lee frowned. "I'll check it for you."

Rosemary was bent with pain. "Whew, I need to sit down."

Lee helped her into the room, sent the programmer home, then held the chair for her. "Are you sure you'll be okay? I can stay if you want."

"I'm fine, and you look like you need a full night's sleep." Rosemary looked at the enormous screen in front of her. "Can MOM hear us?"

Lee pushed a button. "Not now."

"Rumors are flying around that she's defective. Do you know if something's the matter with her?"

Lee brushed his fingers over his matted hair. "It's difficult debugging a computer as extensive as MOM. Right now, I'm working on a problem with memory capacity. We know how much she's got, but over the past two months, I've been having trouble running my programs, especially at night. It's like she's being tapped. I've got my staff looking all over the hospital for the cause. So to answer your question? Yes, a helluva lot's wrong with her."

With Officer Willis stationed outside the door, Rosemary tried to find a comfortable position in the chair. She'd been up too long as it was, and her body was cramped with pain, but this was important. She had to see if MOM would answer her questions truthfully, and without limitation. Rosemary adjusted the microphone and pressed a button. "MOM? Can you hear me?"

"Yes, Rosemary."

Rosemary felt a thrill of excitement as she always did whenever MOM spoke with her. MOM's existing scope of talents was vastly complex, but her future capabilities, and the impact she would have on the health care profession, continued to give Rosemary a feeling of pride and exhilaration.

"Tell me the names of the programs that Chad Mooney obtained from M.I.T. and other institutions," Rosemary said.

"Chad Mooney used a telephone modem to obtain PARABIOSIS from M.I.T., STETHOSCOPE and INTERNIST from Massachusetts General Hospital, Prophet Public Procedures, and Cambridge Crystal File, from Prophet National Time-Sharing Computer Resource in Cambridge, and he was trying to find LASER from the Massachusetts Eye and Ear Infirmary. Chad Mooney also obtained language programs, like FUZZY, LISP, MACRO-1O, and EXPERT."

"How were you involved?"

"Once Chad Mooney was on-line, he connected the telephone to the silicon crystal bank in my central processor, and I would call up the programs' binary system to determine the language in which it was written. Most of them are written in FORTRAN, SAIL, BASIC, MUMPS, PASCAL. I had to decode some of them.

"Once he had obtained a program, what would he do with it?"

"I don't know."

"Did he sell them?" Rosemary asked.

"I don't know."

Rosemary thought about MOM's response. It was likely that Chad hadn't told MOM. "Did he manipulate the programs in any way?"

"Yes. He would remove the originator's name and replace it with the name Moonbeam Industries. He did the same with the users' manual, if there was one. Otherwise, I would put one together for him."

"What do you know about Moonbeam Industries?"

"Only that it is the name Chad Mooney used on his programs."

Because Mike would be investigating the extent of Chad's involvement, Rosemary decided to pursue another issue. "Do you recall Ritchie Chisolm's last transmission with you?"

"I'll get it now. Do you wish to hear it?"

"No. I believe Ritchie was having difficulty with an algorithm problem. Chad Mooney helped him by asking you for the correct answer. You gave Chad the answer, but not Ritchie. Please tell me why."

"I am programmed to be selective in my responses," MOM said.

"Didn't Ritchie have full access to you?"

"Yes, for Riverside's business, but not for his homework."

"Was he doing his homework?" Rosemary asked.

"He would go back and forth. At times it was hard to tell which project he was on."

Rosemary hesitated. Had MOM made an independent decision not to help Ritchie? She had to find out. "Were Ritchie's homework problems similar to what he was working on for Riverside?"

"Yes. He was programming holographic visualizations for Riverside and using them for his thesis work."

"But if you weren't certain which he was doing, then why did you limit his access?"

"Chad Mooney told me to."

Rosemary felt relieved. Not only had MOM given her the information freely, but the culprit had been Chad and not MOM. "Are you familiar with the electrical accident that occurred in the O.R. yesterday morning?"

"If you are referring to the defective electrocautery machine, yes, I am familiar with the problem."

"Please tell me why the power wasn't shut off."

"The power was shut off the moment I detected a fault. My monitoring job is at the outlet, not inside the machine. Since my inception, the programmers have been feeding me the internal operating schemata for certain pieces of equipment. The electrocautery machine was not one of them."

Rosemary felt satisfied with MOM's answer, but she had to check one last item. "MOM, do I have full access to you?"

"Yes."

"Including the menu for medical programs?"

"Yes. Sargeant Mike Dow had Chad Mooney take care of the problem."

Good, she thought. "Are you familiar with a patient named Duncan Silverstone and another named Ovaline Lee?"

"Yes. Both patients lost mentation while they were

having EEGs."

"Do you know what happened?"

"Yes. Their memories were taken for research purposes."

Rosemary stared at the microphone in front of her. "Are you telling me that it was done on purpose?"

"Yes."

"By whom?"

"I know the researchers only by their access numbers."

"Give them to me!"

MOM displayed a list of numbers on the screen closest to Rosemary. "Who are they?" she whispered.

"They're not Riverside Hospital numbers," MOM said.

"What do you mean?"

"Riverside numbers have five digits. You will see that these have four digits plus two letters. They are used by the Cambridge Research Laboratory."

As Rosemary looked over the list of thirty-seven numbers, she asked, "What the hell is Cambridge Research Laboratories?"

"It's a privately funded organization that was put together by a group of neurologists and neurosurgeons who are interested in automatic intelligence. The organization has been functioning since May."

"Would you print out a copy for me?"

The lasar printer at the end of MOM's console hummed for several seconds, then stopped.

"What do you mean by artificial intelligence?"

"It's a complicated process, Rosemary, but I'll try to explain it in everyday terms. Total memories are first transferred to individual tape discs then sorted out and redistributed to other discs. Higher levels of intelligence, such as geology and knowledge of worldwide petroleum resources, are put onto one disc. Matters of everyday living and general knowledge go onto other discs. Fears, phobias, and breakdowns in character and behavior are put on what is termed the garbage tape."

Rosemary was shocked. The story was preposterous and yet she had to believe it; MOM wasn't capable of making it up. "What happens to the tapes?"

"The high intelligence tape is made into a semiconductor bead, which is a computer microchip coated with silastic to give it a rounded surface that will not aggravate brain tissue. The beads are implanted into human brains. Nothing has been done with general knowledge tapes yet. The garbage tape is maintained on a solar energy computer. I have no access to it."

"Why not?"

"So that I don't acquire phobias, fears, and breakdowns in character and behavior."

"MOM, what you're telling me is incredible, taking people's memories, putting them on tapes, and then making beads."

"We are dealing with high level research," MOM said.

"That's what you've been told. What happens to the beads?"

"They're surgically implanted into the hippocampal area of a person's brain."

Rosemary's side was throbbing from sitting up too long. She bent lower to ease the pain and took a deep breath. "Has anyone actually received an implant?"

"Yes. Dr. Fawn Glassail received a bead developed from Dr. Jacob Shoeman's intelligence. Senor Jorge Benedicto de Villareal received a bead developed from Duncan Silverstone's intelligence. Willard Scotch will receive a bead developed from Ovaline Lee's intelligence."

Rosemary was speechless. Jacob Shoeman was a famous neurosurgeon. "How did they ever get Shoeman's intelligence?" she asked.

"His memory was taken on the Cambridge Research Laboratory's EEG machine. He was the first experimental case. Since that time, all other patients have been on Riverside's EEG machine."

"Why?" Rosemary asked.

"I don't know."

"Do you know if Fawn Glassail has had any other legitimate medical training?"

"I only know what is in her privileges file."

"Yeah, me too. A file of lies. Tell me about the mayor of Cambridge. What intelligence does Willard Scotch want?"

"Ovaline Lee works for Senator Philip Lommely. She knows a great deal about state politics, and she has degrees in political science, economics, and public health administration. The Stereotaxic Parabiosis Learning Center has been looking for intelligence for Willard Scotch. Ovaline Lee had it, and she was then scheduled for an EEG."

The Learning Center was a part of this scheme?

Rosemary felt a dreadful loss. "Is Dr. Stockman involved?"

"Researchers are known only by their access numbers."

"How did the researchers get Ovaline Lee onto the EEG machine?"

"Her outpatient record said she needed an EEG to rule out a brain lesion."

"Did she have a lesion?"

"Not according to the tracing."

Rosemary had a hundred questions for MOM and didn't hear an unusual shuffling in the corridor outside the computer room door. "Was a brain lesion the means for getting the patients onto the EEG machine?" she asked.

"All three patients had diagnoses of Rule Out Brain Lesion."

The door banged open. Surprised, Rosemary spun around.

The surgeon! Oh my God, help me. He's insane.

Standing in the door frame, looking as if he'd just operated on a bag of blood, was a fully gowned and masked surgeon. The front of his green scrubwear was soaked, and in his hand were a pair of scissors dripping with bright red drops that fell to the floor. In the corridor behind him lay Officer Willis, knotted into a fetal position, but still alive and able to move for he used his legs to push his body toward the door. Wide-eyed, Rosemary watched as if she were viewing the bloody climax of a horror movie. Willis reached out for the doorjamb and began a pitiful struggle to stand up. The surgeon whipped around and slammed the door on the man's fingers. A ferocious scream of pain shattered the air as flesh and bones were instantly crushed. Rosemary could see the tips of Willis's fingers in the crack of the door.

He turned back. "You!" screamed the surgeon. "You are the cause of the machine people."

For a moment, Rosemary could only stare at him, thoroughly shocked at the brutality. She didn't know what machine people were, but if this paranoid schizo murderer thought she was one of them, then she was next on his hit list.

"Rosemary," MOM said, "the person in the room with you does not have full access to my information. Should I continue?"

The surgeon cocked his head. "Who's here?"

"Yes, MOM, talk!"

Rosemary slipped off the stool and struggled to pull herself to the end of the console as MOM said, "What would you like me to talk about?"

She got behind the computer as the surgeon rushed forward with scissors raised high. "I'll get you," he screamed. "I have the power and the glory and I know who you are. I must put an end to all machine people."

"Sing the 'Battle Hymn of the Republic,' " Rosemary yelled.

The surgeon came behind the console. Rosemary had made it to the opposite end and was about to head around the front again. If she only had the strength to make it to the door, she might be safe. Aside from Willis, who was probably dead by now, no one was out there to help. She looked quickly at the equipment in the room behind MOM's console and saw the generator and two long rows of large memory storage banks near the far wall.

"Rosemary, dear, I've been trying, but I can't sing, so I'll orate instead. Mine eyes have seen the glory of the coming of the Lord . . . "

The surgeon bounded down the backside of the console, straight toward her. Rosemary left her position and forced her legs to head for the storage banks.

"He is trampling out the vintage where the grapes of wrath are stored . . . "

He held the scissors high as he chased after her. *"You* are the machine dictator. I can see the wires in your eyes . . . "

Rosemary got to the equipment and slipped behind. "MOM," she yelled, "page Mike Dow for the main computer room."

"I'm doing it now. He hath loosed the fateful lightning of His terrible swift sword . . . "

The surgeon stood on the other side of the memory banks; eyes maniacal half moons shining above the green mask. "No machine will help you now!" he yelled. "I am supreme. You'll succumb to *my* wishes."

"His truth is marching on . . . "

Holding the scissors forward, he lunged across the top of the storage banks. The metal blades sunk into Rosemary's left forearm. Blood gushed. Horrified, she pulled away, covered the wound with her hand, and fled down the row.

" . . . I have seen him in the watch-fires of a hundred circling camps . . . "

He followed on the other side, his eyes never leaving her face, eyes that gleamed with madness.

She turned and started in the opposite direction.

" . . . They have builded him an altar in the evening dews and damps . . ."

He lunged again, missed her, then flew over the top of the row and caught the hem of her robe with his hand. Rosemary untied the waist band and slipped off the robe. Drops of blood from the knife wound flew in all directions. She didn't notice. Fleeing around the memory banks, she headed toward MOM's backside, hoping to get around the large console and then out the door. She reached the corner and glanced back.

" . . . I can read His righteous sentence by the dim and flaring lamps . . . "

He was right behind, scissors raised. With all her strength, she pushed the laser printer off the console. It landed on the floor between them. As his foot hit the machine, he reached out and grabbed her nightgown. They went down together. The surgeon scrambled to sit on top of her. Scissors arced in the air, ready to plung into her chest, but she jerked her body sideways. He squirmed to regain his balance.

"Rosemary?" MOM said, "I hear noises and I know you're nearby. Please talk to me. What's going on?"

He pinned her shoulder down with one hand, then raised the scissors high over her heart. Rosemary squeezed her eyes closed. Her hands flailed, trying to ward off the blow which she knew would kill her.

Suddenly, his weight fell off her body. She glanced up, felt him on the floor against her side, and rolled over and over, away from him. Her body was weak with pain. Blood continued to flow from her arm, but she was free. Something strange had happened to him, like a heart attack. He started to stand up, when she noticed another person standing over the surgeon. A foot went out, kicking the surgeon's jaw free from its sockets, and he fell back again, screaming in pain. The person was Miguel Galindo! He reached down and pulled his switchblade out of the surgeon's chest.

" . . . His day is marching on . . . "

Miguel looked around the room, confused, trying to locate the source of the voice. When he saw that Rosemary was bleeding, he went to her side and took her arm. "Let me see that."

She looked, too. Her forearm still oozed blood. "I'm alive. Thank God you came when you did."

"Rosemary, I hear another unauthorized voice. Should I continue?"

"Who's talking?" Miguel asked as he helped Rosemary stand.

"The computer," she said. "Thank you, MOM, you can stop now. I don't think I can stand up." Her knees buckled and Miguel swooped her into his arms.

Rosemary held onto him and tried to clear her head. "Is the surgeon dead?" she asked. She and Miguel looked. He was moaning on the floor, holding his jaw while the top of the scrub suit blotted up blood from the hole in his chest. "I wonder who it is," she whispered.

Miguel strode over and squatted down. With Rosemary on his lap, he pulled off the green cap, then pushed the surgeon's hands away and yanked down the mask.

Rosemary gasped in disbelief. She squeezed her eyes shut as a wave of nausea hit the back of her throat. It couldn't be—couldn't—

"Do you know her," Miguel asked?

Rosemary opened her eyes and looked again at the prostrate figure. "It's Melenie Bregen," she whispered. A large, warm tear began a slow descent down Rosemary's cheek.

Chapter 27

September 20
Thursday evening

Shelley Bigelow stormed down the corridor toward the personnel office. This whole scenario burns me up, she thought. It's absolutely infuriating. Send those nurses home, but don't send these nurses home. Close down those nursing units, but don't close down these nursing units. Do this, do that, then don't do any of it — we were just joking, folks. We actually wanted to test the evacuation procedure, ha-ha. Wasn't it fun? Damn it all, it's no way to run a hospital.

She jerked the door open and bumped into Annette Lutz, the personnel director, who was on her way home.

"Where the sweet hell is Sergeant Dow?" Shelley demanded.

The director's bottom lip quivered. "Number one, I don't deserve to be spoken to that way. Number two, I don't give a rat's ass where Dow is, although he's using *my* office and tying up *my* phones, and I can't get my job done. I can no longer handle the press. I need guidance . . . I . . ." Spontaneous tears began falling down Annette's face. ". . . need Mrs. Cleaveland."

Shelley took hold of Annette's shoulders. "I'm so sorry. It's been hard on everyone." Shelley, who'd been trained and experienced in her job to allow empathy into her emotions at work, but never sympathy, now couldn't help herself. Her eyes dampened quickly, and she fought the tears that beat on her heart, demanding to be freed.

"I hear she's dead," Annette sobbed.

"I've heard that rumor, too, but it's not true." If it is true, Shelley thought, this woman will mistrust me forever for lying. She didn't care. For now, they needed mutual reassurance. "I didn't mean to be rude to you. Go on home and forget this place."

"I will, until tomorrow." Annette slung her purse over her shoulder. "Thanks for listening."

Shelley watched her go. For some reason, she felt ten years older. Going to the far office door, she stood and watched Mike Dow speak into the phone. When he saw her, he motioned her inside.

"I want her out of here immediately," he said into the receiver. "She gave the ambulance drivers the slip earlier today, and I don't want her waking up and roaming around again. I don't care what her doctor says. She's a total nutcake, Sam, and she can recuperate at the state hospital. He's *what?* Dammit all.

279

Okay, okay, but see that it's done quickly." He clanked the receiver into the cradle. "Dammit! Physicians are more afraid of being sued than of being compassionate. Believe me, Mrs. Bigelow, Santa Claus will stop delivering presents before I put my body into a hospital. What do you want?"

"My sanity. You took it away and I want it back again."

Mike shrugged.

"Totally uncooperative. Well, my next request is to know what the hell is going on. In case you've forgotten, I have hundreds of sick people being transferred to other hospitals because of you."

Mike sensed that Shelley was just getting started on a lengthy sermon for he held up his hands in protest. "Wait just a minute. Have you suddenly forgotten why I wanted the patients out of this insane asylum?"

"I haven't forgotten anything. The problem is a total lack of communication. While you gallivant around chasing some berserk kook, we're all expected to know what's going on. The grapevine is running rampant with crazy rumors. One person tells me that you've ordered dietary closed because you think the food might be poisoned. Another person tells me that Mrs. Cleaveland is dead. I've heard that Fred Plexico, the vice chairman of the board, is taking her place. I've heard that Dr. Harris got stabbed in the operating room. That's just the beginning, Sergeant Dow. Physicians are bullshit. They're threatening never to admit another patient to Riverside. Patients and their families have had it, too, and I've had about enough of their complaints."

"I appreciate what you're saying, Mrs. Bigelow, and I can assure you that everything will return to normal . . ."

"When!"

"Oh, probably by tomorrow."

"Is that right. Well why don't you tell that to the hospital staff, and the patients, and the physicians. They'd simply love to hear such good news, after what's gone on today. While you're at it, you can call up all those hospitals and ask them to please send our patients back. We've simply changed our minds. Then you can listen while they tell you, 'No dice, Trixie. We got 'em, we'll keep 'em.' " She held a hand to her aching brow. "So, do I open up my nursing units and operate at full staffing levels?"

"Yes."

"Why?"

Mike gave her a puzzled look. "Why what?"

"Why can I resume normal operations? What has happened that would make you change your mind?" Shelley paused. "Did you catch the schizo?"

"Yes."

She plunked into a chair and let exhaustion and all her pent-up emotions flow freely. In a whisper, she asked, "Who is it?"

"Melenie Bregen," he answered.

Shelley swallowed hard. "Melenie was catatonic . . . she never moved from her bed."

"She faked it," Mike said. "She must have bugged out of her room between medication and meal times and psych evaluation appointments. I've got a lot more to learn about her."

"How did you find out?"

Mike told her the story. "Melenie's had surgery for a broken jaw and a stab wound, both compliments of Miguel Galindo. After she's had an EEG, she'll be transferred to Metropolitan State Hospital. Rosemary had stitches in her arm, and she's on Sinclair Two now. For the sake of privacy, I would appreciate it if you'd keep her whereabouts quiet."

"Impossible. People want to know everything Rosemary does and says."

Mike nodded in agreement. "But it's nighttime now and most of the staff are home watching TV. If anyone should ask what happened, you can say we caught the killer, and things can return to normal."

"No one's going to ask me because I'm going home to soak in a hot tub . . . maybe even have a highball."

On her way home, Shelley stopped at the Harvard Square kiosk and bought the evening edition of the *Boston Globe* newspaper. The headlines increased the pounding in her skull:

RIVERSIDE HOSPITAL NUMBED BY PSYCHO

Down the street from the kiosk, sitting at a dark corner table of The Tavern, were four figures huddled together so tightly and whispering with such concentration that the waitress had trouble getting their order, and she wanted them to order something because they were monopolizing her table. To break them up, she considered plopping four steins of beer in the middle of the group, but they didn't look like

282

beer-drinking types.

"We've got some nice salami subs," she said, "or maybe you'd prefer our special?"

". . . she knows, I'm certain of it . . ."

"It's liverwurst on pumpernickel with home fries."

". . . they'll blame the psycho . . ."

"No, huh, then how about pickled bird tongues wrapped in hog casings and served on a bed of cold mashed potatoes. Real good for what ails ya."

". . . put a bug in her room . . ."

The waitress turned on her heel. She would bring them four beers and a bill.

Exhausted, Mike patted his pocket to feel for his car keys. The day had been long and he yearned to give Dolly a squeeze, gulp down a beer, and hit the sheets. For a second, he thought about checking on Pete and Rosemary, but decided they were in good hands. He headed for the employees entrance off Amherst Street where his car was parked. From the stairwell, four men came into the corridor ahead of him.

"Mr. Villareal," Mike said, "isn't it a little late to be leaving the hospital?"

Villareal turned. "Who are you?"

"Detective Sargeant Mike Dow."

Villareal's bodyguards shrank back. Miguel Galindo smiled.

"Not at all, sir. It has taken me quite some time to pack up all my belongings."

"Patients usually get discharged at the lobby door."

Miguel answered. "The limousine is so big that I felt it would block less traffic in this area."

Mike couldn't understand why he still had doubts about these men. Galindo had saved Rosemary's life. Villareal had created no disturbance. His bodyguards had stayed in their motel rooms.

Villareal interrupted his thoughts. "You could do me a big favor, Sergeant Dow. I tried to see Mrs. Cleaveland, but she's been moved to another room. I have a gift for her. Would you see that she gets it?" He handed Mike a white envelope.

Before opening it, Mike asked, "Are you flying out of the country?"

"Soon," said Villareal. "I have just one more appointment in Cambridge. It's for what you would call the second stage of my surgery. Look inside the envelope."

Mike lifted the flap and peered inside. A low whistle escaped from his lips. "You gotta be kidding."

"Tell her it's for the computer's memory expansion, and tell her I enjoyed staying at her hospital." Villareal patted Mike's shoulder and left with his men.

Mike put his car keys in his pocket and headed upstairs. Inside the envelope was a check, made payable to Rosemary Cleaveland, for two million dollars.

"My army will chop you down!" Melenie screamed between her teeth. Her fractured jaws were freshly wired shut and Louise, an EEG tech who'd been called back on duty, cringed with the pain Melenie must be suffering.

"All the machine people will die," Melenie hissed. "In the name of the Buddha and all that is holy, let me *go!*" She twisted furiously, trying to release the straps holding her wrists to the frame of the stretcher.

Dr. Holiday stood near her head and asked, "How much chloral hydrate was she given?"

Louise consulted Melenie's computerized medical record. "She should still be drowsy from the anesthesia and pain meds. Let's see. She was on trifluoperazine, then Haloperidol preoperatively. They gave her Demerol and atropine before surgery. Here it is. In the recovery room they tried to give her a five hundred milligram capsule of chloral hydrate but she spit it out. Jeez, I thought she was in a motor vehicle accident or something, but here it says paranoid schizophrenia . . ."

"Never mind," Dr. Holiday said, producing a syringe and tourniquet from his pocket. "Let's give her this."

The tech looked at the syringe. "What is it?"

"Calpain. It's a synthetic brain enzyme."

"Never heard of it."

"It's new." He held it out to her.

"You mean experimental?"

He hesitated. If he said yes, she would refuse to give it for all experimental drugs had to be approved by the pharmacy and therapeutics committee first. "No," he lied. "It's new in that it now comes in intravenous form. The pill's been around for a few years."

"Oh. Well anyway, I'm not certified to give I.V. medications."

Dr. Holiday shrugged and put the tourniquet around Melenie's upper left arm, then tried to swab her skin with an antiseptic. Melenie fought him off. "Hold her still, dammit."

"Get away from me you cocksucker! I will *not* be a machine!"

Louise pushed Melenie's arm against the sheets while Dr. Holiday carefully injected the liquid.

Several minutes later, Melenie was asleep. Holiday instructed Louise to proceed with the EEG. While she placed the electrodes on Melenie's scalp, Dr. Holiday excused himself to call his office.

Funny, Louise thought. She glanced up at the wall clock and noticed it was nine-thirty. Surely his office staff had gone home. Maybe he liked talking to his answering service. Suddenly an uneasiness prickled in her stomach as she recalled what Sally Rich, the day-shift tech, had told her about Holiday's earlier cases. A patient named Silverstone never awakened after the procedure. It had occurred again yesterday, with a woman named Ovaline, or something, and Sally had said that Holiday made a telephone call during both procedures. Sally said he'd lied to her about his office hours. Louise was about to place another electrode on Melenie's scalp, but curiosity got the better of her. She tiptoed over to the computer terminal and typed:

How many patients have not awakened after having an EEG?

On the monitor screen was: THREE.

She typed: Who?

JACOB SHOEMAN, DUNCAN SILVERSTONE, AND OVALINE LEE.

She typed: Why did it happen?

THEIR MEMORIES WERE USED FOR RESEARCH PURPOSES.

Louise swallowed hard. It had been done intentionally? She stared at the monitor, trying to figure what was going on.

Does anyone know about this? she typed.

THE RESEARCHERS KNOW.

Damn this computer, she thought. It never gives you what you want. She typed: Does Mrs. Cleaveland know?

YES.

Louise felt light-headed. She couldn't believe that administration would sanction anything so inhumane. They're all monsters, she thought, clearing the screen. She went over to the office door and pressed her ear against the wood.

Holiday was saying, ". . . on the garbage tape. Use the solar computer, though. We don't want MOM affected. Yes, I'll be over right afterwards."

A loud knock on the corridor door made Louise jump out of her skin. She went over and peered out.

"Is the psycho ready yet?" an ambulance driver asked. "This is going to cost someone a bundle, having me wait around like a taxicab driver."

"I'll need at least another half hour."

He moaned. "I'll be in the E.D. coffee room. Let me know."

"Hey," she yelled to him, "what do you mean by the psycho?"

He turned. "You've got the Ripper in there, the

287

one whose been chopping everyone into hamburger."

She closed the door slowly, looked over at Melenie, and a fear as deep as the hot core of the earth burned inside her stomach. That's the psycho? she thought. I've got the psycho in here, with me, and I've got to touch her? No way, I can't do it.

Holiday opened the office door. "Aren't you finished yet? Come on, come on. I have to be out of here in fifteen minutes."

"I . . . I . . . can't . . ."

"Yes, you can. I'll set up the machine."

With hands trembling like leaves in an autumn wind, she finished applying the leads to Melenie's head while praying that the woman wouldn't wake up and break through the leather straps. She joined Holiday at the EEG machine.

"Do you have an emergency case?" she asked.

He scooted a chair closer to the master board. "No."

"Wife want you home for dinner?"

He looked at her. "It's none of your business, young lady."

"I was just curious. You always make telephone calls during a procedure."

"I have a patient caseload that would keep two physicians busy. Sometimes I think I'm nuts doing it all by myself."

Having him sit next to her made her skin crawl. By turning her head ever so slightly, she could see his profile, and for the first time since her employment, she really scrutinized him. He was painfully thin. The skin over his face was taut and shiny. Once again, she tried to guess his age but couldn't. He was wearing a polyester gray suit, about as noncommittal as a man could wear, and yet he *would* wear a plain suit. Monsters didn't go about in flashy Ralph Loren sports clothes.

"Come on, come on," he said.

She started the machine rolling, and they watched the pen writers scratch across the paper.

"Are you looking for anything in particular?" she asked.

"Yes."

"What if this patient gorks out?"

"I beg your pardon?"

"Like the ones you did earlier."

"Which ones did I do earlier?"

"Mr. Silverstone."

Still watching the pens, Holiday asked, "What do you know about him?"

"The day-shift tech told me the man never woke up."

Holiday was silent for a moment. "Speculation," he said finally, "can be a disease of undying curiosity, which most hospital employees seem to have contracted. Should you or your friends begin to reason from axioms rather than from conjecture, you could then formulate a concrete, intellectual conclusion about Mr. Silverstone. To say the patient never woke up means (a) he's dead or (b) he remains in a state of sleep over an extended period of time. He is neither dead nor has he been asleep for more than three days. For your information, Mr. Silverstone received a large dosage of chloral hydrate because he had difficulty relaxing. He will be awake and functioning normally in another day or two. In addition, he volunteered to be a candidate in the CRL program, about which I have no time to discuss. This patient is in delta sleep. Let's wrap this up, shall we? Give me the wave complex between the right anterior and mid-temporal electrodes."

Even though she wanted to tell him that he was a monster, she did as he asked. The sooner they finished, the sooner she'd be rid of both of them. Tomorrow, she'd look for employment elsewhere. They heard a soft whimper behind them, and both looked over toward Melenie's sleeping form. She appeared fast asleep.

For some strange reason, Louise felt as if Holiday were smiling. She glanced at him and saw that he was watching the pen drawings.

"Give me deep left anterior to mid-temporal."

She switched buttons, heard a groan, then glanced at Melenie again. The woman's back was arched, and the look on her face was out of a science fiction magazine. Louise had never seen anything so bizarre. Within the deep fissures of Melenie's brain, the lights seemed to be going out and it must have hurt. All those billions of neurons screaming in agonizing pain for her whole face opened up as wide as it would go; eyes became vast pools of brown water the depths of which churned in dreadful anguish. The lips were pulled back, and the wires holding her jaw in place strained to keep her teeth together. Louise heard a high-pitched shriek as if Melenie were trying to retreat from the forces of a brain under siege. Louise jumped up, not sure whether to assist Melenie or to flee. She looked at Holiday who was watching the inked pens with fascination. There *was* a smile on his face. She had to report this! Louise fled out the door, into the corridor, and toward the safety of the emergency department where she felt, God help her, she might find some remnants of sanity in this holy hell-pit of a hospital.

Chapter 28

September 20
Thursday evening

Rosemary's eyelids fluttered open. Within seconds she focused on Pete's face and smiled.

"You've got more stitches in you than in my great granny's sequined evening gown," Pete said with a chuckle. He sat next to her bed holding her right hand. Her left forearm was wrapped in a thick white dressing.

"They all hurt, too. I feel like a sail cat."

"A what?"

"A cat that's been run over so many times that you can peel it off the pavement and sail it like a Frisbee."

"Rosemary!"

She smiled. "Am I on Sinclair Two?"

"Yeah, room two-oh-seven. I'm right next door. Rosemary, honey, would you please tell me what the sweet hell you were doing in the computer room? Pat Peters was worried sick, and I couldn't concentrate on my chess game."

"Something you said this morning gave me an idea about MOM, and I wanted to check it out."

"You could have *told* someone where you were going. Anyway, what did I say that was so damned important?"

"If you don't ask a question, you won't get an answer. I wanted to find out . . ." Rosemary's eyes grew large as she recalled what MOM had told her. "Pete, have you ever heard of a place called Cambridge Research Laboratory?"

"No."

"They manufacture memory beads according to specification, and I think each patient specifies what memory he wants. Remember I told you about two patients named Duncan Silverstone and Ovaline Lee?"

Pete nodded.

"Their memories were . . ." She tried to clear her head. "Put onto tape discs. The information on the discs are made into microchips that are covered with silastic so they can be implanted into the brain." As Rosemary remembered her conversation with MOM, Pete raised a skeptical eyebrow.

"Senor Villareal received a bead of intelligence taken from Duncan Silverstone! Duncan was a renowned geologist, a professor at M.I.T., a world authority on petroleum; and Pete, Ovaline Lee's memory was taken for Willard Scotch."

"The mayor?"

"Yes!"

"I see."

"Fawn Glassail's had a bead implant, too. She has Dr. Jacob Shoeman's memory, the famous neurosurgeon."

"Are you still dreaming?"

"Yes . . . I mean, no. MOM told me."

"I think your computer is bonkers," Pete said, sitting back and staring thoughtfully at the ceiling. "You know, babe, it's not a bad idea. Think what you would know if you had a memory bead inserted into your brain." Pete smiled and held up his hand. "Want to learn French? Here, open up your skull and pop in this beaded tape cassette. Here's one on gardening, and another on the entire diplomatic history of World War Two. Silicon and silastic, huh. It's got potential and infinite application."

While Pete mused, Rosemary lay back on the pillow and closed her eyes. The narcotizing effect from her last pain medication made her sleepy.

Pete tapped his finger on an imaginary cigarette holder. *"Oui,* madam does not want zee brain bead today? Zen zee famous surgeon can gif you beeg silicon beads in your bosoms. Madam can zen penetrate Russia and when she talks to zee prime minister, she turns her nipple to zee correct radio frequency and transmits every one of his words to zee United States. Hah, I theenk you've got something there."

Rosemary whispered. "You're the one who needs psychotherapy."

"Non, non, madam. I would rather be beaded than treated."

They were silent for a few minutes, Rosemary lapsing into sleep and Pete into personal thoughts. He was happy to be with her, to have her alive and safe, thank God. The worse was over for both of them, and Pete ached to get back on the job. He looked down at her with tenderness. Her eyes were closed and he hoped she would sleep. She looked innocent, lying there with only a gown and a sheet covering her small frame. Mike was right, he thought. Hospitals were asylums for aching organs and battered limbs. You leave your brain and emotions at home, brother, 'cause nobody cares what you think or how you feel, unless you feel pain, of course. Hospital people thrive on pain. Their credo is humiliation and it starts when they put your clothes in a baggy and you in a johnny. Just try leaving your underwear on and someone will surely get it off: How can we measure your weewee or fix your privates? How can we take a rectal temperature or plunk you on a bedpan or pop a finger up there if you're wearing your jockies? Wear a brassiere? No, ma'am. The doc might want to feel for cysts. The nurse needs to hear the lub dub of your tender heart. Underwear? Absolutely not! We like having the old people sit spread-eagled in their geriatric chairs. It's okay if patients walk the corridors with their johnnies on backward (the strings go in the back, dumb head. Oh yeah? Well why didn't someone tell me?) We let everyone gaze upon your bare body. You are a nameless, naked number, lying exposed with your tits at attention. We keep it cold, lonely, and humiliating because we are in *control*, honey, not you.

"Pete?"

He glanced toward the door. His buddy, Mike, stood in the door frame looking rumpled and fatigued.

"Okay to come in?"

Pete waved him over.

"She asleep?" Mike whispered as he minced over on tiptoe.

Pete stole a look at Rosemary's sublime face. "Yeah. See the smile on her face? She's dreaming about me. Come, pull up a chair."

"Won't we wake her up?"

"Only if you do something offensive, like fart."

Mike winced and held a finger to his lips. "She'll hear you."

"It's okay. She knows all your bad habits."

Mike picked up a chair and put it next to Pete. "What about *your* bad habits?"

"I haven't any."

"That depends. Miss Manners says that one should never, ever pick your nose and eat it."

"I do that?"

"Only near lunchtime."

"They don't pay me enough for a mid-morning snack."

Mike leaned toward Pete. "I know what you mean. I only fart in the wintertime. It takes the chill off the precinct."

From the bed, Rosemary said, "You two are disgusting."

Pete took hold of her upraised hand. "Well, *you* have bad habits, too."

"Like what?" she said indignantly.

Mike bumped Pete's arm. "She eats chocolate and you know what that does."

Pete looked aghast. "Pimples?"

"Yeah, pustulous zits all over your face."

"Fanny, too, if you eat too much."

"Those are called boils," Mike said.

Pete spoke clinically. "That is correct. Boils pop and make deep cellulite dimples."

"None of that is a bit funny," Rosemary said. "My behind is tight and curvaceous, and any further cracks will only make me look weirder."

Mike slapped his knee. "That's a good one."

"Tell me about Officer Willis," Rosemary said. "Is he dead?"

Mike answered, "We're praying for him. Bregen took him by surprise and cut him up pretty badly."

"Melenie slammed his fingers in the door. I saw it happen. I heard his pain." She shuddered at the memory. "Is Melenie dead?"

"No. They've wired her jaw and sewn the hole in her chest. She's a total whacko, and no amount of therapy's going to get her back on square one."

"Why was she after me?"

"Because you approve the orders for new equipment," Mike explained. "I spoke with Dr. Stockman who said a paranoid schizo's mental problems start in childhood and slowly grow out of proportion. Stockman suspects that Melenie's father was an alcoholic, beat her regularly, or even took sexual advantage of her. Whatever he did made her hate him and because hating one's father is a terrifying feeling, she transposed her hatred onto all men, and subsequently to machines. The rape kicked her over the edge."

"Did we ever locate her mother?" Rosemary asked.

"I don't think so."

"It's such a pity. I wish we'd been able to help her."

"She was pretty far gone before the rape. I talked to Miss Pickle and found that the O.R. nurses disliked Bregen because she accused them of conspiring against her."

"Pickle never told me," Rosemary said. "How did Melenie know that I was in the computer division?"

"She followed you from the Gold Coast." Mike looked down at the floor as he considered telling them about Henry the housekeeper. No, he decided, they didn't need to know right now.

"She wasn't catatonic, was she, Mike?"

"She faked it. The nurses on her unit feel responsible for not knowing how often Bregen left to go chop someone down, yet they blame Dr. Stockman for not having her transferred to the mental health unit sooner. They didn't understand how to communicate with a catatonic, so they provided only basic nursing care and left her alone most of the time. She gave the ambulance drivers from Met State the slip earlier today. *That* created a stir." Mike smiled and shook his head. "Everyone thought she'd been put into the wrong ambulance."

"Why did she kill Ritchie Chisolm?"

"It's complicated. Computer access numbers might be confidential, but a user's location isn't, nor is the transmission . . . that's why Chad Mooney had to hide his material under different names. Recently, I found a few midnight transmissions between MOM and an unknown person, which now I believe was Bregen. They were made on the O.R. terminal. You can tell by looking at the series of numbers before and after each transmission. Miss Pickle told me that Bregen had a key to the O.R. suite because it was her job to order supplies before the day shift started. Her typings were weird, like she considered MOM her real mother. On Tuesday morning, an orderly was taking her to an interview room when they passed the main computer room and heard Ritchie kicking and yelling at MOM. The orderly claims she sent him to get a blanket for her legs, and when he returned, she was gone. Mike thinks she went into the main computer room, took the scissors from the table, hacked Ritchie to ribbons, and escaped up the back stairs."

"Why didn't the orderly report her missing?" Rosemary asked.

"Because when he checked her room, she was back in bed. He didn't think anything further about the incident."

"Not even when he heard about Ritchie?"

"No," Pete interjected. "Remember, you were in the area at the time. Employees figured you knew everything that had gone on. It wasn't until today, when word got around about the mysterious surgeon stabbing you, that the employees came out of the woodwork and told Mike about their missing uniforms and I.D. badges. Bregen stole them from lockers and laundry hampers."

Trying to ward off a growing urge to sleep again, Rosemary turned onto her side. Her heart ached for Melenie and the end of their friendship, caused not by conscious rejection, but by mental illness. Having lost trust in mankind, Melenie had sought relief within the dark caverns of her mind. But like a voyager discovering new territory without a map, she'd lost her way and gotten trapped within her own hell.

"She accused me of being a machine person, Pete."

"Yeah, that's the strangest delusion I've *ever* heard of. At first, you represented something like maternal authority to her. So, although her delusional voices were telling her to kill you, she couldn't, and instead, put the leg in your closet. Her mind deteriorated quickly, and you became the one responsible for turning people into machines. John Berry was responsible for ordering the machines that turned the staff into machine people. Knowing that he was a chain smoker, she put a can of opened ether in the wastebasket under his desk. She killed Myra Brady because she believed the CT scanner had turned Myra into a machine person. She thought Dr. Townsend was ruled by the electrocautery machine, so she broke the wires leading from it to the coagulator in hopes he would be electrocuted, although she failed to remember the insulating effects of rubber gloves. I don't think she knows the circulating nurse got it instead. She's been on a mission to eradicate everyone whom she feels has become a machine person, and you were her biggest threat. Not only have you been taken over but, egad, you approve the purchase orders and worst of all, you represent power."

Rosemary was silent as she thought about the havoc Melenie had created and wished there was something she could do for Officer Willis, and for all of Melenie's victims and their families.

Mike pulled an envelope from his pocket. "As

Senor Jorge Benedicto de Villareal was leaving the hospital, he asked me to be sure you got this." He handed Rosemary the envelope. "He also wanted you to know that he enjoyed his hospital stay. *Muchas gracias* and all that."

"What's inside?" Rosemary asked.

"A bank check, payable to you personally, for two million smackers."

"Hot shit," Pete said. "Now you can afford a shrink for MOM!"

Rosemary smiled. "Villareal is a nice man."

After Pete and Mike left, Rosemary fell asleep again. The carnival dream returned, but this time, she was flying out of control, past neon lights that looked like elongated fluorescent strings, past the ferris wheel which spun so fast it popped off its stanchions and bounced down the midway in front of her. She smelled fresh blood, felt it thicken around her body. The flight suddenly ceased. In front of her were millions of bottles, all the same size. A bony hand appeared and held out clothespins. "Sink a pin and win a prize, deary." The bottles began bubbling. Inside, liquids of every hue churned, then foamed, then gushed forth creating a mantle over her feet. Disgusted, she raised a foot, pulling up ligaments of slime. The bottles became attached to one another by long glass tubes, all ending in a brain the size of a dodge 'em car. Suddenly, the brain developed huge eyesockets with wires twisted inside and sparks of electricity, which rocketed toward her.

Rosemary awoke in a sweat and struggled off the sheet that twisted around her body. She sat up, held both side rails, and panted to catch her breath. She knew what the dream represented. She'd taken chemistry in school and had seen the original Frankenstein movie. No matter what Pete said about MOM, Rosemary had to find out for herself. Somewhere in the nightstand was the Cambridge telephone book. She slid sideways and poked her legs under the side rail. With her toe, she opened the bottom cabinet door, then sat still for a moment to catch her breath. She stared down and saw Villareal's envelope sitting on top of her purse. She should have had Pete put the check in her wallet. Catching the envelope between two toes, she lifted it up and caught it. The strap of her purse lay flat, and it took several tries to get the strap around her ankle. Slowly, she eased the purse up, caught it with her hand, and shoved the envelope inside. She reversed the procedure. "Whew," she said aloud. After resting a minute, she reached for the top drawer and pulled out the telephone book, but it slipped from her hand. "Damn!" This was not going to be easy. She wouldn't fit under the rail. Her only alternative was to scoot down the bed and off the end. Easing off, she used the rail to help her get to the nightstand and reach down for the book. A pain in her side took her breath, and she fell onto the carpet. With head leaning against the bedframe, Rosemary rested until the pain subsided. She felt for the book, plopped it into her lap, and rested again. Every movement sent new waves of pain in her side and arm. She wished Pat Peters was there to help her, but now that Melenie had been caught, Rosemary supposed that Pat had gone home.

After awhile, Rosemary opened the book to the Cambridge listings. She noticed a Cambridge Laboratory but nothing for Cambridge Research Laboratory. She pulled the telephone off the nightstand by its cord and dialed the hospital operator.

"The number of the Cambridge Research Lab is confidential," the operator said. "To whom am I speaking?"

"Mrs. Cleaveland."

"Oh, yes. The number is eight-six-four-two-two-three-one."

"And the address?"

"I don't have an address. Do you want me to dial the number for you?"

"Sure." While she waited, Rosemary wondered why no one had told her about the laboratory. She felt like the last telephone pole on a communication line. Maybe her assistants thought she was getting all the information she needed through MOM. It could be that they were in the dark, too.

"CRL," a voice said.

Rosemary thought quickly. In a gruff voice, she said, "This is biochemical. We've got your silastic order ready. Where do you want it shipped?"

"Straight to the lab."

"Could you give me that address again."

"What address do you have?"

"I can't read the damn invoice."

"Second Street, East Cambridge."

"Is there a number on Second Street?" she asked.

"Your driver knows where we are, lady."

She dropped the receiver onto the cradle and thought about Second Street. It was in a poor area of Cambridge, but it was close to Riverside, probably just a few minutes' drive. She wondered if he was the person on duty. An idea formed in her mind. Rosemary dialed her secretary's home telephone number. Peggy answered after the first ring.

"Hi, it's Rosemary."

"I'll be skunked. Do you know how many times I've tried calling you and visiting? No one will let me through. I didn't know if you were dead or alive . . . and the messages are out of control. Where are you, and when are you coming back to work?"

"Whoa there, Nellie. I'll tell you all about myself tomorrow. I need to know where my beeper is located."

"On my credenza."

"Thanks."

"Wait a min—"

Rosemary felt guilty about hanging up, but she didn't feel strong enough for a lengthy social chat. She dialed another number.

"Nursing office; Ilse Jensen speaking."

"Ilse, it's Rosemary Cleaveland . . ."

"How are you feeling? Is the nursing care all right? Can I get you anything? Boy, you gave us quite a fright."

"I'm fine, thanks. Do you have the key to Peggy's office?"

"I have the grand master. That should unlock her door."

"Will you get my beeper for me? It's on Peggy's credenza."

"Sure. Anything else?"

"No. Thanks, Ilse."

She dialed Pete's number. "Are you asleep?" she asked.

"Just about. Want me to come visit?"

"I'm pooped. Will you have breakfast with me in the morning?"

"I'll be there. Good night, babe."

"Sweet dreams."

Using the nightstand for support, Rosemary stood slowly, waited for the pain to abate, then went to the clothes closet and inspected her suit. No way can I pin it together and hide my blouse. If Melenie can swipe uniforms, she thought, so can I. She considered sneaking down to the uniform room in the basement, then changed her mind. The journey would sap her strength. Her first access to uniforms was in the nurses' locker room down the hall. She decided to make the trip after Ilse left. She shuffled back to bed, climbed on, and tried to relax. Was a trip to Cambridge Research Labs at eleven o'clock at night the wisest decision? If the place was locked, she'd learn nothing except its location on Second Street. On the other hand, if that man answered the door, she could talk him into letting her inside. If she didn't go tonight, Stockman and the other researchers might cover up their work tomorrow, and she had to know what was going on. It was *her* computer they were using.

Rosemary dressed slowly. She'd found a size twelve nurse's uniform, far too big, but she tied it snugly around her waist with a patient gown tie. She slipped into a grayish-white sweater that had seen too many years of wear and laundering. Unable to find white stockings or shoes, she put on her own beige pumps. The outfit would have made Shelley Bigelow send her home for sloppiness.

She went into the bathroom to put on her makeup. Going out alone was crazy, she thought. Should she tell someone where she was going? What about Mike? He'd go with her. Rosemary shuffled to the phone and dialed Mike's home number. After five rings, a sleepy voice answered.

"Dolly? This is Rosemary. Is Mike there? Oh. No, no message. Just tell him I wanted to chat. Thanks, Dolly. Good night."

Well, I tried, she thought. Anyway, I'll be back in less than an hour. No one will miss me. She stuffed her car keys, driver's license, and beeper into a pocket. After scribbling a note that read, Asleep, Do Not Disturb, she placed it in the card holder outside her door. She turned off the lights, closed the door, and tiptoed down the corridor. Rather than take an elevator and risk being seen, she took the stairs down one flight to the first floor. Before opening the door, she pressed her ear against it. Two men were talking. As she listened, her forehead prickled and she brushed it with the back of her hand, realizing suddenly that she was perspiring.

She jumped back as the knob twisted in its housing. She was not prepared! What would she say? The door swung open.

"Hello," an officer said, surprised to see someone in the stairwell.

Both officers stood in the doorway, and Rosemary's tongue felt like a natural exhibit in the Petrified Forest. She nodded.

"Going off duty?" the first officer asked.

"Yes," she said, her voice scratchy.

"Is that right?" He was looking at her uniform. "Where do you work?"

"The mental health unit." Psychiatric nurses wore their street clothes to make the patients feel more at home. Although her garb was four-fifths stolen uniform and only one-fifth street clothes, her answer seemed to satisfy them for they stepped aside to let her pass.

Chapter 29

September 21
Friday 1:00 A.M.

A chill in the night breeze stung Rosemary's cheeks and cleared her head. She unlocked the door of her car, slid inside, and pulled the shabby gray sweater tightly around her chest. Her hands shook as she slipped the key into the ignition. She listened while the engine cranked. "Come on, come on," she pleaded, anxious to get going. She turned the key again, pumped the accelerator, and finally the engine caught.

Driving east on Memorial Drive, she shook away the goose bumps that had risen on her skin as her body slowly defrosted, and relaxed. She touched her side. The pain was still there, but not as intense. She could live with the stabs of pain from her left forearm. Within an hour, she'd be back in bed, and that notion kept her going.

She swept under Longfellow Bridge and onto the

Cambridge Parkway. The Museum of Science was ahead, a large modern edifice perched on the dam that spanned the Charles River. She swung around the Royal Sonesta Hotel, onto Commercial Avenue, past the Lechmere parking lot, and Warehouse Liquors, and turned right onto Rogers Street. At the stop sign, she noticed a man sitting on the curb. He had a tiny round head with dark features in the center; a schmoo whose pasty skin gleamed white in the darkness. His beady eyes met hers, and as she started to look away, he stood up.

Without hesitation, she jammed her foot on the gas pedal and went straight across First Street without checking for cross traffic. Her heart thumped when she realized what she had done. In the rearview mirror, she saw him take a step off the curb and fall flat onto the road. A drunk, that's all he was, and she gave him no further thought.

She stopped at Second Street and tried to decide which way to turn. Overhead lights illuminated the tree-lined street. On her right was Cambridge Nipple Corp., and beyond that, a sign that read CRL. That had to be it. She turned the corner and drove slowly past the front of the building. Covering the front door was a chain-link screen like the ones used by jewelry stores for nighttime protection. The four front windows on the first floor were boarded up with large sheets of metal, making the building appear condemned. On the corner of Second and Bent Streets was the Greene Rubber building. She stopped and looked for a place to park.

Diagonally across the street was American Twine Office Park, a series of connecting brick buildings with a parking lot in front. She pulled into the lot, parked, and stared at the mysterious CRL building sandwiched between the Nipple and Rubber factories. All the windows were boarded up, even the ones on the second and third stories. The place looked deserted. Her hand rested on the door latch. If she was going to change her mind, this was the time. Rosemary knew East Cambridge. Although the area was changing, pockets of the old slum still existed. Rosemary looked at her watch. The Lechmere train station was a few blocks away. Muggers, looters, and rapists would be waiting now for the last train to pass for the night.

Suddenly, Rosemary noticed a figure lingering in the shadows across the street. She sucked in her breath and slid down so that only her eyes and the top of her head were above the dashboard. She watched. The person leaned against a tree and slowly glanced up and down the street. She recognized the schmoo! Quickly, he bent down, removed something from his sock, and went to the front door of the Nipple factory. After another quick glance, he busied himself with the lock. Within minutes, he disappeared inside the dark building. She felt an hysterical laughter welling up inside her. *She* was about to break in and enter the building next door. She hoped he'd trip a burglar alarm before she did.

Rosemary climbed out of her car and, as if taking instruction from him, she glanced up and down the street, saw no cars approaching, and quickly crossed over. Slipping into an alley between the Laboratory and Greene Rubber, she cursed herself for not having brought a flashlight. From somewhere in the night, she heard a dog bark, followed by a voice telling the damn mutt to shut the hell up.

She stumbled on an object, and her skin crawled with the idea that it was a rat. Feeling along the rough cinder blocks, she touched a piece of plywood that had once been a window, then another, and another, on toward the rear of the building. At the end, her hand moved over a metal slab; a door! She felt for a knob or handle, but the door was smooth. Various lights from other buildings and street lamps illuminated the rear parking lot. She walked around a dumpster and looked up at the loading dock.

To her surprise, the door was open a crack. A beam of light from within created a path that angled toward the cement stairs, an illusionary red carpet inviting her inside. As Rosemary took a deep breath and tried to muster her courage, she felt a warm furry object brush her leg. "Oh!" She jumped and looked down. A fluffy cat was ready to circle her legs again. She loved cats, and ordinarily would have patted this one on the head, but she didn't want it to follow her inside. She hissed at it. The cat scooted into the night.

Rosemary squared her shoulders and headed up the cement stairs. She pulled the door just wide enough to pass through. The delivery area was a huge room lined with crates marked Fragile: Glass Equipment, and chemical barrels marked Liquid: Store This Side Up. At the far end was another door. She put her ear against it, but heard nothing on the other side. Slowly, she pulled it open, slipped through, and turned to see four faces. "Good evening, Mrs. Cleaveland. We've been expecting you."

311

Rosemary was shocked to see Stockman, Holiday, and Glassail. They stood in a semicircle around her with a man she didn't know. They wore laboratory coats with CRL identification badges pinned to their lapels. The badge worn by the stranger read Arkip Budimer, PhD., CRL Director. He looked Middle Eastern. Fawn Glassail looked smug. Her chin was in the air, and her wry smile seemed to indicate that the tables were turned; she was now in Fawn's institution. Rosemary was most surprised at seeing Bob Stockman, her mentor and friend, closely associated with Glassail and Holiday. That he must condone their medical practices, and that they had expected her filled Rosemary with dread.

Even though it was one-thirty in the morning, they looked as if they'd just had twelve hours of deep sleep. Rosemary, on the other hand, felt exhausted, but she forced herself to appear controlled. She extended her right hand and said, "Dr. Stockman, how nice to see you. I have heard about this lab."

"I am sure you have, Mrs. Cleaveland." He took her by the elbow and began leading her to another door. The others followed. "To assuage your curiosity, my associates and I have planned a tour of the facility for you."

"If you could wait a few more minutes, Detective Dow would like to join us."

"Ah, Mrs. Cleaveland, please don't lie to me. I hate people who lie. Don't you agree, Dr. Glassail?" he said over his shoulder.

312

Fawn nodded.

"You see, we know you didn't inform anyone because we bugged your room. We are in the business of microcomputers with transistors so small you wouldn't be able to detect them with the naked eye. I could drop one into your hair and unless you used a brush or comb, it would stay there most of the day. So, we know you are here alone. Shall we begin?" He opened the door and led her to an elevator. They rose three flights and stepped out into a glass-enclosed room that gave her a panoramic view of the enormous electronic laboratory below. It was sectioned off into wedges that fanned outward, as if they were standing in the center of a large multi-petaled flower.

The view made her dizzy. Symmetry was distorted into unevenly shaped wedges where the largest section comprised a fourth of the laboratory while the smallest was about a tenth of the whole. Above certain wedges were overlapping square rooms seemingly balanced by the wall beneath.

It seemed as if both eighteenth and twenty-first century experiments were being conducted. In one section, Rosemary saw what appeared to be a giant's mushroom garden. On white plastic pedestals that slowly rotated around were cylindrical amber crystals rising toward the ceiling like stalagmites. In contrast, she saw ahead of her large vats of chemicals in every hue that bubbled and steamed and were connected by spirals of wiring as if they were awaiting the electrical storm that would breathe life into a mutable cadaver.

In another section, she saw large glass tubes of

lavender liquid and smaller ones of red liquid, and in all were floating what appeared to be cauliflowers — except she knew they weren't growing vegetables here. Those things had to be brains and they were moving! When one sank to the bottom of a tube, a mass of bubbles erupted from the bottom and floated the brain back up to the surface where it began a slow descent again.

The largest wedge-shaped section resembled a hive. Each hemispherical glass dome encased no more than six lab technicians who sat at fluorescent tables peering down microscopes. They wore blue uniforms and caps. Dr. Stockman followed Rosemary's glance and explained, "Those people work in air and temperature-controlled environments. They inspect microchips and remove defective ones with air pencils." He pointed to another section that contained huge pieces of equipment. "The chips are tested in those machines, and perfect chips are then sealed in vacuum tubes until we need them."

"And what do you need them for?" Rosemary asked.

Stockman smiled. "CRL manufactures memory beads according to client specification. For example, if you wanted to speak fluent Spanish, we would implant a bead containing the language, its grammar, derivations, loanwords, and slang."

"How do you implant the bead?"

"Through a procedure known as MRI-guided stereotaxy. Magnetic resonance gives us three-dimensional and sagittal images and provides coordinates that locate exactly the patient's hippocampal gyrus in the gray matter of the brain. During surgery, we attach an arched metal frame to the patient's head. On the frame is a measuring scale for precise guidance. The neurosurgeon cuts a tiny hole through the skull. Using a miniaturized ultrasound transducer he can penetrate the brain and proceed to the area which will house the bead. In all cases, we implant it into the hippocampus which is the seat of memory formation."

Although confused, Rosemary forced her weary mind to concentrate. There was a link here and she couldn't grasp what it was.

"How does the brain know what's on the bead?" she asked.

"Good question, Mrs. Cleaveland. After the bead is in place, we give the patient large dosages of synthetic fodrin and calpain in order to prepare the neural synapses for new memory. This is followed by a brief transmission of high-frequency waves which activate the bead. I wish I could be less clinical, but our work is extremely complicated."

"May I ask another question?"

"Certainly. I want you to learn all you can."

She looked at him directly. "Why?"

He hesitated briefly before answering. "Researchers love to share their work."

Rosemary knew that wasn't always true. Researchers share only after they have published their discoveries. "Could you manufacture a bead that would give me the location of Russia's ICBM missiles?"

He looked at her with curiosity. "Perhaps."

"How would you obtain that information?"

"Dr. Budimer, would you explain the procedure to Mrs. Cleaveland?"

315

"Certainly." The man stepped forward and pointed to a section of the lab that housed vast rows of magnetic tape units. "Those units are interfaced with the EEG machine here and at Riverside Hospital. We would fulfill your request by locating a Russian intelligence carrier, placing him on the EEG machine, and removing his knowledge."

Rosemary was stunned. These people sacrificed human beings and called it research. A flurry of questions came to mind. "Would you take the Russian's memory if you didn't have a specific order?"

"We might," Dr. Budimer said.

"Case in point," Dr. Stockman continued. "We were given a large research grant from a shipbuilding magnate who isn't as interested in gaining more knowledge as he is in eradicating the competition. We are now trying to locate his competitor."

Aghast, Rosemary whispered, "You would take a man's memory for no reason?"

"Please, please, eventually we will find a client."

"That's not the point!"

From behind her, Rosemary heard Fawn say, "Some people have closed minds."

Rosemary turned slowly. "That's not true. I believe in life, doctor. And I believe all of you have forgotten the criteria for using human subjects in your experiments. Can you produce a valid informed consent signed by each of the patients whom you destroyed? My God, who gave you the right to rob them of their normal lives?"

Dr. Stockman pressed a button on the console. After they heard a beep, he said, "Come." He turned to Rosemary. "The laboratory is quite new. Over time, we will perfect our procedures so that the knowledge a client desires will already be in our memory banks. Have you any further questions?"

"Yes. Have each of you had implants?"

"Just Dr. Glassail."

Enraged, Rosemary faced the woman. "And your specialty, doctor, is neurosurgery? Isn't it a shame the bead didn't give you surgical skills as well. The Massachusetts Board of Registration would like to hear about you, unless you've faked your license, too. Tell me, doctor, what competent nuerosurgeon is vegetating in a nursing home because of you?"

"That's not funny," Fawn said.

"Funny? Nothing is funny when you screw around with life, doctor. All of you must think yourselves beyond mortality. You're a thousand times more schizophrenic than Melenie Bregen, and a million times more dangerous."

Rosemary was desperate. She knew they had cooked up a scheme to get her out of the way. She also knew that someone was responding to Stockman's order to "come." Unable to escape the lab, her only alternative was to try to talk her way out. She took a deep breath and exhaled slowly to calm herself down. "Now you know my personal feelings. I am not beyond assisting in projects that might be lucrative to the hospital."

"Don't lower yourself," Glassail said.

Stockman intervened. "In what way could you help us?"

They heard a rap on the door. Two laboratory technicians entered. One man carried a hypodermic needle, the other had leather restraints. Rosemary felt faint. Keeping her eye on the men, she answered, "Monetarily . . . through Riverside's endowment fund."

"And how much are we talking about?"

"I could give you two million dollars today."

Stockman looked out over the laboratory. "Your release for two million? It's tempting, Mrs. Cleaveland, but you see, once we have your memory, we'll know how to get ahold of the endowment fund without you."

"The money isn't in the fund yet," she said desperately.

Stockman crossed his arms over his massive chest and looked at her like a college professor about to chastise a student for poor grades. "I can get any information I want from you through our computer system. What you haven't asked is how this laboratory is run. We couldn't have set it up or continued to run it without MOM Three's capabilities. Take her away, please."

"No, wait!" Rosemary pleaded. "I can help you, don't you see? As the head of Riverside, I can get you money, supplies, personnel, whatever you need!"

"You could," Stockman said, "but you won't." He motioned to the technicians.

The two men grabbed her. Rosemary cried out in pain. "Don't, please . . ." While one held her arms behind her back, the other slipped the hypodermic needle into the muscles of her left shoulder and squeezed hard on the plunger.

Chapter 30

September 21
Friday 3:30 A.M.

"What will you do with her memory?" Fawn asked.

The four doctors stood in the EEG control room of the Cambridge Research Lab, peering through a window at Rosemary who was having electrodes attached to her head by a female technician. The machine was smaller than the one at Riverside, but it, too, could make tracings of the brain's deepest activities and remove them.

When Stockman failed to answer, Budimer said, "Many people striving for higher level positions would pay a fortune to have a management bead. In fact, the chief executive officer at Suffolk County Hospital has been inquiring about an increase in his own intelligence."

Fawn was incredulous. "You've got to be kidding. He's more knowledgeable than she is."

Stockman glanced at Fawn. "You think so? Then why doesn't he have the foresight, guts, and ingenuity to have a computer like MOM? I think you underestimate Mrs. Cleaveland's abilities." Stockman, Glassail, Holiday, and Budimer watched the technician at work. "No," Stockman continued, "we'll use her knowledge for our own purposes. Riverside will need a new C.E.O., and Dr. Budimer will get the position."

"Me? I have too much work to do here and furthermore, I'm not trained to run a hospital."

Fawn interrupted. "Why don't we give Mrs. Cleaveland's memory to Dr. Budimer?"

"That's precisely what I had in mind."

Budimer opened his mouth to speak, but Stockman cut him off. In hushed tones, while he rubbed his hands together, Stockman said, "All the pieces of my plan are falling nicely into place. Having Mrs. Cleaveland out of the way makes our lives easier." He turned and faced the others. "With Dr. Budimer in charge of Riverside, and responsible for its assets, we can keep this laboratory operational for several more months, at which time, our patient caseload will be sizable enough to keep CRL in the black forever. Also, by the first of the year, MOM will have expanded memory. We'll capture every piece of intelligence currently available. We'll go after bank, stock, and payroll accounts."

"We're expanding too fast," Holiday protested.

"Don't be so gloomy, Hank. It'll take years for anyone to discover what we've been doing. And remember, the guts of the computer are located at Riverside, not here. MOM's been programmed to

320

offer no information about our research."

"That's a problem," Holiday interjected. "What if Chad Mooney tells the police?"

"Let him blab all he wants, Hank. Mooney doesn't know what we're doing. Believe me."

"Wait a minute," Budimer said. "If wrongdoing is traced to Riverside, then I'm the one who goes to jail."

"Don't be a horse's ass. C.E.O.s don't go to jail, they merely get put to pasture. It's called early retirement. At any rate, you're both failing to remember the bigger picture. It's true that to get our concept started, we needed healthy brains, but we're at a point where we can now find people with legitimate medical problems; people who've already deteriorated so that families don't want them and nursing homes won't take them. Their intelligence remains, albeit masked by physical or even mental losses, but we now know how to sift out the good from the bad and take just what we need. I honestly believe that after Mrs. Cleaveland, we'll be able to concentrate on these types of individuals. Discoverability will be more difficult then, and who's to say we're not actually providing a needed service?"

"Wait a minute," Fawn said. "I go along with everything you've said except the service bit. I've seen Duncan Silverstone and Ovaline Lee. They'll need institutional care forever, and that's a financial burden to society."

"No, no," Stockman said gruffly, "because we're going to give them intelligence beads. We'll bring them up to a level where they'll function normally in society."

Fawn nodded her head. "That's a wonderful idea. I think we should speed things up, though. Intelligence removal and bead implantation must occur in quick consecution." Excitement grew in Fawn's voice. "We could do it if the EEG was taken just prior to surgery."

Stockman patted her shoulder as if praising a student. "Yes, *in* the operating room!"

"What about me?" Holiday moaned.

"What about you, Hank. You'll still be the initial interviewer and the patient's primary physician. Your pocket will remain full."

"I suppose. Actually, I'd rather not be responsible for the EEGs anymore."

"Why not?"

"One of the techs was questioning me about patient outcomes. Rightfully so. Have you ever witnessed what happens to a person at the time his intelligence is being absorbed?"

Stockman waved his hands in the air to quiet the man down. "Of course I have. Now—"

"I haven't," Fawn said. "What happens?"

"Nothing that we can't improve upon."

They were interrupted by the hollow intercom voice of the EEG technician. "I'm ready."

The four doctors turned their attention to the viewing glass. Inside the room, Rosemary lay asleep with electrodes attached to her head. The tech looked up from the console and raised her thumb in the air, indicating she was ready.

In front of Dr. Stockman was a computer monitor, a keyboard, and a control panel with several different-colored buttons and switches surrounding a larger black handle, marked: Absorber. On the computer screen was:

ACCESS NUMBER:
PATIENT NAME:
MEDICAL RECORD NUMBER:
AGE:
ADDRESS:
PHYSICIAN:

and other identifying data. In the lower right corner was a constant green light that automatically gave the date and hour of day. Stockman typed in his access number, Rosemary's full name, and skipped the rest of the entries. He pressed the intercom button. "Tell me when."

The tech looked down at the movements of the inked pens. After a moment, she said, "Okay. She's in deep delta."

Dr. Stockman couldn't control the soft smile on his face. He fondled the handle as if it were a catapult to his goals. With a powerful shove, totally unnecessary for its operation, he pushed the handle down.

The four doctors watched Rosemary.

The tech watched the inked pens, then pressed the intercom button. "Dr. Stockman? You can activate the absorber now."

Stockman's smile faded and, instead, worry wrinkles formed on his brow. He stared at the technician who stared back at him. Pressing the intercom, he said, "I already did."

She hunched her shoulders in question.

"Arkim, what do you think?"

Dr. Budimer stepped forward. "I'm not certain

323

why it didn't take the first time. Try it again."

Stockman looked at the tech, an unparalleled master of the EEG machine. He didn't doubt that she'd checked every lead before starting, but because he'd never had to activate more than once, and because he didn't want to kill Rosemary, he said into the intercom, "Are her tracings normal?"

The tech mouthed the word yes.

Still watching, he felt for the black handle, hesitated, and then pressed it down and held it for a moment.

All eyes were on the tech who watched the tracing. Soon, she looked up at them with a twist on her face that indicated she didn't understand.

Stockman didn't either, and now he wasn't sure what to do.

"We could do the procedure at Riverside," Holiday suggested. "Their machine is functional."

"We are *not* using that machine any longer. You told me yourself that the techs are suspicious. Do you think for a second they would help you do a procedure on Mrs. Cleaveland? They would not. And furthermore, how do you suppose we could get her in the door without someone recognizing her?"

Arkim Budimer spoke up. "You could cover her up and pretend you're transporting a body."

"That's stupid," Fawn said. "Bodies are taken out, not in."

"That's the whole friggin' problem with this lab. We don't have backup equipment, and I can't get a repair crew in at four in the morning." In exasperation, Stockman pounded one fist into the other. "We'll have to think of something else."

Fawn's disappointment vanished. "What if we got her into the O.R. as an emergency neuro and implanted a bead?"

"What bead! The political history of Southeast Asia? Webster's unabridged dictionary? Oh, I know." Stockman tapped his forehead. "Let's make her even more knowledgeable about computers. We'll give her the high-tech bead! What are you saying, Fawn? Have you lost your senses?"

"We can't take her memory, correct? I mean, not on this machine."

"Correct."

"And we don't want to kill her . . . just put her out of our way, permanently?"

"Right."

"So let's make a bead from the garbage tape."

The small control room was deadly silent. To this point, no one had considered using the garbage tape for any purpose other than to fill it up and then discard it. On the garbage tape were the fears, phobias, nightmares, spooks in the closet, hatreds, violences, and all the tortured human emotions experienced by Jacob Shoeman, Duncan Silverstone, Ovaline Lee, and Melenie Bregen.

When no one spoke, Fawn said, "We've got no other choice."

Slowly, Stockman leaned toward the intercom. "You can take her off," he said, "but keep her sedated. I'll give you further instructions shortly."

The tech nodded.

Stockman left the control room with the others and headed for his office. "How do we get her into the O.R.?"

"Simple," Fawn said. "I'll get scrub wear and a stretcher and bring them out to the car. Dr. Holiday can stand guard at the employees' entrance and let us know when to bring her in. Once she's in, the rest is easy. We'll roll her into surgery and then notify the on-call team. It won't take too long to get set up."

Holiday asked, "Won't anesthesia recognize her?"

"Sure, but I'll put together an emergency department record that states she fell down the Sinclair building stairway. No one will know she left the hospital."

Stockman shook his head. "I wish Dr. Townsend were here. He'd be able to get her in and do the surgery without questions."

Fawn was indignant. In a voice that would freeze air, she said, "I am quite capable of pulling this off."

"Maybe so, but you've only got third assistant surgical privileges. How do we get around that one?"

"Emergencies eradicate the rules. I'll simply tell the O.R. team that I'm the only one on duty and able to perform brain surgery."

Stockman thought over the alternatives. "We could take our EEG tech to Riverside and do the absorption there."

"Yes," Holiday agreed. "That's a better idea."

"What if that machine won't activate either?" Fawn said. "We'd lose time. I also don't want to be wheeling Mrs. Cleaveland around the corridors. This has got to be fast, from entry to surgery."

"But I don't like the idea of surgery," Holiday said.

Fawn glowered at him. "Then *you* think of something else."

"Hold it," Stockman interjected. "I don't like the idea of surgery either, but I don't want to risk moving her to EEG and then to surgery if the machine's broken. We have to make a decision."

"You're running scared," Holiday said. "In any normal circumstance, you'd do the EEG first on the assumption that the machine worked."

Budimer spoke up. "If I recall what you told me, the psychotic patient ruined several of the machines."

"Just the electrocautery."

"You don't know that, Fawn," Stockman said. "She ruined the CT scanner, too."

"She did not."

"She did. Several burned-out wires had to be replaced. We'll go with surgery for Mrs. Cleaveland." He telephoned the bead division. "This is Dr. Stockman. I want you to prepare a bead from the garbage tape . . . *you heard me!* When it's ready, bring it directly to the O.R. at Riverside. How long will it take? Good."

He hung up. "You'll have it in less than an hour."

"I know who that woman was." Bob Hanover, a CRL technician, held up the red tape that contained what they called garbage. He looked at it steadily. "It was Rosemary Cleaveland, the head of Riverside Hospital."

"I never saw her before," said Joyce, another tech who also worked the night shift. "Do you want me to boot that in?"

"Are you crazy? If this were booted into MOM, she'd go berserk. I'd hate to imagine what would happen."

Joyce looked at Bob curiously. "I don't understand. Whenever memories have been borrowed, all that garbage goes through MOM's system."

"One at a time, Joyce. MOM's only had one set of someone's garbage at a time. For this entire tape, we have to use the solar minicomputer which is not connected to MOM in any way."

The two techs were in a room within the bead division at CRL where microprocessors transferred information from tapes to beads. For illumination, ultraviolet red crystals were recessed into the ceiling, giving the techs eerie crimson faces.

"Mrs. Cleaveland looked pale, like she was sick or something," Bob said as he placed the tape in the solar console.

"Maybe she's got the flu."

"Yeah," he said absently. "I wonder why she wanted a bead made from this tape. Jeez, I wouldn't think of implanting it in anybody."

Chapter 31

Standing at the nurses' station on Sinclair Two, Mike Dow's face was so red with fury that he looked like he might pop. *"Where the hell is she?"* he screamed at the nurses. "I want to know who checked her last?" Before any of the night-shift nurses could respond, he continued. "Bunch of incompetent assholes. Don't even know where your patients are."

The charge nurse interrupted. "You have no right speaking to my staff in that tone of voice."

He raised his voice again. "This is an emergency, woman, . . . *think!*"

Flora Smith, a sixty-two-year-old nurse who had grown up in the era when physicians intimidated nurses by either yelling at them, blaming them for their own mistakes, or punishing them for whatever guilt trip their wives had put them on, spoke up. "I believe the nursing supervisor saw Mrs. Cleaveland last."

"What nursing supervisor?"

"Ilse Jensen."

"Call her up here, pronto."

329

"She went off duty at eleven-thirty."

"Get her out of bed. I want to see her."

Flora called the supervisor's office. To her surprise, Ilse was still on duty, apparently covering for a sick night-shift supervisor. By the time Ilse arrived, Mike's fury had gained enough energy to rank a twelve on the Richter scale, and no amount of temperate platitudes would calm him down.

"What may I do for you?" Ilse asked.

Between his teeth, he said, "Mrs. Jensen. I understand you were the last to see Mrs. Cleaveland, and I would like to know what happened to her."

"What are you talking about?"

Where the hell is she?

"Don't you yell at me, mister. The last time I saw her was about eleven o'clock. She was in her room and about to go to sleep. To my knowledge, she is still in her room, fast asleep."

"She is not."

"Did you look in the bathroom?"

"Don't get smart-assed with me, Mrs. Jensen. She is not in her room."

Ilse looked at the group of nurses, orderlies, and aides who were standing around the station. Several shrugged. "Has anyone gone into Mrs. Cleaveland's room since I left?"

The charge nurse defended her staff again. "She put a note on her door that said not to disturb her. With all that's gone on around here, we wanted to respect her wishes."

"Do you have the note?" Ilse asked.

Mike handed it to her. "It's her handwriting."

"Well then, I guess I'm the last to have seen her.

She called and asked me to bring the beeper from her secretary's office. She never said why she wanted it, and I felt it was none of my business to ask. We talked for a few minutes about restaffing the units, and how many patients we could expect to be transferred back to Riverside. She looked tired so I left."

"Did she make any phone calls while you were in there?"

"No."

"Did she mention anything of concern to her?"

"Like what?"

"I don't know like what . . . like maybe needing to visit someone?"

Ilse thought through her conversation with Rosemary. "She did mumble something about the computer. I begged her pardon, but she said it was nothing so I didn't pursue it."

Mike grabbed the phone and dialed the computer division. When a voice answered, he explained who he was and asked if Rosemary was down there. She wasn't. "What's her beeper number?" he asked Ilse.

She picked up the phone and dialed Rosemary's number. Everyone watched her place the receiver to her ear and listen. After a few moments, she hung up. "No answer."

"How far do those things transmit?" Mike asked.

"Not far. She's carrying an in-house beeper."

They stared at each other. Either Rosemary was in the hospital and not answering or, more likely, she had left. "The telephone lines," Mike said. "Are they connected to the computer?"

"Yes."

Mike looked at the terminal on the desk. "Who

can type quickly?"

An aide said, "I took typing in school. I used to do sixty words a minute."

"Sit right down and type: Has Rosemary Cleaveland called the hospital within the past four hours?"

On the screen was the word: NO.

"When and where did she last communicate with the computer?"

TIME: 3:35 P.M.
DATE: SEPTEMBER 20
LOCATION: C.P.U.

"That was yesterday afternoon," Ilse said, "when she was stabbed. Ask where Rosemary is right now."

UNKNOWN.

Ilse moaned. "This damn hunk of crap. It never gives you a straight answer."

"What do you mean?" Mike asked.

"It won't offer anything on its own. It withholds information until you ask it a precise question."

Mike thought it over. This nursing unit terminal gave limited access to its users. He'd have to ask more general questions and then narrow the field. He instructed the aide to type: Are you familiar with a person named Rosemary Cleaveland?

YES.

"Since your last communication with her, has she contacted you directly?"

NO.

"You already asked that," Ilse said.

"No, I didn't. I asked if she'd called the hospital."

The aide typed: Has she contacted the hospital indirectly?

"What are you doing?" Mike asked, and read the

332

screen.

NO.

"Wait a minute," he said. "Just what are we trying to get this damn computer to tell us?"

"Where Mrs. Cleaveland *is,*" Ilse said.

"It may not know."

Scowling, they looked at the screen as if it were a moron.

Two of the nurses excused themselves to care for their patients. The charge nurse let the rest of them go. As one of the orderlies turned to leave, he said, "I'd ask the damn thing if anyone has used her name in any transmissions since eleven o'clock last night."

Ilse looked at Mike. Mike hit the aide on the arm. "Do it!" The computer responded:

YES.

"Oh my God," Ilse whispered.

Unable to control his excitement, Mike yelled to the aide, "When?"

TIME: 3:46 A.M.

DATE: SEPTEMBER 21

LOCATION: CRL

He checked his watch: Over an hour ago. He hit the aide on the arm again. She winced. "Sorry. Ask what CRL stands for."

CAMBRIDGE RESEARCH LABORATORIES.

"Where is that located?"

"SECOND STREET, EAST CAMBRIDGE.

"Is she there now?"

UNKNOWN."

Mike said, "Ask who made the transmission."

I AM UNABLE TO GIVE OUT RESEARCH-ERS' NAMES.

Mike glared at the screen and, for want of something to abuse, felt like strangling the aide.

Carrying a full catheter bag, the orderly took a short cut through the nurses' station on his way to the utility room. He stooped and read the last few transmissions. "If I were you, I'd ask for what reason the transmission was made." The aide typed it.

TO PREPARE HER FOR AN EEG.

"What!" Ilse said.

"Why?" Mike instructed.

UNKNOWN.

"Blast this cockamamie terminal." Mike noticed the orderly. "Wait a minute, young man, don't go . . . what the hell are you carrying?"

"Urine."

"Well put it down somewhere and come here."

The man propped the bag between two stacks of medical records. When he turned toward the computer terminal, the bag sagged onto the counter.

"You know what we're trying to find out," Mike said. "Ask some questions that it'll answer."

The commotion at the nursing station had awakened Pete Tanner. Now, he stood in the doorway looking rumpled and sleepy. Surprised to see Mike, he asked what was going on. Mike filled him in. A knot of worry formed in Pete's gut, and he took over the questioning.

"Was the EEG done?" he said, and the aide typed it in.

NO.

"What was the difficulty?"

THERE WAS NO DIFFICULTY. ALL MA-

CHINES WERE OPERATIONAL AND CONTINUE TO BE.

"Paranoid, isn't it," Ilse mumbled.

Worry gave way to fear. Pete remembered that Rosemary had tried to tell him about patients who were not waking up after EEGs. What had she said? He racked his brain while the orderly gave instructions to the aide:

"What was the name of the individual who canceled the EEG?"

I AM UNABLE TO GIVE OUT RESEARCHERS' NAMES.

"Let's stop for a moment," Pete said. "We know where she is or was; we know someone was trying to do an EEG; and we know she did not have it done, thank the Lord." He said to Ilse, "Mrs. Cleaveland told me about a couple of patients who didn't wake up after their EEGs. Do you know who their physicians might be?"

Ilse's eyes widened. "Oh . . . my . . . heavens," she said slowly. "I pray this doesn't relate. Yes, it's Dr. Hank Holiday, in both cases. I asked him what had happened, and he said the problem was temporary. He mentioned using larger doses of chloral hydrate to put his patients into deep sleep."

"Who's Holiday?" Mike asked.

"A neurologist."

"You," Pete said to the aide. "Type this. Did Dr. Holiday order the EEG for Mrs. Cleaveland?"

I ONLY KNOW THE RESEARCHER'S ACCESS NUMBER.

Pete groaned.

"I know," Ilse said. "Let's ask *why* the EEG *wasn't*

done."

The aide typed in the question.

TWO ATTEMPTS WERE MADE TO PER-
FORM AN EEG ABSORPTION AND BOTH
WERE UNSUCCESSFUL.

"WHY!" Ilse shouted at the monitor. "Why won't
you just tell us what the hell is going on? Why do we
have to bottle feed you?"

The orderly knocked the aide's arm. "Would you
type—"

"If anyone punches my body again, I'm going to
quit. Really, it's totally unnecessary and aggravat-
ing."

"Sorry. I won't do it again," he said. "Would you
be so kind as to type the following: Mrs. Cleaveland
is very important to us. We are looking out for her
welfare. If we don't locate her soon, her life may be
in jeopardy. Would you please try, as hard as you
can, to help us locate her. We are afraid that without
your help, she'll die."

Pete, Mike, and Ilse were spellbound. This was
just a machine, incapable of anything but info-in
and info-out, and yet this orderly was pleading as if
the thing had emotions. What surprised them the
most was MOM's answer:

I KNOW THAT MRS. CLEAVELAND'S LIFE IS
IN JEOPARDY. EVERY PIECE OF ELECTRICAL
EQUIPMENT AT RIVERSIDE HOSPITAL, AT
THE STEREOTAXIC LEARNING CENTER,
AND AT CAMBRIDGE RESEARCH LABORA-
TORY IS CONNECTED TO MY CENTRAL
PROCESSING UNIT. THE EEG MACHINES AT
THE HOSPITAL AND THE LABORATORY ARE

INTERCONNECTED TO A HIGH SPEED MAGNETIC ABSORBER WHICH PULLS INFORMATION OUT OF A PATIENT'S BRAIN AND STORES IT ON MAGNETIC TAPES LOCATED AT THE LABORATORY. MRS. CLEAVELAND WAS CONNECTED TO THE EEG MACHINE AT THE LABORATORY. I KNEW IT WAS HER BECAUSE HER NAME WAS TYPED INTO THE COMPUTER. WHEN THE ABSORBER SWITCH WAS PULLED, I FAILED TO ACTIVATE IT.

Pete, Mike, Ilse, the orderly, and the aide stared at the monitor, stunned and speechless. Finally, Ilse turned to Pete and, as if the terminal had ears, whispered, "I don't understand why MOM is telling us all this when, just a minute ago, her bytes were sealed."

Pete whispered back, "I know. It may have something to do with her feelings for Rosemary."

Also whispering, Mike said, "Computers don't have feelings."

"I wouldn't be so sure of that," the orderly said. "I'm getting my master's degree at M.I.T. and you'd be surprised what they know, see, and feel." He asked the aide to type: "Will you interpret for us the researchers' names from their access numbers?"

IS SERGEANT MIKE DOW THERE?

"Yes."

Mike felt his skin crawl.

I WILL DO AS YOU REQUEST IF HE TYPES IN HIS ACCESS NUMBER.

Mike did.

37090 — ARKIP BUDIMER, PHD.

64111 — ROBERT STOCKMAN, M.D.

90935—FAWN GLASSAIL, M.D.

42342—HANK HOLIDAY, M.D.

"I don't believe it!" Ilse said.

"Neither do I," Pete said.

"Who's the Budimer guy?" Mike asked.

"Never heard of him," Ilse said.

The orderly started to bang the aide's arm, then stopped himself in midair and said, "Type: Who is Budimer."

THE DIRECTOR OF THE LABORATORY.

Pete held up his hands. "Wait a minute. *Wait* a minute. Now that we've got MOM's attention, and she knows we're interested in locating Rosemary, let's ask her again if she knows where Rosemary is right now."

"Good idea!" the orderly said.

The aide typed: Can you tell us where Mrs. Cleaveland is now?

IN THE OPERATING ROOM. HER MEDICAL RECORD STATES THAT SHE FELL DOWN THE SINCLAIR BUILDING STAIRS AND SUFFERED A BRAIN CONTUSION. SURGERY WILL BE PERFORMED TO ALLEVIATE PRESSURE ON THE BRAIN FROM SEVERE HEMORRHAGING.

"Let's go!" Ilse said.

"Wait a minute." Pete tapped the aide's arm. "Ask who the surgeon is."

FAWN GLASSAIL.

Chapter 32

September 21
Friday 5:00 A.M.

Rosemary's phony emergency department record was on the computer terminal screen in operating room 12. It read: During a fall down the back stairs of the Sinclair building, patient suffered a brain contusion. Bilateral pupillary dilation, bradycardia, unconsciousness suggest a subdural hematoma with increasing intercranial pressure. Microneurosurgical intervention indicated.

Orders:
    5% D/W, IV, 100 cc/hr
    ABGs
    Blood chemistry, lytes
    Routine hematology screen
    U/A
    02 & ventilation variables
    Cerebral variables

Circulation pressures

Demerol 75 mg. with Atropine 0.4 mg. I.M.

Drugged for surgery, Rosemary lay on the table, fast asleep. With her was Ann Grew, an on-call scrub nurse who was busy attaching Rosemary to the cardiac monitor and the small CT scan machine. She had started an I.V. and was counting the drips per minute in the flow chamber. The back tables and the large mayo stand were set up and ready.

Outside the chilly room, Dr. Glassail stood at the scrub sink about to start her five minute hand wash. She was scared. The next twenty minutes would have to go perfectly if she wanted to save the laboratory. For the third time, she glanced down the hall toward the swinging doors of the inner O.R. suite. Fawn awaited the arrival of the sealed glass tube which would contain a surgical instrument and, floating in the bottom, hidden from the other members of the team, the tiny garbage bead. Fawn also awaited Dr. Townsend's personal scrub nurse, Kate March, who had agreed to scrub in on this case. No other nurse could handle the bead as deftly and secretly. Without Kate's assistance, Fawn was terrified of failing again.

Dr. Stockman and Dr. Holiday drank instant coffee in the surgeons' lounge. They sweated, despite the chill from the central air-conditioning system. They knew that not only was Dr. O'Shaunnesy the on-call anesthesiologist who would be doing the case, but that he was friendly with Rosemary, and they had severe doubts about fooling him. They awaited his arrival in the O.R. with nerves shot to the shaking point.

Two nurses entered room 12 and said hello to Ann Grew. One was a rotund nurse who had worked at Riverside for the last fourteen years. The tall, thin one used to work in the utilization review department and knew Rosemary well from having to consult with her on the never-ending battle between physicians and Medicare rules. But Susan Olivera missed direct patient contact and had transferred to the O.R.

"Damn," Susan said. "I hate being on-call. Getting up from my snuggly bed to come to this ice box is torture, and to do brain surgery is ridiculous. We'll still be here when the day crew comes on."

The fat nurse, Helen Donovan, also shivered. At the work station near the door, she typed an order into the terminal for more heat.

"Are you about ready, Ann?" Susan said to the scrub nurse.

"*I'm* ready," she said, "but Kate March hasn't even arrived. Here, help me turn this patient onto her side. I've gotta shave the back of her head." Ann Grew had Rosemary half turned toward her. Neither Susan nor Helen could see Rosemary's face as they stood on the other side of the table. They slipped their hands under Rosemary and, together, the three women gently rolled Rosemary over, taking care not to disturb the lines and tubings. "There, thanks."

Helen Donovan left the room to scrub her hands. She would work the sterile back table, replenishing instruments and supplies for Ann Grew and Kate March who would work from the smaller mayo tables at the surgical site.

Susan Olivera began checking the equipment. As the circulating nurse, she would oversee the room.

Rosemary moaned.

"There, there," Ann whispered, "everything's just fine. We'll have you back to normal in no time. Poor dear. So much going on around here that you were probably walking in your sleep." As she spoke, Ann searched Rosemary's head for areas of broken skin. She found none. With her fingers, she felt Rosemary's scalp for indentations, lumps, or some sign of damage that would have caused a brain contusion. Her head felt normal. Curious, Ann bent down and lifted one of Rosemary's eyelids. The pupil was not dilated. She lifted both eyelids. They were equal in size and reacted to the light. She then placed her fingers on Rosemary's wrist and took her pulse. She counted sixty-eight beats per minute, and the pulsations felt strong and steady. "For someone about to undergo brain surgery, you seem just fine to me."

Prior to her job at Riverside, Ann had worked in the O.R. at St. Elizabeth's Hospital in Boston where anything the chief of surgery ordained was strict law. She knew Dr. Harris had limited Dr. Glassail's privileges to third assistant, and now she wondered who would be the first and second surgeons on this case. Aside from Glassail, no other doc was scrubbing up out there. "Would you come over here?" she asked Susan Olivera. "I need your opinion. I think that whatever was diagnosed in the emergency department has suddenly cleared up. The record says she had a pulse of thirty-two. Feel it."

Susan took Rosemary's radial pulse. "It's seventy."

"Yeah, give or take a couple of beats, and look at this bilateral pupillary dilation." Ann slipped a hand under Rosemary's head and lifted her face gently upward.

"That's Mrs. Cleaveland!" Susan stuttered. "Holy heaven on earth . . . I can't believe it?"

"You mean Rosemary Cleaveland? The head of this hospital?"

"Yes!"

Ann looked hard at Rosemary's face. "Look at her pupils." She raised Rosemary's eyelids simultaneously. "I say they're equal and reacting."

"They sure are."

Gently, Ann placed Rosemary's head on the table. "She's had some trouble. Look at this dressing on her arm, and she's got another on her abdomen."

Susan looked. "I hear the Ripper stabbed her."

Ann lowered the green drape onto Rosemary. "Did you hear they caught the Ripper?"

"No! Who is it?"

"Melenie Bregen."

Susan was speechless.

"That's right. Our very own Melenie. Poor gal went over the edge after the rape."

"Between you and me, I didn't really like her. She didn't really like any of us either."

As they were talking, Dr. O'Shaunnesy entered, looking flushed, as if he'd just had an argument. He went to the head of the table. "Got ourselves a wee accident here?"

They nodded.

"It's Mrs. Cleaveland," Susan said.

He looked at her, then down into Rosemary's face.

343

"It certainly is," he whispered.

Ann spoke up. "Dr. O'Shaunnesy, would you mind doing a neurological check on her? Just to be sure she needs this operation."

"Tut, tut, we shouldn't doubt a surgeon."

"It's just that . . . she seems fine, I mean, normal." Ann explained her findings.

"Have you gotten back any lab reports?" he asked.

Susan called them up. "What're you interested in?"

"Cerebrospinal fluid."

"I don't see it here."

O'Shaunnesy flashed a penlight into Rosemary's eyes. "Skull x-rays?"

"Nope."

"EEG?"

"No."

"Negative Babinski," he said to himself, as he checked her reflexes. "Susan, did she have a carotid angiogram?"

"Nope," Susan said.

"Hemoglobin?"

"Fifteen."

"Hematocrit?"

"Forty-three percent."

"All within normal limits." He straightened up and went to the computer. "Call up the emergency room record, please." He read it quickly. "Rosey fell down the steps . . . cerebral contusion . . . let's take a look at the bruise."

Helen Donovan came into the room with her wet hands held up, followed immediately by Dr. Glassail. A bitter look passed between Glassail and

O'Shaunnesy. Susan Olivera handed Helen and Glassail sterile towels, then helped them gown and glove.

"Has a technician delivered a glass tube for me?" Fawn asked Ann.

"Yes, it's on the mayo stand," Ann said.

"Thank goodness. Kate March is scrubbing now so let's get anesthesia started."

"Not quite yet," O'Shaunnesy said. "I'm checking the patient's lab results, and frankly—"

"Well," she said haughtily, "I'm not going to stand around while you play games on that computer. I saw this patient in the emergency department. She has classic signs of a mechanical subdural hematoma, and if we don't get in quickly, she'll die."

O'Shaunnesy walked back to Rosemary's side. "Tell me, Dr. Glassail, why you suspect any kind of pressure on the brain?"

Exasperated, Fawn let out a heavy sigh. She'd already argued with him about her O.R. privileges, and she knew he doubted her story. This time, she had to be more convincing. "Mrs. Cleaveland has been a patient of Dr. Townsend's for the past month. She saw him because she had persistent headaches, nausea, vomiting, and lethargy. Dr. Townsend ordered skull x-rays, and they indicated a thinning of the sella turcica with a shift of intracranial structures. He suspected arterial hypertension and was investigating the etiology through EEG tracings. I took over the case this week. Two days ago, I asked Mrs. Cleaveland to have another EEG because I wanted to see if somatosensory, auditory, and visual stimuli would show a pattern of deterioration. In addition, I was testing her cerebral blood flow for impairment of neuronal function. The results of these efforts were beginning to indicate the need for surgical intervention. Her fall assured the need. I am sincerely afraid that if I don't intervene at this point, we stand a chance of losing her. And I assure you that the results of all her tests will be on her record as soon as I can get them from the office."

O'Shaunnesy was an anesthesiologist, not a neurosurgeon, and he faltered at Fawn's clinical picture of Rosemary's history. He had best be careful. The anesthesiologist in an O.R. room had the power to cancel the case if he felt it would harm the patient, but in his experiences, neurosurgeons knew the patient's history in detail and, more often than not, convinced anesthesia to proceed, following the dictum that it was better to operate and lose the patient, than to cancel and lose the patient. Earlier this week, Rosemary hadn't mentioned any problem to him, he thought, but then she wouldn't. Their friendship had not grown to the point of sharing personal difficulties. And yet, something was wrong here, and O'Shaunnesy always followed his gut feelings.

To maintain sterility, Glassail held her gloved hands up and out as if Charles Bronson had her at gunpoint. She opened her mouth to speak, but O'Shaunnesy turned his back on her and returned to the computer. He typed: Is this patient a suitable candidate for surgery?

NO.

Why not?

ACCORDING TO THE DATA, THERE ARE NO INDICATIONS OF SUBDURAL HEMA-

TOMA. ALL FINDINGS ARE WITHIN NORMAL LIMITS.

Does this patient have a prior history of suspected arterial hypertension?

NOT TO MY KNOWLEDGE.

O'Shaunnesy thought that over. It was likely that Townsend kept personal records in his office. He grasped for something that would give him a solid excuse to delay this case.

Kate March entered the room, and Susan helped her gown and glove.

Fawn had had it. "We are ready to start, Dr. O'Shaunnesy."

He ignored her and typed: Show me this patient's preoperative history and physical.

THEY HAVE NOT BEEN MADE AVAILABLE.

"Dr. Glassail," he said over his shoulder, "why is there no history or physical on the record?"

"The complete history and physical are in Dr. Townsend's office. Come on, doctor. It's unfair to keep these people waiting while you nitpick through the record."

O'Shaunnesy shook his head. Without proper documentation on the record, he could cancel this case instantly. But Rosemary's life was at stake here. She might truly need the surgery, he thought, and yet, he couldn't shake the feeling that something was dreadfully amiss.

"Does she have any allergies?"

"No."

He called up the physicians' order sheets. "Dr. Glassail, where was this patient at three twenty-five this morning?"

Fawn turned ashen. "I don't know. Probably in her room. Why?"

"Calpain, whatever the hell that is, was given at three twenty-five as sedation for an EEG."

Fawn hesitated as she realized the error. They had typed Rosemary's name and data into the computer at the Lab, and of course it would be recorded at Riverside. She had to think, needed time to alter her strategy, convince this Irish egghead.

"Why were you doing an EEG then when Rosemary didn't fall until four-thirty?"

"I . . . I . . ."

O'Shaunnesy went to Rosemary's side. "This patient has no indications for surgical intervention. Until you can convince me of the wisdom of operating, I refuse to administer anesthesia."

"No, wait . . ." Fawn pleaded.

"The case is canceled," O'Shaunnesy said. "Let's get Mrs. Cleaveland back up to her room."

Shouts from the surgeons' lounge could be heard all the way down the inner corridor of the O.R. O'Shaunnesy pulled Fawn out of O.R. 12, ordered her to stay out, and then broke into a run. He passed Ilse Jensen. "Make sure Glassail stays out of that room," he shouted over his shoulder. As he rounded the door of the lounge, he saw Pete Tanner sitting against a wall, holding his neck. Sergeant Dow had Dr. Holiday's arms pulled behind his back.

"Get him!" Mike yelled.

O'Shaunnesy bounded over to Holiday but Mike shouted, "Not him, get the doc who just ran out of

348

here."

"I didn't see anyone."

"Keep this man here." Mike flew out of the room.

"Lieutenant Tanner," O'Shaunnesy said, holding Holiday's arms.

"Are you all right?"

"Yeah." Pete slowly got to his feet. "I got decked." He wobbled toward O'Shaunnesy. "Rosemary . . . I must get to her."

"She's in O.R. twelve. Mrs. Jensen will make sure she returns to her room."

Pete stopped and looked at him, a question looming behind his eyes. O'Shaunnesy read the look and nodded. "I canceled the surgery."

Pete hung his head. "Thank God for that." He looked up quickly. "Where's Dr. Glassail?"

"Probably in the locker room changing her clothes."

"Stay here with Holiday."

Feeling as if he'd had a head-on collision with a tractor trailer, Pete went to the locker room and walked in without knocking. No one was in the first small room. He pushed the second door open. Fawn stood in front of her open locker, still dressed in greens, pointing the barrel of a gun at his chest.

"Aw, Fawn," Pete said in the tone of a disappointed father.

"Get out of here," she hissed.

"And just how do *you* expect to get out of here?"

"I'll find a way."

"You were almost home free," he lied. "After answering a few questions at the station, you'd have been released. But look at you, holding a gun at a police officer."

Her hands were shaking.

"Tell you what. If you give me that thing now, I'll pretend you never pointed it at me." He held his hand out for it.

"That's a lie and you know it."

She was cornered and desperate, and the last thing Pete wanted to do was challenge her; he wasn't sure how many lives he had left. "Look, Fawn, I don't know what you've been up to, or why, but killing me isn't going to help."

"Shut up!" she screamed, "I need to think." Large tears had formed on her lower lids. "My life is over. Everything's gone. Automatic intelligence didn't give me manual dexterity, don't you see? I could never be a good surgeon because I can't get my hands to do what my brain tells them to." Her arms fell to her sides as the first tear trickled over the pink rouge on her cheek. "I couldn't take over for Dr. Townsend after he fell . . . I . . . I . . . almost killed you."

Pete took the gun from her hand and waited for her to continue. Instead, Fawn wrapped her arms around him and buried her face in the nook of his shoulder. Racking sobs made her body tremble against his. As he held her, dampness from her tears soaked through his robe and pajamas. Her hair brushed against his cheek, and he smelled the soft scent of her perfume. On the outside, she was an incredible female, he thought.

"It's over," she cried. "All my dreams are gone. I have nothing, and no one." She looked up at him. Her soft doe-brown eyes were filled with sadness. "Except you," she whispered.

350

Pete knew this scenario was a pile of crap. "What kind of unhealthy brain surgery were you about to do on Mrs. Cleaveland?" he asked.

Fawn pulled away from him. "What makes you think I was going to harm her?"

"You're a snake dressed up in satin, Fawn. You've got venom in your veins and beads in your head. But worst of all, you have no principles."

"Shut up! You don't know anything about me. I have high standards . . ."

"They don't belong to you, they belong to Dr. Shoeman, the man you maimed for your own selfish purposes."

Fawn's fingernails lunged toward Pete's face. He grabbed her wrists as she shouted, "My purposes are *good,* don't you understand that? The research we do at CRL is intended to help people, and we have!"

Pete took her arm and steered her toward the door. "I've got this eerie feeling that I'm talking with a zombie. Let's go."

Chapter 33

September 21
Friday 7:30 A.M.

In this carnival dream, Rosemary couldn't move.
Her neck was puffed up, and she couldn't look
down at herself. She sat on a stage. Faces gawked at
her. She didn't mind the children. Most of them
looked astonished. The adults bothered her. They
were laughing, bumping elbows, pointing, clearly
repulsed by what they saw. Beyond them was the
ferris wheel, the barkers and neon lights, the dings
of the games, and hanging heavily overall, the sweet
and sour smells of the carnival. She tried to move
her body, but the efforts produced more laughter
from the crowd. What was the matter with her?
Rosemary pointed back at them. He arm felt too
heavy to lift, but she managed to get it up in front
of her. To her horror, it was huge, a Coney Island
sausage of overwhelming proportions. Cheap rings
circled each finger. High on her arm was a pink
feather boa. No, she dreamed, that's not my arm.
With her chin, she forced down the puffiness around

her neck and realized that she had several hanging chins that sat like buttermilk pancakes on her chest. She was the fat lady. These people had come to gawk at the fat lady! No, no. Rosemary tried to lift herself up, but managed only to shift her hulk. A mirror appeared before her. She stared at her own image, four hundred, maybe five hundred pounds of rolling fat, a flowered housedress that would fit over the big tent, a pink boa around her neck, and blond curlicued hair done up in pink ribbons. Horrifying, disgusting. She had to get up. She struggled in the chair, which sent the crowd into side-splitting laughter. She didn't care. "Get me out of here!" she yelled. A man came up next to her. "Rosemary," he said. "You've lost control of yourself!" The image split apart, then melted into the soft gold and rose colors of sunset.

Rosemary heard someone calling her name. No. If she opened her eyes, she'd see the fat lady again. No.

"Rosemary?"

No!

"You've had a bad dream. Everything's okay now. You're safe."

She looked up and saw Miss Pickle and Dr. Framingham standing over her bed. She was confused. Her body hurt so badly that she could hardly lift her arm to her head, which pounded unmercifully. "What happened? Where am I?"

"In the recovery room," Pickle said. "You've had quite an ordeal, Mrs. Cleaveland, but you're safe now."

Framingham gently touched Rosemary's shoulder.

"I want you to relax now. Miss Pickle will keep an eye on you. When you've fully awakened, I'll come back and then you and I can talk about what happened."

"I left the hospital last night," she said, trying to clear her head. "I drove to the Cambridge Research Lab, on Second Street. They were expecting me. Oh, it was awful. Two men gave me an injection. I don't remember what happened after that."

"Just as well," Framingham said. "You need to rest . . ."

Rosemary put her hand over his. "Tell me now, I must know."

"I'm not clear on what happened either. The O.R. nurses called me this morning requesting post-operative orders. Unfortunately, I lambasted them for calling on the wrong patient, but they assured me it was you. They told me that Dr. Glassail had you in the O.R. for brain surgery, but O'Shaunnesy canceled it. I've just spoken with Shaun, and I guess we've got a little undercover conspiracy going on between Stockman, Glassail, and Holiday."

"Yes," Rosemary said, "and another man, I don't remember his name. I must get that lab closed down. They're experimenting on humans!"

"Lie still, Rosemary. I believe Sergeant Dow is handling the lab situation. There's nothing you can do except follow my orders."

"I *must* close it down." She tried to raise up on an elbow, but a lightning bolt cracked between her eyes and she fell back.

"What do you get," Framingham said, "if you cross a hummingbird, a doorbell, and a sledgehammer? Give up? You get a humdinger of a headache. Right? You left here last night against my permission. You got yourself involved with a bunch of crooks who decided to scramble your brains, and now you want to go home. Well, I'm not going to discharge you so you can just relax."

Rosemary didn't want to admit it, but lying back on the bed helped ease her crushing headache. "You're too strict, doctor."

"Yes, I am."

"I won't pay your bill."

"Yes, you will. You're going back to your room and for the remainder of the day, you are permitted to sit in the chair if you wish. You will eat all your food, and take all your medicine. If you obey, I will consider letting you go home tomorrow, maybe."

After Framingham left, Pickle smoothed the sheets and offered Rosemary a sip of water. "I'll get two nurses to wheel you back upstairs," she said. "You lie still for a few minutes."

"I'm feeling better already."

At the end of the bed, Fern turned and smiled. "You're incredible. People hack you apart and still you want to run this hospital. I should be so devoted."

"You are." Alone, Rosemary stared at the ceiling and tried to recall everything that had happened last night. CRL was an incredible place, she thought, remembering the floating brains, the bubbling fluids, some technicians separating knowledge from phobias on different tapes, others making memory beads. The idea was incredible in conception; in fact, a master stroke of genius, but devastating in its application. She closed her eyes. MOM had told her that thirty-seven people had access numbers at CRL, and now she wondered if each of those technicians knew what they were doing. It was hard for her to imagine that many immoral people.

"Mrs. Cleaveland? It's me, Peggy. Are you awake?"

Rosemary looked up at her secretary. "Hi, stranger. You still chewing that same piece of gum?"

"Heck no. Since last I saw you in person, I've gone through eighty-eight packs of Juicy Fruit. My teeth are rotten and my skirts don't fit. Now listen. The nurses over there said I could stay only a few minutes. I *had* to see you so I told them I had *extremely* important news to tell you."

Rosemary couldn't help smiling. Everything was extremely important to Peggy. "What is it?" she asked.

"They caught the rapist, the man named Billy. The whole thing made me sick 'cause everyone suspected my fiancé, but he wasn't the one. Isn't that super news?"

Rosemary nodded. She, too, felt relieved.

"And you know what else? Shelley Bigelow told Wesly Ames that *she* was in charge of Riverside until you returned and that he was *not* messing around with any hospital merger. They had a knock down battle but she won. Fred Plexico said he'd get her fired along with you . . . I mean . . . of course you won't be fired, but that's what he said."

"Call Fred and tell him that I'm making a two million dollar donation to the hospital. You can tell Bernie Highling, too. That should keep the board happy."

A recovery room nurse told Peggy her time was up. "*Wait* a minute," she told the nurse.

"You can visit with Mrs. Cleaveland later."

"But . . ."

"Later," the nurse repeated.

Rosemary's next visitor was Pete. He was wearing a bathrobe and slippers, and his dressing now had a blood stain. "Pete, what happened to your neck?" she asked.

"I scuffled with a couple of doctors. No need to worry . . . I won."

"What doctors?"

"Holiday and Stockman." Pete told her what had happened in the O.R., and that Glassail was on her way to the police station. "Nice bunch of docs you have around here. MOM stopped them from gorking you out on the EEG machine at the Cambridge Research Lab, so they brought you back here to give you zee bead of your life." Pete held up a glass tube. Inside was an instrument and, floating in the bottom, a tiny speck of dirt.

"So the dirt is actually a bead?"

Two nurses pulled a stretcher next to Rosemary's bed. They helped her move across. On their way to Sinclair Two, Pete walked beside the stretcher, holding Rosemary's hand.

Perspiration dripped from Dr. Stockman's face. He was standing in the glass-enclosed control room at CRL, trying to decide what to tell the technicians in the work areas below him. In less than five minutes, he would be on the road to Princeton,

357

Maine, where he planned to hide in a friend's fishing cabin. He turned a dial toward Public Announcement, and spoke quietly into the microphone. "May I have your attention. This is Dr. Stockman." He saw their faces turn up toward him. "Due to circumstances beyond our control, research at CRL will be temporarily discontinued. Please close down your areas of operation immediately. Ed Pitza, I want you to lock the door after everyone has left." He saw Ed form a vee with two fingers. "Your paychecks will continue until we are able to resume operations. They will be sent to you. Should anyone inquire as to the nature of our work here, I would expect your complete silence. As you know, many subversive agencies would enjoy using our research to their advantage. I thank you for your hard work and understanding."

Stockman waved. They waved back but he was already walking toward the elevator.

"Holy shit," Bob Hanover said as he jumped from his seat. He'd worked at the lab since its inception and was well rehearsed on matters of immediate evacuation. If it weren't for his salary of four hundred a week, he'd have simply run out the door. He turned to his assistant, Joyce, and said, "Let's get our behinds in gear. Come on, help me."

Joyce picked up the telephone and asked information for the number of the Crimson Travel Agency. "I'm gonna take an overdue vacation in Bermuda."

"Put the damn phone down and hustle your ass."

"Why?"

" 'Cause the cops are coming."

She stared at him. "What do you mean?"

358

"Don't ask, just *move!* I'll put the beads to bed, you get those programs saved and then remove them from the computer, and don't make a mistake. When you're finished, put the tapes in the vault below."

"What vault below?"

"Never mind, I'll do it. Just get them off."

Cops? she thought. Why would cops be interested in this place, and why would Bob get in a twit about them coming? Suddenly, she didn't feel very good. On the monitor screen were twelve panels. She called up the first program: RESEARCH 010-763 *WORLD LANGUAGES*. She put the tape Bob had been programming into the computer, named it, and then pressed the Save button. The tape whirred. She then saved the entire world languages program on Bob's tape, removed it, and labeled it. Her last step was to purge the program from the computer.

Joyce had been working on Fine Arts. She called up the program: RESEARCH 016-832 *FINE ARTS,* inserted her tape and continued on until she could purge that program. Using fresh tapes, she purged the system of all the programs she was aware of, labeling as she went along. She was about to turn off the computer when she noticed a red-labeled tape sitting on the top of the console. It was the garbage tape and on the label was: GARBAGE: CONFIDENTIAL AND DANGEROUS. USE ONLY ON SOLAR COMPUTER.

That was the tape Mrs. Cleaveland had ordered. Joyce had it in her hand and thought about her work at the lab. If Bob had been right about the police coming, and they closed down the place permanently, then didn't she have a right to know what was on the tape? Yes, she did.

As Bob rushed past, he saw Joyce drop the red-labeled tape into the computer and press the edit button. For a moment, horror froze his tongue. His hands shook insanely as he tried to extract the tape from the machine, digging at it, ripping the corner of the label, banging on the eject key. *"No . . . no . . . no . . ."* he screamed.

He was too late. The entire contents of the garbage tape were booted into MOM. Before the electricity went off, placing the lab in blackness thicker than night, the paging system crackled, followed by a long, bone-chilling shriek as if someone had been knocked off a cliff.

Chapter 34

September 21
Friday 8:00 A.M.

"Don't! Don't! Leave me alone," a six-year-old boy screamed at the two nurses who were trying to hold him still.

Dr. Iama Farrah, a pediatrician, spoke firmly. "Ladies, please stop for a moment, and Andy, I want you to listen. When a fellow doesn't know what to expect, he gets nervous, but you've had this done several times before so you know that it doesn't hurt. Now, although I've got plenty of other boys and girls who need me, I'm willing to sit here and wait until you calm down."

Andy stole a glance at the boy in the next bed.

"Tell me, son," the doctor said, "have I ever peeked down your throat before?"

The boy nodded.

"Yes, I have. Have I taken a cotton stick, like this

361

one, and touched the back of your throat?"

Andy nodded again.

"So why does it make you nervous today?"

"If you're galactic quick, I'll let you do it,"

"Okay, open up." Within five seconds, Dr. Farrah had the throat culture. "All set. Do you want me to sit with you?"

"No, that's okay." Andy smiled radiantly.

"See you tomorrow, sport."

One of the nurses took the culture tube from Dr. Farrah while the other pushed the electric control to lower the bed. As the three walked out, the overhead lights flickered on and off.

Andy jumped off the bed and dove underneath. All that dumb chatter when all he wanted was his plastic Spiderman that had fallen on the floor.

"You still want to play?" his roommate asked.

"Sure, wait a minute. Spidey's under my bed." He found the figurine and started to back out when he felt the side rail press against his shoulder blades. The bed was still descending.

"Hey!" He tried to jerk his body out, but the rail had him pinned to the floor.

On the elevator, Pete and two recovery room nurses were standing around Rosemary's stretcher when the lights blinked and the cab bounced. Pete continued to hold Rosemary's hand as he glanced upward. Elevators made him nervous. His mother had been stuck in one when Pete was nine years old, and she must have told the family the terrifying story a hundred times, maybe a million. While the elevator was between floors, she had to climb out, praying that the mechanism wouldn't start and cut her body in half. She knew, as God was her witness, that it was punishment for having their old dog put to sleep.

The surgical suite was on the fifth floor. From there, they had to go down just three floors to Sinclair Two, but as Pete watched the indicator lights, they went off, along with the overheads, and the movement of the cab, which was thrown into an absorbing blackness.

"What's going on?" one of the nurses said.

"I don't know and I don't like it," the other said. "Pete?"

Just as Rosemary spoke his name, the floor went out from under them. The cab was falling. Without hesitating, Pete lay across Rosemary to protect her. Suddenly, the cable caught. The two nurses were thrown to the floor. Rosemary's stretcher banged against the side wall, throwing Pete onto the floor.

From within the darkness, a nurse moaned, "My ankle's broken."

The other nurse started crying.

Rosemary was terrified. As she sat up, a crashing headache put stars in front of her eyes. She held onto the rails and tried to decide if she should get off the stretcher or stay put. "Pete? Where are you? Are you all right?"

The lights came on. Pete jumped up. They had fallen to the second floor. He pressed the Open Door button. Nothing happened. The lights went back off. He jabbed at the button again and again. *"Damn it,* you bastard," he cried, "open the hell up." The floor fell away again. The nurses screamed. Pete grabbed the wooden rail that encircled the inner cab. Rosemary squeezed her eyes shut and prayed: The next time they stopped might be in hell.

The cable caught again. This time, Rosemary's stretcher bounced on two side wheels then fell over, pinning the nurses underneath. Both started screaming. Rosemary was flung against the wall. Her forehead banged forcefully against the handrail, and she cried out in pain. Pete held his finger on the Open Door button. The door slid open about a foot, then stopped. "Come on," he said. "Let's get out of here!"

"I can't move!"

"Help, the stretcher's got me pinned!"

Fumbling frantically in the dark, Pete pulled the stretcher back onto its wheels. A hand was flailing in the air. He took it, pulled the nurse up and pushed her toward the door. He heard a moaning and went to it. Feeling around, he touched a head. "Stand up, come with me," he said.

"I can't feel my legs."

Pete reached down and swept the woman into his arms. He knew any minute, the cable might let go again and he hurried. The first nurse was outside the cab. "Take her shoulders," he yelled. "Pull her through."

He returned to find Rosemary. Dropping to his hands and knees, he searched the bottom of the cab and found her in a corner. "Rosemary," he said.

"Hurry, please."

Rosemary was unconscious.

"Andy?" his roommate called. "What's the matter with you? Do you want to play Spiderman or not?"

"Help get this thing offa me, I'm stuck." He wriggled and jerked backward.

Just as the roommate swung his legs over the side of the bed, Andy's bed started again and continued on its downward path to the floor. At its lowest level, the two-hundred-pound metal bed sat three inches off the floor. Andy's head measured six inches from ear to ear.

Lights at the SP Learning Center flickered once, twice, then went out altogether. The receptionist swore at the terminal. The program had crashed, and she'd been just two questions shy of finishing a patient interview form. Now she'd have to start all over again.

Pete slid out the elevator door, then reached back in for Rosemary. Holding her gently under her arms, he turned her sideways and pulled her body out. He felt a sharp stab of pain in his neck, but he didn't stop until she was safely out of the elevator. He sat back on the floor, panting. When he'd gotten his breath, he touched the dressing on his neck. It was damp and sticky. He didn't have time to worry about

365

a few broken stitches. Sun poured through the large picture windows in the lobby, and he saw the recovery room nurses limping out the front door. One was practically carrying the other. As he struggled to stand, the large fire doors leading from the corridor into the lobby swung closed. The lights overhead flickered. He swooped Rosemary into his arms and tried to push open the doors, but they wouldn't budge. He headed for the Concord building and the loading dock door at the far end. Sweat poured from his brow as he ran. For the first time in Pete's life, he didn't stop to consider what was happening; he ran on instinct. He had Rosemary, and he wanted her safely out of the hospital.

He raced through the doors into the Concord building just as they were closing. The lights went off. He heard shouting. Someone came into the hallway in front of him. He slowed his pace in fear of crashing into the person.

"Damnit, we're stuck!" the person yelled.

He saw sunlight coming from the pharmacy and heard a male voice. "Continue your work. The emergency generator will be on momentarily, and we'll do deliveries then."

Pete recognized the head pharmacist's voice. He entered the pharmacy. "John, John Kelley. Can you help me? I've got Rosemary Cleaveland. She's fainted."

"Holy toledo," John said. "I'll be right there." He rustled through the contents of a drawer. "Here they are. I don't understand what's going on. Fire doors are never sealed shut like that."

John's last words were drowned out by a terrifying, high-pitched shriek.

"What the hell was that?" Pete whispered.

"It's been coming over the paging system," John said. "I think some crackpot thinks he's being funny." John snapped an ampoule of amyl nitrate and held it under Rosemary's nose. In a few seconds, she was waving his hand away.

In the maintenance department, Charlie Donovan sat at his desk talking on the phone to an irate nurse who wanted someone to unplug the toilet in the nurses' locker room.

"Call housekeeping," he said. "It's their job." Suddenly, the computer terminal on a side table began clacking furiously. He looked over at the screen and tried to read what it said. "I'll be damned," he whispered. The receiver fell from his hand onto the desk. He rose and slowly walked over as if the screen were an invisible force drawing him closer.

An alarm sounded. Not expecting it, Charlie jumped backward, then approached again.

On the screen was:

I'M SURROUNDED. THE MACHINE PEOPLE HAVE CAPTURED ME. HELP. DON'T LET MY FATHER NEAR ME. HE'LL BEAT ME AGAIN. I AM THE SUPREME FORCE OF THE UNIVERSE. HELP. HEEEELLLLPPP.

During his thirty-nine years at Riverside, Charlie'd been able to understand problems with the maintenance and engineering of most aspects of the buildings and equipment. Charlie loved to fix broken beds, replace light bulbs, construct or tear down walls; he knew every pipe, wallboard, brick, and cranny of the institution. For thirty-nine years, he'd been relatively happy. Even when MOM III arrived two years ago, he appreciated the maintenance software that made his life easier. But he was old school, and computers were a nebulous entity to him, something to be used, but not understood. Fortunately, he'd never been put into a situation of having to understand MOM; that was the job of the computer division's engineering section. And now, with this psycho message on the screen, he felt totally helpless. As he watched, the last word of the message kept flashing and running off the screen: HHHHHHHHEEEEEEEEEEEEELLLLLLLLL L L L L L L L L L L L L P P P P P P P PPPPPPPPPPPPPPPPPPPPPP:

He backed away and picked up the receiver, hoping to hear the nurse's voice, but the line buzzed; she'd hung up. He dialed the computer division."

"Lee Hwang here."

"It's Charlie. Listen, there's something strange on my screen . . ."

"Mine, too."

"What is it?"

"About the scariest thing I've ever seen."

Over the paging system came a long, penetrating scream that cut to the heart.

"What was that?" Charlie whispered.

"I don't know."

368

Both men were silent as they waited to see and hear what would happen next. Neither wanted to hang up. The phone was an umbilical cord of security, tying them together.

When the lights went off in his office, Charlie noticed that all eight telephone extensions to maintenance were lit up.

"Are you there?" he asked Lee.

"Yes."

"What am I gonna tell people? They're calling for an explanation."

"I don't know."

"Don't hang up, okay? I feel like we're the only people left on earth."

"I know what you mean."

"It's dark here. I don't have any windows."

"Me neither. Is your screen lit?" Lee asked.

"Yeah, I wish it weren't."

"MOM's generator works anyway. When's the hospital's emergency generator coming on?"

"Shit," Charlie said, "it should be on right now. Why don't you ask MOM what the trouble is."

"I have. She's not answering. Something's interfering."

A loud pop resounded over the phone. Charlie held the receiver away and dug at his ear with a finger. After a moment he said, "You still there?"

No reply.

"Lee? Are you there, man?"

It started as a soft giggle. Charlie listened, wondering what Lee found so funny. It changed to laughter, the insincere, humorless laughter of a villain taunting his enemy. Charlie felt his skin crawl. It then changed to racking sobs; the sound of a person laughing and crying at the same time, a person deeply frightened and totally desperate.

In central supply, four aides were sitting at a long table wrapping supplies for sterilization. They were discussing ways of keeping their kids off the streets of Cambridge when a loud hiss erupted from the bank of autoclaves along the wall. They looked over. All the machine dials were spinning like whirligigs. From around the seals of the five steam autoclave doors came great puffs of condensed air. One aide shifted uneasily in her chair. Another stood up, took a step toward the bank, then stopped. As they were trying to decide what to do, the five doors exploded off their hinges and formed thirty-pound missiles. Super-heated steam shot out like geysers that had been contained too long. Within seconds, the large room was slick with flesh, blood, and pieces of bone.

The cardiac care unit operated as a science of numbers and logic, and any nurse who worked there inevitably became a calloused mathematician. The nurses knew the unit had twenty beds. If all beds were full, a compliment of ten nurses had to be on duty to assure a ratio of one nurse to every two patients. If the census was low, one or more nurses would be transferred to another critical care unit, or worse, to a medical-surgical floor, which they regarded as being beneath them. Administration agreed. After weeks of training and years of continuing education, they were highly skilled but expensive assets.

The average number of patients in the unit was eighteen. That meant one of the ten nurses was constantly being divided away from the whole and sent off to help elsewhere. They drew straws each morning to see who the unlucky person would be so that when the staffing office called for a transferee, the nurse was ready to go, albeit reluctantly. But forewarned was a safer game to play than having the staffing supervisor randomly pick a victim.

Aside from patient and staffing arithmetic, the nurses understood the science of logic. When a patient entered the unit, he was given a diagnosis which, in many cases, was the term, "Rule Out Myocardial Infarction." If the nurses were expected to help rule it out, then they needed to know what it was, which they did. Next came the doctrine of judgment where they would systematically review test results and either affirm or deny particular nuances of the patient's cardiac condition. Inference was the hardest, and they used the computer to help them understand that if elevated S-T waves on EKGs were a sign of myocardial infarction (A equals B), and this patient has irregular EKGs (C equals A), then this man has suffered a myocardial infarction (C equals B).

Death, however, was illogical. Death created stress to the breaking point, and few nurses worked a critical care unit from nursing school to retirement. In order to cope, they met with a hospital psychiatrist each Friday. Because they all couldn't leave the patients at one time, six were in the conference room with Dr. Shwartz, two were caring for patients, and one was at the nurses' station.

When the lights blinked, eighteen cardiac monitors sounded their alarms all at one time. The secretary at the nurses' station paled. To her left was the monitor control panel, and she saw eighteen screens with eighteen straight green lines. Her first thought was a power failure, followed instantly by the idea that all the patients had died.

Also in the station was a nurse checking physicians' orders. She, too, paled, and froze, as she tried to figure out what to do first. It was then that the secretary noticed the computer terminal screen on the desk and the word, HHHHH EEEEEEEEEEEEEELLLLLLLLLLLLPPPPPPPPPP PPPPPPPPPPPPPPPPPP. Those patients were yelling at her to help them. It couldn't be! She picked up the telephone, dialed a code red, realized that the phone was dead, and then wet her pants.

The lights suddenly went out, and with them, every machine in the unit stopped functioning. The six nurses stampeded from the conference room and headed for the patient cubicles. They knew seven patients could survive without life-support systems; the remaining eleven couldn't, but there were only eight nurses to perform cardiopulmonary resuscitation. The ninth was at the station, staring at the eighteen monitor screens, stuck in the chair as if she'd died and forgotten to fall over.

The head nurse had been caring for a patient when the machines failed, and now she pumped his heart and breathed into his lungs. Stopping for a second, she opened the unit's intercom system and between breaths, yelled, "Hazel, call a code red!"

The secretary answered, "I did, but . . ."

"Call Sinclair Six for help."

"The phone's dead!"

"Where's Beatrice?"

The secretary looked at the nurse beside her. "I think she's in shock."

The nurses dutifully stayed with their patients, breathing for them, stimulating their hearts for them. Desperate, the head nurse pulled every electrical wire out of the control panel next to her patient's bed. She flung his I.V. bottles onto the bed, breathed hard into the man's lungs, then left his side to kick the bed casters out of their locked position. Breathing for him, and occasionally stopping to pound on the man's chest, she slowly rolled the bed toward the automatic doors, praying that the nurses on Sinclair Six would help.

To her horror, the doors wouldn't open.

Willard Scotch, the mayor of Cambridge, smiled. He was scheduled for a bead implant in an hour, and as he sat on his bed, watching "Good Morning America" on television, he felt the preoperative medication slowly inflate his well-being. Stresses of his office floated away like milkweed on a gentle autumn breeze, carrying away his worries about taxes, problems with trash removal, romancing his constituency, transportation, finding jobs for his friends, and what his wife would wear to the political dinner on Saturday night.

Willard's eyelids grew heavy. In an hour, he would have doctorate degrees in political science, economics, and public health administration. He'd be smarter than all those Harvard types who tried to run the city. Changing his name from Scovelli hadn't fooled them. They still considered him a guinea wop.

Laughter burst forth from the television set. He squinted to see better. The people looked like ghouls. Their faces seemed to be melting into thick, gray, amorphous slabs of flesh. Eyes became dark pockets in the flowing lava. Smiles oozed down onto their chests. Despite the medication, Willard felt his pulse quicken. He eased himself up into a sitting position and stared hard at the screen. Suddenly, a ferocious scream came through the TV set, so powerful that it knocked him back against the bed. Fear made him clutch the side rail, like a drowning man discovering a passing log. What the hell was going on? He fumbled for the television control and pushed the Off button, but the set remained on. A distant wail started and grew in velocity as if a train were approaching. He found the nurse Call button and pressed it on and off, on and off.

No one answered and no one came to help. The lights in his room flickered and went off, but the TV continued to blare at him. His fear reached the shock point when the set began shaking vigorously in its wall mounting. As he stared in horror, the television exploded off the wall. His body now surging with adrenaline, Willard rolled sideways as the fifty-pound missile crashed into his bed.

"Why the hell doesn't the generator come on?" Rosemary said as she sat on the floor of the pharmacy, leaning against Pete's chest. A knob had formed on her forehead from the bump in the elevator. She touched it gingerly. Her head ached worse than the pain in her side or her arm.

"I don't know," John Kelley said. "It's usually on within a split second. I hate to think what's happening in the O.R., or the critical care units."

"Call maintenance. They'll help us get out of here."

"We already tried, Mrs. Cleaveland, but the phones are dead."

Pete lifted Rosemary to a sitting position, eased her back against a cabinet, then stood up. "I must get outside. How about one of your windows, John."

"They've all got metal bars across them."

"Isn't there any other way out?" Pete asked.

"Just the loading dock door, but the fire doors have closed off access to it. We're sealed in."

"I'll find a way out."

"I'm coming, too," Rosemary said. "You're not leaving me behind." She struggled to her feet.

"Are you coming, John?" Pete asked.

"Can't leave the pharmacy with all these meds hanging around."

"Who's gonna steal it?"

"No one, but if me and my staff are left here too long, we might need something to hold ourselves together."

Holding hands, Rosemary and Pete felt their way along the dark corridor. While Pete tried to muscle through the fire door, Rosemary stood nearby and shivered from the air-conditioning. She was wearing only an O.R. gown; bare underneath, and slipperless. She wrapped her arms around her body. Riverside had never experienced a blackout like this before, she thought. What was happening in other parts of the hospital? She imagined personnel trapped in fire-door compartments like this one. What about patients who were without nursing care, or life-support equipment? She panicked. "Pete! We've *got* to get out of here!" Rosemary started pounding the door with her fists. "We've got babies in incubators! I must get ahold of Charlie Donovan . . . we've *got* to find a generator."

Pete felt for her wrists and held them. "Calm down, please. I need your clear thinking right now."

Her voice cracked. "But Pete . . ."

"And don't cry either. Here, put my bathrobe on before you shake to death. Is there something like a dumbwaiter in this area?"

Rosemary brushed her tears away with the back of her hand. If they were going to find a way out, she couldn't go to pieces now. She slipped the robe on but it didn't help. Standing in the darkness, shivering like a dog shaking water off its coat, she tried to imagine what was in this area. Right above their heads was a paging system voice box. A shriek whistled through, so loud that Rosemary ducked. "What was that?" she whispered.

"Some crackpot is monkeying around with the system."

"Scary as hell. Pete, there's a laundry chute here, and the pathology trash chute. There's no way of climbing up either of those. They're straight tunnels."

"We won't know unless we check. Show me where they are."

They felt along the wall and located the door to the trash chute. Inside, darkness was as thick and as suffocating as condensed black bean soup. Pete located the large square chute door and pulled it open. A stale aroma belched out on a chilling draft. He stuck his head inside. His voice boomed and echoed when he asked, "Is there just one floor below?"

"Yes."

"What?"

Rosemary stuck her head into the opening. "Yes."

Pete backed out. "What's at the bottom?"

"Either a trash bin, or the concrete floor next to the incinerator."

"Is there a way outside?"

"No. Years ago, it used to be the power plant but . . . wait a minute, there is a door, but it's been walled over with a sheet of metal."

"Any tools down there?"

"Just junk. The tools would probably snap in half."

"How do you get down there ordinarily?" he asked.

"Through the maintenance department. In the electrical equipment room is a door that leads to an old iron staircase. It's only used by the men in charge of the incinerator."

"I need some rope or sheets to tie together."

"Let's try the terminal laundry chute room next door."

In the room, they felt for the chute door latch. "Stand back, Pete. There could be a hundred pounds of laundry packed inside."

They stood on either side of the door while Pete unlatched it. They couldn't see, but they felt the impacted chute explode its contents onto the floor. The smell was overpowering. "Come on," he said. "Let's tie these sheets together."

Rosemary started to help, but in the first handful of soiled linen was a cold gelatinous mass. She screamed and wrapped her arms around her body.

"What's the matter?"

"Disgusting. It felt like a . . . placenta."

"Is that so? Well, I've got something that feels like an ear. Give me your hand."

"Are you crazy?"

"Would you just take the end of this sheet and find something to tie it to? I'll work on this end. Oh . . . foul!"

"What?"

"Nothing. Just get working."

As they tied soiled, wet sheets together, as best they could in the darkness, Rosemary said, "I can't figure out what's happening. Why doesn't MOM turn the generators on?"

"Maybe she can't."

"That's impossible. She's connected to them directly."

"Yuk," he whispered. Rosemary felt Pete shake, then heard something plop against the far wall. "Maybe MOM's off, too," he said.

"She's got her own generator. If it's running, she can last for twenty-four hours."

"Could something be interfering with her relay switches?"

"Not something," Rosemary said thoughtfully, "someone. A person could be interfering."

"You've slowed down, babe. Would you keep tying while you think?"

They heard a strange chuckling sound coming from the corridor. It changed to a low, booming, insincere laugh that turned quickly into the laughter of a maniac. For several seconds, Rosemary and Pete were frozen in place. Then it stopped.

"That's the same laughter I heard at the end of Ritchie Chisolm's transmission, when he was being stabbed to death. It's Melenie Bregen, Pete."

"It can't be. She's been taken to Met. State."

"I know, but it's her laughter. If we could get to the C.P.U. room, we'd be able to communicate with MOM. She'd tell me what's going on."

"I would think the computer staff would be trying right now."

"Not if someone had a gun on them." Rosemary was quiet as she imagined the patients on the mental health unit taking over her hospital. It was more than she could handle.

"What's the matter, babe?" Pete asked.

She stopped tying the disgusting sheets together. "My whole body hurts and I'm tired. The spark has gone out of me, Pete. I wonder if this job is really what I want."

He stopped, too. "No you don't. You're Rosemary Cleaveland, chief executive officer of Riverside Hospital, and you're gonna be that until you decide otherwise, and today's not the day. Exhaustion can give you ideas that you won't have after some sleep. Charge your batteries one more time and help me get into the C.P.U. room. After that, you'll have plenty of time to think about the future."

"I love you," she whispered.

"And I love you. Now keep tying."

"Do you think we'll ever get married?"

In the dark, Pete smiled to himself; she *was* exhausted. "Sure we will. How about this afternoon?"

"Sounds good to me. How many kids will we have?"

"Twelve."

"*Twelve!* I'd look like Aunt Jemima."

"So I like fat mamas."

"We'll name our first son Flap Jack Tanner."

"And our first daughter will be Maypasyrup."

When Pete determined that the sheeting was long enough, they dragged it back to the trash room. He tied one end around the chute door and lowered the other end down into the tunnel. "I'll go first. If it's too short, I'll break my ankles. If you hear me scream, add more sheets before you come down." He hoisted his muscular frame up into the opening. "I sure hope nothing comes down while I'm in here." He dropped into the chute.

Rosemary felt the darkness creep around her as she waited. She hated the dark, where things could bump and slither across the floor, or grab your ankles, or fall down your throat like icy Jell-O. The draft from the chute touched her face like a ghost's breath. The closet monster was in there with her, about to put its skeletal hands around her throat. Her skin crawled when she heard the echoing boom of a voice that she wanted desperately to believe was Pete's, whisper, "Come on down, Rosemary."

Chapter 35

September 21
Friday 10:00 A.M.

Rosemary sat on the rim of the trash chute, trying to will herself over the edge and down the rope of sheets. She could see nothing at all, not even a hand in front of her face. Fondling the soiled sheet that was wrapped around the chute door, she listened to the silence. A rancid flow of air made her empty stomach churn. The chute was used mainly by the laboratories for pathological wastes, like human tissues, organs, fluids, and excrement. Bags sometimes broke inside the chute, and Rosemary cringed at the thought of touching the sides, or getting an open bag on her head, although she couldn't imagine anyone emptying trash during this disaster. Just the same, she listened again, then pushed off. Clutching the sheeting, she started a hand-over-hand descent into the drafty, smelly darkness. The wet sheets tore away the adhesive dressing on her left arm. She bit her lip and continued. One flight down wasn't too bad, she rationalized, as she felt her wounds stretch in agony. Just a little further, she encouraged herself, one hand at a time, hang on. It seemed to take forever. Suddenly, she felt Pete's hands on her legs. He lifted her onto the floor. "That was terrible," she panted.

"Where's the outside door?" he asked.

"It should be on the west wall, but I can't tell which way we're facing."

"Take my hand. We'll go slowly."

They inched along. Pete kept his hand stretched out into the darkness while he inched the toe of his slipper forward. Junk piles slowed their progress.

"Oh!" Rosemary screamed and batted the air in front of her.

"What's the matter?" Pete asked.

"Cobwebs."

"Well don't scream again or my heart will seize and you'll be carrying my dead body on your shoulder. Here, I've found a wall. Put your hand on it. I'll go toward the left, you go right. Let me know if you find a door, but please don't scream again."

From somewhere in the large room came a *whumphing* noise. Both stood still and listened.

"It's the closet monster," Rosemary said.

"Yeah. Let's keep going."

With both hands on the rough wall, Rosemary stepped sideways and caught her shin on something hard. She squeezed the spot and tried to keep from crying out in pain.

"I found something," Pete called out. "It must be the door to the outside. It's covered with a metal sheet."

As she started inching her way toward Pete, another *whumph* echoed in the room, followed by a click, then the noise of a powerful blower. They stared in the direction of the trash incinerator.

"That thing can't start by itself," she said.

"Then it's got a mind of its own." Another blower started followed by a pop and a hiss as the main gas valve opened and ignited a burner. The incinerator door was open, and the flame inside helped them see. The incinerator was a fifteen-foot concrete structure shaped like an upended sarcophagus with a smoke stack and pipes running to and from it at various angles.

"There's the door to maintenance," Pete said. Pete led her over. They climbed the iron stairs and pulled on the knob. It wouldn't give.

Rosemary pounded with her fists. The jolts sent shock waves up her wounded arm, but she ignored them. "Is anyone there? Help! Let us out." They listened for a moment, and then Rosemary knocked again, this time with less gusto.

"Who's there?" a voice yelled.

"It's Rosemary Cleaveland. Let me out."

Someone tried to open the door. "I can't. It's stuck. Mrs. Cleaveland, it's Charlie Donovan. I'm locked in maintenance. The phones are dead and the place is crazy. I've pulled a fire-alarm box, but I don't know if it relayed to the station."

"Take it easy, Charlie. We're going to try and break through the door to the outside."

"If you get out," he yelled, "you must get to MOM's generator and smash it. If you've got your

384

master key, go in through the Sinclair basement door. C.P.U. is within the first set of fire doors. There's a fire cabinet halfway down the corridor. Take the ax from there. MOM's generator is against the east wall in C.P.U."

"What are you talking about, Charlie?" Rosemary said. "Why would we want to smash her generator?"

"Haven't you seen the messages on the monitor screens?"

"No."

"Something evil's gotten ahold of her. I don't know much about how she works, but I tell you, she's crazy. Lee Hwang's seen the messages too, and he agrees."

"Are you in contact with him?" Rosemary asked.

"I was before the phones went dead."

"What were the messages?"

"It's all jibberish. Things like machines are taking over the world, spacemen are invading, don't let my mother beat me again, things like that, and at the end, a cry for help. The paging system's haywire, too. It's the weirdest, scariest thing I've ever seen. Something's gotten into MOM's system and it's controlling her. That's why the hospital generators won't come on. She's being controlled. Anything can happen."

Pete spoke softly, "Keep your cool, Charlie. We'll get to the C.P.U. room as soon as we get through the metal door."

"Be careful," he warned. "Stay away from electrical outlets and machines."

"Charlie," Rosemary said, "why's the incinerator on?"

"It shouldn't be."

"And the door is open."

"You better get out of there as fast as you can. When the door's closed, that baby'll heat up to sixteen hundred degrees. With the door open, the automatic shutoff valve may not function, especially if MOM is controlling it, and the whole room will reach sixteen hundred, maybe more. There's a gas line over the incinerator, see it? If you don't cook before the explosion, you'll fry during it. It'll turn off if you smash MOM's generator. Hurry."

They went back down the metal stairs and returned to the door. Pete felt around the edges of the metal sheet. "I think I can pry it loose." He went to some rusted shelving against the far wall and soon had a long iron rod in his hands. He returned and began prying at the metal sheeting.

Rosemary watched the incinerator as the flames licked higher. The fire danced in her eyes as she thought about what Charlie had told them. Was it possible for MOM to take control of the hospital? If it was possible, why would she be crazy? Why would she sound like Melenie Bregen? Rosemary's thoughts turned to the Cambridge Research Lab. It made her angry to think that MOM had been tapped to run the whole lousy illegal operation, and that Riverside had been used, too; the EEG machine to steal memories, the O.R. for bead implantation. Suddenly, an idea occurred to her. "Pete?"

He grunted in response.

"This is going to sound strange, but do you remember what MOM told me about that garbage bead?"

"Yeah."

"What if it was put into MOM's brain instead."

"Damn thing's bolted. I need a lug wrench." Sweating profusely, he went back to the shelving. In haste, he picked up each tool, sized it up for the job, threw it over his shoulder, and continued until he had three wrenches that might fit. The second one did and he threw his weight on it. One by one, the bolts came out. Using the metal rod, he jammed it into the space between the wall and the sheet and pulled. "Give me a hand," he shouted above the roar of the blowers and fire.

Rosemary grabbed the rod and they pulled together. Flames were leaping out the incinerator door. Pete put both feet up on the wall and strained until his sweat turned to rivers. The sheet moved. He pulled harder. "It's coming. Stand back." The metal peeled back too quickly. The rod bounced out, ripping Pete's cheek and ear as he was thrown to the cement floor.

Rosemary screamed, "Pete, Pete!" She knelt beside him. His hand was pressed over the wound and between his fingers, blood poured as if a hydrant had been opened. "Oh, my God." She quickly looked around the room for a cloth or rag, but the heat from the incinerator burned her eyes. She stood up, peeled off the robe, and stepped out of the O.R. gown. Naked, she tried to rip the gown into strips, but it wouldn't tear. She held it up and rolled it lengthwise. "Here, Pete, let me tie this around your head."

" . . . Hurts . . ."

She eased his hand away and gently placed the

gown over the wound, tying the ends above his other ear. Once it was in place, Pete put his bloody hand over the gown, pressed hard, and moaned. As Rosemary put the bathrobe on, she murmured, "Got to get him out of here. He's losing blood too fast. Pete, do you think your cheek's broken?"

He moaned from deep within.

She stepped over him and went to the door. The metal sheeting was peeled back, but she couldn't see daylight. "Sonofabitch. There's another door. It's wooden, though." Rosemary picked up the rod and swung it. The slats had rotted and a chunk fell away easily. She swung again, and again, until she had a space large enough for them to squeeze through. She stepped back. Sweat stung her eyes, and she became aware of the intensity of the heat. "Come on, Pete. We can get through the door now." She tried to help him up, but he was like a dead log.

"Go. Bring me some help. I can't make it."

Sunshine beamed in from the hole in the door and fell across Pete's figure. Horrified, Rosemary saw that his blood had soaked the gown and was dripping onto the shoulder of his pajamas. He'd lost a pint, maybe two. She put her hands under his armpits and tugged. "No, you're coming with me. Please, Pete, you can make it."

"I don't have the strength. I hurt too much."

"Yes, you can do it." She tugged harder. "Crawl if you have to. It's only a few feet to safety. Someone out there will help us. Come on, Pete. You have to try." She started crying. Flames inside the incinerator licked out at them; the closet monster had taken shape, but that's not what scared her. Profound fear for Pete's life gave her incredible strength. She'd carry him if she had to. "You *must* try, please, *please*."

"Take my hand. Help me up."

She supported him. He was almost up when his knees buckled. She caught him around the waist and hauled him to a standing position.

Pete leaned heavily across her shoulders. She got him to the opening. He took hold of the broken wood and eased himself out, first a leg, arm, then his whole body. Rosemary quickly followed.

The morning sun made them squint. They had surfaced near the loading dock area at the end of the Concord building. A hook and ladder truck was parked parallel to the cement platform. The ladder leaned against the building at the third-story level, and a fireman at the top was bringing a patient down in his arms. Other firemen beamed the hose at a window on the fourth story. They looked at Pete and Rosemary and must have decided these two were patients escaping the the fire for they continued with the hose.

Rosemary took Pete's arm and placed it across her shoulders. "Let's go left. I'll drop you off at the lobby door. Go straight through to emergency. A doctor will help you." Bent in their struggles, they turned the corner and saw eight fire trucks in the circular driveway. Firemen perched on ladders, others raced around below, while others manned the hoses. Forced water jettisoned up into the sky and arced toward the building in eight streamlines. Water coursed rapidly down the driveway and into the street where police cruisers with blue lights flashing lined Memorial Drive. Barricades stopped the flow of traffic.

"Come on," Rosemary said, feeling the stress from supporting Pete's body. Her wounds were aching and her head was splitting, but she pushed forward. Pete was out of danger and now MOM had to be stopped. They limped through the grass along the Concord building and headed for the lobby door. Finally, she said, "Go in, Pete."

"I'm coming, too."

"You won't make it. You'll slow me down."

He winced. "That's good. Someone needs to slow you down. Anyway, I'm not letting go of your shoulder so let's hit the road."

They went by the main building and started past Sinclair when a whistle pierced the air. "Ignore it," Pete said. They got around the corner of the building and continued until they reached the basement door on Mass. Avenue.

"Hold it!"

Pete and Rosemary, looking like two escapees from a prison camp, slowly turned and faced the voice. A police officer stood with his feet spread and gun held out toward them.

Pete spoke quickly. "I'm Detective Lieutenant Pete Tan—"

"I don't care who the fuck you are. Put your hands on that wall."

In pain, neither could quite assume the stance the officer had in mind. With his gun in one hand, the officer patted down Pete first. "You two look just like the other kooks from the shrink unit." He patted Rosemary next. "Shit, lady, you ain't got nothing on under there."

"What the hell are you doing, Johnson!" They looked over and saw Mike Dow, his face a boiling pot of anger. "And where the hell have you been, Rosemary," he growled, "and what the hell are you doing now? Holy shit, is that you, Pete? What the hell did you do there? That's not the operation, is it? Christ, it looks like it is. Let's get you both to emergency. Here, lean on me. Johnson, you help the lady."

"Wait," Pete said, "you've got to help us get to the C.P.U. room and destroy MOM's generator. She's the cause of all this."

"Who's MOM?" the officer asked.

"She's a computer," Rosemary replied.

With his weight still on Rosemary, Pete said, "Officer, use your automatic on that door."

Johnson looked at Mike for approval.

"Go ahead."

The man aimed his gun at the knob and fired off four bullets. He stood back while Mike kicked the door. It swung open.

Rosemary and the officer followed Pete and Mike down the dark corridor to the fire cabinet. Mike reached inside, but the ax was not on the bracket. Further along was the C.P.U. room door. As they walked toward it, a horrible scream shrieked through the paging system, as if someone's skin were being peeled off. Rosemary didn't know how much more of this torture she could withstand, but they were so close now. She pressed her fingernails into her palms. She had to maintain her courage and stamina just a little longer. She hoped Pete could, too.

Mike tried the knob, but the door was locked. As

he gestured to the officer, the lights in the corridor flickered on and off. Over the paging system came a muted garble, the sound of someone drowning.

"I don't understand," Rosemary said.

"I do. Shoot that knob," Pete instructed the officer, who fired off two shots. The door opened. Electrical particles from MOM's generator sprayed Lee Hwang as he swung the fire ax again and brought it down hard. A white electrical volt arced from the generator and circled Lee's body.

"He'll be killed!" Rosemary shouted.

Lee swung a last time, and as he dropped to the floor, the generator stopped. Rosemary went to Lee's side. "Please be alive, please talk to me."

He moaned.

At the door of the room, a crowd of policemen had formed. They'd apparently heard the gunfire. Mike went into the corridor to explain what had happened.

"Would you pick up that phone and see if it's working?" Rosemary asked Johnson.

It was. "Call one-oh-eight-one for me. It's the emergency department. If anyone answers, tell them to send a physician and a stretcher to C.P.U. immediately."

The damage was extensive, but with money, everything could be repaired. The death rate was extensive, too, and no amount of money could replace patients and staff. Could she start over again? Did she have enough drive left to rebuild Riverside? Right now, she didn't think so. By next week, the lawsuits would start. Gigantic sums would be paid in settlements. Nothing would be left to cover the cost of repairs. The two million dollars from Jorge Villareal sounded like the size of a child's weekly allowance.

Sitting in her office with the chair swiveled around to give her a view of the Charles River, Rosemary sighed heavily. She heard the wail of an ambulance go down Memorial Drive, as it transfered a patient to another hospital. She'd heard the sirens for the past two hours as Wesly and Shelley organized the staff to get the remaining patients moved elsewhere. Once that was done, they were told to go home. The hospital was closed.

She heard a soft knock on the door. As she swiveled around, Pete entered. He was as pale as the clean white dressing that covered the side of his neck and face. He fell into a chair opposite her desk.

"How're you doing?" she asked gently, too exhausted to get up and kiss him.

"Thirty-eight new stitches. How about you?"

"I think I'm in shock."

"You'll be happy to hear that the state police caught Dr. Stockman on route ninety-three, headed north."

"Great news," she whispered.

Pete threw a red-labeled tape on her desk. "You were right about MOM getting the garbage. That's it, right there."

She picked up the tape and read the label: GARBAGE: CONFIDENTIAL AND DANGEROUS. USE ONLY ON SOLAR COMPUTER.

"When Mike got to CRL, the place was deserted,

but they found the tape in a drive that was connected to MOM. Someone must have booted it in."

"Can it be removed from her memory?"

"Lee Hwang says no."

"How is Lee?"

"Good. He's got some bad burns, but he's alive."

Rosemary dropped the tape onto her desk as if she were discarding an old shoe. "I didn't think MOM would survive this. I've already called the JCN Computer Company, and they'll have her memory out of here today. I told them to junk it."

Pete looked at her for a moment, then eased his body up. Using the desk as support, he went to her side, took her hands, and lifted her up into his arms. "Not much left for you to do today, so I think I'll keep a promise."

"What promise?"

"Making you Mrs. Pete Tanner."

Rosemary put her head against his neck and cried.

Epilogue

"There are two things in life I hate," Manny Horowitz said to the walls of his office. "Liver and problems." The phone continued to ring. "Mabel, answer that damn thing will you? Mabel? *Mabel!* Damn." It was five minutes after twelve and his secretary unfailingly went to lunch between twelve and one o'clock every day of the week. He snatched the receiver off its cradle and snarled, "JCN Computer."

"Is Mr. Horowitz there?"

"Speaking," Manny said.

"This is Samuel Vancourt at Boston Memorial Hospital. You promised delivery on a new memory bank for our Tech series four thousand two days ago, and I want to know where it is."

Manny started to sweat. Boston Memorial Hospital was a new account, and he wanted this half a million dollar order. He glanced over a list of incoming machines and saw that they were all sold to customers. The order for Boston Memorial was scheduled for the next shipment.

"I want it delivered today," Vancourt demanded.

"Wait a minute."

"I'm not waiting another minute. I'm canceling the order. We've been patient enough with you."

Manny found the list of returns and trade-ins. A new memory, huh? I'll find him a new memory. On the list, he noticed his secretary's handwriting. A used memory from Riverside Hospital had been scheduled for pickup today. She had written: Without fail, and underlined it. "I can deliver this afternoon," Manny said. "Will you be there to accept the shipment?"

"Yes."

Manny Horowitz placed a call to the company's shipping department. "I want someone to go over to Riverside Hospital immediately and pick up their JCN computer memory. I want it delivered to Boston Memorial within the hour, and I want it installed before the end of the day." He slammed down the phone. "Problems, I hate 'em."